SECRETS OF THE TUDOR COURT

⇢ Between Two Queens ⇠

Secrets

of the
TUDOR COURT

→ Between Two Queens ←

KATE
EMERSON

POCKET BOOKS
New York London Toronto Sydney

Pocket Books
A Division of Simon & Schuster, Inc.
1230 Avenue of the Americas
New York, NY 10020

First Pocket Books trade paperback edition January 2010

POCKET and colophon are registered trademarks of Simon & Schuster, Inc.

For information about special discounts for bulk purchases, please contact Simon & Schuster Special Sales at 1-866-506-1949 or business@simonandschuster.com.

The Simon & Schuster Speakers Bureau can bring authors to your live event. For more information or to book an event contact the Simon & Schuster Speakers Bureau at 1-866-248-3049 or visit our website at www.simonspeakers.com.

Manufactured in the United States of America

1   3   5   7   9   10   8   6   4   2

Library of Congress Cataloging-in-Publication Data
Emerson, Kate.
Secrets of the Tudor court: between two queens / Kate Emerson.—1st Pocket Books trade paperback ed.
p. cm.
1. Henry VIII, King of England, 1491–1547—Fiction. 2. Great Britain—Kings and rulers—Paramours—Fiction. 3. Great Britain—Court and courtiers—Fiction. I. Title. II. Title: Between two queens.
PS3555.M414S425   2009
813'.54—dc22
2009022622

ISBN 978-1-4165-8327-1

ISBN 978-1-4165-8359-2 (ebook)

To Kathy Sagan

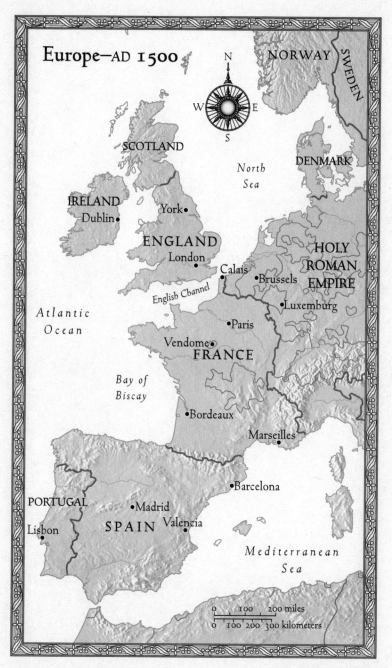

Europe—AD 1500

NORWAY

SWEDEN

N

W E

S

SCOTLAND

DENMARK

North
Sea

IRELAND
Dublin •

York •

ENGLAND

London •

Calais

Brussels •

HOLY
ROMAN
EMPIRE

Atlantic
Ocean

English Channel

Luxemburg •

Paris •

Vendome •

FRANCE

Bay of
Biscay

Bordeaux •

Marseilles •

Barcelona •

PORTUGAL

Madrid •

SPAIN

Valencia •

Mediterranean
Sea

Lisbon •

0   100   200 miles

0   100 200 300 kilometers

Map by Paul J. Pugliese.

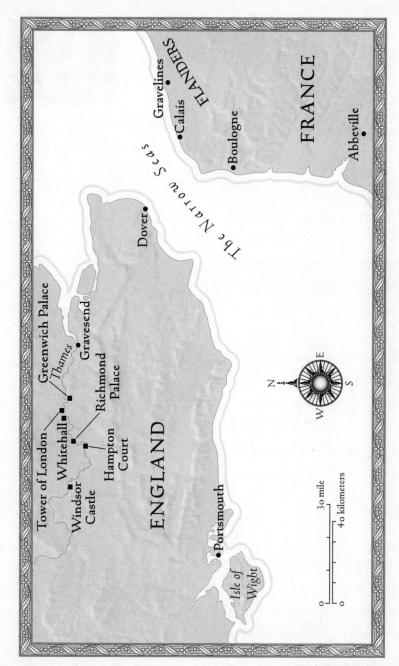

FLANDERS

Gravelines •

Calais •

Boulogne •

FRANCE

Abbeville •

The Narrow Seas

Dover •

Greenwich Palace

Thames

Gravesend •

Richmond Palace

Tower of London

Whitehall

Hampton Court

ENGLAND

Windsor Castle

Portsmouth •

Isle of Wight

N
E
W
S

30 mile
40 kilometers

0
0

Map by Paul J. Pugliese.

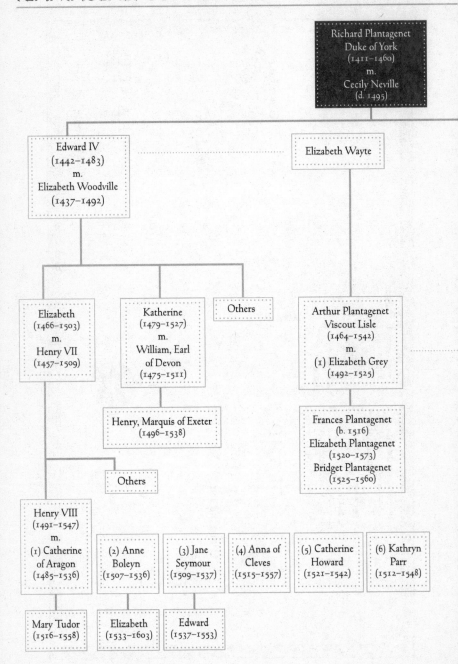

Richard Plantagenet
Duke of York
(1411–1460)
m.
Cecily Neville
(d. 1495)

Edward IV
(1442–1483)
m.
Elizabeth Woodville
(1437–1492)

Elizabeth Wayte

Elizabeth
(1466–1503)
m.
Henry VII
(1457–1509)

Katherine
(1479–1527)
m.
William, Earl
of Devon
(1475–1511)

Others

Arthur Plantagenet
Viscout Lisle
(1464–1542)
m.
(1) Elizabeth Grey
(1492–1525)

Henry, Marquis of Exeter
(1496–1538)

Frances Plantagenet
(b. 1516)
Elizabeth Plantagenet
(1520–1573)
Bridget Plantagenet
(1525–1560)

Others

Henry VIII
(1491–1547)
m.
(1) Catherine
of Aragon
(1485–1536)

(2) Anne
Boleyn
(1507–1536)

(3) Jane
Seymour
(1509–1537)

(4) Anna of
Cleves
(1515–1557)

(5) Catherine
Howard
(1521–1542)

(6) Kathryn
Parr
(1512–1548)

Mary Tudor
(1516–1558)

Elizabeth
(1533–1603)

Edward
(1537–1553)

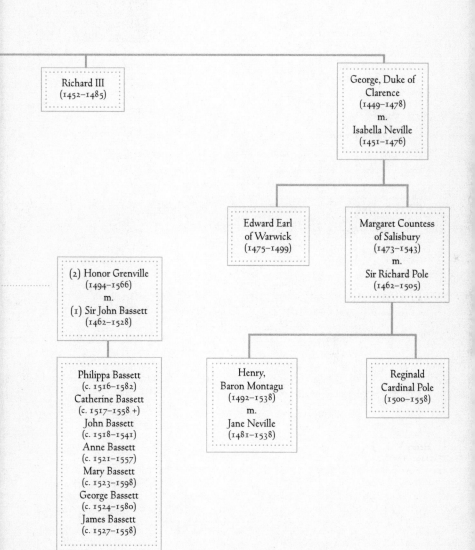

Richard III
(1452–1485)

George, Duke of
Clarence
(1449–1478)
m.
Isabella Neville
(1451–1476)

Edward Earl
of Warwick
(1475–1499)

Margaret Countess
of Salisbury
(1473–1543)
m.
Sir Richard Pole
(1462–1505)

(2) Honor Grenville
(1494–1566)
m.
(1) Sir John Bassett
(1462–1528)

Philippa Bassett
(c. 1516–1582)
Catherine Bassett
(c. 1517–1558 +)
John Bassett
(c. 1518–1541)
Anne Bassett
(c. 1521–1557)
Mary Bassett
(c. 1523–1598)
George Bassett
(c. 1524–1580)
James Bassett
(c. 1527–1558)

Henry,
Baron Montagu
(1492–1538)
m.
Jane Neville
(1481–1538)

Reginald
Cardinal Pole
(1500–1558)

SECRETS OF THE TUDOR COURT

✦ *Between Two Queens* ✦

Her Grace made grant to have one of your daughters; and the matter is thus concluded that your ladyship shall send them both over, for Her Grace will first see them and know their manners, fashions and conditions, and take which of them shall like Her Grace best; and they must be sent over about six weeks hence, and your ladyship shall not need too much cost on them till time you know which of them Her Grace will have. But two honest changes they must have, the one of satin, the other of damask. And at their coming the one shall be in my Lady of Rutland's chamber and the other in my Lady Sussex's chamber; and once known which the Queen will have, the other to be with the Duchess of Suffolk, and then to be apparelled according to their degrees. But madam, the Queen will be at no more cost with her but wages and livery, and so I am commanded to write unto your ladyship.

—John Husee to Lady Lisle, 17 July 1537

The distance across the Narrow Seas between Calais, the last English outpost on the coast of France, and the town of Dover, in Kent, was less than twenty-five miles. On a clear day, with the wind in the right direction, the journey could be made in a matter of hours. If a storm came up, the crossing could take days. On this particular morning in early September 1537, a cold wind gusted and ominously dark clouds scudded across a bleak sky. The three people huddled together on the deck of the fishing boat regarded the choppy water that surrounded them with varying degrees of dismay.

Edward Corbett, known to his friends as Ned, was in charge of the party. He was a young man, just turned twenty-two, and one of the gentlemen servitors in the household of Arthur Plantagenet, Viscount Lisle, lord Deputy of Calais, and uncle to King Henry VIII. Dogsbody would be a better name for what he was. He served at the beck and call of his master, performing whatever menial task Lord Lisle set for him. But the post was not all bad, and it would sustain him until there was an opening in the elite guard known as the Calais Spears. In the interim, his main duty was to take letters back and forth between Calais and England and deliver gifts—or more accurately, bribes—to those with influence at the court of King Henry VIII. On this journey he had been put in charge of the most precious gift of all. He was to escort two of the lord deputy's stepdaughters to be interviewed by Queen Jane, Henry's third wife. Her Majesty had a vacancy among the maids of honor.

The older sister, Catherine Bassett, called Cat by her family, was twenty and prodigiously plain in appearance. Her face was as pale as new-fallen snow, and her eyes, a blue so washed out as to look gray, had dark shadows beneath them. Even tightly wrapped in her heavy wool cloak, she shivered violently. "We will sink," Cat whispered in a voice that trembled. "I know it. We will not live long enough to see England again."

Her younger sister, Anne Bassett, whom everyone called Nan, was just sixteen and the acknowledged beauty of the family. Nan shot a contemptuous look in Cat's direction. She showed no fear and no sign of succumbing to seasickness. A lass after his own heart, Ned thought, bold and perhaps just a trifle foolhardy.

"Do stop whining, Cat," Nan said. "Master Nele's boat has made this trip across the Narrow Seas hundreds of times. We are perfectly safe."

"If the sight of the waves disturbs you, Mistress Bassett, there is a cabin in the stern," Ned suggested. "You might feel better out of the wind and weather." Salt spray coated their clothing, making everything feel damp and clammy.

Cat sent him a look of such gratitude that Ned felt guilty for not thinking to send her indoors earlier. But Nan's glare took him aback.

"If she goes in, I will have to go with her," Nan announced, "and I wish to remain where I am."

Ned frowned, torn between sending Cat off alone and leaving Nan by herself at the rail. In good conscience he could abandon neither of the sisters. They were his responsibility until he delivered them to the London house of John Husee, the lord deputy's man of business.

Cat heaved a great sigh. "The stink will be worse inside," she said, "and Nan is much affected by strong smells."

On a vessel of only thirteen tons, nowhere was free of the stench of tar and the strong odor of brine. But until Cat brought it to his attention, Ned had barely noticed. Master Nele's fishing boat was sweet smelling compared to most, used as often to carry passengers and cargoes of wine as it was for its original purpose.

Nan looked pleased by her easy victory, but Cat cast a wary glance at the sky. "Do you think we will reach Dover ahead of the storm?"

"Let us consult the frog." Ned led the way to a barrel secured near the beakhead. A frog was kept in a wooden cage nearby. Ned extracted it and dropped it into the barrel, which was filled with water. "Frogs always swim toward land," he explained, ignoring the fact that at this point the vessel was probably equidistant from France and England. "If a storm is coming, the frog will swim near the bottom of the barrel. If good weather is on the way, it will swim near the top."

Ned grinned as the two sisters leaned closer to stare at the frog. The peaks of their French hoods nearly touched midway over the barrel. At the front of each headdress a narrow strip of hair showed. Nan's was light brown dusted with gold, while Cat's more closely resembled the color of spring mud.

Nan turned her head, fixing eyes of a vivid popinjay blue on Ned's face. She pouted. "This frog is swimming in the middle of the water in the barrel."

"Then our fate is in God's hands. If the winds favor us, we will arrive before the weather worsens."

A bit of color had come back into Cat's cheeks. "Do you believe in signs and portents, Master Corbett? Nan and I are undecided on the subject."

He laughed. "Only when it suits me. Some superstitions are merely foolish. Do you know why most mariners refuse to learn to swim?"

Both sisters shook their heads. Cat looked genuinely curious. Nan's pretty face was a study in skepticism.

"They believe that once the sea gets a taste of you, it will come back for more. Those who willingly go into the water to swim are therefore more likely to drown."

"But ships do sink and men do drown, whether they can swim or not," Cat said, her expression solemn.

Ned herded the two young women back to the rail. The sky overhead had grown lighter in the last few moments. "Look there," he said, pointing. "If you squint, you can just see the cliffs at Dover."

"Look there," Nan shot back, as a wave broke against the side of the boat and cold mist sprayed over the rail. "We are not out of danger yet."

"I vow I will rescue you both if we sink," he promised. "I will turn myself into a dolphin and, like the old legend, carry you on my back to safety on the nearest shore."

"You can swim, then?" Nan asked.

"I can."

"Could you teach me how to stay afloat on my own?"

Wicked thoughts coursed through his mind as his admiring gaze slid over her. He could see very little of her shape beneath her cloak, but he had caught glimpses of her often enough in Calais to know she had a trim figure. He lowered his voice. "You would have to take lessons wearing nothing but your shift. Otherwise the weight of your clothing would pull you under the sea."

She turned a pretty shade of pink, but he saw in her eyes that she was not truly offended. "And you, sir? What would you wear?"

"That, mistress, I leave to your imagination."

"You are wicked, sir." More embarrassed than her sister, Cat avoided meeting his eyes. After a moment, she turned away, ostensibly to go back to the barrel for another look at the frog.

Nan's gaze remained fixed on Ned. "I would like to learn to swim, but I suppose I will have no time for such things when I become a maid of honor."

"Are you so certain you will be chosen? The queen sent for both of you."

"I should already have had a place among the maids." Nan could not hide her frustration. Her words tumbled out in a rush. "It was all arranged. More than a year ago, when I was fifteen, all the appropriate bribes had been paid, all the courtiers courted. My stepfather had sufficient rank as Viscount Lisle to entitle me to the position. Under Queen Catherine of Aragon, or even Queen Anne Boleyn, my age would not have been a drawback, but Queen Jane Seymour decided that I was too young. Only then did anyone suggest that Cat apply to enter royal service."

Ned made sympathetic noises and waited, leaning casually against the rail. His manner invited further confidences.

"It is most unfair that I should have to compete with my own sister for the single opening in the ranks of the queen's damsels, but I have one advantage." She lowered her voice and leaned a little closer. "I have been trained in a noble French household. I understand the ways of powerful and wealthy people. My sister was educated solely by our mother and has never left Calais once in the four years our stepfather has been in charge there."

Cat Bassett had stayed well in the background even in Lord Lisle's household. Ned had rarely been aware of her presence. Then again, it was hard to notice anyone else when Lady Lisle was in the vicinity. She was an altogether formidable woman.

Born plain Honor Grenville, a gentleman's daughter, Lady Lisle had been wed first to a simple West Country knight named Bassett, who'd died when her children were very young. Only by her second marriage had she become a viscountess and the wife of the lord deputy of Calais. She'd done well by the match. Not only had she pushed her new spouse into seeking advancement, but she had vastly improved her first family's fortunes. She took full advantage of the fact that her husband was King Henry's uncle.

Ned smiled to himself. That sounded much grander than it was. It was true that Arthur Plantagenet had been sired by King Edward IV, but he'd been born on the wrong side of the blanket. For decades he'd lived at court and been virtually ignored, just another royal bastard. Only during the last few years had he achieved any rank or position worth noting, and that had doubtless been due to the machinations of his ambitious second wife.

"Cat is shown favor simply because she is older." Nan's comment and the heartfelt sigh that accompanied it instantly reclaimed Ned's attention.

"What sort of favor?" he asked.

"While we wait for the queen to summon us, she is to be in the keeping of Eleanor, Countess of Rutland. I must stay with the Countess of Sussex."

"As they are both countesses, where is the difference?"

"Lady Rutland is more experienced. She has more influence at court. Lady Sussex is our cousin and only a few years older than I am. She was plain Mary Arundell less than a year ago, one of the maids of honor herself."

"Then perhaps she is the best person you could find to teach you how to succeed at court."

Nan considered that for a moment before nodding slowly. "Mayhap you have the right of it. I do hope so. A place at court has been my dream from the moment I was old enough to realize that royal service could open the gates to even greater things."

"Greater?" Ned already knew the answer, but he was enjoying this conversation with Nan. Even when she complained, her voice had a pleasant, musical lilt.

"Maids of honor are on display to make a colorful background for the queen. Sooner or later every maid of honor comes to the attention of all the important and wealthy noblemen in the land." Nan had a dreamy look in her eyes, clearly imagining herself being showered with gifts and proposals of marriage.

Ned grinned. He could find no fault with her goal. He'd be at the royal court himself if he had anyone to sponsor him. A courtier's advancement was limited only by his or her ambition. Win the queen's affection—or, better yet, the king's—and a word in the royal ear became a marketable commodity. The maids of honor were wont to make good marriages. Indeed, two previous members of that elite group—Anne Boleyn and Jane Seymour—had gone on to marry the king himself.

Nan Bassett's combination of beauty and ambition would take her far, Ned thought. A pity the position of queen was already filled.

ON SATURDAY, THE fifteenth day of September, Queen Jane summoned the Bassett sisters to her privy chamber at Hampton Court, the grandest of King Henry's palaces. She kept them before her on their knees for what seemed like hours. It took every ounce of self-control Nan possessed not to fidget.

I am blessed with a pretty face, she thought. *Everyone who meets me says so. But will that be enough?*

Her knees throbbed. In spite of the thick layers of fine linen and soft damask that separated them from the tiled floor, she could feel that hard and unyielding surface press against her flesh with bruising force. .

Holding herself otherwise perfectly still, Nan glanced sideways at her sister. Cat's eyes were demurely lowered. Her demeanor was all that was calm and composed. True, her face was pale, but then it always was.

Nan's gaze dropped to Cat's hands. Clasped together just at her waist, they trembled slightly. At once Nan felt better, but it still rankled that she had been forced into a competition with her sister for the single opening in the ranks of the royal maids of honor.

Why has the queen not yet decided? Can she not see that I am the one she should choose? Nan could not bear to contemplate her own future if Her Grace selected Cat.

Time stretched toward the breaking point. Nan was skilled at controlling her facial expression, but there was not enough willpower in the world to prevent the sheen of sweat that now appeared upon her brow.

The queen's presence chamber was overly warm . . . and it smelled faintly of cooking meat. Nan had always been sensitive to smells. The sweet scent of strewn herbs could not quite mask the stronger odors wafting up from the privy kitchens located directly below Her Grace's apartments.

The queen shifted in her gilded chair and her satin skirt rustled against the cloth-of-gold cushion. The faint sound seemed abnormally loud in the subdued quiet. Nan risked a glance at the woman who had been naught but Mistress Seymour before she supplanted Queen Anne in the king's affections. Although she sat beneath a canopy, just one of many symbols of her exalted position, and was surrounded by a bevy of attractive maids of honor and ladies-in-waiting, the queen herself was exceedingly plain. Her sumptuous clothing only emphasized her lack of physical beauty.

Everything Her Grace wore was heavily embroidered and sparkled with jewels. Pearls studded her old-fashioned gable headdress, their luminescent paleness emphasizing the lack of color in Queen Jane's skin. Pearls were supposed to have a slimming effect on plump features, but they did nothing to diminish the dimensions of the queen's large, round face, especially now that she was with child.

What on earth could it have been about Jane Seymour that had so appealed to the king? In Nan's experience, men responded to beauty. Pink-and-white complexions and delicate features like her own were the fashion, not a ghostlike pallor and a long nose such as the queen's, which became thicker near the point. The queen had high cheekbones, thin lips, and a roll of flesh beneath her chin, presumably the result of being hugely pregnant.

Nan was about to lower her gaze to the tiles once more when the edge of the tapestry directly behind the queen suddenly moved. A blue-gray eye peered out from the narrow gap between one section of the hangings and the next. Startled, Nan forgot it was not her place to stare. The eye fixed on her in return.

At once, a laugh rang out. A loud, booming guffaw echoed off the high, painted ceiling. The sound made the queen grimace, but only for an instant.

Cat gasped as the king emerged from his hiding place and stepped out into the sunlight. But Nan did not. She had already guessed whose eye it must be. Who else would dare conceal himself in the queen's lodgings?

Queen Jane's maids of honor and waiting gentlewomen hastily made an obeisance. Already on their knees, Nan and Cat should have bowed their heads. Cat did. But Nan, smiling, continued to stare at His Majesty.

Her admiration was genuine. King Henry was the tallest man she'd ever seen, taller even than her stepfather, and massively built. His doublet, gloriously decorated with roses embroidered in gold thread and rubies that caught the light, covered an impressively firm, barrel-shaped chest. His lower limbs were shapely and encased in the finest hose.

The king was no longer young, already in his forty-sixth year, but he was still a magnificent and awe-inspiring sight. Nan knew she should lower her eyes, and her head. It was only proper in the presence of royalty. But she found she could not tear her gaze away from the man striding across the chamber toward her.

His square-cut beard was a golden red, just as it appeared in the portraits Nan had seen. She could not help but notice that it contained a few stray flecks of gray, but that did not seem to matter. His Majesty was ageless. His skin was fair and still as smooth as a much younger man's. Her breath caught at the expression in his eyes. Her bold stare had apparently given no offense. On the contrary. His gaze was both amused and admiring.

"Rise, mistress." The king thrust out a large hand adorned with an assortment of glittering rings. His touch was gentle but firm, and Nan's fingers quite disappeared in his.

Her senses reeled. An exotic blend of perfumes wafted out from his person. She recognized musk and rose water and ambergris, but there was another ingredient as well that rendered the combination unusually heady and potent. It produced in Nan a disconcerting swell of desire and she nearly lost her balance as she came upright.

"Mistress Bassett," the king murmured. He kept hold of Nan's hand and drew her close, as if to inspect her face for flaws. "But which Mistress Bassett are you?"

Her fingertips burned from his heat. Suddenly, she ached to feel the brush of his soft beard against her skin. By some miracle she found her voice, although it emerged as a throaty whisper. "I am called Anne, if it please Your Grace."

The king frowned.

Utter stillness filled the presence chamber.

Nan instantly realized what the trouble must be. She had the same Christian name as the queen King Henry had so recently cast off and had executed. She told herself that it should not matter, would not make a difference in her fate. Anne was as common a name as Catherine—and half the girls in England had been named after Catherine of Aragon, the king's first wife, the woman he had divorced in order to marry Anne Boleyn.

"Do you enjoy dancing, Mistress Anne?"

The mundane question had Nan fighting not to laugh aloud with relief. The king was not displeased with her after all. She sent him her most brilliant smile. "I do, Your Grace."

"And music? Are you adept with lute or virginals?" Sliding one hand beneath her elbow, he steered her toward Queen Jane.

"I play both, Your Grace." Modesty had no place at court.

"Excellent. I will depend upon you to provide soothing songs for my queen while she awaits the birth of my son and heir."

"Have you chosen, then, Your Grace?" The queen's voice was low and carefully modulated so as to reveal nothing of her personal opinion.

The king's admiring gaze never left Nan's face. "She will do nicely, my heart."

With that, Nan's own heart beat so fast and loud that she feared she might swoon. His Grace had the most penetrating eyes, and at the moment they revealed the full extent of his interest in her. The king of England wanted her, and not just as a maid of honor for his wife.

The queen spoke again. This time her voice was stronger and brooked no disobedience. "Come forward, Mistress Anne Bassett."

As Nan approached the gilded chair, she saw that Queen Jane had blue eyes, too—but they had narrowed to slits. Nan felt heat creep into her cheeks. Along with it came the certainty that, if the decision had been left up to Queen Jane, she'd have chosen Cat to join her household.

Schooling her features to present a picture of demure obedience, Nan knelt before the queen.

"Do you swear to serve me faithfully, Mistress Bassett?"

"I do, Your Grace."

"Then you may kiss my hand as a pledge of your fealty." Queen Jane extended her fingers, which were almost as heavily laden with rings as the king's, toward Nan.

By this act, Nan was sworn in as one of the maids of honor. But when her lips actually brushed the queen's skin, as dry and cracked as old leather, she had her first good look at what lay beyond the glitter. Queen Jane had bitten her fingernails down to the quick.

"You need not put on airs," Cat said the moment they left the queen's presence chamber. "I know why you were chosen."

In spite of her sister's critical tone, Nan preened a bit. She was a maid of honor. Every time Queen Jane appeared in public, Nan would be one of the six richly dressed young women accompanying her, petals to her flower. In private she would be at the center of a whirl of activity—disguisings, dances, tournaments. The king himself would partner her. He was known to participate with great enthusiasm in all the entertainments at court.

"Neither one of us would have been considered for the post," Cat added, "if Her Grace did not have a fondness for quails."

Irritated, Nan turned on her sister, heedless of the stares this sudden movement attracted. They were in the queen's watching chamber, a large, ornately furnished room crowded with guards, courtiers, and servants. Recent rebuilding had left behind the faint scent of newly hewn wood and burnt brick.

"It is of no importance why the queen sent for us. All that matters is that one of us was chosen."

Still, Cat's reminder stung. The pregnant queen had developed a craving for quails. Providing a constant supply of the birds from Calais had given their mother a convenient means by which to remind Her Grace, over and over again, that she had four Bassett daughters, any one of whom would be delighted to accept a post at court. Honor Lisle's largesse—she sent tokens to influential courtiers, as well—had led directly to the summons to be interviewed by the queen.

Small gifts, Mother called them, but some were not so small. Tokens could be anything from a personal offering, such as a ring, given out of friendship, to a present that acknowledged a similar gift received, to an offering made in the hope that the recipient would do the sender a favor. Sometimes this favor was specified; sometimes the note that went with the token only hinted at what the sender really wanted, especially if the gift was sent directly to the king.

Nan told herself that, in the end, her looks were what had won her the post. And it would be her appearance and her manners that would attract a suitable husband. That was, after all, why most mothers wanted their daughters to be maids of honor. The queen's damsels enjoyed superior opportunities to entice wealthy, titled gentlemen into marriage. A faint smile curved her lips.

"I do not see anything funny about those quails!" Cat's sharp tone abruptly made Nan once again aware of her surroundings.

"The quails assured our welcome. My beauty won the queen's favor."

"The *king's* favor, you mean!"

As soon as the hasty words were out, Cat's eyes widened with regret and alarm. They had both forgotten how easy it was to be overheard. Seizing Nan's arm, Cat towed her out of the watching chamber and down a flight of stairs. She did not speak again until they reached the relative privacy of the open air. They were not alone out of doors, either, but at least no one was paying close attention to them.

"Have a care, Nan. Do not be too brazen in His Grace's presence."

Nan frowned at her, puzzled by Cat's marked shift from resentment to concern. She stopped midway across the courtyard. Her hands, curled into fists, rested lightly at her hips and she turned a fulminating glare on her sister. "Speak plain if you must speak at all. I have no time for riddles."

"Lady Rutland says the king always strays when one of his queens is great with child. He began the practice in Queen Catherine of Aragon's time and was just as quick to take a mistress when Queen Anne Boleyn was increasing. It is most unusual that he has not done so this time, but mayhap that is about to change. He chose *you*, the pretty one, to replace Mistress Mewtas, Anne." Bitterness returned to Cat's voice.

"The queen's damsels are *supposed* to be attractive!" While waiting on her knees for the queen's decision, Nan had caught a glimpse of the other five and seen them watching her with speculative looks. None was as pretty as she was, Nan thought, but they were all comely enough, as was Jane Mewtas, the woman whose marriage had created a vacancy. Jane was a small, slender, fine-boned beauty.

"Should you not ask yourself why?" Cat demanded.

"The maids are ornamental. Decorative. There is nothing wrong with that."

Her sister's sniff spoke volumes. "Lady Rutland says—"

"A fig for what Lady Rutland says and less for what she thinks!"

Stalking off ahead of Cat, Nan reentered the palace by another door and began to thread her way through the maze of connecting rooms toward her temporary lodgings.

With her longer stride, Cat easily overtook her sister. She kept her voice low. "Lady Rutland has been at court for years. She knows how things are done."

Nan increased her speed. She was anxious to return to Cousin Mary's chambers and collect her belongings. Tonight she would lodge in the maids' dormitory.

"She says another maid of honor will marry soon. Anne Parr."

"And you think *you* will be chosen to replace this Mistress Parr?"

"I no longer *wish* to be chosen! I would rather remain with Lady Rutland. She has already told me that I would be a welcome addition to her household."

"Well, if you are satisfied with that . . ." Nan shrugged to express her indifference and walked even faster.

"Lady Rutland says—"

"Do you intend to parrot every word Lady Rutland speaks or have you a mind of your own?" Nan found it most annoying that Cat had no trouble keeping pace with her.

"If you do not wish to have the benefit of her wisdom, that is your loss. I intend to learn all I can from her. And I will have the advantage of my freedom during the next month."

Confused by this last comment, Nan faltered in her steps. She debated only a moment before she gave in to her need to know what Cat meant. "Explain yourself, sister."

"Did you not realize?" Cat smirked. "On the morrow, Queen Jane goes into seclusion in her chambers until the babe is born. No men will be admitted there, not even the king."

"I know expectant mothers sequester themselves." Nan had experience with the custom from her days in the household of the sieur de Riou. She frowned, remembering what the last weeks of Madame de Riou's pregnancy had entailed.

"There will be a most impressive ceremony to mark the queen's withdrawal," Cat continued. "Lady Rutland says that first Her Grace will hear Mass. Then she will be escorted to her presence chamber by all the lords and ladies of her household and led to her chair of estate. She will sit there and be served spices and wine, after which her two highest-ranking lords will lead her to the door of her bedchamber and take formal leave of her. Only Her Grace's ladies and gentlewomen will be permitted to follow her inside. After that, no men will be admitted except, I suppose, for the royal physicians. Anything Her Grace needs will be brought to the chamber door, where her women will receive it and take it inside. Even the humblest male servants must stay away for the duration. I am told there is a narrow spiral staircase leading from the queen's apartments to the ground floor where the privy kitchens and the royal wardrobe are located. It permits waiters to bring food and yeomen to deliver clothing without ever entering Her Grace's private rooms."

During her sister's recitation, Nan came to an abrupt halt. In an instant, all her joy, all her triumph, fled. The sour taste of disappointment filled her mouth. "I will be no better off than a cloistered nun," she whispered. That was not how she had hoped to spend her first weeks as a maid of honor! "How long? When will the child be born?"

"Lady Rutland thinks Her Grace's time is three or four weeks hence, but who can say? Babies come when they will."

Nearly a month? That was a very long time to be locked away from the world of men. Longer than Nan had ever gone without male company before. There had been a goodly assortment of personable young men in the de Riou household in France, including young Gabriel de Montmorency, the heir to the de Bours title. More recently, in Calais, all the young, personable gentlemen her stepfather kept on petty wages had vied with one another to pay her pretty compliments.

"Ah, well," Cat said as they resumed walking. "I am certain you will be so busy that the time will fly by. I will try not to envy you as I spend my time with the courtiers who attend upon the king."

"Much good that will do you!" As far as Nan had been able to observe, Cat had little aptitude for flirtation.

They had nearly reached the Countess of Sussex's lodgings. With each step Cat looked more smugly pleased with herself. "I did not manage too badly with Master Corbett on the journey from Calais," she said.

Nan gave a disdainful sniff. "He spent more time talking with me than with you. Not that it matters. Ned Corbett is naught but a country gentleman's younger son."

And yet, even before he'd escorted them across the Narrow Seas, Nan had taken notice of him. In appearance Ned was most appealing—a head taller than she was and well proportioned, with thick, dark hair; a fine, thick beard; and laugh lines around his eyes. Nan liked his irreverent sense of humor, too. She had noticed he was careful to repress that side of himself when he was in the presence of Nan's mother or stepfather or their man in London, John Husee. That fact alone intrigued her.

Ned's devil-may-care attitude had been much in evidence during the trip from Calais to London. Nan had appreciated the wicked and admiring glint in his eyes when he'd talked of teaching her to swim, she in her shift and Ned—or so she imagined—wearing nothing at all. She liked his natural smell, too. Unlike the king, who, she noticed, doused himself in heavy perfumes, Ned's scent consisted of his own body's musk underscored by a hint of leather and augmented by the herbs he used to wash his face and beard. The combination was most pleasing.

Nan's thoughts abruptly returned to the present when Cat embraced her. "Enjoy your prize," she whispered. "I know how much it meant to you to win it."

Realizing that she would be locked away from Cat, too, Nan hugged her sister tightly in return. When she stepped back, she held Cat at arm's length for one last, long look before they parted. Unexpected tears sprang into Nan's eyes.

"Lady Rutland says each maid of honor is allowed a spaniel." Cat injected laughter into her voice, striving to lighten the mood. "And a maid, so you'll no longer have to share a servant with me."

"I would rather have a linnet or a monkey than a dog," Nan said, forcing a smile of her own. Their mother kept both in the household at Calais, together with several hounds and a one-eared cat.

"Lady Rutland says that although maids of honor are paid ten pounds per annum and provided with meals and livery, you must supply your own bedding. And you will likely need to amend your clothing," she added as she moved away.

Amend her clothing? Before Nan could ask her sister what she meant by that, Cat had scurried off in the direction of Lady Rutland's lodgings.

Nothing needs amending, Nan told herself. Everything she had was new and in the latest fashion. Mother had taken particular care in acquiring it. Or rather, John Husee, carrying out his employer's orders to the letter, had done so. And he had sought advice from both countesses—Sussex *and* Rutland—before making his purchases.

Nan's cousin Mary, the Countess of Sussex, was waiting for her. She had already heard of Nan's appointment and enveloped her in a warm embrace and a cloud of her distinctive rose-water scent when she arrived. The top of Mary's head came just level with Nan's nose.

"Well deserved, coz," Mary said. "I was certain you would be the one the queen chose."

"Is there something wrong with my clothing?" Nan blurted out.

"Ah, well, that may present a small problem." Cousin Mary lifted a hand to her cumbersome gable headdress, a wistful look in her coal black eyes. "The queen does not care for French hoods. No doubt her aversion has something to do with Anne Boleyn's fondness for the style."

"But . . . but I have no other bonnets." Nan's spirits plunged again. She felt as if she could not get her footing. Every time she took a step in confidence, some new obstacle appeared in her path.

"I will provide you with one of velvet, and a frontlet of the same, such as the other maids wear," Cousin Mary said, "but you will need to acquire a second and it should have an edge of pearl."

"I thank you, cousin. You are most kind."

Looking amused by Nan's obvious lack of enthusiasm, Cousin Mary drew her into the inner chamber and closed the curtain behind them. The Sussex servants, including two waiting gentlewomen, remained in the outer room. "What do you have against gable headdresses?" Mary asked.

"Aside from the unflattering shape and awkward construction?" Nan said.

Mary chuckled and opened the wardrobe chest that held the garments she wore at court.

"What good is it to have beautiful hair," Nan asked, "if no one can see it?" A gable headdress had two pieces of fabric at the front to cover every strand.

"It is a great pity, I agree," Mary offered.

Nan knew Mary meant what she said. Her cousin's hair was long and luxuriant and as black as her eyes. Nan sighed. "What else will I have to give up to conform to royal whims?"

"The queen has sent word that she will allow you to wear out the remainder of your French apparel, but it is possible she may change her mind. Indeed, it is likely she will. Her moods of late have been as unpredictable as the weather. You are fortunate she did not take a dislike to your looks, out of fear you might capture the king's interest while she is indisposed."

This remark, following so closely upon Cat's observations, sent heat rushing into Nan's face. "I did not come to court to become anyone's mistress, not even the king's. I am seeking a rich, titled, future husband, such as the one you yourself found." *Only younger and better looking*, Nan added to herself. Cousin Mary was the earl's third wife, and he was some thirty years older than she was.

"His Majesty admires pretty things," Mary mused as she held up a pair of sleeves heavily embroidered with flowers in a rainbow of colors.

"I am certain the king intended no more than an avuncular interest in my well-being," Nan said stiffly. She did not like being forced to defend herself this way.

Mary laughed. "I would not be so sure of that, but the matter will not arise for the immediate future. As for your wardrobe . . ." She produced a kirtle of crimson damask and sleeves of the same. "You may have these, as my gift. And I have already sent for Master Husee, so that he may send word to your mother that you have been chosen. Do you wish to write to her yourself?"

"I cannot." At her cousin's look of surprise, Nan felt obliged to explain. "I read both French and English, but in the de Riou household I was only taught to write in French. Since Mother does not understand that language in either its written or spoken form, it would be far better if Master Husee wrote to her in English on my behalf."

Lips pursed, Mary shook her head in a disapproving manner. Nan was not surprised by the reaction. Cousin Mary was very clever with languages. She had learned to read and write in Greek and Latin as well as English and French. "Amend the oversight if you can, Nan," she advised. "A knowledge of French is all very well, but you are in England now."

"Indeed I am!" The smile Nan flashed was wide with triumph and delight. "Not only am I in England, but I am at the English court. And from this day forward, I am one of the queen of England's maids of honor!"

JANE MEWTAS CAME to Lady Sussex's chamber to escort Nan to her new quarters. At Hampton Court, the queen's suite of rooms stretched along the entire south end of the east front of an inner court and extended into a long gallery that faced out upon the park. There were many interconnected chambers, including a maid's dormitory that contained three large beds and a scattering of other furniture. Two mullioned windows let in light and air, but shutters on the outside and heavy curtains within were already in place, ready to be closed tight. During the queen's confinement, every room in her lodgings would be kept dark and airless.

After two men in Sussex livery delivered Nan's wardrobe trunk, Jane led Nan back to the queen's privy chamber. The maids of honor Nan had glimpsed earlier, together with several other waiting gentlewomen, were still there, but the queen herself had gone to lie down.

Mistress Mewtas began introductions with a stern-faced, unfriendly looking woman who appeared to be at least thirty years old and regarded Nan with deep suspicion in her light gray eyes. "This is Mistress Jane Arundell," she said. "She and Lady Sussex are half sisters."

Nan found it difficult to conceal her surprise. The two women were nothing alike. Where Cousin Mary had been warm and welcoming, Mistress Arundell held herself stiffly and acknowledged Nan with naught but a curt nod.

"Kinswoman," Nan said, inclining her head.

"We are only very distantly related." With those few clipped words, Jane Arundell went back to hemming a cambric shirt.

Linking her arm through Nan's, Jane Mewtas steered her toward three considerably younger women seated on cushions on the floor. They looked up from their embroidery with equal parts curiosity and wariness.

"This is Anne Parr, who will be your bedfellow," Jane Mewtas said, indicating a young woman who would have been beautiful if not for an off-center nose and a profusion of freckles across her cheeks. She was older than Nan by only a few years.

"Welcome, Mistress Bassett," said Mistress Parr. "Now we will have two Annes in our number, as well as two Janes and two Marys."

"Until recently there were three Janes," Jane Mewtas interjected. "At times it is very confusing."

"My friends call me Nan," Nan said.

"Well, Nan it shall be then." Anne Parr looked pleased. "This is Bess Jerningham." She indicated the young woman sitting beside her. "Our only Elizabeth. She came to us when Mary Arundell left to wed the Earl of Sussex."

"And I am Mary Norris," said the third young woman. Even seated, her height was apparent. So was her antipathy. She regarded Nan with an owlish gaze and did not smile.

"I am pleased to meet all of you," Nan said.

"The other Mary," Jane Mewtas said as she led Nan toward a flat-topped chest beneath a window, "is Mary Zouche, who has been a maid of honor longer than any of the rest. She is the daughter of Lord Zouche of Harringworth. Back when Catherine of Aragon was queen, Mary begged to be taken into royal service because she had a new stepmother who was cruel to her."

Mistress Zouche was busily embroidering roses on a handkerchief. She appeared to be no more than twenty-five and had been blessed with a clear complexion and good features, although Nan thought her chin a trifle too square for true beauty.

She greeted Nan with a haughty sniff and looked her up and down before speaking. "You will need to alter your clothing. Your garments are cut in the French fashion. That will not suit the queen."

"The matter is already in hand." Although Nan hid her resentment, the criticism stung.

"And that accent!" Mary Zouche exclaimed. "You scarcely sound English."

"I am as English as you are, Mistress Zouche."

"Where were you raised?"

"In France, but—"

"You see!" The other woman gave an airy wave of the hand holding her needle. "French. It makes one wonder if you have foreign sympathies, as well. Or worse, papist leanings." This speculation provoked nervous titters from the maids of honor and other gentlewomen in the queen's privy chamber.

Nan bit back an angry response. It was scarcely her fault that she'd been sent from Calais into France at the age of twelve. At the time, her mother had thought a French upbringing would be an advantage for her. After all, Queen Anne Boleyn had been trained in France.

"Mary," Jane Mewtas said sternly. "Enough. You have no cause to question Mistress Bassett's loyalty."

"And is her moral character also beyond reproach? We all saw how she flaunted herself before the king, *and* how he responded."

Nan glared at her accuser, but she knew better than to lose her temper. "I should think it most unwise to question His Majesty's intentions," she murmured with feigned shock and innocence. "I am certain King Henry can do no wrong, being God's anointed one on earth as he is."

Mary Zouche said nothing, apparently unable to think of a reply that would not be taken for criticism of the king. So Nan smiled sweetly and walked away. On the surface, Nan knew she appeared confident and self-assured, but inside she had gone cold with dread.

Yes, she was one of the maids of honor, but all of a sudden she realized that this could be cause for concern. The maids lived in each other's pockets, day and night. How would she manage if, as it now seemed, they all disliked her?

Nan's steps faltered. She felt she had nowhere to go save back to the little group of embroiderers who sat on their cushions. Uncertain of her reception, she braced herself for more barbed comments.

Anne Parr looked up, a twinkle in her gray eyes. "If you have other matters to tend to, Jane," she said to Mistress Mewtas, who had trailed along after Nan, a look of concern on her face, "I will be happy to acquaint Nan with her duties."

Her overt friendliness eased Nan's mind, and her suggestion that they retire to the privacy of the maids' dormitory was even more welcome. As they entered, Anne plucked a handful of sugar-coated nuts from a bowl. Carrying them with her, she scrambled atop one of the high beds, tucked her legs beneath her, and patted the coverlet at her side.

"Come and be comfortable," she invited, and tossed one of the nuts to Nan.

Nan caught it and popped it into her mouth, relishing the burst of sweetness. "You were going to tell me about my duties."

"They are simple enough. We present ourselves in the queen's privy chamber every morning by eight of the clock and remain close at hand until we are dismissed for the night. We are at the queen's beck and call."

Nan climbed up to sit beside her mentor on a quilted, yellow sarcenet counterpane. "I expect to be asked to perform all manner of services for Her Grace."

Anne made a little snorting sound. "You will be surprised, then. Menial tasks such as lighting fires and bringing in torches and lights are done by underlings. On occasion, you may be permitted to supervise them."

"What about helping the queen dress and undress?"

"The chamberers do that."

"Serving meals?"

"We are not important enough to undertake that task. The queen is waited upon by noblewomen—countesses at the least. You might be allowed to set mats on the table when the queen's board is laid or bring in water for her to wash with before she eats. But as a mere maid of honor, you will not even be permitted to hand the basin directly to Her Grace."

Anne polished off the last of the sugared nuts and licked her fingers. "After you take the water away again, you may occasionally have the honor of fetching bread, ale, and wine for the queen's ladies."

"That sounds simple enough."

Anne slanted a look Nan's way. "For the most part, we have a pleasant life. You must not let what Mary Zouche said trouble you."

"I did not try to entice the king." Nan grew weary of denial.

"It would not matter if you did." Anne sounded matter-of-fact. "By the time the queen gives birth, King Henry will have forgotten all about you."

Nan did not know whether to be relieved by this prediction, or insulted.

... touching all other particular ceremonies at the christening, Corbett can inform your ladyship, for he stood by and saw all things. . . . on Sunday last my Lady Sussex sent to me with all speed to make for Mrs. Anne either a new gown of lion tawny velvet, or else one of black velvet turned up with yellow satin, the which with much work I have done; . . . she wore the same at the Christening. So that this notwithstanding, she must have against the Queen's churching a new satin gown and against Christmas a new gown of lion tawny velvet.

—John Husee to Lady Lisle, 16 October 1537

The bay windows in Queen Jane's bedchamber were covered by thick damask curtains, making the room dark, airless, and overly warm. Behind the screen that shielded her bed, the queen herself was a study in misery. But she had an advantage over the women trapped with her. Queen Jane was free to express her displeasure. She could take out her frustration on those around her.

"You there," she called in an imperious tone. "Bassett. You claim to be skilled on the lute. Play a soothing song for me."

Nan knew she was not the most accomplished musician at court, but the king's minstrels, all men, were not permitted near the queen during her lying-in. Nan took up her instrument and sang along as she strummed a tune King Henry himself had composed—"Pastance With Good Company."

Queen Jane listened without comment to the end, but the expression on her pale, bloated face did not bode well. "Your playing is inferior," she complained as Nan set the lute aside.

The queen's cutting criticism stung. Nan bowed her head to hide the single tear that rolled down her cheek.

"Begone," the queen ordered. "Get out of my sight."

As she backed away from the royal bed, Nan never saw the pillow the queen threw at her. It struck the side of her head and knocked her gable headdress askew, but did no real damage. Muffled laughter from the other maids followed her retreat.

As soon as she was clear of the bedchamber, her steps faltered. *Begone?* How far away did the queen expect her to go? And for how long? Her hands shook as she adjusted her attire and gathered her shattered composure. Surely Her Grace did not mean she was banished from the household. Nan had been a maid of honor for only a bit more than a week.

Anne Parr slipped through the door that separated the bedchamber from the privy chamber. She caught Nan's hand in passing. "Her Grace has sent for her poppets," Anne whispered. "Come and help me fetch them."

"Poppets?" Nan echoed. "You mean toys?" She envisioned straw bodies and wooden heads, similar to the playthings she and her sisters had pretended were babies when they were very young.

"The queen collects them. They are her passion."

The poppets were kept in a cedar chest in a small room deep within the queen's lodgings. It was filled to the brim with little figures cleverly made to resemble miniature ladies and gentlemen. Some were carved from wood while others had been constructed of clay.

Enchanted, Nan lifted out one dressed in white cloth-of-silver with an underskirt of green velvet. Beneath was another poppet wearing a white velvet gown. A third was garbed in crimson satin.

"They have finer clothing than we do," Nan observed.

Anne chuckled. "And more of it. Coffers full. Gather up a half dozen and I will bring their spare garments."

By the time the two maids of honor returned to the queen's bedchamber, Her Grace seemed to have forgotten her pique with Nan. Her attention fixed on playing with her poppets, she sent most of her attendants away.

Nan returned to the privy chamber wishing she could leave the queen's apartments entirely, just for a little while. The great ladies of the household and the ladies of the privy chamber did not have to attend Her Grace every day. Most had separate lodgings at court. Some shared apartments with their husbands, if those gentlemen waited on the king. A few even kept private houses nearby.

She sighed. Maids of honor had no such luxury.

"Mistress Bassett?"

Nan had not heard anyone approach and was surprised to find Eleanor, Countess of Rutland, standing next to her. The countess was a plump, matronly woman in her midforties, the mother of numerous children. The most recent had been born earlier that year. Nan narrowed her eyes. Unless she was much mistaken, the loosened laces on the countess's kirtle meant she was pregnant yet again.

"I trust the pillow did not do any serious damage."

"Only to my pride. It is kind of you to ask." Nan dipped low in acknowledgment of the countess's superior status.

"Your sister sends her regards," Lady Rutland said.

"Cat is still with you, then?" When Nan came upright again, she found herself eye to eye with the countess. They were almost exactly the same height.

"I have told her that she is welcome to stay as long as she wishes."

"As one of your waiting gentlewomen?" Nan knew that the queen's ladies were allowed two gentlewomen apiece to wait upon them in their quarters, just as the maids of honor could each employ one servant. Nan's newly acquired tiring maid, whose main duty was to help Nan in and out of her attire, was a girl named Constance Ware. She had been supplied by Cousin Mary.

"Not officially, but you will have noticed that most noblewomen at court keep more than the two attendants they are permitted. Cat's company delights me. I will be sad to part with her if your mother arranges a more prestigious place for her."

Nan listened politely as Lady Rutland sang Cat's praises. Clearly the countess was fond of Cat, much fonder than Queen Jane was of Nan. Nan began to feel the unmistakable burn of envy. She was glad to escape when the queen summoned her maids of honor back to the royal bedchamber.

Queen Jane had tired of her poppets and looked sulky. She brightened when she caught sight of Nan. "Ah, there you are, Bassett. Come closer."

She peered at Nan for a long moment. Then she reached out and fingered the embroidered linen of Nan's chemise. It had been designed to show in a froth of white just above the bodice of her kirtle.

"You must replace your linen," the queen declared. "The cloth used to make your smocks is far too coarse."

Biting back a protest—since her mother had paid dearly to have her daughters' undergarments made of the finest fabric available—Nan bowed her head. "As you wish, Your Grace. I will send for replacements at once."

"See that you do." Queen Jane flapped one hand in dismissal and plucked the nearest poppet off the coverlet. A look of satisfaction played across her pale face.

Once again, Nan backed out of the room. This time she went straight to the maids' dormitory to find Constance. She would have to send the girl to Cousin Mary and ask that the Countess of Sussex dispatch new orders to John Husee. The family's man of business was already engaged in procuring a second gable headdress for Nan and had ordered new gowns, sleeves, bodices, and kirtles. Now he would have to dredge up replacements for her undergarments, as well.

"Look at the bright side, Mistress Nan," Constance consoled her when Nan passed on the queen's latest demand. "At least you have new clothes, even if they are not of your own choosing."

IN THE UNFAMILIAR vastness of Lord Cromwell's house in Austin Friars, near the north wall of London, young Wat Hungerford found it difficult to settle down for the night. He was twelve years old and had been issued Cromwell livery only a week earlier. Before that he had always lived at Farleigh Castle in rural Wiltshire, his father's country seat.

Using the excuse of a trip to the privy, Wat left the bed he shared with two other boys and set about exploring his new home. With the help of a full moon and the occasional rush light in a wall sconce, he poked into unused chambers and storage rooms and discovered a half-hidden stairway that took him to the kitchens. At length he made his way into the wing that contained his master's private chambers.

Thomas Cromwell was Henry VIII's Lord Privy Seal and the most powerful man in England after the king. He had been the one responsible for obtaining the king's divorce from Anne Boleyn and had masterminded the dissolution of the monasteries, with the claim that they were breeding grounds for sin and corruption.

Wat's father, Lord Hungerford of Heytesbury, had told Wat over and over that a place in Lord Cromwell's household was a grand opportunity for advancement. He'd ordered Wat to make himself indispensable to his new master. Exactly how he was supposed to do that, Wat did not know, but it seemed to him that it would be an advantage to know the lay of the land. At home he'd had a dozen hiding places and knew all the best listening posts.

Wat entered Lord Cromwell's private study cautiously. It was past midnight. He did not expect to encounter anyone, so long as he stayed indoors where there were no guards. He had been a casualty in an ongoing war between his father and his stepmother—subject to blows from one and slaps from the other—and had learned at a young age to keep to the shadows.

The faint rustle of rushes was the only warning he had that someone was approaching. Wat ducked behind the nearest arras. The heavy wall hanging concealed him completely, but when two men entered, one carrying a lantern, he found he could see into the room through a worn patch in the weave.

With a start, Wat recognized the man with the light as Lord Cromwell himself. The boy wondered why he was skulking about in his own house. The answer was not long in coming. Cromwell did not want anyone to know about this meeting.

A thrill of excitement made Wat shiver in anticipation. He had heard that his new master employed spies and secret agents to do his bidding. There were even rumors to the effect that if evidence of misconduct was lacking at some of the wealthier religious houses, Lord Cromwell contrived to make sure that something untoward would still be found on the premises. Barely able to contain his curiosity, Wat held himself as silent and still as a little mouse and listened hard.

At first he could not make out what the two men were saying. They kept their voices low until Lord Cromwell raised his in a show of temper.

"You are a thief and a heretic."

"My lord, you wrong me," the other man protested.

"You stole silver and gold plate from the church of St. Gregory in Canterbury when you were a canon there. Cups and chalices meant for holy use. I could have you arrested for that crime at any time."

A sharply indrawn breath was followed by a lengthy silence. Wat risked peering around the edge of the arras for a better look, but there was not enough light to make out the stranger's features. All he could discern was that the fellow was tall and dressed like a priest.

"What is it you want of me, my lord?" The stranger's voice sounded subdued, almost subservient.

"I have a task in mind," Cromwell said. "One you are well suited to perform, since you seem to revel in conspiracy for its own sake."

"I am determined to advance myself. Is that so unusual?"

Cromwell gave a short bark of laughter. "You are an unscrupulous, irresponsible rogue, completely unsuited to being a clergyman."

"And yet that is what I became. Younger sons have little choice."

"Especially younger sons who are the black sheep of otherwise respectable families. Do not try to work your smooth-tongued charm on me. Save it for the purpose I have devised."

To Wat's frustration, Cromwell lowered his voice again. The boy caught only a few words of the ensuing dialogue, although those he did overhear intrigued him. Lord Cromwell said, "Calais," and later, "the lord deputy's wife."

After some little while, filled with more mumbling, the stranger said, "It will be as you wish, my lord," and took his leave. Wat thought he detected a note of sarcasm in the words, but if Lord Cromwell noticed, he did not comment. A few moments later, Cromwell also left. The study became noticeably darker.

Wat stepped out from behind the arras. The movement stirred dust in the air and he sneezed. Horrified, he froze. Had Cromwell heard? Would he return to investigate?

When nothing happened for several minutes, Wat thought he was safe. Belatedly, he realized the enormity of what he had done. He had witnessed Lord Cromwell coercing a priest into entering his employ. Whatever the man was to do, it involved Calais, the last English outpost on the Continent. Even though Wat had not understood most of what he had overheard, he knew too much. If he'd been caught . . .

Wat did not want to think about that. He took deep breaths to steady himself, then crept out of the study and back to his own bed. Best to forget what he'd heard, he decided. Just as he always put what he knew about his own father out of his mind.

*   *   *

AT COURT, NAN'S days passed with mind-numbing sameness until, at last, the queen's labor began. Her women rejoiced, but when it continued throughout the following day and the next night and into the day after that, worry replaced elation. No one dared voice the thoughts that were on all their minds—what if the queen should die? What if the child were stillborn?

"Where is the king?" Nan asked Anne Parr. "Does he know what is happening?"

"No doubt he does, and no doubt that is why he is at his hunting lodge at Esher and not here. He is close enough that he can reach Hampton Court quickly when he needs to, but far enough away that he does not have to see"—she broke off as another agonized scream rent the air—"or hear the queen's suffering." She lowered her voice. "The king has an aversion to illness of any kind. He will never go near anyone who is sick."

"He must protect himself from contagion," Nan said, defending His Grace, but at the same time could not help thinking him cowardly. He could scarcely catch what ailed the queen.

When more than fifty hours had passed and the queen's labor was well into its third night, a royal visitor did arrive, but it was the king's eldest daughter, not His Majesty. Even though she had never seen the Lady Mary Tudor before, Nan had no difficulty in recognizing her. Her clothes alone announced her status. Over the cloth-of-gold kirtle, the Lady Mary wore a violet velvet gown. Her headdress sparkled with precious gems. At her throat a jeweled *M* was set with rubies, diamonds, and a gigantic pearl.

At twenty-one, thin, and of middling stature, Mary Tudor was in no way beautiful, but she had a presence that was unmistakably royal. That did not surprise Nan. The Lady Mary had spent most of her life—until Mistress Anne Boleyn came along—being groomed to rule England.

Mary Zouche, who had once been a maid of honor to the Lady Mary's mother, scrambled to her feet and sank into a curtsy. After the slightest hesitation, everyone else followed her lead. Mary Tudor *was* the king's child, even if both she and her four-year-old half sister, Elizabeth, Anne Boleyn's daughter, had been disinherited and declared illegitimate by their father. The king claimed his marriage to Queen Jane was the only one that was legal.

The Lady Mary stared at Mistress Zouche with large, pale hazel eyes. She seemed to be trying to place the maid of honor. After a moment, Nan realized that Mary Tudor's intent gaze was actually a symptom of poor eyesight.

"Rise," said the Lady Mary in a surprisingly deep voice. "All of you. Mistress Zouche, how does the queen fare?"

When Mary Tudor drew Mary Zouche aside to hear her answer, Nan's attention wandered to the older woman who had accompanied the Lady Mary. The woman and Bess Jerningham were whispering together in a most familiar manner.

"Who is that?" Nan asked Anne Parr.

"Lady Kingston. She is Bess's mother. When she was still Lady Jerningham, she was one of Catherine of Aragon's ladies. This past year, she joined the Lady Mary's household." Now that she was looking for it, Nan saw the strong physical resemblance between the two women. Both had large brown eyes, wide mouths, and small, turned-up noses.

"My mother served Queen Catherine, too," Anne added in a low voice. "Mother devoted her life to royal service. Although she sought rich marriages for my sister and brother, she trained me to follow in her footsteps."

"Then you can find a wealthy and influential husband for yourself at court, as she must have done."

Anne chuckled. "My father died when I was two, so I do not remember him, but as far as I can tell his most outstanding accomplishment was to take the part of one of the Merry Men when King Henry disguised himself as Robin Hood and crept into Queen Catherine's bedchamber early one morning to demand that she rise and dance with him. Father had no title and no great wealth, either."

Her interest caught, Nan studied her friend. "Did your mother succeed in making good matches for your siblings?"

Anne nodded. "She arranged for my sister, Kathryn, to marry old Lord Burgh's son. After he died, Kathryn wed Lord Latimer. And our brother is married to the Earl of Essex's only child. Will has every expectation that the king will grant him that title when his father-in-law dies. But what of you, Nan? Have you brothers and sisters?"

"Three of each, and none of them wed, although my oldest brother is betrothed to my stepfather's daughter, Frances Plantagenet."

Anne's eyebrows lifted.

"My stepfather, Lord Lisle, is Arthur Plantagenet, a natural son of King Edward the Fourth. My stepfather has three daughters by his first wife—Frances, Elizabeth, and Bridget."

"And your own sisters?"

"Philippa is the eldest, Catherine next, and we have a younger sister, Mary, who is being brought up in the household of a French gentlewoman of my mother's acquaintance."

"The same family you were sent to?"

"Kin to them."

Nan's French upbringing had not produced the rich results her mother had hoped for, since England and France were again at odds. It had been Nan's charge to win and keep Queen Jane's favor. She was to promote her siblings and find a rich, titled husband for herself. But what if the queen and her baby did not survive childbirth? Who would advance the Bassetts then? Who would be worth cultivating?

Nan's gaze went to Mary Tudor. Would Catherine of Aragon's daughter be reinstated as King Henry's heir? If there was even the slightest possibility of that, then Nan would do well to meet the once and future princess and make a good impression on her.

It was not difficult for Nan to persuade Anne Parr to present her to Lady Kingston. As soon as Nan mentioned that she was Lady Lisle's daughter, Lady Kingston embraced Nan like a long-lost cousin. Both Lady Kingston and her second husband, who was constable of the Tower

of London, were among Honor Lisle's correspondents. After a few minutes of conversation, Lady Kingston presented Nan to the Lady Mary.

Mary Tudor's myopic hazel eyes fixed on Nan's face in a most disconcerting fashion. Nan wondered what the other woman was thinking. Most likely, she was reviewing what she knew about Nan's family.
Would she hold it against Nan that Lady Lisle had been one of Anne
Boleyn's attendants during the visit Anne made to France before she
became queen? Or would she remember hearing that Nan's mother still
clung to the old ways in religion? Doubtless, the Lady Mary knew both
these things.

Another agonized scream from the queen's bedchamber put an
abrupt end to Nan's hope of having a conversation with the king's daughter. Turning to Lady Kingston, the Lady Mary ordered the older woman
to investigate. Then she retreated to the far side of the privy chamber,
well away from any member of Queen Jane's household.

The waiting resumed. It lasted until nearly two o'clock in the morning on the twelfth day of October, when Queen Jane at last gave birth to
a healthy, fair-haired baby boy. Nan was ecstatic. All would be well now.
Soon she would have the life she'd dreamed of.

King Henry rode in all haste from Esher to Hampton Court, arriving
just at dawn. Nan was present in the royal bedchamber, now flooded
with light, when the king lifted his new son from the cradle and held him
in his arms for the first time. There were tears in His Grace's eyes.

"His name shall be Edward," Henry VIII proclaimed. "For my grandfather, and because he was born on the eve of St. Edward's Day."

The king lavished praise upon his exhausted wife, but as far
as Nan could see, Queen Jane was far too tired to care what her
husband thought. Nor did she react when he gave orders for every
courtyard and hallway near the nursery to be washed down and swept
daily.

"The king has a surprising passion for cleanliness," Nan observed
when His Grace had departed.

"He has good reason to fear contagion," Anne Parr said. "He had another son once. Catherine of Aragon's child. The boy lived only eleven days before he fell ill and died."

Nan did not quite see what washing and sweeping had to do with keeping a baby healthy, but she knew already that the king was more fastidious than most people. She'd heard from the other maids of honor that he took regular baths, in spite of the risks associated with immersing one's self in water. And he washed his hands far more often than was usual.

"Did you hear?" Anne asked, interrupting Nan's musings. "The queen wants everyone in lion tawny velvet or black velvet turned up with yellow satin for the christening."

Nan stared at her, appalled. "Do you mean to say that I will need *another* new gown?"

Anne nodded. "And in three days' time, too."

Nan groaned. If the queen commanded it, it would be done, but Master Husee was not going to be pleased.

ON THE EVENING of Monday, the fifteenth day of October, in the hours before the christening, nearly four hundred persons gathered outside the queen's apartments. Presently, they would be allowed in to pay their respects. Then they would move on into the Chapel Royal for the actual ceremony.

Arranged in a half circle behind Queen Jane, who reclined on a daybed covered with crimson damask lined with cloth-of-gold, the maids of honor stilled, smiled, and held their poses. Nan wore a new gown of black velvet trimmed with yellow satin. She loved the feel of the soft fabric. For all that Master Husee had been obliged to rush the needlewomen who made it, the workmanship was as fine as that on any of her companions' clothing.

Although she was otherwise motionless, her gaze roved. The same crimson that decorated the daybed was repeated in the mantle the queen wore around her shoulders. Nan envied her its ermine trim. Even at court, where servants dressed according to the rank of their masters, that particular fur was not for the likes of a mere gentlewoman.

When Nan's gaze came to rest on Her Grace's hair, she nearly sighed aloud. Queen Jane wore it uncovered and flowing free. In spite of her extreme paleness—or perhaps because of it—those long tresses, so light a brown as to be almost blond, gave her an ethereal beauty. In contrast, her maids of honor still wore their ugly, old-fashioned, unflattering gable headdresses.

A familiar scent tickled Nan's nose. Belatedly, her attention shifted to the king as he took his seat on an ornately carved and elaborately upholstered chair at the queen's side. He was so close to Nan that, had she dared, she could have reached out and touched him. Propping one foot on a stool, King Henry took his wife's right hand in both of his, the picture of husbandly devotion.

Careful not to attract unwanted attention, Nan looked her fill. She found the king's person just as appealing now as she had during their first encounter. Only with a supreme effort of will was she able to redirect her attention toward the door.

The first guests to enter were those of highest rank. Sequestered as she had been, Nan had not had many opportunities to match courtiers' names to their faces. Now she struggled to commit features to memory as each person was announced.

The Lady Mary was there, resplendent in a richly embroidered cloth-of-silver kirtle. She was the newborn Prince Edward's half sister and was to be his godmother. The Duke and Duchess of Suffolk and the Duke of Norfolk came in next. Aside from the prince, who would hold the titles Duke of Cornwall and Prince of Wales, the baby's godfathers, Norfolk and Suffolk, were the only two dukes in England. Neither of them was royal.

Nan stared at the Duchess of Suffolk. Blue eyed, with fair coloring, she was only two years Nan's senior, while the duke was in his fifties. It was not uncommon for an old man to take a young wife, especially if she had wealth as well as beauty, but it could not be pleasant for the bride. Nan shuddered delicately before she remembered that if she was successful here at court, she might well end up with a husband just as old and fat as Charles Brandon. But rich, she reminded herself. And titled. She suspected she could put up with a great deal to be a duchess.

She stole another glance at the Duke of Norfolk. His wife was not with him. Nan had heard that she was confined to a manor house in Hertfordshire because she'd dared object, loudly and in public, when the duke installed his mistress at the family seat of Kenninghall.

Norfolk had a stern and forbidding manner that went well with his hawk nose and tightly pursed lips. At present, his face wore a pained expression. That did not surprise Nan. Queen Anne Boleyn had been his niece. All her family had lost the king's favor when she was arrested, charged with adultery, and executed. It must be a bitter honor to stand godfather to a prince born to Queen Anne's successor, especially when the duke had thought to see his own kin poised to inherit the throne.

Having examined the three most important personages in the crowd, Nan shifted her attention to lesser noblemen. The Marquess of Exeter came next in precedence and entered the queen's apartments right after the two dukes. England's only other marquess, Dorset, was not in attendance. He, his mother, and his wife had been ordered to stay away because there was plague in the vicinity of the dowager Lady Dorset's manor house at Croydon. The king refused to take any risks with the health of his son and heir.

Earls came next. Nan already knew Sussex and Rutland on sight. Robert Radcliffe, Earl of Sussex, was a homely man past his prime, with deep-set eyes, a prominent nose, and a gray beard trimmed to a point. His oldest son and heir, Lord Fitzwalter, was a widower, but he was twice Nan's age and looked a good deal like his father. She hoped to do better.

The Earl of Rutland, Thomas Manners by name, was younger than Sussex, but not by much. His beard, square cut, was going gray. Lady

Rutland had been married to him for nearly fifteen years and had presented him with numerous children. The two oldest had recently been married off, despite their young ages, to other young people of noble birth.

Seeking better prospects, Nan shifted her focus to three other earls—Arundel, Oxford, and Wiltshire—but none of them were prospective husbands either. They already had wives and the latter had another count against him. He was Anne Boleyn's father.

Also married were the next two noblemen to be announced, Lord William Howard, a younger son of the Duke of Norfolk, and Edward, Lord Beauchamp, Queen Jane's oldest brother. The queen's younger brother, Thomas Seymour, was a different kettle of fish. Not only was he still single, but he was a fine-looking man. Nan's gaze lingered on his muscular physique. A pity that, so far, he was not even a knight. She moved on to the next group of courtiers.

Nan skipped over Thomas Cranmer, archbishop of Canterbury—no marriage prospect there! In England, clergymen were not allowed to marry, although some secretly had wives. Next to Cranmer was Thomas, Lord Cromwell, the king's Lord Privy Seal and most trusted advisor. Cromwell's son had recently married Queen Jane's widowed sister. Cromwell was himself a widower, Nan recalled, but she did not for one moment consider him as a prospective husband. Like the Earl of Sussex, he had seen more than fifty summers. Besides, he was at odds with her stepfather.

Nan looked quickly away when Cromwell noticed her staring at him. Even with her eyes modestly downcast, she knew she was being watched. But when she peeked at Cromwell again, he had lost interest in her. Through lowered lashes, she searched the crowd. With a sense of pleasure, she identified several courtiers of lesser rank, both knights and plain gentlemen, who were looking her way. Nan wished they could see her in her French wardrobe, instead of the dull styles Queen Jane had mandated. Then she reminded herself that a mere gentleman or knight would not do. She wanted a man with a title.

Nan's gaze fell next on Lord Montagu, grandson of that infamous Duke of Clarence who had been the brother of Edward IV and Richard III and had been—so it was said—drowned in a butt of Malmsey wine while a prisoner in the Tower of London. She stifled a smile at the thought.

Nan glanced at Lord Cromwell again, but this time the Lord Privy Seal was too absorbed in his conversation with the archbishop to notice her interest. Someone else did, though. A boy in Cromwell's livery stood next to him, watching Nan intently. She stared back. She had no idea who he was, although it seemed likely that he was some gentleman's son sent to finish his education in Cromwell's service. He looked to be twelve or thirteen, a gangly lad with little to recommend him beyond a head of thick and wavy dark brown hair.

When Peter Mewtas was announced, Nan lost interest in the boy. She studied Mewtas with considerable interest. What was it about him, she wondered, that had prompted Jane to give up her post as a maid of honor and marry him? He was nothing remarkable to look at. Tall, yes, and athletic. So were most courtiers. Mewtas had yellow hair and a long, yellow beard. He was a gentleman of the privy chamber, but as yet he had not been knighted and he had no particular prospects. His grandfather, so Nan had been told, had been a native of Picardy and had been employed as French secretary by King Henry's father.

Nan was still contemplating Peter Mewtas when a slight movement at her elbow distracted her. Anne Parr leaned forward, her gaze fixed upon a man wearing the livery of the King's Spears, Henry VIII's elite bodyguard. A rather ordinary-looking fellow of thirty or so, he was tall and lanky and had a shock of red hair.

Nan was about to ask Anne who he was—she had not been paying attention when he was announced—when she caught a glimpse of the man next in line to enter the chamber. The sight drove every other thought out of her head. It was Ned Corbett.

In honor of the occasion, Ned wore his finest doublet and hose. A brilliant jewel sparkled on the hat he swept from his tousled hair to make his bow to the king and queen. He offered felicitations to the royal couple on behalf of Lord and Lady Lisle. Then, to Nan's horror, he asked to speak with her, saying he had messages for her from her family in Calais. Nan felt her cheeks flame as Ned looked her way and winked.

The queen graciously granted permission. She had been in a mellow mood ever since she'd fulfilled her duty and produced an heir. She'd also been indulging herself by eating her favorite foods, including an enormous quantity of sweets.

As deftly as any accomplished courtier, Ned whisked Nan away from the other maids of honor, threading his way through the crowd until he reached a secluded corner where they would have a modicum of privacy. Keeping one hand on her elbow, as if he were afraid she might bolt, he grinned down at her.

Nan glowered back. "Did you just lie to the king and queen of England?"

"I did," he said. And if Ned felt any guilt in the matter, it did not show. The mischievous glint in his eyes was impossible to resist. "I confess. I wanted an excuse to speak with you, Mistress Nan Bassett."

"Why?"

His gaze slid downward. "To praise your new attire? Master Husee outdid himself in procuring so many garments in so little time. I cannot repeat the language he used when word came that you must have yet another new gown."

In spite of her irritation with him, Nan smiled back. "Then he will be wroth indeed when he learns that I must have two more, one of them in time for the queen's churching and the other by Christmas."

"Oh, that *will* delight him! And does Queen Jane have particular requirements as to color and fabric?"

She made a face at him. "Does that not go without saying? We are all to wear satin at the churching, and gowns of lion tawny velvet for Yuletide."

"You will look well in lion tawny. The color will bring out the gold in your hair."

"That scarcely matters when no one can see it. The queen requires us to wear these cumbersome, all-concealing headdresses."

That one restriction still irked her more than all the others combined. Nan knew how well she looked in a French hood, especially with her unbound hair flowing freely down her back. It reached nearly to her hips and was of an excellent texture.

"I return to Calais tomorrow," Ned said. "Have you any message for Lady Lisle?"

"Tell Mother to send more quails if she would keep Her Majesty sweet."

Chuckling, Ned left her and bowed his way out of the chamber. He walked backward, as protocol demanded. The sight amused Nan until the door opened and she caught sight of her sister waiting in the chamber beyond. Ned turned, smiled at Cat, then went straight to her side. Cat greeted him with obvious pleasure and considerable familiarity. As the guards eased the portal closed again, Nan was left to wonder just how often the two of them had met during the weeks she had been sequestered.

CAT SMILED SHYLY at Ned Corbett. Truly he was a lovely man. He was under no obligation to spend time with her when he delivered messages to personages at court from her mother and stepfather, and yet he did. They'd gone for long walks in the royal gardens and now he was escorting her to witness Prince Edward's christening.

"We'd best hurry," he said, taking her arm. "There will be hundreds of people all trying to crowd into the Chapel Royal at once. If we want to be able to see everything, we need to get there early and claim the best spot."

"Lady Rutland says they'll progress two by two, just like the animals going to Noah's ark." She'd also warned Cat that the pageantry and ceremony combined would last five or six hours.

Ned chuckled as he swept her along. She had to trot to keep pace with him as they passed through corridors illuminated as bright as day by men-at-arms holding torches.

"Did you speak with Nan? Is she well?" Lady Rutland had said she was, but Cat worried about her younger sister. Nan was not accustomed to being shut in. Cat knew that physicians said the air, especially the night air, carried all manner of contagions, but she also knew from firsthand experience that she felt better when she could indulge in a daily constitutional out of doors. Cat had been very grateful these last few weeks that she was not the one Queen Jane had chosen as a maid of honor.

"She seems in excellent health and spirits," Ned said.

Cat heard the admiration in his voice and had to stifle a sigh. She should be accustomed to this by now. Gentlemen always preferred Nan. They were drawn to her vivaciousness as well as her beauty.

Ned found a place for them near the entrance to the chapel. They had scarcely settled themselves when the first gentlemen of the household appeared carrying torches—two by two, just as Lady Rutland had predicted. The members of the chapel choir followed, then the dean, abbots, chaplains, and bishops.

Members of the privy council came next, followed by assorted noblemen, the lord treasurer and the controller of the household, a group of foreign ambassadors, the lord chamberlain, the Lord Privy Seal, and the lord chancellor. Ned whispered names as they passed, identifying them for Cat, but she paid little attention. Their identities were unimportant to her. The spectacle was all.

The baby's godfathers and the archbishop of Canterbury, who was to officiate at the christening, were followed by two earls carrying silver basins and two more bearing a wax taper and a gold saltcellar. The Lady Elizabeth, only four years old, came next, carrying the heavily embroidered and bejeweled chrisom-cloth. No one seeing her could ever doubt that she was King Henry's child. She had the Tudor red hair and something of the king's petulance, as well. Clearly she wanted to fulfill her role in the ceremony unaided, but the chrisom-cloth was too bulky for her to manage alone. When she faltered, the queen's brother, Lord Beauchamp, picked her up. He carried both child and chrisom-cloth into the chapel.

At last the baby Prince Edward appeared in the arms of the Marchioness of Exeter. She walked under a canopy supported by three other noblewomen. The baby prince was dressed in a long, white gown with a train so long that it had to be carried by two noblemen. The Lady Mary followed with her ladies. Bringing up the rear were the baby's wet nurse and the midwife. They walked under a canopy, too, this one held by six gentlemen.

Tears began to flow down Cat's cheeks. Ned produced a square of linen and gently patted them dry. "Why are you sad?" he asked.

"I am not," she said, sniffling. "I am crying because it is all so beautiful. Truly, the royal court is full of wonders!"

My Lady of Rutland has commanded me to tarry and to come back again to Hampton Court, and so to wait upon Mistress Katherine and to bring her to her house, because she hath but a few servants there. My lady herself and all the ladies must ride to Windsor to the burial, and so from thence for to come to London. She would have taken Mistress Katherine with her, but that she had no mourning gown.

—Edward Corbett to Lady Lisle, 10 November 1537

3

Had Anne Parr not elbowed Nan in the ribs, the queen would have caught her woolgathering. Nan barely managed not to cry out. She had no idea how much time had passed. Ned and all the rest had long since departed for the Chapel Royal. Only the king, the queen, the maids of honor, and a few yeomen of the guard had remained behind.

By tradition, a baby's parents did not attend their child's christening. Their Graces awaited the return of all and sundry at the end of the ceremony, when refreshments would be served—hippocras and wafers to the nobility and bread and sweet wine to the gentry. It would be close to midnight by then.

The king and queen had been engaged in quiet conversation when Nan's mind wandered. Now the king rose and stretched.

"My dear," he said to Queen Jane, "I fear I grow stiff with all this sitting. I must move about a bit."

"As you wish, Your Grace. With your leave, I will remain as I am. My strength has not yet fully returned." She reached for another comfit from the silver dish beside her.

After kissing his wife's hand, His Majesty turned to the maids of honor. "Scatter, my pretties. There is no need for you to stand at attention. My guards do enough of that for everyone."

Obediently, they all laughed at his quip. Five of the six maids were equally quick to comply with the royal command. Even the most limber person soon tired of staying in one position for too long. Only Mary Zouche elected to remain with the queen.

Anne Parr caught Nan's arm and tugged her toward a window embrasure. Her wide-spaced gray eyes were alight with pleasure. "Well? Is he not wonderful?"

"The king? Why, that goes without saying."

Anne rapped Nan lightly on the shoulder. "I mean Will Herbert, and well you know it."

It took Nan a moment to connect the name to the tall redhead Anne had been admiring earlier. "He is somewhat bony for my taste," she remarked.

"He is stronger than he looks." Anne blushed becomingly.

"Why, Anne!" Nan pretended to be shocked.

In truth, she *was* a trifle surprised. It was abundantly clear from the way Anne had leapt to Will Herbert's defense, and the dreamy look that came into her eyes when she said his name, that she was in love with Master William Herbert. Nan remembered then that Cat had told her Anne was likely to be the next maid of honor to wed.

"Tell me about him," Nan prompted. "Who is he? What are his prospects?"

"He is Welsh. His father was an earl's bastard, but that does not mean much in Wales."

"Still—"

"Will has made a career for himself here at court. But that is not important, either. Oh, Nan—he cares for me as deeply as I do for him. We plan to marry."

Nan opened her mouth to point out that if neither of them had any money, they would have nothing upon which to live. At the last moment, she held her tongue. Of all the maids of honor, Anne had been the only one to go out of her way to show kindness to a newcomer. Romantic love always made people do stupid things. That was why Nan was determined to avoid its pitfalls in her own life. But voicing that opinion would only annoy Anne and do nothing to change her mind about marrying Will Herbert.

Linking arms with her friend, Nan commenced to stroll. They made one circuit of the room, then another, as Anne continued to laud Will's virtues. On the third, their paths crossed that of the king.

"Mistress Bassett," King Henry said as both women sank into deep curtsies. "I trust you have settled into your new position without difficulty."

Her head almost touching the floor, Nan murmured, "I have, Your Grace. Your Grace is most kind to ask."

Ignoring Anne Parr, the king tugged Nan to her feet and kept hold of her hand once she was standing. Smiling down at her, he tucked her arm through his and began a slow promenade. Everyone they passed bowed low. To Nan, it seemed almost as if they were bowing to her. Was this what it was like for Queen Jane? Nan took particular delight in seeing Mary Zouche and Jane Arundell dip their heads.

"We are most indebted to your lady mother," the king said as he began a second circuit of the chamber. "Her gifts are always a delight."

"She is pleased to be of service, Your Majesty."

"She would have liked to place both you and your sister with the queen, I think."

"She wishes to see all of us well provided for," Nan temporized.

"Tell me, Nan, did you leave many suitors behind in Calais?"

"None, Your Majesty. And even if I had, how could they compare to the lords at Your Grace's court?" The king's genial manner had dispelled Nan's nervousness but this question set off warning bells. Did he have some personal reason for asking? That His Grace seemed extraordinarily pleased by this answer caused a frisson of alarm to snake through her. She was flattered by the king's attention, but by custom he would not return to his wife's bed for some weeks yet, not until after she was churched—purified by a special church service. If His Grace's interest *was* amorous in nature, Nan had no idea how to respond. She had come to court to find a husband, not a lover. She'd not set out to seduce the king, either, but only to charm him into looking favorably on any request she might make on her mother's behalf.

Nan's heart speeded up, beating far too loudly. She was certain the king could hear it. She felt heat creep into her cheeks and her palms began to sweat. She did not know if her reaction came from attraction or trepidation but suspected it was a little of both.

When they passed the queen's daybed, Nan darted a glance that way. At once, she wished she had not. Queen Jane's glare did not bode well, nor did the suspicious expression on Mary Zouche's square-jawed face.

THROUGHOUT ENGLAND, AND even as far away as Calais, bells pealed and bonfires blazed in honor of the new prince. But on the afternoon of the day after the christening, Queen Jane fell ill. By Wednesday morning, her ladies were deeply concerned.

"What ails Her Grace?" Nan asked, waylaying her cousin Mary, the Countess of Sussex, as Mary passed through the privy chamber.

"Is it childbed fever?" Mary Zouche voiced the question all of them had already asked themselves.

"It may be." The countess's tear-ravaged features and bleak expression made her look a decade older. "I am sent to fetch the king's personal physicians."

Queen Jane rallied on Thursday. The king went ahead with the investiture ceremony that created Edward Seymour, Queen Jane's elder brother, Earl of Hertford, and knighted the younger, Thomas Seymour.

On Friday evening, while celebrations of Prince Edward's birth continued throughout the realm, the queen became feverish once again. Delirium followed, growing steadily worse on Saturday, Sunday, and Monday.

Nan did not hold out much hope that the queen would recover. She knew full well how often women died after childbirth. And if Queen Jane died, her household would be disbanded. Without a queen, there was no need for maids of honor. Nan would be obliged to leave the court before she'd had the opportunity to enjoy any of its pleasures.

Despondent, she sought solitude in one of the palace gardens. At last she was free to go wherever she would at Hampton Court. Much good it did her! With the queen dying, no wealthy, titled nobleman would dare be seen flirting with one of the maids of honor. They must all be respectful and sorrowful and wear long faces.

Nan kicked a stone out of her way and watched it bounce into the shrubbery. She wanted to scream in frustration. She might have given in to the impulse had she not suddenly realized that she was not alone amid the flower beds and topiary work.

As King Henry approached, trailed by his usual escort of gentlemen and guards, Nan dropped into a curtsy. She expected His Grace to pass by. Instead, he stopped in front of her, hesitated a moment, and then ordered his attendants to fall back to give him privacy.

"Walk with me," the king commanded.

For several minutes, he said nothing more. The only sound was the crunch of their leather-shod feet on the gravel path. But when they reached a small, ornate bridge over a man-made pond, the king stopped to look down at her, his face a study in consternation.

"How does Queen Jane fare today, Mistress Bassett?"

Nan hesitated. It was not wise to tell a king something he did not want to hear, but lying would avail her nothing. "No better, Your Grace."

"I had intended to return to Esher on the morrow," he murmured, "but I cannot find it in my heart to leave her."

It was on the tip of Nan's tongue to tell the king that he should visit his wife, but she did not dare be that bold. She remembered what Anne Parr had said about King Henry's aversion to sickness of any kind. If His Grace could not abide being near anyone who was ill, she did not suppose he'd have much tolerance for deathbed vigils.

"She gave me a son."

"Yes, Your Grace. A beautiful boy."

"She has done her duty."

Nan was not sure how to respond to that statement. It was almost as if the king thought Queen Jane might as well go ahead and die, now that she had provided him with his much-desired male heir.

Abruptly, King Henry bid Nan adieu and left her there on the bridge. She heard him call for his escort and then he was out of sight, behind a hedge. Her mind awash with confusion, she fled back to the queen's apartments.

LESS THAN TWO weeks after giving birth to Prince Edward, two days after Nan's encounter with King Henry in the garden, Queen Jane tragically died. The king left Hampton Court as soon as he was told of her passing. Grief? Nan wondered as she watched His Grace's departure for Windsor Castle from an upper window. King Henry was all in blue, the color English royalty wore for mourning, but that signified nothing.

Nan was not certain what she felt, either, other than a sense of being set adrift with neither compass nor rudder. She had no idea what would happen to her next. She might be sent back to the Pale of Calais, England's last tiny stronghold on the Continent. Or she could be offered a position in some noble household. That would be better than returning to her mother, but not as good as being at court. A tear trickled down her cheek as she contemplated all she had lost.

Cousin Mary came to stand beside her. Her eyes were red and

swollen and her voice was husky. "Come, Nan. Seamstresses await us in my chamber."

Nan sighed and followed her. "I suppose we must all wear black for mourning."

"Not only that, but there are very particular rules for those who rank above a knight's wife."

Nan pretended to be interested, but her mind was fuzzy with weariness, her wits clouded with disappointment. She caught only bits of her cousin's discourse, something about a mantle, a surcoat, and a plain hood, all in black, over a Paris headdress and a pleated white linen barbe that would cover Mary's chin as well as the front of her neck. Nan thought longingly of the new lion tawny velvet gown and the satin one—a lovely crimson shade—that Master Husee had so diligently procured for her. It would be months now before she'd be able to wear either.

Cousin Mary was smiling ruefully when Nan's attention returned to her cousin. "I am glad I am not a duchess," Mary said with a wry chuckle. "The greater the rank, the longer the train."

"Am I to have a train?" Nan asked.

"You have not heard a word I've said, have you?" Sounding exasperated, Cousin Mary pushed open the door to her own chamber. "Knights' wives and gentlewomen of the household must wear surcoats with moderate front trains and no mantles."

"And what is a surcoat?" She was not familiar with the term.

"It is an old-fashioned garment such as they wore in the days of King Edward IV. It is made like a close-bodied gown."

Inside the countess's rooms, a servant was just closing the window and preparing to drape it in black cloth. The maids had already packed away Mary's usual assortment of colorful clothing.

The tears that sprang into Nan's eyes were heartfelt, as were her whispered words: "It is most unfair that Queen Jane should die."

The queen's lying-in-state began on the day following her death. For a week, she lay in her own Presence Chamber, where her ladies took turns keeping vigil day and night. Then, on the last day of October, the body was taken by torchlight to the Chapel Royal, where it would remain until the twelfth of November, when it would be transported to Windsor Castle for the funeral and burial. The queen's ladies continued to keep vigil during the day, but now gentlemen took their places at night.

On the last day of that duty, Lady Rutland took Cat Bassett aside. "I have asked Master Corbett to escort you to Rutland House in Shoreditch," the countess said. "I will join you there as soon as the queen's household is officially dispersed."

"But why, my lady?" Cat asked in alarm. "Have I offended you?"

"Not at all, my dear. But you lack the proper clothing to accompany the funeral cortege to Windsor Castle." As the third gentlewoman serving the Countess of Rutland when she was only supposed to keep two ladies-in-waiting at court, Cat had not been provided with mourning by the Crown.

"What will happen to my sister?" Cat asked. "Where is Nan to go?"

"Lady Sussex will house her for the time being, just as I will continue to look out for you. You know already that your mother has been seeking a position for you in the household of the Duchess of Suffolk. The Countess of Hertford is another possibility. So is the Lady Mary. Never fear. In time, you and Nan will both find good places."

"I would rather remain with you than serve another," Cat said.

Lady Rutland patted her cheek with one plump hand. "You are a sweet child. Now, go and pack your belongings and be ready to depart on the morrow just as soon as the funeral cortege leaves Hampton Court."

Cat did as she was told. At five o'clock the next morning—a full two hours before dawn—she stood next to Ned Corbett to watch Queen Jane leave Hampton Court for the last time.

Guards, household officers, officials, and a hundred paupers came first, followed by noblemen, ambassadors, heralds, and gentlemen of the court, some of them holding banners aloft. Six lords rode, three on a side, with the chariot that contained the queen's casket. It was drawn by six horses with black trappings beneath a canopy of black velvet fringed with black silk and decorated with a white satin cross.

The queen's effigy was prominently displayed on top of the casket, clothed in robes of state and holding a scepter in a hand that had real rings on the fingers. There were golden shoes on its feet and the head wearing the crown rested on a golden pillow.

More noblemen came next, then the Lady Mary. As chief mourner, she was mounted on a horse trapped with black velvet. The king would not take part in any of the ceremonies. According to custom, a husband did not attend the funeral of his wife.

Some of the ladies and gentlewomen of the court had gone ahead to Windsor, but all those who had not—and who had proper mourning garments—followed the king's daughter in the procession. Some were on horseback. Others rode in black chariots. Lady Sussex and Lady Rutland both had places in the first one. Nan sat inside the fifth and last chariot with some of the other maids of honor. Cat had a clear view of her sister's ravaged face, staring straight ahead.

"She has been deeply affected by the queen's death," Cat murmured.

"Indeed," Ned agreed. "She did not plan for this."

Cat frowned at his tone, but his expression was properly somber. When the last of the cortege had passed by, he took her arm and led her to the water stairs where a boat waited to take them downriver.

Ned said little during their journey on the Thames. Cat found herself remembering the last death to touch her closely, that of her father when she was only nine years old. For Cat's mother, the loss of a spouse had meant she must find a new husband, someone who could help her provide dowries for four daughters and two stepdaughters and find employment for two younger sons. Once upon a time, one of the boys and one or more of the girls would have gone into the church. After King Henry's break with Rome, that had no longer been a choice. These days becoming a nun or a Catholic priest meant living in exile, branded a traitor, like Lord Lisle's cousin, Cardinal Pole. One by one, the monasteries and nunneries were being closed. Soon there would be none left in England.

The sound of bells ringing penetrated Cat's reverie.

"London," Ned said.

"But the city is still miles away," she protested.

"That is the sound of every church bell in a hundred parishes, tolling in memory of Queen Jane."

The din was deafening when they disembarked for the ride through London on horseback to the Earl of Rutland's house in Shoreditch, a northern suburb of the city. But just as they reached their destination, an eerie quiet descended.

The mansion itself was not only silent, but nearly deserted, and permeated by an icy chill. Ned set the cook to preparing a light supper and started a fire in Lady Rutland's parlor with his own hands. He was adept at the task, clearly accustomed to looking out for himself.

"You do not seem much disturbed by being sent away from court," he observed as he balanced a small piece of wood on the stack of burning kindling.

"It matters little to me where I am," Cat said, "although I do enjoy Lady Rutland's company."

"After the queen is buried, her household will be dispersed. I suppose your sister will go to the Countess of Sussex?"

"So we expect. Temporarily, at least." Cat supposed she should not be surprised that Ned asked about her beautiful younger sister, but she did not want to talk about Nan. To change the subject, she asked him when he was due to depart for Calais.

"Not for some time." His blue eyes twinkled in the firelight. "While John Husee meets with Lord Lisle in Calais, I remain here in his place."

"How pleasant for you."

"For you, too, I hope. You know how I enjoy spending time with you."

Absurdly pleased by his comment, Cat felt herself flush. "You are welcome to visit me here as often as you like during your sojourn on this side of the Narrow Seas."

"I look forward to seeing a great deal more of you."

A shy smile curved her lips when he winked at her. His added responsibilities meant her stepfather trusted Ned and meant to advance him. Did she dare hope Lord Lisle might consider Ned worthy to court one of his stepdaughters? It would be very easy, Cat thought, for her to fall in love with Ned Corbett.

PLAIN FACED AS Cat Bassett was, Ned Corbett thought, it was inevitable that she would fall for his flattery. A few days after he'd brought her to the Earl of Rutland's house in Shoreditch, they walked together in the gallery, just as they had each day she'd been in residence. When they came to the far end, Ned tugged Cat into his arms and took advantage of the shadows to give her a lingering kiss on the lips.

The clatter of hooves and wheels on the cobblestone courtyard of Rutland House interrupted him before he could do more. He cursed under his breath. The commotion could mean only one thing—Lady Rutland had arrived home.

A short time later, Ned and Cat took their turn greeting the countess. She gave him a narrow-eyed look, but addressed her words to Cat. "Lady Sussex traveled with me from Windsor. Even now she is at her husband's house in London. Your sister is with her."

Ned hid his elation. Here was a piece of luck. He had expected the Countess of Sussex to go to the earl's manor in Chelsea. The place was easily accessible by boat, but would have been expensive for him to visit on a regular basis. The cost of hiring wherries mounted quickly and Ned had to hoard his pennies. Having Nan Bassett in London meant she'd be only a short walk from John Husee's house, where Ned lodged. He could continue to court Cat Bassett and at the same time pay frequent visits to her sister without incurring any appreciable expense.

The next day Ned made his first call on Lady Sussex. She received him in a bright, sunny room luxuriously furnished with not one, but two chairs. There were Turkey carpets atop the tables and richly woven tapestries on the walls. And it was overflowing with females in all shapes and sizes.

Ned's gaze went first to Nan. She had abandoned her gable headdress for a French hood and was all in mourning black. The dark garments flattered her pink-and-white complexion.

Seated next to Nan on a low, padded bench was the countess's half sister, Jane Arundell, another displaced maid of honor. On a cushion on the floor sat the countess's orphaned niece, Kate Stradling. Kate had the dark hair and eyes of the Arundells and a heart-shaped face that would have been appealing had it not been spoiled by a rather sallow complexion. On the window seat Ned identified one of the countess's cousins, Isabel Staynings, who had lost her husband to the most recent outbreak of the plague and was great with child besides. He recalled that Nan was kin to both Kate and Isabel through her mother.

Ned bowed to Lady Sussex and explained that he had been appointed to fill in for Master Husee during Husee's sojourn in Calais. "I bring letters from Lady Lisle," he added.

The countess took the one inscribed "To the right honorable and my very good Lady of Sussex." The other was for Nan.

Offered refreshments, Ned munched on marchpane made with blanched almonds and sugar and sipped barley water while the two women read. Nan's eyes lifted briefly from the paper to meet his. He winked to let her know that he was aware of the letter's contents.

"Honor invites you to join her in Calais, Isabel," Lady Sussex announced. "She writes: 'If my niece Stayning will take the pain to come over hither, she shall be as welcome as heart can think, and her woman with her.' That is a generous offer."

"Lady Lisle always seems to be in need of waiting gentlewomen. None stay long if they have the means to escape her service," said Jane Arundell. Her acid-tongued remark created an expression of sheer panic on Isabel's face.

"You are welcome to remain at Sussex House as long as you wish," Lady Sussex assured her. "I enjoy your company."

Isabel's relief was painfully obvious, but so was her embarrassment. "Your mother has always been kind to me," she said to Nan in a soft, almost inaudible voice, "but I fear she would be a . . . difficult mistress."

Nan started to deny it, then shrugged. "Her reputation precedes her. I just hope she does not decide to send for me next. I do not have the liberty of refusing."

"She will not take you away, not when she knows that we are bound to have a new queen soon," the countess said. "The king must marry again. He cannot place all his hopes on young Prince Edward. He must beget more sons to secure the succession."

"He has daughters," Nan pointed out. "Queen Catherine gave him Mary, and Anne Boleyn's daughter, Elizabeth, is the very image of her father."

The countess looked at her askance. "They are both barred from inheriting on the grounds they are illegitimate."

"It will be months yet before the king is out of mourning," Ned remarked. He watched Nan closely, trying to gauge her state of mind. He admired Cat Bassett's serenity, but she was a dull stick compared to her sister. Even when Nan was out of sorts, she had a vibrant quality Cat lacked. And it went without saying that Nan was by far the prettier of the two sisters.

"It may take years to negotiate with some foreign power for a new queen," Jane said. "She will have to be a princess this time. The king's marriage is too valuable a tool of diplomacy to waste on another English girl."

Nan did not look pleased by the prospect of a long delay. Ned took another swallow of barley water to hide his smile. Nan's discontent suited him, for it provided him with an excellent opportunity.

The next time he visited Sussex House, Ned asked the countess's permission to stroll with Nan in the walled garden at the back. It contained several small trees, and an expanse of turf had a fountain at its center. Now that it was November, the fountain was dry and empty. No flowers bloomed. The grass was brown. The only color came from plants that stayed green all year round—rosemary, lavender, myrtle, and germander.

Near the far wall, a gardener worked with his spade. Whether he was digging something up or planting it, Ned could not tell.

"Earlier in the week," Nan said, "I saw a woman weeding a flower bed. These days watching servants work passes for entertainment."

"Things cannot be so bad as all that." He was careful to keep the satisfaction out of his voice. She'd been in London less than a week and already she was chafing at the bit.

"Cousin Mary is expecting a child and is loath to do anything to endanger the babe," Nan said. "For that reason, she has declared that November is a bleak month best spent indoors. When I said I did not wish to pass the time embroidering, she suggested that I play the lute instead." Nan grimaced and related her last experience with that instrument. Time and distance allowed her to laugh at herself, but her voice also held a deep sadness as she recalled Queen Jane's reaction to her performance.

"So she threw a pillow at you," Ned repeated, shaking his head. "Did you play so very poorly?"

"I am an excellent musician. She'd have admitted that, had she lived."

Having reached a bower, Ned stopped and drew Nan down beside him on a stone bench. "It is a great pity the queen died," he said, "but at least you had the opportunity to live at court for a little while."

"All I have to show for my short tenure as a maid of honor are clothes I cannot abide and the services of a tiring maid."

"No spaniel?" He tried to tease her bitterness away.

"I did not choose to acquire one."

"Tell me about your maidservant, then."

"Why?" She held herself stiffly, her eyes suddenly wary.

"So that I may assure myself that she serves you well. While Husee is in Calais, it is my responsibility to see to your every need."

"Find me a queen to serve, then!"

"Tell me about your maid," he insisted, certain that any knowledge of the person closest to Nan on a daily basis would prove useful to him.

"Oh, very well! Her name is Constance Ware. She is a girl from the countryside near one of the earl's estates. Cousin Mary selected her. Constance is a year younger than I am and still as gangly as a colt. Cousin Mary's tiring maid has taken her in hand to teach her all she needs to know to dress me and look after my belongings."

"Are you satisfied with her?"

"She'll do well enough." Nan toyed with the embroidered band trimming her sleeves. "Will my sister stay with Lady Rutland, do you think? At one time there was talk that whichever of us failed to become a maid of honor would go to the Duchess of Suffolk, but Mother thought she was too young. The duchess, not Cat. Lady Suffolk is only two years older than I am."

"Who can say? Cat seems happy where she is."

"I could go to the duchess in her stead."

"If not a queen, then a duchess will do? Well, why not? A duchess takes precedence over every countess in the land. But I thought you wanted to be at court. The Duchess of Suffolk remains in the country for some time yet, since she is also expecting a child."

Nan grimaced. "More babies! It is an epidemic."

"There has been talk of placing your sister in the household of the Lady Mary."

Nan's look of dismay amused Ned, although he was careful not to let his reaction show. A princess, even one who had been eliminated from the succession, still took precedence over a duchess. "Never tell me you want that post for yourself?"

Nan mulled it over. "I suppose not, since the prince appears to thrive. And the Lady Mary is hardly ever at court. They say the king has never forgiven her for siding with her mother over the divorce."

Ned gave a bark of laughter. "Always thinking. Always planning. Always looking for the best way to get what you want. You are the most determined woman I've ever met, Nan Bassett."

"There is nothing wrong with ambition!" A tinge of pink colored her cheeks as her temper flared.

"Indeed, there is not." He slid one arm around her waist.

"You grow bold, sir." But she did not pull away from him.

He tugged her close against his side. "I must make certain you are warm enough. It grows colder by the minute on this gray November day."

"A paltry excuse for such familiarity," she chided him, "but it will serve, I think. You do realize that at least one of my kinswomen is certain to be spying on us from that convenient window in the ground-floor parlor?"

He had not. A glance showed him that it overlooked the garden. Ned wished they could adjourn to somewhere more private, but that was like asking for the moon. He would have to content himself with conversation . . . for now.

"Why are you so unhappy?" he asked.

"What have I to be cheerful about? All my hopes have been dashed. Soon Cousin Mary will go into seclusion, just as Queen Jane did. Once again, I will be cut off from all light, all air, all amusement."

"Surely that will not happen for some time yet." He'd not have guessed the countess was expecting a child if Nan had not told him.

"Mary expects to give birth sometime in March."

"Months away! Perhaps by then the Earl of Sussex may have found you a husband."

Nan sent an annoyed glare his way. "The earl may have been thrice married himself, but he is no one's choice as a matchmaker. His idea of a suitable spouse would likely be some minor lord's youngest son!"

"Ah, my poor Nan!" He waggled his eyebrows at her. "Great heavens! If that is the case, you might as well marry me."

Irritated, she pulled free of his embrace. "I would rather die a maid than wed a man with no money."

Ned winced. "What a waste that would be! No one with any sense, my sweet, would voluntarily choose chastity if they had any other alternative. Do you seriously think you can live all your life without ever sampling the joys of love? Dearest Nan, I can imagine no worse fate."

She punched him lightly on the arm. "Far worse to live a life of abject poverty. Or one of servitude. Or of utter boredom."

When Nan stood, Ned followed suit. They began to stroll again, weaving in and out among the raised flower beds. "I am sorry you are so unhappy with your lot."

"I thought my life would be full of excitement once I escaped Calais. Even if I cannot be at court just now, there should be other pleasures. London is right out there." She gestured toward the garden wall. Very faintly, they could hear the noises of the city beyond. "It is so near, and yet I cannot venture into its streets. I vow I am wasting away for want of freedom. When I lived in France as a child, we often left the château. I rode out into the countryside, just for the exercise. And once Madame de Riou took me to the French court and I saw King Francis himself."

"Did you now?"

A mischievous look came into her eyes. "Only from a distance. Madame was full of warnings. She did not want the French king to see me. He is said to be very fond of pretty young ladies, and not above ordering them into his bed."

"Poor Nan," he repeated. "No chance to catch a king."

"Not *that* one," she quipped.

He laughed again. "You do deserve to have some fun. Has it occurred to you that you might simply *ask* to go out?"

Having planted that suggestion in Nan's mind, Ned went away from Sussex House well satisfied with his day's work.

THE MORNING AFTER Nan walked with Ned Corbett in the garden, she asked Cousin Mary for permission to explore London. "I would like to visit the shops, even if I cannot afford to buy," she said, "and take in the sights and sounds."

"You cannot just wander about the city on your own!" Mary was appalled by the very idea.

"I will take Constance with me."

"Your tiring maid? She knows less about avoiding the dangers of London than you do."

Nan pouted. "I will pine away if I am confined in one place much longer!"

Mary smiled at this exaggeration, but Nan also saw a hint of sympathy in her cousin's dark eyes. Tapping her fingers against the arm of her chair, Mary reconsidered Nan's request. "You may go out for a few hours to visit some of the more respectable shops, but only if you take Kate with you in addition to your maid and are accompanied by at least two grooms."

Nan leapt at the chance. Of all the women in the household, she got along best with Kate Stradling. Kate was nine years Nan's senior and Welsh by birth, so they had little in common, but Kate was very fond of sweets. She was amenable to the expedition so long as it included a stop at a confectioner's shop.

They set out at midmorning the next day, after taking formal leave of Cousin Mary in the parlor. Their little procession made its way through the hall into the screens passage and across the yard to the entry where a liveried servant waited to open the gate to the street. He dipped his head as Nan and Kate went through. Heedless of pedestrians and horses alike, Nan set off at a brisk pace. She wanted to see everything at once.

It was the smell of London that slowed her down. Fumbling for the decorative pomander ball that hung from her waist, she pressed it firmly to her nose so that, after a moment, the most unpalatable odors—she refused to try to identify any of them!—weakened in intensity. Filtered through the soothing scent of hartshorn, they became endurable.

Nan felt a trifle foolish. She should have remembered how London stank. Still, some things were worth putting up with, so long as the reward was great enough. Linking her arm through Kate's, she marched on, determined to make the most of her hours of freedom. Constance trailed behind with the two burly grooms Cousin Mary insisted they take with them.

Nan made frequent use of her pomander ball at first, but before long she became accustomed to the stench and could manage with only an occasional restorative sniff. They stopped to view the Great Conduit in

Cheapside and the Eleanor Cross, the latter erected to commemorate the passing of the funeral cortege of a long-ago queen. Nan wondered if King Henry planned any such memorials for Queen Jane. If he did, she had not heard about them.

Some streets were cobbled. Others were paved. Some merely had a layer of gravel over hard-packed dirt. Nan suspected the latter turned into quagmires every spring. All the roads and byways were crowded with persons of every sort, from rough farmers in town to sell their produce to expensively dressed gallants on richly caparisoned horses. Nan wished she had been at court long enough to recognize individuals in the latter group. After all, it would do her no good to attract the attention of some scoundrel who was deep in debt or, worse, already had a wife.

The noise of the city made conversation difficult. Hawkers shouting out inducements to buy their wares competed with the clop of horses' hooves and the clatter of wheeled carts and wagons. Church bells in dozens of churches rang out the time, adding to the din. Everywhere there was bustle and confusion.

Nan was happier than she had been in weeks. After two hours of walking, however, even she began to flag, and Cousin Kate had been limping for the past quarter hour. Nan looked around, thinking to find a respectable hostelry in the vicinity. A tavern or an alehouse would not do, but inns that catered to travelers had rooms for hire where a gentlewoman could sit down for a bit and even order food and drink.

There were no inns in sight, but there was something familiar about Nan's surroundings. She looked more carefully at the buildings and realized that one of them was Master Husee's house. The tall, narrow structure rising cheek by jowl with its neighbors was not distinctive in any way, but Nan remembered it from her last visit. She and Cat and Ned had stopped at Husee's lodgings to break the journey from Dover to Hampton Court.

Sheer chance that she had ended up here, Nan told herself. She had not intended to search out familiar landmarks. But fate had taken a hand, and here was a place to rest awhile, just when they needed it.

If Husee had been in residence, Nan might have continued to search for an inn, but he was still in Calais. That made her decision a foregone conclusion. "We must stop for a bit before we return to Sussex House," she announced, "and here is just the place to do it. If Master Corbett is not at home, then Master Husee's servants will make us welcome."

"Master Corbett?" Kate's dark eyes widened in surprise. "How . . . fortuitous."

"I have always been lucky," Nan agreed.

As for Ned, he seemed delighted to find two young gentlewomen on his doorstep and obligingly offered them refreshments and the chance to rest their feet. At the first opportunity, he bent to whisper in Nan's ear, "Clever girl to find this place again."

A teasing smile played across Nan's lips as she inhaled his fresh, clean scent. "I hoped you would welcome me."

His eyes gleamed and his voice turned husky. "I'd have given you an even warmer welcome, Nan, had you arrived without an escort."

They both looked at Kate. Nan's cousin was watching them with gimlet-eyed intensity, her suspicion that Nan had arranged this meeting with Ned as obvious as if she had lettered it on a sign.

"I would such a thing were possible," Nan murmured as she stepped away, depriving him of the opportunity to say more.

Her intent had been to match Ned's lighthearted flirtation. But the moment she spoke those words, it came to Nan that she'd meant them. The epiphany stunned her.

She stared hard at Ned, now bantering with Cousin Kate. She told herself that Ned's brown hair and blue eyes were unremarkable. And hundreds of men had a physique as excellent. *He was penniless.* That was what she had to remember. And she must not lose sight of her goal. She had left Calais to set her traps for a man who possessed both wealth and a title.

Ned Corbett had neither.

. . . by the report of all the gentlewomen, Mrs. Anne is clearly altered, and in manner no fault can be found in her. So that I doubt not but that the worst is past, and from henceforth she will use herself as demurely and discreetly as the best of her fellows. My Lady Sussex willeth me to make her a gown of lion tawny satin, turned up with velvet of the same colour, and also to buy her a standard for her gowns, which shall be done, God willing, against Christmas. And there is no doubt, whensoever the time shall come, she shall enjoy her accustomed place . . .

—John Husee to Lady Lisle, 14 December 1537

4

A few dull days in the exclusive company of women, embroidering baby clothes and making plans for a quiet Yuletide, made Nan restless. She proposed another shopping expedition, but this time Cousin Kate had no interest in such a venture.

"Why go out?" Kate asked without looking up from her needlework. "London is noisy, crowded, filthy, and smelly and we have only to express an interest and Cousin Mary will ask tradesmen to bring their wares here for us to examine. Cloth. Ribbons. Even jewelry. Not that either of us can afford to buy much." She frowned over a stitch. "Does this look straight to you?"

With barely a glance, Nan told her it was perfect.

"We both know why you want to go out," Kate said.

Nan went still, suddenly wary. "Do we?"

"It is only an excuse to visit Master Corbett again. I can understand the desire. He is a well-made man and clever with words, as well." She took several more careful stitches in the sleeve she was embroidering with tiny rosebuds. "But I see no advantage to myself in venturing out into London so that you can dally with your stepfather's man."

"You are mistaken," Nan lied. "I have no interest in Master Corbett. And I would not dream of disturbing your work by asking you to accompany me." She walked stiffly away, annoyed with her cousin and even more annoyed with herself. She had dreamed of Ned the previous night, a dream filled with longing . . . and fulfillment. But she had not thought her interest in Ned was so obvious to others.

Next Nan tried to persuade Jane Arundell to accompany her, but Jane, too, preferred to remain indoors, as did Isabel Staynings. Since Nan would lack the company of another gentlewoman, Cousin Mary refused her request for a second outing.

Frustrated, Nan brooded for the rest of the day and was still in ill humor by the time Constance appeared to help her get ready for bed. Kate was already sound asleep and snoring lightly. She had also appropriated all of the blankets, wrapping herself in a cocoon of wool. When Nan climbed into bed beside her, she'd have a struggle to free enough of the fabric to cover herself.

"I vow," Nan grumbled, "I shall soon die of boredom. Then they will be sorry they kept me confined!"

Constance paused in the act of untying the points that held Nan's sleeves to her bodice. "Are you a prisoner, mistress?"

"I might as well be!"

"Even prisoners in the Tower of London are allowed to walk on the leads for fresh air." Constance's voice was muffled as she fought a knot in the laces holding bodice to kirtle.

"Are they? Who told you that?"

"John Browne did, mistress. He knows all sorts of things. He says more than men are locked up in the Tower. There are beasts, too. Lions and—"

"John Browne? Who is he?"

"Why, he is Master Corbett's man, mistress. His servant."

Nan had a vague recollection of a manservant in Calais and at Master Husee's lodgings, but she had not paid any attention to him. Big and brawny, she thought. Had he been on the boat from Calais with them? She supposed he must have been. And it appeared he'd entertained her maid while his master had been occupied with Constance's mistress.

As Constance finished undressing her, the first glimmer of an idea formed in Nan's mind.

THEY LEFT SUSSEX House through the garden. Since it was broad daylight, Nan expected to be caught at any moment, but luck was on her side. She and Constance reached the lych-gate unnoticed and stepped out into a narrow alley. All the way from Sussex House to Master Husee's dwelling, Nan was certain she would be challenged, or robbed, or assaulted. The potential for danger made the adventure all the more exciting.

"Slow your steps, mistress," Constance hissed, scurrying to keep up with her, "lest you draw unwelcome attention to yourself."

Seeing the sense in her advice, Nan forced herself to walk at a sedate pace. Head held high, she pretended she had every right to be out on the streets of London with her maid. Fortunately, no one they passed could see how her hands were trembling inside her muff.

Forewarned by John Browne, Ned was expecting them. If he had any qualms about entertaining Nan without the presence of Cousin Kate and the two Sussex grooms, he hid them well. Indeed, it seemed to Nan that he regarded her clandestine visit as a great lark. They spent a pleasant hour sharing stories about their childhoods and laughing over Nan's mother's latest unsuccessful effort to secure the services of a waiting gentlewoman.

"She sent an enameled pomander containing cinnamon balls to Lady

Wallop to sweeten her," Ned said with a chuckle. "Lady Wallop has a niece of the right age and disposition."

"Lady Wallop is fond of my mother. They met when her husband was the English ambassador to France. Never tell me that she failed to deliver the girl."

"Worse than that." He waited a beat, then slid closer to her on the window seat they shared. "The clasp on the pomander was faulty. It broke, scattering the cinnamon and quite ruining Lady Wallop's favorite damask gown."

Nan's fingers flew to her mouth, but it was too late to hold back the explosion of mirth. "I can just imagine the expression on her face," Nan sputtered when she could catch enough breath to speak. Lady Wallop affronted would be a comical sight even without cinnamon spilling down her ample bosom.

Ned's laughter mingled with her own. His hand came to rest on Nan's shoulder, as if to steady himself. Or her.

The touch, light as it was, sparked a conflagration. Nan's cheeks warmed. Her heart raced. She leaned closer to Ned, face lifting until their eyes locked.

She recognized an answering heat in Ned's gaze. And then she saw no more because he'd closed the distance between them and was kissing her. His lips settled over hers, warm and sure. His soft beard and mustache brushed her skin, sensitizing it almost beyond bearing. She heard someone moan and realized with a sense of wonder that she had made the small sound of arousal.

All too soon for Nan's liking, Ned pulled away from her. "You had best return to Sussex House before someone notices you are missing."

She struggled to get her breath back and to adjust to the sudden loss of Ned's embrace. "I pled a headache," she blurted out. "They think I am lying down with the bed hangings closed to keep out the light and with a poultice of banewort leaves on my brow."

"And if Lady Sussex should decide to offer comfort to her dear young cousin?"

Nan turned away from him, suddenly chilled. She knew he was right. To stay away too long was to court discovery.

An hour later, having collected Constance from John Browne's bedchamber, she returned to Sussex House the same way she had left.

THE SECOND TIME Nan crept out to meet Ned Corbett, the kisses were more intense. "I love the way you smell," she whispered.

She felt him smile against her cheek. "I am a noxious weed compared to you, my flower. I never knew lavender could be so sweet."

Again they parted too soon to suit Nan, and the third time she visited Master Husee's little house, Ned greeted her with the news that this must be their last meeting. "Husee intends to make the crossing on the first of December. I am to meet him at Gravesend, in Kent."

"Must you return to Calais?" The aching, empty feeling inside her was far worse than any hunger for food.

"I am one of your stepfather's regular couriers," Ned reminded her. "That means I will come back from time to time."

"But we will never have this house to ourselves again." Tears sprang into her eyes. First she had lost her best chance at attracting a wealthy, titled husband. Now she would lose Ned's company. It was not fair!

Ned took her in his arms and kissed her damp cheeks. When his gentle, comforting embrace turned passionate, the lure was irresistible. Nan tugged at his laces even as he began to undo her kirtle.

"Are you certain?" he whispered. "I would not hurt you for the world."

Nan did not reply in words. Caught up in a whirl of new and fascinating sensations, she seized his face in both hands and pulled until his lips met hers. Her world tilted and spun and by the time the tumult slowed enough for her to think again, she was naked in Ned's bed and he was pushing himself into her.

The intrusion hurt . . . until Ned slid one hand down her body. The waves of renewed arousal lashed at every place he touched. She had never experienced anything like what he did to her, never imagined such pleasure was possible. She had no name for what she felt. She only knew that the moment of pain was quickly replaced by shudders of ecstasy.

Only later, when they lay sated and smiling, did Nan realize the enormity of what she had just done. Men wanted wives who were virgins. How could she have allowed herself to become so caught up in passion that she'd lost all common sense? How was she to catch any husband now, let alone one who was rich and titled?

Nan sat straight up, fumbling for her smock. Tears pricked at the backs of her eyes, but this time she was determined not to let them fall. She dared not look at Ned, although she could feel him watching her.

"Wounds of Christ," he swore. "I'd never have taken you for a puling infant. Is it really so terrible to have given yourself to a lover? Great ladies do it all the time, and so do maids of honor!"

"I am not a maid of honor any longer!" Nor was she a maid. Nan met his gaze at last and read concern there, as well as frustration.

"Did I not please you, Nan?"

"You know you did," she whispered.

"Then what is it that troubles you?"

"This . . . this is not . . . acceptable behavior."

Startled, he blinked once and then began to laugh. Nan glared at him, but after a moment she saw the humor in her choice of words and her prim tone of voice and joined in the mirth. Acceptable or unacceptable did not begin to define what they had just shared. And if she had truly cared a fig for what was "acceptable," she would never have crept out of Sussex House to be with Ned in the first place.

What was done, was done. Her maidenhead was gone. That being so, Nan reasoned, why should she not enjoy herself while she could? Scooting closer to Ned, she rained kisses down his chest. He responded with enthusiasm.

They had two days before he had to leave to meet John Husee. They made the best of them, spending both afternoons in his bed. What Cousin Mary thought of Nan's sudden spate of headaches, Nan neither knew nor cared. She did not trouble herself overmuch with worrying about it. She had discovered the delights of coupling with her lover and was far too eager to be with Ned to concern herself with the consequences if she were found out.

The only thing Nan dreaded was the moment when they must say farewell. Inevitably, it arrived. They made love for what would have to be the last time. Then Ned, his face wearing the most serious expression she had ever seen there, took her hands in his and drew her up so that they were kneeling face-to-face upon the bed. Hangings closed them in, away from the rest of the world, but they could still hear the faint sounds of London beyond. A death knell began to toll the years of a deceased parishioner's life.

"We can go through a private form of marriage here and now, Nan, if you are willing. None will ever be able to part us if we do."

What Ned was suggesting made Nan's limbs go stiff with shock. "We cannot marry!" she blurted out.

"Formal trothplight is the only answer. It is not a ceremony in church or the presence of witnesses that makes a marriage binding. We have only to pledge ourselves *per verba de praesenti*, as they call it, and we will have made a legal precontract. That done, neither of us can ever marry anyone else." He grinned. "We have already taken care of the consummation that seals the bargain."

"We cannot!" Her voice rose in panic.

"Why not? I love you, Nan. And you love me."

"What has love to do with marriage? My dowry is but one hundred marks and you have no prospects at all."

A spasm of displeasure momentarily turned his handsome features ugly. "What if you are with child?"

Nan jerked her hands free of his and scrambled off the bed. "Was that your plan? To force a marriage? Well, it will not work." Surely it was not that easy to conceive. Her mother and Lord Lisle had tried without success for years. Nor had the king been notably successful at getting his wives with child.

More slowly, Ned followed her from the bed. They dressed in silence, his brooding, hers a mixture of anger and trepidation. In spite of living with two pregnant women, her cousins Mary and Isabel, it had never crossed her mind that she might quicken with Ned's child. Such an outcome was unlikely, she told herself firmly, and dismissed the possibility from her thoughts.

She was more concerned that Ned would betray her. If he told her stepfather that they'd been meeting in secret and that he'd taken her maidenhead . . . Lord Lisle *could* force them to wed. More likely, he'd turn Ned out for his effrontery. She did not think Ned would risk that. She hoped he would not.

"I love you, Nan," Ned said as she was about to leave, "and I think you love me."

"That may be, Ned. But marriage is a business arrangement. A contract negotiated by parents for their children. Love, if it happens at all in a marriage, comes after the wedding and bedding." So she'd been taught her whole life.

"And what we've shared?"

"A mistake?"

She heard the regret in his voice and was sorry for it, but he should never have pressed for marriage. "Go on, then. Run back to the countess. Pretend none of this ever happened," he said bitterly.

Nan walked rapidly through the gathering dusk, trying to outrun her troubled thoughts. She left Constance at the lych-gate, bidding John Browne a tearful farewell, and hurried through the house to the safety of her own bedchamber. She saw no one along the way and was certain her absence had gone unnoticed . . . until she caught a whiff of Cousin Mary's rose-water scent.

Curled up on the window seat, her face shadowed in the twilight, the Countess of Sussex watched Nan close the door. Nan had the sense that her cousin had been waiting for her return for some time.

"Where have you been, Nan?"

"I went for a walk." Perhaps there was still a chance to bluff her way out of trouble. Mary could not possibly guess where she had been or what she had been doing. All she'd know for certain was that Nan had not spent the afternoon prostrate on her bed, laid low by a megrim.

"Alone?" Mary's displeasure was a palpable force in the room.

"I took Constance with me. I was most desperate for relief and, indeed, the air and exercise seem to have done wonders for my aching head."

"This is not the first time you have left the grounds with only your maid for company. Do not trouble to deny it. Yesterday one of the gardeners found the lych-gate unlatched."

"I did go out. Just for a few moments. That is how I came to realize that venturing beyond the gates does more to ease my pain than bane-wort leaves moistened with wine and laid to my temple, or bloodwort made into a plaster, or even infusions of cowslip juice."

"It is not meet for you to venture into the city without a proper escort." Cousin Mary's voice dripped icicles.

Nan winced. In truth, her head *had* begun to throb. "It will not happen again. I promise."

Mary patted the cushioned seat beside her, indicating that Nan should come and sit. She was far from mollified, but Nan thought her cousin might believe her. She was certain Mary *wanted* to. It did not reflect well on the Countess of Sussex if one of her household misbehaved.

"My Lord Sussex and I have worked hard on your behalf, trying to convince the king that he should guarantee you a place with the next queen, whoever she may be. It would be a great pity if you ruined your reputation before her arrival in England."

Nan bowed her head. She *had* been foolish. If she was to return to court, she must engage in no more dalliances. Moreover, she must take care to appear both biddable and virtuous. No one, least of all Cousin Mary, must ever discover that she was no longer a virgin.

"I devoutly hope we will have a new queen soon," Mary said as Nan took the place beside her on the window seat. "There is talk of a young woman at the court in Burgundy—Christina, daughter of the deposed king of Denmark. She is your age, Nan, but already a widow. A virgin bride, or so they say, but by that marriage she became Duchess of Milan. As such, she would be a most suitable wife for the king of England."

Mary rambled on, extolling Christina of Milan's many reported virtues. Nan had only to nod and smile. She agreed with everything Mary said for the next hour, but for much of that time a part of her mind was elsewhere.

As soon as her cousin had gone, Nan sent for Constance. "I think she believed me," Nan said when she'd repeated the first part of her conversation with Mary, "but just in case she asks you, you must confirm all I told her. We ventured no farther into London than a few yards from the garden gate."

"You have naught to fear from me, mistress," Constance vowed. "And I've no doubt Lady Sussex is so wroth with you only because she is great with child and uncomfortable with it. Mayhap you should ask your mother to send her more gifts."

Cousin Mary had not developed a craving for quails, but she did love pretty trinkets. For once, Nan wished she *could* write a letter in English in her own hand. She resolved to have Master Husee set quill to paper for her as soon as he presented himself. She'd ask Mother to send whatever tokens she thought would keep the countess sweet.

"If everything goes well," she said, as much to convince herself as to reassure Constance, "it will only be a matter of time before I am back at court where I belong." Pageants. Dancing. Disguisings. Tournaments. A little sigh of anticipation escaped her as she contemplated all the pleasures of life at Hampton Court and Greenwich Palace and Windsor Castle.

And then she pictured King Henry in her mind's eye. Tall. Muscular. Smiling. She could almost smell that wonderful scent he wore. And the thought of encountering His Majesty again in the flesh, of seeing admiration in those blue-gray eyes, produced a distinct flutter in Nan's belly and set all her female parts to tingling.

LESS THAN TWO weeks after Nan had resolved to turn over a new leaf, King Henry sent word that her place as a maid of honor to the next queen was secure. Nan was elated. She saw this news as proof that the king remembered her fondly and that she had done the right thing by refusing Ned's offer of marriage.

December passed quietly and, save for the servants, entirely in the company of women. Then, in early January, the Earl of Sussex rode into London from Whitehall Palace, in the City of Westminster, where the court was, to pay a visit to his wife. Eager for news of the king's search for a bride, every gentlewoman in the household, Nan included, immediately surrounded him.

"We will not have a moment alone until you have satisfied their curiosity," the countess warned her husband. "And I, too, am eager to hear of the doings of the court."

"The king leaves for Greenwich Palace in two days' time," the earl said. "He will celebrate Twelfth Night there."

Disguisings, Nan thought. And a Lord of Misrule to preside over the Yuletide festivities. She longed to be there.

"He is still in mourning for Queen Jane," Jane Arundell objected. "How much celebration can there be?" Then she saw something in the earl's expression that made her light gray eyes go wide. "Who?"

Nan watched the earl's expression change as he glanced around the circle of eager faces. He seemed to be debating with himself, but in the end he relented. "No doubt you will hear of it soon enough. The election lies between Mistress Mary Shelton and Mistress Margaret Skipwith. I pray Jesu that the king will choose the one who will give him greatest comfort."

"You cannot mean he intends to *marry* one of them!" Kate Stradling exclaimed.

"He is supposed to wed a foreign princess," Nan added.

The earl shook his head. "It is a mistress His Grace is after from among the gentlewomen of his acquaintance, not a wife."

"MARY SHELTON," JANE Arundell mused when the earl and countess had retired. "Well, well."

"Do you know her?" Nan sat with her legs curled under her on a cushion on the floor.

Isabel, whose pregnancy weighed heavily on her, had claimed the window seat that overlooked the garden, while Kate occupied a stool. Jane took the countess's chair.

"I have never met the woman, but I know who she is. One of her sisters, Margaret, was at court when Anne Boleyn was queen. Madge, they called her. That one was no better than she should be." Jane paused to glance over her shoulder at the door, making sure there was no one else listening. Then she lowered her voice to a conspiratorial whisper. "Madge Shelton warmed the king's bed throughout one of Queen Anne's pregnancies."

Isabel fanned herself with her embroidery hoop. "Oh, my! Well, I do not suppose His Grace minds tupping sisters. He has done so before."

"There are some who say that the two children Queen Anne's sister bore during her first marriage were really fathered by the king," Jane explained, noticing the puzzled expression on Nan's face.

More tales of Anne Boleyn's sister, and other women who had reportedly been King Henry's mistresses, followed hard and fast. Nan was fascinated. Her mother had told many stories about people at the English court but, with one exception, she had not included illicit liaisons in her lessons. She had mentioned a woman named Bessie Blount, but only because Bessie had given birth to King Henry's bastard, Henry FitzRoy, a boy who had died about a year before Nan arrived at court.

"The first mistress anyone knows by name," Jane continued, preening a bit because she had been a maid of honor long enough to know, "was the Duke of Buckingham's sister. That was way back in the first year of King Henry's reign. The duke very nearly caught them together and afterward he had his sister confined to a nunnery for her sins."

"Is she still there?" Kate asked.

"Not likely," Nan interjected. "Most of the nunneries have been dissolved."

"And the Duke of Buckingham is long gone—executed for treason years ago." Jane lowered her voice again, obliging the others to lean closer. "But his wayward sister, as you suggested, Nan, did not remain long in confinement, and these days she is the Countess of Huntingdon!"

"Whatever happened to Bessie Blount?" Nan asked.

"She was married off to Lord Talboys, and after he died she wed Lord Clinton."

"So one former mistress has married an earl and another became a baroness twice over," Nan mused aloud. "It would seem that the king's castoffs do not fare too badly."

"Not *all* of them married peers. Mary Boleyn was wed to a mere knight and her second husband is the same."

Jane's answer only piqued Nan's curiosity. "And Madge Shelton? What happened to her?"

"I've no idea," Jane admitted.

"Have there been others?" Nan persisted.

Jane's eyebrows rose. "Surely we have enumerated quite enough for one man! Any more would be excessive."

"Not so," Nan said with a laugh. "Why, the number of mistresses the king of England has taken pales beside the legions of women so honored by the king of France." Finding herself the center of attention, Nan regaled the others with stories of King Frances and his conquests until it was time for supper.

That night Nan dreamed she was at court. King Henry walked right past shadowy figures that Nan somehow knew were Mary Shelton and Margaret Skipwith, and chose Nan instead. And not just to be his mistress, either. It was a crown he offered her, and his hand in marriage.

Nan could not help but feel chagrined a few weeks later when she heard that the king had made Margaret Skipwith his mistress. She took care to hide her reaction, but Constance knew her too well.

"Why do you care what Mistress Skipwith does?" the maid asked as she dressed Nan's hair for the day.

"She won the prize before I even knew there was a contest," Nan muttered. They were alone in the bedchamber. Kate had risen early and was already in attendance upon Cousin Mary.

"You cannot have wanted to be the king's mistress. Not after knowing Master Ned. The king is old and getting older. Fat and getting fatter. What pleasure would there be in going to bed with the likes of him?"

"A great deal if he could be persuaded into marriage," Nan replied.

"You want to be *queen*?" In the mirror, Nan saw the girl's eyes widen.

"A woman can aspire no higher," said Nan. "And surely a king would be a superlative lover."

Nan did not mention the way King Henry affected her. She did not think Constance would understand that she had been drawn to the king's person every bit as powerfully as she had been to Ned's. True, Ned was younger and better looking, but Nan had no difficulty at all imagining herself in Henry Tudor's bed.

Constance snorted and pulled a little too hard as the comb caught a snarl. "Climb too high and a fall from that height will be the death of you. King Henry has killed three wives already, one by neglect, one by beheading, and the third in childbed. Where's the pleasure, or the profit, in joining that company?"

Nan considered for a moment. "There's pleasure, profit, and power, too, just in being at court, and to have the king's attention means more of all three. Whatever woman he takes as his mistress has more influence than other women at court, at least for a time. A wife would have even more."

"For a time," Constance amended under her breath. Satisfied with Nan's hair, she went to the wardrobe chest to collect kirtle, bodice, sleeves, gown, and shoes. Nan was already wearing her stockings and garters and chemise and petticoats.

"Perhaps I aim too high." Nan heaved a gusty sigh. "Even to dream of replacing Mistress Skipwith is likely presumptuous. And foolish, as well," she acknowledged, catching sight of Constance's expression. "And yet I do know one thing—I will never be content to spend my life living as a poor relation in a wealthy cousin's household."

Most assuredly she could do better than that!

FOR THE NEXT few months, Nan busied herself making baby clothes, attempting to learn to write in English, and planning the garments she would have when she was once more a maid of honor at the royal court. She was least successful with the writing, since she had little true interest in acquiring that skill. Given that her own mother corresponded with dozens of people, always employing a secretary to write for her, Nan had no real need to make the effort. Nor did she have anyone to whom she had a great desire to send a letter. Except, perhaps, for Ned. But she knew that was not a good idea.

But if she had written to someone, she mused, she might have said that Isabel Staynings had been delivered of a healthy girl and that Cousin Mary, the Countess of Sussex, still awaited the birth of her child. Mary had taken to her bedchamber in mid-February. Since Nan was not obliged to stay with Mary all the time, she could take walks in the garden, despite the cold weather, if she so desired. For some reason, however, she found she lacked the energy to venture outside.

She'd felt listless for several weeks—she blamed the weather—when John Husee arrived on the fifteenth of March with letters and tokens from Nan's family in Calais. The news that he was accompanied by Ned Corbett made Nan's heart flutter with anticipation, but she was determined to show no weakness where he was concerned.

Jane Arundell remained with her half sister while Nan and Kate went to greet their visitors. Since the king had left off wearing mourning on the third day of February, the day after Candlemas, thus permitting his subjects to do the same, Nan had on the gown of lion tawny satin turned up with velvet of the same color. It was one that Master Husee had supplied against her return to court as a maid of honor. With it she wore a flattering French hood. Her headdress still lacked an appropriately rich decorative border, but she had already begun a campaign to amend that lack.

"Has Mother sent the pearls?" she asked before Husee had a chance to say a word beyond his greeting. She pretended to ignore Ned entirely.

John Husee was a stolid individual in his early thirties, plainly dressed. There was nothing memorable about his brown hair and brown eyes. His other features, including a short, neatly trimmed beard, were equally unremarkable. He was skilled at effacing himself and eager to please without being obsequious. He had been in the employ of Lord and Lady Lisle since Nan was twelve and deferred to her just as he did to her mother and stepfather. If any of them asked for something, he procured it, whether it be goods or information. He always knew the best places to find both.

A pained expression on his face, Husee shook his head. "It grieves me to tell you, Mistress Anne, that she has not yet done so."

"I need them by Easter." Easter Sunday fell on the twenty-first day of April, only a little more than a month away.

Although Nan could feel Ned's intense gaze boring into her, she refused to look at him. He'd no doubt try to steal a moment alone with her, but she did not intend to let him succeed. She did not dare allow him close to her, not when just knowing he was in the same room shook her resolution to avoid him.

"What news of the king's search for a queen?" Kate cast a flirtatious look Ned's way. Nan frowned at her, but Kate took no notice.

John Husee answered, "The king has sent Master Hans Holbein abroad to make portraits of several noblewomen considered worthy to be queen of England."

"Including Christina of Milan?" Kate wanted to know.

"Including Christina. Wagering at court favors her five to one over any other candidate."

"There is news closer to home," Ned cut in impatiently. He stepped in front of Nan so that she was forced to meet his steady gaze. "Your eldest brother, John Bassett, has married your stepsister, Frances Plantagenet."

Nan kept her expression carefully blank. "That is no great surprise. They have been betrothed ever since my mother married Frances's father. I imagine they were only waiting until John reached his eigh-teenth birthday."

"I suppose you do not care, either, that your youngest sister, Mary Bassett, has been ill. She was sent home to Calais last week in the hope that your mother could nurse her back to health."

Nan stared at him with concern, but said nothing. She felt as if she barely knew Mary anymore, having seen her only a handful of times dur-ing the last four years.

Master Husee hastened to assure her that her sister would recover.

"In spite of her ill health," Ned remarked, "she is quite the beauty, by far the prettiest of Lady Lisle's daughters."

Nan went rigid as a fireplace poker, but she refused to be baited. She would not oblige Ned Corbett by quarreling with him.

"Perhaps," Ned continued, as if unaware of her irritation, "you will soon be able to judge for yourself. It has been suggested that when she regains her health, Mary should join you here in the Sussex household."

Caught off guard, Nan struggled to find a polite reply. "It would be pleasant to see my youngest sister again," she said after a moment, "but I would not want her to make such a long journey if she is not well."

"We have news of your sister Catherine, too." The hard glint in Ned's eyes belied his casual tone of voice and reminded Nan that he'd once shown a marked interest in Cat. "There is talk of a marriage for her with one of Sir Edward Baynton's sons."

"Baynton," Nan mused aloud. "He was vice chancellor to Queen Jane. No doubt he will assume the same post under the next queen." Baynton had wealth and influence, but he was merely a knight and his sons lacked even that distinction. Still, Cat must be well pleased at the prospect of such an alliance. Plain as she was, she'd never have much choice in a husband.

"I've heard no names bandied about for you, Mistress Anne."

Nan ignored Ned's taunt. Andrew Baynton, she recalled, the old-est of Sir Edward's sons, was about Cat's age. There were at least two younger boys. Nan hoped her mother would not suggest doubling the alliance—two sisters for two brothers.

"The Bayntons are wealthy and growing more so all the time," Master Husee chimed in. He looked from Ned to Nan and back again with a puzzled expression on his face.

"How fortunate for Cat." Nan smiled sweetly. "For as we all know, there is never any point to marrying a man who has no ready money."

THE COUNTESS OF Sussex gave birth to a son on the eighteenth day of March. That same day Master Holbein returned to court and showed King Henry his drawing of Christina of Milan.

"This put His Grace in an excellent mood," the Earl of Sussex reported to his wife and her attendant ladies. "The king has agreed to be our new son's godfather."

Nan's spirits soared. If King Henry came to the boy's christening, she might have an opportunity to speak with him.

"His Grace will send a deputy," Sussex continued.

Disappointed, Nan repressed a sigh.

"Did you see the sketch of Duchess Christina, my lord?" Kate Stradling asked. "What does she look like?"

Sussex considered that in thoughtful silence for a few moments. Then his deep-set eyes crinkled and he gave a snort of laughter. "A great deal like Madge Shelton, if you want to know the truth. Pretty girl, that Madge. I hear she married a country gentleman by the name of Wodehouse. I wonder if that resemblance accounts for the king's enchantment with the duchess's portrait? Whatever the cause, he has ordered negotiations to proceed apace. With luck, we could have a new queen as early as Whitsuntide."

Whit Sunday was the ninth of June, not very far away at all. Nan resolved to send a reminder to Calais. Her mother must send the pearls at once. Everything must be in order before the new queen of England arrived.

I have been in hand with Mrs. Anne, who, I assure your ladyship, making not a little moan for your ladyship's displeasure, but weepeth and taketh on right heavily. Mrs. Katharine Stradling hath the pearls, part of them as lent and part of gift. Mrs. Anne sayeth that she putteth no doubt to have them again, if your ladyship's pleasure had not been that I should have monished her the contrary. She sayeth that the said gentlewoman hath been ever most loving and glad to do her pleasure, and always ready to help and assist her in all her proceedings and doings.

—John Husee to Lady Lisle, 5 May 1538

5

John Husee's next visit to Sussex House did not occur until early April. He was accompanied by several gentlemen, but Ned Corbett was not one of them. It irritated Nan that she cared.

She had been out of sorts quite a lot of late.

As Cousin Mary had not yet been churched, she remained in her chamber. Once again, Kate accompanied Nan to greet their guests, but this time Isabel and Jane also joined them in the ground-floor parlor.

Master Husee's companions were Tom Warley, another of Lord Lisle's gentleman servitors, and two men Nan had never met. Husee introduced the first as Master Clement Philpott and the second as Sir

Gregory Botolph, who was slated to become Lord Lisle's new domestic chaplain at Calais.

That meant the "sir" was only honorary. Sir Gregory was a priest. A pity the English church did not allow clergy to wed, Nan thought. She found herself intrigued by Sir Gregory's air of confidence. He appealed to her in a way she found hard to define and seemed to have the same effect on the other gentlewomen. Frowning, Nan tried to determine what it was that drew her. Sir Gregory was not as tall or as well built as Ned, nor was his face as pleasing to look at.

"In what part of England were you born?" Jane Arundell asked him. "I cannot place your accent."

"The Botolphs are an old Suffolk family, but I left home many years ago. Most recently I served as a canon in Canterbury."

"At the cathedral?" There was a hint of awe in Jane's voice.

Affecting modesty, Sir Gregory shook his head. "At St. Gregory's. Do you not find it apt that I served in a church that bears my own Christian name?"

Everyone agreed that they did, and Kate, Jane, and Isabel began to pepper him with questions about Canterbury, long a popular spot for pilgrimages. Nan listened to his answers as much to hear his voice—low, mellow, and persuasive—as for what he said. This priest's voice could probably convert heathens with its timbre alone.

"Is the shrine of St. Thomas à Becket truly encrusted with magnificent jewels?" Kate's question caught Nan's attention. She had a particular interest these days in precious stones.

"Great, huge gems of astonishing brilliance," Sir Gregory assured her. "Sufficiently gaudy to make any man covetous."

"Or woman," Kate said with a laugh.

But Botolph had stopped smiling. "For hundreds of years, pilgrims visited Canterbury to kiss the martyr's silver-encased skull and make offerings at his gilded coffin." His intense gaze raked over the company, as if he were weighing each one's worthiness. "There will be a great outcry if the king allows the tomb to be stripped, the shrine demolished, and the relics burnt. It is sacrilege even to consider despoiling such a holy place."

A hush fell over the company. Sir Gregory's words came perilously close to criticizing His Majesty. King Henry had been closing religious houses ever since his break with Rome. That was no secret. Monastery churches in London had been put to secular uses, everything from storage rooms to stables. Others were being torn down to provide building materials for noblemen's houses. But the tomb of Thomas à Becket was the holiest shrine in Christendom. So far, King Henry had spared it.

"Who will care for the poor when they are sick or give them alms when they have no food?" the priest demanded. "Where will they go to be educated? In city and country alike, abbeys and monasteries are being dissolved, and with them their chantries. Nothing that has been so generously provided by religious houses will remain."

The gleam of religious fervor in Sir Gregory's eyes alarmed Nan and shattered whatever spell he'd cast over her. He seemed poised to deliver a sermon on the evils of King Henry's decision to break with the pope. Although many people would agree with him, Nan's own mother included, it was not safe to speak of such things. A few words more, and Sir Gregory would be guilty of treason.

Husee saw the danger, too. There was a hint of panic in his voice as he produced a small casket from his pack and thrust it at Nan. "Here are the pearls you asked for, mistress."

Eagerly, Nan took the small wooden box and opened it. She stared at the contents, unable at first to believe what she was seeing. The pearls were ill matched and inferior and there were too few of them. Bad enough that she had to wait so long to return to court. The least her mother could do was to provide her with the proper accessories.

Nan saw Husee's anxious expression through a red haze, felt her temper spike, surging beyond her control. Furious words erupted before she could stop them, shrill and imperious. "How dare you deliver such a paltry offering! I need pearls fit to wear in the queen's service." She slammed the offending container down on a table.

"Surely there are sufficient to make a decorative border at the front of a French hood." Husee held both hands in front of him, palms out, as if to ward off a physical attack. "The casket contains six score."

"There are not enough, I tell you. And these are of poor quality." Nan could hear herself screeching at him but could not seem to stop.

"Calm yourself, mistress, I beg you. I will write to your mother for more." Husee began to back away. Isabel and Jane also retreated, slipping out through a side door.

Nan fixed her victim with a withering stare. "See that you do. I am to be a maid of honor to the next queen. I must be prepared for her coming."

Signaling for the other gentlemen to follow him, Husee bolted, leaving Nan alone save for Kate Stradling.

Nan closed her eyes and took several deep breaths. What had come over her? For a few minutes, for no good reason, she'd been as irrational as a madwoman.

She opened her eyes to find Kate examining the contents of the casket. Her face wore the look of a contented cat. Dark eyes alight with pleasure, she scooped up a handful of the pearls. "Inferior, without a doubt, Nan, but if you do not want them, I will gladly take them off your hands."

"They are not entirely without value to me!" Nan's control over her own voice was still uncertain. She willed herself to be calm. It was not like her to behave in this way. She often *wanted* to scream at those around her, but she did not do so. Annoyed at herself, she kicked a nearby stool, sending it bouncing across the rush-strewn floor.

"I will have at least some of them," Kate said.

Nan whirled around to stare at her. Her cousin's expression was cold enough to chill Nan's bones.

Kate stepped closer, lowering her voice. "You will share, Nan, because if you do not, I will tell the Earl and Countess of Sussex that you are with child by Ned Corbett."

Nan gaped at her, shocked. "That . . . that . . . I am not! I *cannot* be!"

Kate burst into laughter. "You really did not know? Think back, Nan. When did you last have your courses?"

Nan felt as if all the air had been sucked out of the room. Dizzy, she collapsed on Cousin Mary's chair. It was not possible. Was it? She had never considered that pregnancy might be the explanation for her moodiness, her lack of energy . . . her uncontrollable outbursts.

The horrible sinking feeling in the pit of her stomach convinced Nan that Kate was right. She counted. She'd last shared Ned's bed at the end of November—over four months ago.

"You could *tell* Corbett," Kate said. "He'll marry you for certain."

In Nan's state of mind, her cousin seemed the very devil, offering temptation. Kate was right. Ned would. But they'd be poor. She shuddered. She'd seen too many women worn down by poverty and constant childbearing. Even spending the rest of her life dependent on one of her more affluent relatives would be better than that!

Nan watched her hand move, seemingly of its own volition, and come to rest on her belly. There was as yet little outward sign that a child grew within her. Could she conceal her pregnancy for five more months? It might be possible, if the new queen did not arrive before the child did.

Nan drew in a deep, steadying breath and stood. She walked to the table, picked up the casket of pearls, and handed it to Kate, catching and holding her cousin's gaze. "Will you help me hide my condition?"

Cradling the small box to her bosom, a smile of satisfaction on her lips, Kate promised that she would.

THE PALE OF Calais included all the territory from the downs of Wissant on the west to the fields overlooked by Gravelines on the east—the towns of Calais and Guisnes and some twenty-five neighboring parishes. This small piece carved out of the continent of Europe between France and Flanders was all that was left of England's possessions on the French side of the Narrow Seas.

Arthur Plantagenet, Viscount Lisle, maintained order in Calais as King Henry's lord deputy. His household resembled nothing so much as a miniature court. On a cold April morning, he sent Ned Corbett to the docks to meet his new chaplain and the latest addition to the gentleman servitors.

Ned studied the two men as they were rowed ashore. They were both brown haired and of medium build, both about Ned's own age, but one—the priest—caught his attention even from a distance. There was an aura of command about him that was almost military in nature. Ned was certain he'd have no trouble holding the attention of his congregation.

"I am to escort you back to the lord deputy's house and see you settled in your new quarters," Ned told the newcomers after he'd introduced himself. "My man will collect your belongings." John Browne had already begun loading trunks and boxes into a cart.

"It is only a short walk to Lord Lisle's house," Ned continued, leading the way. "Nothing is very far away from anything else in Calais."

"The town is more crowded than I expected," Sir Gregory Botolph remarked as they made their way through the marketplace. His voice was the sort that captivated listeners. Ned grinned, pleased by the prospect of sermons more interesting than those preached by old Sir Oliver.

"Much more crowded." Clement Philpott twisted his head this way and that, looking for all the world like a country bumpkin on his first visit to a big city. Botolph was equally interested in his surroundings, but he was more subtle about it.

"There are some twelve thousands souls of various nationalities living in the Pale, about half of them English. All are protected by an English garrison a thousand men strong. In addition, there are twenty-four royal spears. They hold most of the administrative posts in the town."

The royal spears were men of good family and the elite of the outpost. Like most of the gentlemen in Lord Lisle's service, Ned aspired to be named to their ranks one day. A Calais spear was not a prestigious post when compared to maid of honor to a queen, but there were advantages to standing on the top rung of a small ladder.

"Up ahead," he said, "is the residence of Lord and Lady Lisle, the finest building in the Pale." Three stories high and built around a large courtyard, it stood just inside the south wall of the town. Ned led his charges through the massive north gateway and straight up to the Great Chamber where Lord and Lady Lisle awaited them.

Botolph studied his new employers with cynical eyes before they went in. "They look like a king and queen giving an audience," he observed.

Ned suppressed a smile. The priest was right. Surrounded by members of the household, the couple sat in matching Glastonbury chairs on a dais. All they lacked was a royal canopy over their heads.

Honor Lisle was resplendent in a crimson velvet gown and wore such an abundance of jewelry that she glittered in the sunbeams that fell on her through the oriel window. She was a small, plump woman in her midforties, more than thirty years younger than her husband.

Arthur, Lord Lisle, was less pretentiously dressed. The deep lines inscribed in his face and the stoop of his shoulders betrayed the weight of his responsibilities at Calais.

Ned glanced at the two portraits hung against the tapestry that covered the wall behind the chairs. One showed King Henry VIII. The other was of Henry's grandfather King Edward IV. Only a blind man could miss the resemblance between the painted likenesses and the lord deputy of Calais. Although Lord Lisle's hair was now losing its color, it had clearly once been the same burnished golden red shown in King Henry's portrait. The similarities between Lisle and his father, King Edward, were even more remarkable. The taint of bastardy had done nothing to dilute the most distinctive royal features.

Lisle stood, revealing himself to be a head taller than most men— another inheritance from the Plantagenet line. "Welcome to Calais, gentlemen. Sir Gregory, you will be joining these gentlemen as my domestic chaplains." He indicated two somberly clad individuals hovering behind his chair. "Sir Oliver and Sir Richard."

Ned noted with mild amusement how warily old Sir Oliver behaved toward Botolph. Fearful he might lose his post as senior chaplain, no doubt.

Lord Lisle addressed Clement Philpott next, informing him that he would meet Mistress Philippa Bassett at supper. Apparently the rumor that Philpott was being considered as a husband for the oldest of Lady Lisle's daughters was true.

Ned took a closer look at Philpott. The fellow was unremarkable in appearance. Brown eyes matched the brown hair in a long, thin face that was vaguely horselike.

"Be in my lady's dining chamber in good time," Lisle instructed. "Corbett will show you the way."

He was about to dismiss them when Lady Lisle spoke up. "Have you brought letters?" Her voice was pleasant, well modulated and low pitched, but it carried easily to every corner of the chamber.

"We have, my lady." Botolph motioned for Philpott to produce them. That gentleman's fingers trembled as he handed them over to one of Lady Lisle's waiting women to give to her mistress, making Ned wonder just what was contained in the latest missives from England.

Dismissed by Lord Lisle with orders to show the newcomers to the chamber they would share, Ned took them first on a tour of the residence.

"All the chief rooms are hung with fine tapestries," Botolph noted with pleasure. For a priest, he seemed to have a deep appreciation of creature comforts.

"There are little chambers opening off my lord's room and my lady's dining chamber," Ned said. "Two gentlewomen's chambers and a maidens' chamber and a chamber reserved for noble guests. At any given time there are about seventy persons living here. Fifty menservants, not including the chaplains and members of Lord Lisle's personal retinue."

"And the women?" Botolph asked.

"Two of Lady Lisle's daughters live with their mother and stepfather, the eldest and the youngest, and also Lord Lisle's daughter, Frances, who was recently married to Lady Lisle's oldest son. Young Bassett is in England, studying law at Lincoln's Inn. Lady Lisle also has several waiting gentlewomen, and a number of chamberers and laundresses."

As was usual in most noble households, male servants far outnum-
bered the females.

Ned showed them the chapel, with its fine altar cloth of gold paned
with crimson velvet, and the armory, and pointed out the stables, the
stilling-house, the bakehouse, and the laundry. After a quick tour of
the kitchen and other domestic offices, including the countinghouse,
he delivered his charges to a small chamber furnished with a field bed,
a Flanders chair, a cupboard, and a closestool. The boxes and trunks
Botolph and Philpott had brought with them from England were stacked
in a corner.

"I vow, Corbett, I am parched," Botolph said. "Where might a man
find a drink in this place?"

"Parched," Philpott echoed.

"I could do with a cup of beer myself," Ned allowed.

The route to the grooms' chamber, where Lord Lisle's men took their
ease when not on duty, led past Lady Lisle's parlor. The soft murmur of
feminine voices drifted out. Just as they were about to descend the stairs,
a shriek of outrage suddenly rent the air.

"Ungrateful child!" Lady Lisle screeched. "How dare she belittle my
gift?"

"It would be unwise to linger," Ned warned, all too familiar with
Honor Lisle's temper. "Anyone in the wrong place at the wrong time is
likely to find my lady's venom aimed at him."

Botolph did not argue, and Philpott followed his lead like an obedient
puppy. A few minutes later they were safe in the grooms' chamber. They
had the room to themselves. Ned filled three cups with beer and they
settled in on stools around a sturdy table.

"What do you think of Lady Lisle?" Ned asked.

"A virtuous woman," Botolph said. "Sound in her beliefs."

Meaning she clung to the old ways in religion. Ned himself was content to go along with whatever observances his betters required of him.

"I see now where her daughter got her temper," Botolph remarked
after a few swigs of beer.

Ned lifted a questioning eyebrow. "Which daughter?"

"The one who lives with the Countess of Sussex. Anne, is it?"

"Nan," Ned murmured.

"A pretty girl, but of somewhat sour disposition."

"I shall be much distressed if her sister has the same temperament," Philpott said. "Philippa, that is."

Poor Mistress Philippa, Ned thought. About to be courted by a man who did not look as if he'd ever had an original thought in his head. The fellow could not have met Sir Gregory Botolph more than a few days earlier and already he deferred to the priest in everything. "Philippa is the quiet one," he said aloud.

"Cowed into silence by her mother, no doubt," said Botolph.

"Quiet would suit me." Philpott's head bobbed up and down to emphasize the claim. "Biddable."

Ned smiled to himself. Biddable was something Nan would never be, although seducing her had not been difficult. He was certain he could tempt her into his bed again if he tried. Mayhap get her with child and force the issue of marriage. But what if they did wed? She'd never forgive him for the loss of her dream. She wanted a husband with wealth and a title. He'd never be a nobleman, and to be rich he'd have to marry money. What Nan did not understand was that, to him, *she* was well to do.

Philpott was still rambling on about courting Philippa. Ned was content to let him have her. There were two more Bassett girls. He pictured Mary, beautiful but sickly. She had suffered several relapses since her return to Calais from France. Such a wife might soon make him a widower, free to marry again and obtain yet another dowry. But Lady Lisle guarded her youngest chick like a mother hen. He'd have better luck turning himself into a fox and raiding the coop. Amused by his own wit, Ned refilled his cup.

So, Cat Bassett it must be, and her courtship would have to wait until the next time Ned crossed the Narrow Seas.

It was a pity about Nan, though. He *liked* Nan. They had much in common, both being determined to better themselves. He supposed that was why they'd never make a match of it.

And yet he was unable to stop himself from asking about her. "What makes you say Mistress Nan Bassett has a sour disposition? Did something untoward occur in the Sussex household?"

Botolph obliged him with a tale Ned found hard to believe. "And so," he concluded, "Husee retreated in haste while Mistress Nan railed at him like the proverbial fishwife."

"All that fuss over pearls?"

"Indeed." Philpott's head bobbed up and down to confirm it. "It was just as Sir Gregory says. She is a termagant, that one. A virago."

"There will be more trouble here over the matter, too, for I've no doubt that was the cause of Lady Lisle's distress." Botolph's mouth quirked. "Husee wrote to her ladyship of the incident, couching the story in careful words so as not to offend. But Master Warley also sent an account, and he is a fellow who does not know how to be subtle. His letter quoted the exact words Mistress Nan used to disparage the pearls her mother sent."

Ned set his cup on the table with exaggerated care. "You read the letters?"

Botolph's expression blossomed into a conspiratorial grin. "How else are humble servants such as ourselves to make our way in the world? Never tell me you do not do the same yourself."

Ned did not deny it, but neither did he admit to the practice. "You are right about one thing," he conceded. "The furor over those pearls is not likely to die down for weeks." Ned had never met a woman more concerned with her own reputation than Honor Lisle. She would not tolerate criticism, especially from members of her own family.

Nan was just as stubborn.

In the course of the next hour, Ned consumed a considerable amount of beer and learned a great deal about the secret lives of priests. Sir Gregory Botolph liked to listen at keyholes and had no qualms about repeating scandal. He'd regaled his companions with a half dozen bawdy tales before Ned realized that all the priests he ridiculed were staunch supporters of religious reform.

A NEW MOTHER'S churching was the celebration of the end of the month of rest she was entitled to after giving birth. It was also a signal that she could once more participate in the sacraments and could resume her conjugal duties.

Nan's cousin Mary wore a white veil and carried a lighted candle. She approached the church door accompanied by two other married women. There she knelt, waiting for the priest to sprinkle her with holy water. Thus purified, she was permitted to enter the church for the service in her honor.

Throughout the psalms and the sermon of thanksgiving for the Countess of Sussex's safe delivery, Nan watched Mother Gristwood, the midwife who had delivered young Henry. Both she and the month-old baby were honored guests. The Earl of Sussex was also present, but on this occasion he effaced himself. His countess was the center of attention.

After the service, everyone returned to Sussex House for a feast. The company, Mary's friends and relations, consisted almost entirely of women. There was eating and drinking and entertainment by minstrels and jugglers. Several hours passed before anyone thought of leaving.

Mother Gristwood was a strapping woman in the prime of life who enjoyed the celebrations as much as anyone else. At last, however, she departed. Accompanied by Cousin Kate, Nan hurried out by way of the lych-gate. They caught the midwife before she'd gone more than a few yards beyond the gatehouse.

Nan, walking a little behind Kate, was careful to keep her cloak wrapped around her to hide her fine clothing. She let her cousin do the talking. They had worked everything out in advance. Nan was certain she could carry off the deception, but she was so nervous she was shaking. Everything depended upon how convincing Kate could be.

Kate had promised to help, so long as she continued to share in the gifts Lady Lisle sent from Calais. Nan did not fully trust her cousin, but Kate was all she had.

"My serving woman is with child by a scoundrel who abandoned her," Kate told the midwife, gesturing toward Nan. "I will not have her suffer for it."

"I'll not kill the child for you," Mother Gristwood said.

"Will you deliver the babe in secret and find a family to adopt it?"

Mother Gristwood peered at Nan through the gathering darkness, a calculating look on her face. Giving a curt nod, she named a price for her services. It was high, but less than Nan had feared. If she pawned one of her court gowns, she could raise the money.

"Agreed," Kate said. "Constance will come to you on the morrow to be examined, accompanied by another maidservant." The real Constance. Nan's maid was willing to help her mistress in any way she could, even loaning Nan her name.

"And the delivery?" Mother Gristwood asked. "Am I to be summoned to Sussex House for that?"

"You will be summoned, but I do not yet know to what place." Kate's haughty tone of voice discouraged further questions.

The truth was that they had not yet contrived a way to hide the birthing. Bringing a child into the world was a long, painful, noisy process. Even if Nan bit down on a strip of leather to stifle her screams, her secret might well be discovered just when she was at her most vulnerable.

But that was a worry for another time. They had months yet to find a solution to the problem. For now all that mattered was that the midwife had agreed to keep the pregnancy secret.

On the fourth day of May, Nan was in the parlor with the other gentlewomen when Ned Corbett arrived at Sussex House. She had not seen him since mid-March. His very presence in the same room stirred her blood, but she was careful not to let anyone, least of all Ned, guess at her reaction.

John Husee was with him. As usual, he brought news of her family.

"Mistress Catherine is about to leave for Belvoir with my lord and lady of Rutland," he announced.

Only because she was watching Ned so closely did Nan see the flash of disappointment that crossed his face. She frowned. She'd always suspected that he'd courted Cat as well as herself.

"Has a match been made with Sir Edward Baynton's son?" Lady Sussex asked.

Husee shook his head. "The Bayntons say Mistress Catherine's dowry is not large enough."

Again Ned's reaction was easy to read—relief. Nan felt her temper rise. Had he taken Cat into his bed, as he had her? Had he gotten *her* with child? Did he plan to ask Cat to enter into a clandestine marriage? Perhaps they already had.

At her first opportunity, Nan dragged Ned into the relative privacy of a window alcove. "Leave my sister alone," she hissed at him. "She is too innocent for the likes of you."

In a most annoying fashion, he lifted one eyebrow. "Jealous, Nan?"

She answered with a derisive snort.

"Then why should I heed your desires?"

For one mad moment, she considered telling him about the baby. She even toyed with the idea of agreeing to marry him. But before she could make such a fatal mistake, he leaned in close to whisper in her ear.

"Let us not quarrel, Nan. I have come round to your way of thinking. We were most unwise to give in to passion."

She frowned, but did not interrupt him.

"You are a beautiful woman, Nan, and I cannot help but desire your body. But neither of us would be happy if we were bound together forever. You belong at court, and I have my own advancement to consider. We are both best served if we refrain from repeating our mistakes."

"So, what we shared was a . . . mistake?" She was proud that she kept her voice level. She did not rail at him. She did not strike him. She did not allow a single tear to fall.

"It was. As you yourself concluded."

For a moment, she almost hated him. Then she glimpsed the deep sadness in his eyes. When Ned immediately made an excuse to leave, Nan was certain it was because he was distraught over losing her. It was strangely pleasant to know she'd had such an effect on him.

Lost in sweet memories of their time together, Nan barely listened to the exchange of news going on all around her. John Husee had to repeat her name several times before she realized that he was addressing her.

"Your pardon, Master Husee. I was woolgathering."

"Will you walk with me to the gate? I would have a word with you in private." Husee waited until they were out of earshot before he spoke. "Your mother was most upset to learn that you had given away the pearls she sent you." His voice was sharper than usual.

"I am sorry to have displeased her." Nan attempted to sound penitent, even affecting a catch in her voice.

"Why would you do such a thing?" Husee demanded.

"The giving of gifts is part of courtiership."

"Only when such gifts advance your own interests. I cannot see how Kate Stradling can be of any help to you. She is nothing but a poor relation."

Nan thought quickly. She could hardly tell Husee the truth. "I am certain Kate will return the pearls if I ask her to. She has them partly as a loan and partly as a gift. I wished to reward her. She has been a most loving friend, always happy to do me a kindness, always ready to help and assist me in any way she can." *For a price.*

"You must be more sensible in future when you bestow your favors." Husee spoke sternly, obviously more afraid of Lady Lisle than he was of her daughter. "After all your mother has done for you, you must not disappoint her."

The reminder of just how reckless she had been to bestow her favors on Ned shook Nan's self-control. She was going to have his child. The burden of keeping that secret became heavier with each passing day. The constant threat of discovery, of ruin, kept her emotions in turmoil. Without warning, tears filled her eyes and streamed down her cheeks.

Appalled, Husee stared at her. "Mistress Nan! You must not carry on this way. All will be well. I will intercede with your mother on your behalf."

Nan fought to stem the flood, grateful that Husee misunderstood the reason she was crying. He would not be so sympathetic if he knew what had happened with Ned . . . or its consequences. She took the handkerchief he proffered, mopped her face, and blew her nose.

"I must win back Mother's favor, Master Husee," she said, sniffling. "I will do anything she asks. I cannot bear to have her think ill of me."

"There, there, child." Awkwardly, he patted her shoulder. "I will ask Lady Lisle to write you a comforting letter. I am certain that if you amend your ways she will forgive you. But no more overgenerous gifts, eh? And you must show proper gratitude for anything else your lady mother chooses to send you."

"I will be her obedient servant in all things, Master Husee. She will never have further cause to despair of me." Nan put every ounce of sincerity she could muster into the pledge and silently prayed she would be able to keep her word.

The next few months would be the most difficult. The midwife had told her that her baby would be born toward the end of August. Until then, with the help of tight lacing of undergarments and loose clothing for outerwear, she had to deceive everyone into thinking she suffered from nothing more serious than a spate of debilitating megrims. She'd be spending a great deal of time alone in a darkened room, but it would be worth the effort. No one would suspect that she was with child and, in the end, she would have her life back.

As touching Mrs. Anne Basset, it is showed me that she is well amended. I will see her, by God's grace, within this four days, and declare unto her your ladyship's full pleasure.

—John Husee to Lady Lisle, 27 September 1538

On a bright mid-June morning, perfect for hunting partridge, a small party rode out of the town of Calais. When Mistress Philippa Bassett had insisted upon bringing her sister Mary along, Clement Philipott had asked Ned Corbett to come with them to keep the younger girl occupied.

Ned had agreed willingly enough. He even had a merlin perched on his forearm, ready to fly, although he did not much care for the sport. Trailing behind came two servants on mules. Their packs contained food and drink for an informal midday meal in the fields. The Pale of Calais did not encompass a huge area, but it was more than sufficient for their purposes.

Ned slanted a glance at Mary Bassett as they rode through the countryside beyond the wall. She was just sixteen, a bit more than a year younger than Nan. She was just as pretty, perhaps more so, although she was still too pale. Mary had been plagued by intermittent fevers even after being returned to her mother's care in March, but at the moment she seemed in good health as well as high spirits.

Ned urged his horse a bit closer to her palfrey and spoke in a low voice. "Shall we endeavor to give them a bit of privacy?" He inclined his head in the direction of their two companions. "Philpott would appreciate an opportunity to speak with your sister alone."

"As you wish." Mary's voice was low and well modulated and reminded him of Nan's.

They reined in atop a grassy knoll to watch Philpott fly his merlin. Mary signaled for two servants to follow when he and Philippa rode after it. Then she turned curious eyes on Ned.

"Did you come along to distract me? It will not make any difference, you know. Philippa will not have him. She thinks Clement Philpott is a silly ass."

Ned swallowed a laugh. "Lord Lisle must have been of another opinion or he'd not have brought Philpott here."

"My stepfather had not met him. He relied upon the opinions of his friends in England." She seemed confident that her sister would not be forced into marriage with someone she could not like. Ned hoped Mary's innocent faith in Lord Lisle was not misplaced. Philpott was, if not an ass, at least a sheep, easily led and credulous.

Urging his horse onward, they rode in the direction Philpott's bird had flown, keeping their progress at a crawl. Ned idly stroked the merlin he had borrowed from Lord Lisle's mews. It shifted restlessly on his gauntleted fist, anxious to take wing. "All in good time," Ned murmured.

At his side, Mary Bassett seemed lost in thought. He studied her, trying to recall the little he knew about her. She'd spent nearly four years living with the de Bours family. Madame de Bours was now a widow, Nicholas de Montmorency, seigneur de Bours, having died during the time Mary lived in his household. The de Bours lands were near Abbeville, but the family often visited Pont de Remy, a few miles farther along the river, where Nan had once lived in the household of Madame de Bours's brother, the Sieur de Riou.

At the thought of Nan, Ned's grip tightened on the reins and the big gelding he rode shied, startling the merlin.

"I do not want to go to England," Mary said abruptly.

Ned stared at her in surprise. "You would be in the service of a countess, at the least. Scarcely a hardship. And if the king marries again, as they say he will, you could be a maid of honor to his new queen." The current rumors had several French noblewomen in the running, along with Christina of Milan.

"But England is so far away." Mary's heartfelt sigh and the expression of deep longing on her face made the reason for her reluctance as clear as day.

"A Frenchman, I presume?"

"How did you—?" Her hands flew to her mouth, her eyes wide with alarm.

Ned chuckled. Mary was too open and honest to be able to hide her feelings. Her vulnerability made him feel oddly protective. "You can trust me, Mistress Mary. I'll not betray you."

His reward was a brilliant smile. "I love him, Master Corbett. He is the other half of myself. I knew it from the moment we first met, the very day I arrived at his father's house."

"Gabriel de Montmorency?" The young man had become seigneur de Bours upon his father's death.

She nodded. "When he has established himself at the French court, he will ask to marry me."

Ned raised a skeptical eyebrow. Was Mary deluding herself? If the young man truly wished to have her for his wife, he should already have spoken to Lord Lisle.

"He sent me these sleeves." Mary ran a hand over the soft yellow velvet. "And another pair in linen with cuffs of gold."

"Very generous gifts." But not necessarily those of a man interested in marriage.

"I had nothing so lovely to give in return," she confided, "but I did send him a silk flower and he wrote to say that he looks at it hourly and thinks of me."

"You sent a flower and he returned flowery words."

Oblivious to his sarcasm, Mary rambled on, revealing that she kept her love letters in a box in her chamber. Her face came alive when she spoke of her suitor.

Ned flew the merlin and let her go on talking. She seemed grateful that he did not react like a typical Englishman, with prejudice against anything French.

She was a foolish young woman to speak so freely to him when she did not know him well enough to be certain he would not betray her secret to her mother and stepfather. She'd taken him at his word. Something about Mary Bassett's naive faith in him touched Ned's heart. He wanted her to stay as sweet and innocent as she was now. He even hoped that, someday, she would find the happiness she dreamed of with her Frenchman.

NAN SHIFTED RESTLESSLY on the bed, unable to find a comfortable position. The heat and humidity of an afternoon in late August invaded the chamber, increasing her misery. Her hair hung in limp, damp snarls and she did not have the energy to shove it away from her sweat-streaked face.

Her time was near. Soon this torment would be over. She knew she should not complain. Through the misfortune of others, she had been granted her dearest wish. No one but Kate and Constance were aware that Anne Bassett, once and future maid of honor to the queen of England, was about to give birth to a bastard child.

They had the house to themselves, save for the servants and the midwife. Cousin Mary had gone up the Thames by barge to the earl's house at Mortlake, eight miles distant from London. Mary had been too distraught, and too anxious to see her son, who had been sent to Mortlake soon after his birth, to argue when Nan insisted she must remain behind in order to meet Lord and Lady Lisle when they landed at Dover.

Mary had conceived a second time within weeks of her churching, then lost the child to a miscarriage. She had very nearly died herself. Nan wished no harm to anyone, but Mary's second pregnancy and its tragic outcome had been fortuitous. In their concern over the countess's health, no one had paid the least attention to Nan's burgeoning belly.

Nan had not put on a great deal of weight, the way some women did. She had been able to hide most of the bulk by letting out her kirtles and wearing loose-bodied gowns. She'd claimed to have a stomach complaint, along with her megrims, and therefore could not abide tight lacing. No one had questioned the lie, no more than they did her claim that the summer heat was the cause of her frequent headaches. Nan had kept to her chamber, out of sight, for a considerable portion of the last five months.

She only wished she had also been lying when she'd said her mother and stepfather were coming to England. They were due to arrive any day and Lady Lisle had ordered Nan to Dover to meet them. Cat had also been summoned and would travel there in the company of the Earl and Countess of Rutland.

"There must be some way to hurry this child along," she gasped as Constance wiped beads of perspiration from her brow with a damp cloth.

"I have told you before," Mother Gristwood said, "that I do not use potions to bring on labor."

Nan subsided. The midwife might be the best in London—that was why Cousin Mary had selected her and why Mother Gristwood had moved into Sussex House a full month before little Henry's birth—but Nan was not certain she trusted the woman. They had long since abandoned the fiction that she was "Constance Ware" and a servant. Mother Gristwood knew everything except the identity of the baby's father.

In spite of the heat, Nan shivered. Her position was perilous and would continue to be until her baby was safely delivered to one Barnabas Carver and his wife. Mother Gristwood had found this childless couple and maintained that they would make excellent parents for Nan's child, but she would not permit Nan to meet them.

Master Carver was a London silversmith, well respected and well to do. The arrangements were all in place. Mistress Carver would answer a knock and discover a foundling on her doorstep. After a brief and fruitless search for the person who had abandoned the child, the Carvers would adopt the baby. He would be christened James. Or Jane, if she was a girl.

My son, Nan thought. *My* daughter.

She struggled to sit up, her thoughts in turmoil. She did not want to give the child away. Her baby had been a part of her for many long months. She had felt it kick, sensed its life force.

"There has to be a way," she muttered as pain lanced through her body. Another sort of agony tore at her heart when she thought of never seeing her baby grow up, never knowing what kind of person he or she became.

After the contraction passed, Nan turned her head to stare at the midwife. Her vision blurred with tears. "There has to be a way to remain part of my child's life. There has to be. A godmother—"

"Nan! Such foolishness!" Kate Stradling's voice came from the other side of the bed. Nan had all but forgotten she was there. As usual, her cousin was hard at work on a piece of embroidery. She had not spoken for hours. "You cannot be associated with the Carvers in any way lest there be suspicion that you have some connection to their foundling."

"I could pretend to be Constance." Nan kept her eyes on the midwife, hoping for some encouragement.

Mother Gristwood shook her head. "I have told you before, Mistress Nan. We must take great care with your secret. Women who give birth out of wedlock face public humiliation. They are whipped, and worse. And the punishment is even more severe if they will not name the child's father."

"But that is only if a bastard is likely to become a burden on the community," Nan objected. "That is not the case here."

"The law does not differentiate. That is why midwives are charged with the task of learning the paternity of every illegitimate child they deliver."

Nan scowled at her. "Since you have promised not to betray me, you have no need to know."

Mother Gristwood permitted herself a small smile. "Consider it part of the payment for my silence."

"So that you may then extort money and favors from me for the rest of my life? I do not think so!"

Another contraction prevented further speech. By the time it passed, Nan had reluctantly accepted that she could not serve as her child's godmother, a role that would require her appearance at the christening to vow that the child would receive a Christian upbringing.

A stool scraped the floor as it was dragged close to the bed. Kate rearranged her skirts and squinted at her embroidery. Since no one was supposed to know that Nan was with child, her bedchamber had not been turned into a dark cave. Sunlight poured in through the open window, but so did hot, moist air.

"Master Husee was here this morning," Kate said. "He is not best pleased with you. He arrived expecting to escort you to Dover to meet your mother."

"You told him I was confined to bed with a megrim?"

"I did. And he told me the latest news from court. Negotiations for King Henry to wed Christina of Milan are still limping along, but no one now believes that marriage will come about. A French match does not seem any more likely. Christina's uncle, Emperor Charles the Fifth, and the king of France have formed an alliance. As a result of their treaty, neither one will give the king of England what he wants in a marriage settlement." Kate gave Nan's belly a speaking glance. "Just as well."

Oh, yes, Nan thought glumly. She was fortunate. As much as she wanted to return to court, she could not risk being seen in her present condition. She'd been relieved when King Henry had gone on progress in mid-July. The entire court would be on the move, visiting southern ports, until sometime in September. Unfortunately, His Grace had arranged to meet this week with her stepfather in Dover. Her mother had seen this as an excellent opportunity to bring two of her daughters to the king's attention. Curse Ned Corbett! But for him, she'd be in Dover now, flirting with the king of England, perhaps even winning him away from his current mistress.

The next pain hit with agonizing force, leaving no room for any thought beyond the torment of giving birth. Punishment for Eve's sin, the preachers said. She was supposed to suffer. Whether from compassion or from the desire to keep the few Sussex servants who remained in London from hearing Nan's screams, Mother Gristwood dosed her with poppy syrup before she moved her to the birthing chair.

Hours later, dazed and dizzy, Nan lay in bed and watched the midwife bathe her newborn son in a lukewarm mixture of ten parts water, one part milk, mallow, and sweet butter. The solution was supposed to defend the baby's body from all noisome things.

"Is he healthy?" Nan's throat felt raw and the words came out as a croak.

"He is perfect." Mother Gristwood removed him from the bath, dried him, and swaddled him tightly in the linen bands she had ready for that purpose. When she had made the sign of the cross over him, she brought him to the bed and placed him next to Nan.

He *was* perfect. Now that he was swaddled, Nan could not count fingers or toes, but his tiny face was round and pink and he had a tuft of pale hair.

"It is likely superstition," Mother Gristwood said, "but some believe that if a child lies at his mother's left side near her heart before she gives suck, she draws into herself all the diseases present in his body."

Nan looked up in alarm.

Mother Gristwood chuckled. "Have no fear. You will expel whatever evil you attract by the flux and issue of your womb, without any hurt to yourself."

For a few golden moments, Nan held her infant son and imagined what it would be like to keep him, to build a life with him and his father. Tears welled in her eyes. Such a future was impossible. She had refused Ned's offer. There was no going back. And in her heart, she knew she did not want to. Her course had been mapped out years before. She was not destined to marry a poor man.

"Time to take him to his parents," Mother Gristwood said.

"In a moment." Nan hugged the small, squirming body, fighting for self-control.

He was hungry. Mistress Carver had been given the name of a wet nurse, but she would not be able to send for the woman until after she discovered the foundling on her doorstep. Nan's breasts ached with the need to feed her son, but when Mother Gristwood reached for the child, Nan let him go.

"I have left strengthening broths and caudles for you," the midwife said, "as well as plasters and ointments to reduce inflammation and quell the bleeding. Expect afterpains and a bloody flux, both of which may continue for more than a month. A woman who has just had a child has no business traveling for at least a week."

"But I must leave by tomorrow at the latest. My mother expects me to meet her."

Mother Gristwood fixed her with a cold, implacable stare. "Would you risk your life? That is what it amounts to if you make a journey of any length before your body has time to heal." With that last admonishment, she swept out of the room.

Kate appeared at Nan's side with a restorative drink in a pewter goblet. "You were foolish to suggest traveling so soon and mad to think you could serve as the boy's godmother. You must have nothing to do with him, nothing to do with his new family."

Nan swallowed the medicine, but in spite of Kate's advice she knew she could not simply hand her baby over to strangers and forget she'd ever given birth. Somehow, she must find a way to see her son again.

"A SLIGHT INDISPOSITION?" Honor Lisle repeated John Husee's words in a tone that dripped disdain.

"A megrim, or so her cousin told me."

"Ungrateful chit. She has no proper respect for me." Honor had neither forgotten nor forgiven Nan's reaction to the pearls she'd sent. Even after several months, the insult still rankled. "And she need not think I will travel to London to see her."

"I am sure I do not know what Mistress Anne is thinking, my lady," John Husee temporized.

Honor sat at one end of the parlor of the Angel, the inn where the Lisles were lodged in Dover. She occupied the room's only chair. Her man of business hovered nearby, nervously wringing his hands, while her husband and her other daughter, slim and elegant in clothing the Countess of Rutland had given her, stood talking at the opposite side of the room.

"I will not coddle the girl," Honor muttered. "I have weightier matters on my mind."

"As to that," Husee said, "there is something you should know before you meet with the king." Honor made an impatient gesture with one heavily beringed hand to indicate that he should continue. "Your husband's cousin, Sir Geoffrey Pole, was arrested yesterday and taken to the Tower of London. He is charged with corresponding with his brother without making the king privy to his letters." Husee leaned closer. "Madam, if you have, by any small chance, even for the most innocent of reasons, written to that same gentleman, I would advise you to inform the king of it of your own volition and to cease all future contact."

Honor frowned. Sir Geoffrey Pole had more than one brother, but the only one of interest to the king was Reginald, *Cardinal* Pole. His position in the Roman Catholic church had forced him into exile on the Continent. The cardinal's place in the succession increased the threat he posed to King Henry. He and his brothers were descended from King Edward IV's younger brother.

"I do not see why Pole's arrest should affect me or my husband," Honor Lisle told Husee. "Arthur has no claim on the throne."

She had more pressing matters to concern her. There were problems with money—never enough. Arthur was in dire need of an annuity. Honor's youngest son, James Bassett, also required an income. And how was John Bassett, the oldest of her boys, to support his new wife and the child they were expecting in the manner Frances Plantagenet deserved?

There was the dispute over Painswick Manor, too. That matter would have been settled long ago if not for the interference of that upstart Thomas Cromwell.

Honor was an old hand at courtiership. Social gatherings, private meetings over business, the exchange of tidbits of news—all those were familiar ground. Familiar, too, was the snail's pace at which things proceeded. Nothing could be accomplished quickly and, in a court without a queen, there were far fewer opportunities for a woman to influence the king's decisions. All the same, Honor had high hopes for this visit to Dover. King Henry himself had sent for them and today they had been summoned to the castle east of the town to meet with His Grace.

When she'd dealt with the remaining business Husee had brought to her, Honor ordered their horses brought around. With the king in residence, all of Dover's inns were filled to capacity. The Angel was an excellent hostelry, but it had no stabling of its own. They had a long, frustrating wait before they could set out.

The last time Honor had visited the royal apartments in Dover Castle, she had been in attendance upon Anne Boleyn. Not yet queen, the king's notorious concubine had been about to accompany His Grace to France. Honor had embarked on the voyage with mixed feelings. Her religious upbringing required that she side with Queen Catherine of Aragon and deny the possibility of divorce. But the ambitions she harbored for herself and her family were powerful. To win and keep royal favor, she'd been prepared to be flexible. She still was.

Together with her husband and daughter, Honor entered the king's apartment by way of a spiral staircase in the southwest corner. The chamber was well lit and boasted an enormous fireplace decorated with old King Edward IV's badge of the rose *en soleil.* Honor's spirits soared. It seemed to her that they were being shown special favor . . . until she recognized one of the other people in the room. Thomas Cromwell emerged from a dark corner to stand at King Henry's elbow. Several persons in Cromwell's livery accompanied him.

Honor had not expected to be alone with the king. There were always attendants about. But she had planned to complain to His Grace about Cromwell's meddling. That was impossible now, and Honor suspected their long-anticipated "private" meeting with the king would be both public and disappointingly brief.

"But where is Mistress Nan?" the king asked when he had welcomed Honor and Cat with light kisses. "We looked forward to seeing both of your daughters again, Lady Lisle."

"A trifling indisposition, Your Grace, but sufficient to prevent her from traveling."

"What a pity," said the king.

At a nudge from his wife, Arthur attempted to raise the issue of Painswick. And he hinted delicately at the matter of an annuity. His Grace ignored both overtures. When he dismissed them a few minutes later, nothing whatsoever had been settled.

Dissatisfaction made Honor's manner curt when a lad in Cromwell's livery followed them out into the passageway and tried to speak to her. She continued on without acknowledging his presence. Cat, however, out of courtesy, stopped to listen to what he had to say.

"That did not go so badly," Arthur said as Cat caught up with her mother and stepfather.

Honor opened her mouth to contradict him, then closed it again. Let him retain his foolish optimism. She knew better. She did not object, either, when he suggested climbing up to the roof of the keep before they left the castle. He wanted to show Cat the view.

From that height, they could see the town and port, the shallows known as the Downs, and miles of undulating countryside. "That is St. Margaret's Bay below," Arthur said. "At low tide you can walk under the base of the cliffs, but there is always the risk of being cut off."

"Is that Calais?" Cat asked, shading her eyes against the glare of the sun. At the far side of waters that leapt and sparkled, the distant coastline shimmered, more illusion than reality. Only about twenty-five miles separated England from the Continent.

"It is," Arthur said. "On rare occasions, one can see these very chalk cliffs from the walls of Calais, and sometimes even make out the shapes of men walking on the battlements." He peered intently toward the far shore. For a few minutes, the only sounds to be heard were the cries of gulls and guillemots.

Losing interest, Cat drifted over to the spot where her mother stood. "Our Nan has made another conquest," she said.

"What do you mean?"

"That boy. The one who followed us when we left the king's presence. He was most anxious about my sister's health. He heard you tell His Grace she was ill and wished reassurance that it was nothing serious and that she would recover."

"He looked to be thirteen or fourteen at the most. Somewhat young to have formed a romantic attachment."

"Still growing," Cat agreed, "and awkward with it. Color flamed in his face when he said Nan's name. He's encountered her somewhere and been taken with her beauty. We should not be surprised. Half the retinue at Calais fell under Nan's spell during the short time she lived there before leaving for England."

Belatedly, Honor thought to ask who the lad was.

"He's Lord Hungerford's son and heir," Cat said.

"That does nothing to recommend him. I have no high opinion of his father. He was elevated to the peerage through Cromwell's influence." Honor frowned. What was it she'd heard? Some rumor about Hungerford's mistreatment of his wife? She could not quite call the details to mind.

When a salty breeze came up, lifting the lappets on her headdress and making her skirts billow around her ankles, Honor dismissed both Hungerfords from her thoughts. It was past time to return to the inn.

There were letters waiting for her at the Angel. One came from Arthur's daughter, Frances, in Calais. Honor's entire body went tight with dread as she read what the girl who was both her stepdaughter and her daughter-in-law had written.

"Mary is gravely ill." For Cat's benefit, she added, "Your sister has been plagued by an intermittent fever ever since she returned to Calais in March. It is some sort of ague. I hoped it would pass, but Mary was in her fourth week of daily fevers when we left and Frances reports that she has taken a sudden turn for the worse." Honor had only been gone a few days. She'd never have left if she'd thought Mary's fever would rise. In most cases, agues became less severe over time.

"You should be with her," Cat said. "Everyone in the household at Calais looks to you for treatment of their ailments. Even some of your friends in England write to you for advice when they are ill."

"But I have obligations here," Honor objected. "And I am not sure how much more I can do for our Mary. I have tried every cure I know for agues and fevers and none has worked for more than a short time."

Cat looked thoughtful. "I have heard of something they use in the Fenland called 'the stuff.' It is opium poppy juice coagulated into pellets. Perhaps you can locate a supply here in Calais. It is said to be a sovereign remedy for all sorts of agues."

Arthur, who had been listening to the exchange without comment, at last spoke up: "If you can obtain some of these pellets, you had best deliver them to Calais yourself."

"But, my dear—"

"No, sweetheart. I can manage well enough here on my own, and Mary needs you." He frowned. "Unless you think Nan has more need for your skills?"

Honor snorted. "Nan has no need of anyone or anything. That wretched girl is the most independent creature I have ever met."

As soon as Nan was able to travel, she, Kate, and Constance joined her cousin Mary and the rest of the household at the Earl of Sussex's house at Mortlake. News from court reached them there only belatedly, but provided many happy hours of speculation. When it came time to return to London, Nan and the others were still marveling over King Henry's demand to personally inspect seven or eight potential French brides. He'd suggested bringing them together under a marquee to be pitched on the border between France and the English Pale of Calais. The king and queen of France had been invited to chaperone. King Francis had angrily rejected the suggestion, ordering his ambassador to inform the king of England that it was not the custom in France to send damsels of noble and princely families to be passed in review as if they were horses for sale.

In the nearly two months she'd spent at Mortlake, Nan had devised a plan that would allow her access to her son. At her first opportunity, she slipped away from her cousin's house and made her way to Cheapside, the widest thoroughfare in London. All along the way the houses and shops were the most fashionable . . . and the tallest . . . in the city. Some rose as many as five stories.

Nan hurried past the elaborate buildings, barely aware of them. She could see her destination ahead, near where the west end of Cheapside led into Newgate Street—the shop of Barnabas Carver, silversmith.

"There is no need for this," Constance muttered as she trotted along behind her mistress. "He's well cared for. Well loved. The midwife said so."

Nan turned aside, entering the Liberty of St. Martins le Grand. She had not changed her mind. She had one stop to make before she entered the silversmith's shop.

The area was one in which many foreign craftsmen had settled. Nan could hear snippets of conversation in Flemish and Italian and French. She was fluent in the latter and a few judicious questions led her to a tiny shop that sold jewelry.

The Liberty of St. Martins le Grand was exempt from the jurisdiction of the lord mayor of London. The ancient rights of sanctuary applied there, although Nan was not sure why. That scarcely mattered. What was important was that these craftsmen were not bound by the regulations of the Goldsmith's Company. As she'd hoped, the merchant she found sold counterfeit jewelry, both silver and the long strands of fake gold links popularly known as St. Martin's chains.

"This is not pure silver," she said, selecting a pretty bracelet from an array of such trinkets. Lying next to it was a carcanet, a jeweled collar studded with fake jewels. Colored foil had been set behind glass to make it resemble precious stones.

The shopkeeper assured Nan that she was mistaken.

"I do hope not, since it is silver-gilt jewelry I seek."

The Frenchman shrugged. Speaking in his native language, as she had, he sang the praises of imitations that looked like the real thing. When he quoted a reasonable price for the bracelet, Nan paid it. Then she asked for the loan of a knife with which to scrape off enough of the thin silver coating to reveal the dull metal beneath.

A few minutes later, Nan was back in Cheapside and entering Master Carver's shop. Her heart raced in anticipation. She warned herself that she had to be careful. She must not appear too eager, or even mention the child the Carvers had adopted. To display overt interest would arouse suspicion.

"May I help you, mistress?" asked the man Nan assumed was Barnabas Carver. He had a slight build and wore little silver spectacles perched on the bridge of his nose. His hands were small, too, but he had long, graceful fingers. Nan supposed he needed a delicate touch to create the jewelry and other beautiful silver objects he had on display. There were cups and spoons, ewers and saltcellars, candlesticks and elaborate standing cups. From the back of the premises, she could hear the steady sound of hammering as apprentices shaped new pieces for sale.

Nan produced the bracelet she had just purchased. "A gentleman who seeks to marry me gave me this." The fabrication came easily to her lips. "He claimed it was pure silver but, as you can see, I have reason to suspect he lied."

Shaking his head and making a *tsk*ing sound, Carver took the bracelet. He ran one finger over the scratch Nan had made with the knife. "Alas, mistress, this is only silver gilt. The piece is not nearly as valuable as your suitor would have you suppose."

"Oh!" Nan cried in a distraught voice. "Oh, it is too cruel."

She wished she could coax forth tears at will, but had to settle for hiding her eyes behind a handkerchief and choking out sobs. Constance fussed over her, wringing her hands and beseeching the shopkeeper to find a place for her mistress to lie down.

"I know her well, sir." Constance's whisper contained just the right amount of urgency. "She will work herself into a terrible state if she's given half a chance. There's nothing for it but to take her somewhere private, and quickly. And perhaps a sip of wine to restore her?"

Peeking through her fingers, Nan watched Carver panic. Her plan was working. Within moments, she had been transferred from the ground-floor shop to the first-floor living quarters. She was led to Mistress Carver's very fine bed—in truth, it was better than Nan's own—and urged to lie down. She did so, but only until she heard the unmistakable sound of a baby crying.

"You have a child!" Abruptly, she sat up. Genuine tears threatened to undo her.

Regarding her warily, Mistress Carver nodded. "My son, Jamie."

"May I see him?" She sniffed and scrubbed at her eyes. "I love children. It would calm me if I could spend a few moments with your little one."

Mistress Carver looked as if she'd like to refuse, but since Nan was clearly a gentlewoman, not to mention a potential customer, she reluctantly agreed to fetch him and scurried out of the room.

Nan told herself she approved of the other woman's caution. She wanted her son's mother to feel protective toward him. Hastily, she got to her feet, smoothed her skirts, and righted her French hood. Her nervousness returned tenfold. She had little experience with babies.

Mistress Carver returned carrying a tightly swaddled child. Jamie was bigger than Nan expected and the tiny cap he wore completely covered his hair. She would not have known him for her own if she had not found him here.

Without giving Mistress Carver the chance to object, Nan tugged the baby out of the other woman's arms and hugged him tight. Jamie blinked up at her with Ned Corbett's eyes. Then he began to wail. Nan hastily handed him back to the silversmith's wife.

The baby calmed as Mistress Carver crooned to him. "He is a good baby."

"A healthy child with lusty lungs," Nan agreed. "He is more precious than gold or silver. Guard him well."

Her son would never lack for material things. More important, the little boy would have love and attention in abundance. Reassured, Nan knew she should make a clean break. Instead she heard herself asking Mistress Carver if she might call on her again and bring a small gift for Jamie.

The King's Grace removed from Westminster Tuesday the nineteenth day of November, and thanked be to God was never merrier. And the Wednesday before he made a banquet to certain lords and ladies, which was first the Duke of Suffolk and my lady his wife, my lord my master and my lady, the Earl of Hertford and his wife, and my Lady Lisle, with others, maids, which were the Queen's women. And there they lay all night in the Court, and their chambers gorgeously dressed, and everyone had banquets in their chambers and the King's servants to wait upon them: and the next day they tarried their dinner, and after the King showed them all the pleasures of his house, which dured till it was four of the clock. And then they departed and were on their way.

—a servant of the Earl of Sussex to Sussex's eldest son, 21 November 1538

I am back at court!

Jubilant, Nan wanted to whirl in a circle and sing, but she restrained her impulse. Her mother would surely not approve.

In retrospect, it seemed to Nan that her actions had been preordained. She had been meant to escape discovery. She'd had only to wait for a new opportunity to catch the king's eye. How ironic that it should be her mother's return visit to England, two months after the last one, that brought about that much-desired result. Honor Lisle had crossed again from Calais just a week earlier and taken a house in the Lothbury section of London.

It was a clear, cold November day when their party entered

Whitehall Palace through the court gate, just to the north of the northern gatehouse on the east side of King Street. "His Grace has made improvements," Honor Lisle remarked when they reached a courtyard. On one side was the great hall. Beyond that were the royal apartments, outer rooms leading into privy lodgings said to be more lavish than in any other royal residence.

"The changes are even more extensive on the western side of King Street," the Earl of Sussex said. "There are four tennis plays, two bowling alleys, a cockpit, a pheasant yard, and a gallery for viewing tournaments in the tiltyard."

King Street, which ran through Westminster to Charing Cross, neatly divided Whitehall, officially "the king's palace at Westminster," into two halves. They were linked by the northern gatehouse that stretched over the street. Nan craned her neck, trying to see everything at once. She had spent her brief stint as a maid of honor at Hampton Court, with a brief visit only to Windsor Castle. This was her first glimpse of Whitehall.

Together with her mother and the Earl and Countess of Sussex, Nan had been summoned to sup with the king. They would spend the night at the palace. Other noble couples made up the company, together with a few more former maids of honor.

Nan's sense of anticipation grew as they neared the king's presence chamber. She had not seen King Henry since she'd watched him ride away from Hampton Court following the queen's death.

She heard his big, booming laugh first. Then she saw him. He was as gloriously attired as ever, although he did seem a little larger than she remembered. One of his gentlemen—the one standing next to him wearing green silk trimmed with black fur—had clearly just said something that amused him.

"Who is that fellow?" Nan asked her cousin Mary.

"Anthony Denny. He is a groom of the chamber and keeper of the king's privy purse."

"Close to the king, then."

"And distantly related to us though his wife," Nan's mother whispered. "He may be of some help in the matter of Painswick."

Nan grimaced at the reminder that Lady Lisle had her own agenda. She wished her mother luck holding on to Painswick Manor in Gloucestershire. According to Master Husee, Lord Cromwell had made Lord Lisle an offer for the property, a very low offer. To put pressure on Nan's stepfather to sell, he was delaying payment of the annuity King Henry had promised Lisle when they'd met in Dover.

When it came time for Nan to approach the king and dip into her curtsy, she was pleased to see a look of delight on his florid face. "Mistress Bassett," King Henry said. "It is a great pleasure to see you again and looking so hale and hearty, too. Rumor had it that you were ill." He gestured for her to stand and face him.

Nan kept her smile firmly in place. "I suffered from nothing of any import, Your Grace, but I did not wish to bring any hint of sickness into your presence."

"Very considerate of you, my dear. You are wise as well as beautiful." Dismissing her with those pretty words, the king turned his attention to the next guest in line.

Among the glittering company already assembled were the Duke and Duchess of Suffolk and the Earl and Countess of Hertford. Each of those noblemen had at one time been the king's brother-in-law. Charles Brandon, Duke of Suffolk, had been married to King Henry's late sister, Mary, while Edward Seymour, Earl of Hertford, was one of Queen Jane's brothers. Nan realized with a sense of pleasure that, as such things went at court, this could very nearly be called an intimate family gathering. After all, Nan's stepfather was King Henry's uncle.

After supper, Nan returned to the luxuriously furnished double lodging assigned to her and her mother. The king's own servants waited upon them to serve a sumptuous banquet. The next day, they shared dinner with the king and afterward His Grace insisted upon showing off the wonders of Whitehall.

In the course of the tour, King Henry led them to a bank of windows that looked out across the Thames toward Lambeth. He deftly singled Nan out and maneuvered her into a deep embrasure. For a few moments, their privacy was absolute.

"I would have you back at court, Mistress Bassett," the king said. "It is a dull and dreary place without the maids of honor."

"Pray God we will soon have a new queen," Nan answered. "I look forward to entering her service."

"And what of *my* service, Nan?"

His voice was so low that for a moment Nan wondered if she'd imagined the invitation. Uncertain as to what she'd see there, she was afraid to meet the king's eyes. She wondered, suddenly, what had become of Margaret Skipwith.

Before she could decide how to respond, a rustle of fabric heralded Lady Lisle's intrusion. "Your Grace," Honor Lisle gushed as she dropped into a perfunctory curtsy and bobbed back up again. "Is my daughter not the prettiest girl you've ever seen? Why, I vow, being here at court has put roses in her cheeks."

Only by a slight stiffening of his shoulders did the king show his displeasure. Nan held her breath, fearing a display of the infamous Tudor temper, but he said only, courteously, "Mistress Nan takes after her mother."

"Your Grace flatters me." She sent a flirtatious smile his way. "I am emboldened to ask, on my husband's behalf, about one or two small matters that Lord Lisle discussed with you in Dover."

The king's expression darkened and he cut her off before she could elaborate. "You must settle such details with Cromwell." With a curt nod at Nan, His Grace abruptly left them.

Nan's mother, rigid with fury, looked nearly as formidable as the king. "For all his graciousness," she muttered, "for all his pretty compliments, we are no better off than before."

"Perhaps Lord Cromwell can be persuaded—"

"Hah! We have sent that upstart enough French wine to last a year and still he thwarts us."

"He *is* preoccupied with matters of state."

This reminder had its effect. Nan's mother subsided into brooding silence broken only when she informed Nan that she was to spend the night in Lothbury rather than return to Sussex House with Cousin Mary.

Lothbury was a largely residential section of the city and boasted spacious houses with fine gardens. But it was hard by the foundries that made chafing dishes, candles, spice mortars, and the like. During the day, the noise was appalling.

After a light supper, Nan was not surprised to find herself alone with her mother in a small private parlor. She curled her legs beneath her on the window seat, braced her back against the closed shutters, and waited. There was something on Lady Lisle's mind. Until she'd unburdened herself, Nan would be a captive audience.

"Last week," Lady Lisle began, "Lord Montagu, the Marquis of Exeter, and Sir Edward Neville were arrested. Do you know why they were taken to the Tower?"

"I've heard that they wrote letters to Cardinal Pole without the king's permission." Nan fought a yawn. "Montagu is the cardinal's eldest brother. Neville is Lady Montagu's brother. Exeter is also related to the Poles and to the king." His mother, like King Henry's, had been one of King Edward IV's daughters.

"At the time of my last visit to England, Sir Geoffrey Pole was arrested for carrying on a similar correspondence and failing to make the king privy to the contents of his letters. It seems such a small thing." Pacing, Nan's mother began to twist one of the many rings that adorned her hands.

Nan kept her head down and studied her fingernails. One of them was broken. "The king is wary of plots against the realm, and Cardinal Pole did vow to usurp the throne and return Catholicism to England. That being so, anyone who writes to him is suspected of treason."

"Such foolishness!" her mother said. With a glower for Nan, Lady Lisle launched into a rant on the difficulty of corresponding with friends when one had to think how every word might be misinterpreted.

Nan barely listened. Her thoughts had drifted to her son, as they often did. She had visited her baby again, this time taking him the gift of a rattle containing a toadstone. It was supposed to be a powerful charm, particularly effective in protecting infants from harm. She hoped to visit Cheapside again, but it was not that easy to escape Cousin Mary's house without an escort.

"Assassins," Lady Lisle said.

The word brought Nan back to the present with a start. "What did you say?"

"It is well known in Calais. King Henry gave orders to assassinate Cardinal Pole. I've been told it was Peter Mewtas, one of the king's gentlemen of the privy chamber, who was designated to shoot the cardinal with a handgun. By God's grace, he never had the opportunity."

"A gun? What a very haphazard way to kill someone!" Nan had lived long enough in a garrison town to know that small guns were notorious for misfiring. They were difficult to aim, as well. "When did this attempt take place?"

"In April of last year. Officially, Mewtas was in France to persuade King Francis that he should evict Cardinal Pole from the country. The assassination plan was secret."

"Not for long."

Her mother shrugged. "It is difficult to keep anything quiet if you tell more than one person. The point is, King Henry wants Cardinal Pole removed because His Grace considers the cardinal a threat to the throne. Now, I fear, he believes that anyone with Plantagenet blood in his veins endangers the Tudor dynasty."

Nan supposed her mother's deduction made sense. If King Henry was to be replaced along with the new religion, then a new king would have to be found. Cardinal Pole and his brothers had the best claim and, after them, the Marquis of Exeter. "Do you think the king will execute them?" That was the time-honored method of ridding the kingdom of rivals to the throne.

"I fear so. Their families are also in custody. Montagu's wife and son, as well as the Marchioness of Exeter and her boy. Even the old Countess of Salisbury, Cardinal Pole's mother, has been questioned. Where will it end, Nan? What if your stepfather is accused of treason?"

"Has he been in contact with Cardinal Pole?" Nan asked. That was the root of her mother's concern—Arthur Plantagenet, Lord Lisle.

"Certainly not!"

"Then you have nothing to worry about."

"Arthur's father was King Edward IV."

"Yes, but he is the king's *illegitimate* son."

Nan heard the faint clack of rosary beads as her mother fingered them. "Bastards have taken the throne of England before. And bastard lines have been legitimized."

Nan left the window seat to cross the room to wrap her arms around the older woman. "You worry too much, Mother. My stepfather is not the sort to plot rebellion. Lord Lisle is a quiet, plodding sort of man, content with his lot." Nan's mother was the one with ambition. "No one could possibly believe him capable of conspiring to overthrow the king."

"You always were a blunt-spoken child," Lady Lisle complained, but she seemed to take comfort in Nan's assurances.

"There is no reason for you to be concerned about him, Mother."

"I suppose not, but what if Lord Cromwell is behind the arrests of so many of the king's kin? I came to England determined to oppose him in the matter of Painswick Manor."

"If you truly fear Cromwell's influence, then let him have Painswick!"

Lady Lisle went rigid with anger and Nan hastily stepped back. "I may be persuaded to sell it to him in the end, but not for the paltry price he's offering. And I am prepared to stay in England as long as is necessary to obtain the 400 pounds Arthur was promised as an annuity."

"How do you hope to accomplish that? The king has already told you that you must deal with Lord Cromwell."

"I need another opportunity to speak with the king alone, when he is in a receptive mood." She eyed Nan speculatively. "He seems quite taken with you."

"I may not have been at court long, Mother, but it was time enough to learn that the king does not like to be pressured. He is known for his volatile temper. Push too hard and you will incur the very fate you fear most."

It clearly galled Lady Lisle to accept advice from her daughter, but she was, above all else, a sensible woman. Charges of treason were nothing to trifle with. She swallowed her protests.

"The promise of a post as a maid of honor to the next queen will put you in place to court royal favor for many years to come," she said after a few moments of silence. "You have done well so far," she added grudgingly. "The king admires you. I can see that."

Impatient with her mother's histrionics, Nan spoke before she thought: "He already has a mistress."

"Is that what he wants of you?" Shock reverberated in the words.

"So I must suppose."

"I did not labor to send you to court to turn whore. It is a sin to bed any man but your husband. Both the old religion and the new agree on that point."

It was good to know how her mother felt on the subject, Nan thought. She chose her next words with care. "The king admires wit as well as beauty. I can do nothing until he marries and I am once more part of a queen's household. But then, I am certain, I will be able to find honorable ways to persuade him to grant me favors."

"You have a responsibility, Nan. You must not only advance yourself, but your brothers and sisters as well."

This was the start of another lecture, one Nan already knew by heart. She nodded from time to time to convince her mother she was listening, but her thoughts quickly returned to that afternoon, when she'd stood beside the king in the window alcove. Had he really been inviting her to become his mistress?

How odd, she thought, that her mother believed bribes of wine or quails or jewelry were acceptable, but that offering one's self in return for favors was a sin. Just now, Nan found the idea of becoming King Henry's mistress tempting. Even more tempting was the possibility that, if she could please His Grace sufficiently, she might not have to settle for that role. Was it possible she might be able to follow in the footsteps of Anne Boleyn and Jane Seymour . . . without the fatal consequences?

Nan returned to Sussex House the next day, determined to further her future. She'd have liked to begin at once, but was constrained by her mother's continued presence in England. She resolved to be patient, to wait until her mother returned to Calais before she began her campaign to seduce the king.

When Lady Lisle was still in Lothbury at the end of November, Nan worried that her mother would never leave. Troubling in another way was the reason her mother stayed on. She was unable to obtain an interview with Lord Cromwell and settle the matters of Painswick Manor and Lord Lisle's annuity because Cromwell was busy gathering evidence against the king's cousins.

On the second of December, Lord Montagu was tried for treason. On the third, it was Exeter's turn. On the fourth, trials were held for Sir Edward Neville and Sir Geoffrey Pole. All were found guilty and all but Sir Geoffrey sentenced to death. Nan, and everyone else who heard of it, assumed he'd escaped that fate because he'd given evidence against his family and friends.

Lord Cromwell finally found time to see Lady Lisle on the seventh of December. He offered her an unappealing bargain. He would guarantee an annuity of £200—half what Lord Lisle had been promised—in return for which she would agree to sell him Painswick for a fraction of its worth. Persuaded by the fact that Montagu, Exeter, and Neville were about to be executed, Lady Lisle conceded defeat and agreed. She did not want to make an enemy of Lord Cromwell. At last, in mid-December, she left London, freeing Nan to pursue her own inclinations.

CHRISTMAS AT GREENWICH Palace was everything Nan had hoped for. There were masques and games and, every evening, dancing. The palace itself was all that was wonderful, with its gardens and tiltyard and its hunting park. Even in December, its beauty was unsurpassed, and Nan saw it through a golden haze.

The king was most attentive, riding at her side during one of the hunts and seeking her out as a dance partner as often as he did Margaret Skipwith. But Margaret Skipwith was present, and apparently in as much favor as ever.

Nan studied the king's mistress when she thought no one was watching. Her rival was small, plump, and amiable. She flirted with the king, admired the things he admired, and spoke of nothing but inconsequential matters. Nan took heart when she heard the rumor that Margaret was to have young Lord Talboys as her husband. Her reward, Nan assumed, and a sign that the king had grown tired of her.

On the day before Twelfth Night, Cousin Mary took it upon herself to interfere in Nan's plans. She dismissed Kate and Isabel and Jane so that she could speak with Nan in private. As soon as they were alone in Mary's inner chamber, she rounded on Nan. "You will ruin yourself for a good marriage!"

"Hardly."

Nan went to the sideboard and selected two wineglasses with gilt decoration. She filled both from a covered crystal flagon and offered one to her cousin. "Say what is on your mind, cousin."

"A virtuous woman lies only with her husband, and then only after marriage vows have been exchanged. You have nothing to gain by attracting the king's interest but the loss of your most precious possession."

Nan took a steadying sip of the wine—a fine Rhenish—to give herself time to think. Mary clearly meant what she said. She'd be no help at all in winning the king's heart. "I have been trying to pique His Grace's interest," she admitted, "but not for the reason you think." Nan lowered her voice, even though they seemed to be alone. They were, after all, at court. "As long as King Henry is not yet married to some foreign princess, it follows that any true-born English gentlewoman has a chance of marrying him. Would you deny me my opportunity?"

"The king must take a foreign princess to wife. He'll not wed you, Nan, only make you his mistress and endanger your immortal soul. Just because he is the king, you cannot allow yourself to break God's laws."

Mary put aside her wine and went to her looking glass to adjust the crossed bands of amber-colored velvet arranged at the front of her French hood. They were supposed to make her look as if she had light-colored hair, far more fashionable than her own black locks.

"I suppose you are right," Nan said. "I was flattered by His Grace's attention and did not think matters through."

To placate her cousin, she pretended to abandon her attempts to win the king's affection. In truth, she had no intention of doing so.

The next day, Nan paid a visit her old friend Anne Parr. She was Anne Herbert now and shared her husband's lodgings at court. Nan's heart sank when she saw how small and cramped the space was. Will Herbert had but one room. The only place to sleep was a single flock bed with a bolster and coverlet.

Perched atop the ship's chest used to store clothing, drinking an inferior Gascon wine from a beaker of plain glass, Nan hastily made further adjustments to her plans. If she could not move in with Anne and Will, she must find somewhere else to stay, a place where her every move would not be scrutinized.

"I am charged to advance my stepfather's cause at court," she confided to Anne, "and I hope to secure my own future as well. To succeed in both, I need access to the king. *Private* access."

Anne blinked her wide-spaced gray eyes once in surprise, but Nan read neither shock nor disapproval in her expression.

"You must remember how the king sought me out, even before Queen Jane died."

"I do." Anne sipped her wine. "So, you want to replace Mistress Skipwith, do you?"

"Perhaps."

"Be very sure, Nan. His Grace is not easy to please and there will be a new queen soon. What if she takes his fancy? She might persuade him to banish *all* his former mistresses from court."

"I need your help, Anne. I must find someplace to live where the king can visit me without causing comment."

"Mary will be wroth with you if you leave Sussex House."

Nan grimaced. "She has been good to me and I hate to disappoint her, but she has not been able to arrange the sort of marriage I want for myself, and she has made it clear that she does not approve of my . . . flirtation with the king."

Anne looked thoughtful. "I suppose you could go to my sister Kathryn."

"Lady Latimer? But she hardly ever comes to court except to visit you. I need someone with lodgings at court. Or nearby. Or someone whose husband is close enough to the king that His Grace might pay frequent visits to his house."

"What about Jane Mewtas? Her husband is high in King Henry's favor."

And a would-be assassin! Nan quickly suppressed the thought. If Peter Mewtas had earned the king's trust by his willingness to shoot Cardinal Pole, so be it. "An excellent idea," she said aloud.

"I will see what I can do," Anne promised, "but you must be patient. After all, Margaret Skipwith is still at court, and the king, in his own way, is monogamous."

THE NEXT WEEKS passed with excruciating slowness. Then Anne Herbert and Jane Mewtas paid a visit to Sussex House. Jane lived beside Our

Lady of Barking in Tower Street, not far distant, and since both women had been maids of honor at the same time as Mary and Jane Arundell, no one saw anything unusual in subsequent visits, singly and together, over the next weeks.

On her second visit to Sussex House, Jane pressed a small packet into Nan's hand. "His Grace sends his best regards," she whispered, "and looks forward to the day when your beauty will once more grace his court."

The gift was a small likeness of His Grace. The miniature portrait was exquisite, Master Hans Holbein's work, painted on vellum that had been glued to a playing card and then cut into an oval shape to fit into a small gold frame. Nan kept it hidden, since she did not want to arouse Cousin Mary's suspicions, but she took it out often in private to stare at it and daydream.

Gatherings of the former maids of honor at Sussex House soon became a regular event. They speculated about the identity of the next queen, talked about clothes, and exchanged news of the court: Anthony Denny had been appointed as chief gentleman of the privy chamber; Margaret Skipwith had left court to marry Lord Talboys; the king had been excommunicated by Pope Paul III.

"More rumors of treason are afoot," Jane Mewtas reported in early April, "even after last month's executions."

Another plot, Nan thought without much interest. New ones seemed to spring up daily, each one more insubstantial than the last. But the king took no chances. The penalty for expressing a treasonous opinion was the same as for fomenting rebellion—death.

"There are times," Cousin Mary said, "when I am glad to be away from court. There is too much intrigue. Nor are we free of it in London. I am well pleased that we will soon be leaving here."

Startled, Nan dropped a stitch.

"Where are we going?" Kate Stradling asked, equally surprised.

"My lord husband informs me that in a few days' time we will travel into Essex to spend several months at the new property he has acquired near Boreham."

Go away? For *months*? That would not do. Nan sent a beseeching glance in Jane Mewtas's direction. Jane hesitated, then gave an almost imperceptible nod. It was time to put into effect the plan they had been hatching since Anne and Jane first came to call at Sussex House.

That evening, Nan's old complaint, the megrim, returned with a vengeance. Or so Nan told anyone who would listen. Such acute headaches, accompanied by dizziness and extreme sensitivity to light, had been strangely absent since the previous autumn. Although Kate was clearly suspicious, she could not voice her doubts without revealing her own complicity in Nan's earlier deception.

When Jane Mewtas called again the next day, Nan was still abed, the red-and-white damask curtains drawn and all the candles save one snuffed out. Cousin Mary was in a state, concerned for Nan but reluctant to delay her own departure.

"You will have to travel to Essex in a litter," Nan's cousin decided.

Nan shielded her eyes with one arm and injected a pitiful quaver in her voice. "Let me stay here, coz, I beg you. Constance can look after me until I am able to ride."

"Impossible!"

On cue, Jane Mewtas spoke up. "She cannot stay here unchaperoned, but neither can she make such a long journey in her present state. Surely there is somewhere here in London where she can stay until she is fit again."

"Her sister is with Lady Rutland, but they are presently at Enfield."

"Then let her come to me. Peter and I have room and we would be glad to have her."

"Even ill?" Cousin Mary sounded doubtful.

"A megrim does not last forever. It only seems like it. Why, this is the perfect solution. Nan can be moved the short distance to Tower Street, together with her maid, and the rest of your household can depart on schedule."

Mary did not hesitate long. She gave orders for Constance to pack Nan's belongings. That very afternoon, Nan went home with Jane.

Her new lodgings were small and cramped compared with the old, but the Mewtas house stood close to the Thames and could easily be accessed by the royal barge. Nan's bedchamber under the eaves was tiny, but she had it all to herself.

Two days after her arrival, she was sitting on the window seat, passing the time by hemming a handkerchief, when the door abruptly opened to reveal the king.

"Your Grace!" Nan rose in a flurry of skirts and sank into a curtsy. The handkerchief and a pair of shears, in a case of crimson velvet, tumbled to the floor.

The king lifted her by the elbows and greeted her with a kiss. In itself, that was nothing out of the ordinary. The exchange of kisses was as common as the clasping of hands. But this was no brief brushing of lips. King Henry lingered. When he stepped away, his eyes gleamed, anticipating more kisses to come.

"It is a delight to see you again, Mistress Nan."

"Your delight cannot surpass my own, Your Majesty." This was the first time she'd been completely alone with him. A sudden attack of nervousness had her trembling. More than three months had passed since their last encounter. What if she had been wrong about the intensity of his interest in her?

His great booming laugh was both startling and reassuring. "Do you strive to outdo your king in compliments, sweetheart? I say my delight is the greater."

Nan bobbed a second curtsy. "Your pardon, Your Grace. I am no doubt mistaken. And yet, I take such pleasure in your company that I feel as if the sun has just come out after forty days and forty nights of rain."

"Saucy minx." He linked his arm through hers and guided her back to the long, padded bench beneath the window. "Sit, my dear."

He settled himself beside her and took her hands in his, caressing them lightly. He frowned at the lack of rings on her fingers. She wore no jewelry at all except for the miniature of himself as a pendant. Her gown was plain, too, made of violet cloth lined with red saye.

In contrast, the king's fingers were heavy with jewelry, as were other parts of his person. His gown was scarlet and gold brocade, slashed so that puffs of white satin, held with gold clasps, came through the openings. He wore a white satin sash and a collar of twisted pearls with ruby medallions. Even the linen shirt that showed above the neckline of his doublet was heavily embroidered with gold thread.

King Henry slipped an arm around Nan's waist and drew her close for another kiss. Nan found it pleasant, although not as stimulating as the kisses she'd shared with Ned. She returned it with as much fervor as she could manage, but even as she willed herself to encourage him to seduce her, she had to fight an urge to pull back. It had been easy to imagine being intimate with the king, but the reality was far more difficult.

The king might wear fine clothing, but he was much older than she. He was also alarmingly large and heavy. There was a great deal more of him than she'd remembered! Fingers that suddenly put her in mind of sausages stroked her arm and toyed with the pins that held her cuffs in place. She inhaled deeply, reassured when she caught a whiff of the same wonderful scent he always wore. But when he embraced her, she could not suppress a small sound of distress. She felt overwhelmed by his massive physical presence and intimidated by the thought that *this was her king*.

King Henry responded to her whimper with a sigh. Releasing her, he sat back, as if to study her. He did not seem angry, but when Nan looked at him, dismay cascaded over her. How had she ever thought this man was handsome? He had piglike eyes in a jowly face. Just as Constance had said, he was a fat old man.

Struck by a mixture of terror and confusion, Nan's eyes filled with tears. Her entire body trembled. When she spoke, her voice shook. "I . . . do want to please you, Your Grace."

His touch was gentle as he used his own handkerchief to brush moisture from her cheek. "You please me greatly, Nan, and you would please me even more if you were to become my mistress, but to find you so innocent of the ways of men gives me pleasure, too."

Nan bowed her head to keep him from reading her expression. He had misinterpreted her reaction. He thought her sudden revulsion was the fear some brides experienced. *He thought she was a virgin.*

Unable to bring herself to admit that she was not, Nan struggled to clear her mind. She needed time. She needed to think through what the king's misreading might mean. But he was waiting for her to say something.

"To be your mistress would be a g-g-great honor, Your Grace."

Her nervousness seemed to amuse him. She could hear it in his voice. "You have no experience by which to judge, dear Nan."

She did not correct him. One did not contradict the king of England. "Your Grace flatters me," she whispered, still avoiding his eyes. "I know not what to say. I would fain keep your good opinion of me, and your friendship."

"I would be a *very* good friend to you, Nan." Again, he sighed. "What a great pity it is that I must make a foreign alliance. I cannot marry an Englishwoman, but if I could, I would need to look no further for my bride."

Nan's head jerked up and she stared at him in amazement. She'd dreamed of hearing him say such a thing to her, but she had not really believed it was possible. Knowing that he considered her worthy to be his queen left Nan feeling breathless.

"But I am not free to wed where I will," the king continued, caressing her palm with his thumb as he spoke. "My agents abroad have at last found a suitable princess for me to marry."

King Henry's gaze shifted away from Nan. He was staring at the busy street below her window and the view of the Tower of London beyond, but Nan doubted he noticed any details. His eyes had a faraway look in them.

"Her name is Anna of Cleves. One of my agents who has met with her says that she outshines the Duchess of Milan as the golden sun surpasses the silver moon."

"It is good that we will soon have a new queen," Nan whispered. She wished she believed it.

Swift as a striking snake, the king's attention shifted back to her. "Nothing will happen quickly."

Nan's heart stuttered. Her mind raced through tangled thoughts. In a moment, His Grace would embrace her again. For the interim, until his new bride arrived in England, he wanted a woman to warm his bed. He craved feminine company, someone to pamper and amuse him.

She could be that person. She'd be a fool to refuse the honor. And yet, if she did not send him away at once, he would discover the truth about her virginity. Would he care that she was not the innocent he'd supposed? Nan was afraid to find out. She shuddered to think what he would do if he decided that she had deliberately misled him.

King Henry kissed her again, more fervently than before. Nan willed herself not to respond in any way. Had he only been paying lip service to high ideals when he'd stopped before, or did he truly admire women who went to their marriage beds with their maidenheads intact? He was the king. He could slake his lust with her whether she showed any inclination to participate or not, and no one would reprimand him. Besides, she'd made it plain enough that she was his for the taking. But she did not want this, not now. Rigid with tension, she felt his lips move to her throat, his hands caress her breasts.

When he abruptly released her and stood, Nan kept her eyes tightly closed. Had her lack of response angered him? Worse, had she just lost any chance to advance herself and her family? Silence stretched between them until she thought she would scream.

At last he spoke. "Will you join Lady Sussex at Boreham?"

Slowly, Nan opened her eyes, where tears once more shimmered. "I would rather remain here."

The king's smile was tinged with lingering desire and what Nan thought was regret, but she saw no temper there, no threat of retribution. "I would rather that you remain here, too. I crave more from you, Nan, but for the nonce I will hold you to your offer of friendship."

With that, he left her. Nan retrieved the partially hemmed handkerchief from the floor and used it to dry her tears. By the time Jane Mewtas arrived a few minutes later, she had control of herself again.

"His Grace did not stay very long." Worry creased Jane's brow. She and her husband had their own stake in Nan's success with the king.

"Not this time." Nan reached for the fallen shears with unsteady fingers. She was not sure what she wanted anymore, but she had time to consider. Nothing had to be decided today.

"Will he return?" Jane asked.

"Yes," Nan said. She was certain of that much. The king of England had promised her his friendship.

I have delivered your token to my Lady Sussex, who doth heartily thank
your ladyship for the same. Her ladyship is somewhat acrased, and as far
as I can learn she is not well pleased with Mrs. Anne; and though the
matter be forgiven I do perceive she hath not forgotten it.

—John Husee to Lady Lisle, 26 May 1539

On the twenty-first day of May, Cat Bassett returned to court.
She came at the invitation of the king, but without Lady Rutland, who was due to give birth to yet another child in only two months'
time. King Henry was hosting a banquet that evening for a group of his
late wife's gentlewomen. Cat was not quite certain how she'd come to be
included in their number. She could only suppose that it was because,
had Queen Jane lived, Cat would have had the place Anne Parr vacated
to marry Will Herbert.

A yeoman of the guard escorted Cat to the lodgings she was to share
with her sister. She'd been looking forward to the chance to spend time

with Nan. They'd not seen each other since shortly after Queen Jane's death.

She heard the racket well before they reached their destination—laughter, high-pitched feminine voices, and the clink of glassware. Grinning, the yeoman of the guard opened the door for her and took his leave.

There was scarcely space in the room for another person to squeeze in. Cat recognized three former maids of honor—Nan and Jane Mewtas and Anne Herbert. She also knew Joan Denny slightly, since Joan was a distant Bassett cousin, but the other woman was a stranger to her.

"Cat!" With that exclamation of delight, Nan drained the last of the Malmsey from her goblet, tossed it carelessly aside, and rushed forward to embrace her sister.

Hugs from Anne, Jane, and Joan followed. They'd been imbibing freely and their greetings were effusive.

"Do you know Kathryn Latimer?" Nan asked, presenting Cat to a tiny woman smaller in stature than any of the others. "She is Anne's sister."

Dashing off to refill goblets, Nan abandoned them. Cat frowned. Her sister had always been exuberant, but there was a fevered quality about her now, a hectic energy that was not quite natural.

The conversation in the bedchamber ranged from new dance steps, to the fashion in hats, to the relative merits of various precious stones.

"I have a passion for jewels, especially diamonds," Lady Latimer confessed.

"Rubies suit me better." Nan held her right hand out in front of her, the better to admire the ring she wore on one finger. The ruby, mounted in white enamel, was an expensive bauble. Cat wondered who had given it to her sister.

"Jewelry is all very well," Jane Mewtas said, "but I would trade a handful of emeralds to have Kathryn's beautiful soft skin."

"You need not impoverish yourself to learn my secret," Kathryn said with a chuckle. "Twice a week, I fill a leaden bathtub with milk and soak in it for an hour."

Astonished cries greeted this revelation. Joan Denny looked alarmed. "If frequent immersion in water can endanger the health, surely it is even more of a risk to bathe in milk."

"No harm has ever come to me," Kathryn assured her, "although I have noticed that my new kitten seems extremely fond of me right after I emerge from the tub."

Cat joined in the general laughter that followed, much taken with her new acquaintance. Kathryn Latimer was a little older than the others, and quieter. Especially when compared to Nan, Kathryn seemed to be a very calm and contented sort of person.

That might have made her dull, but when the conversation turned to hunting, Kathryn's hazel eyes lit up with pleasure. "I miss riding out to hunt when we are in London," she admitted.

"Kathryn is an excellent shot with a crossbow," her sister boasted.

"The king means to hunt tomorrow," Nan said. "I hope he will invite some of us to ride out with him."

"It seems likely he will ask at least one of us," Jane Mewtas said with a giggle and a knowing look that sparked Cat's curiosity. The polite laughter and speculative glances from the others were even more intriguing, and Nan's expression made Cat think of cats and cream.

They all supped together that evening and afterward all but Lady Latimer adjourned to the king's banquet. "I was not invited, since I have never lived at court or attended upon a queen," she explained to Cat, "although I did visit a time or two when my mother was in Queen Catherine's service. I do not mind. In truth, I am glad to make an early night of it in the lodgings Will Herbert secured for me for the duration of my visit with Anne. I must leave in the morning to return to the house my husband leases in the Blackfriars section of London. We live there while Parliament is in session."

Kathryn Latimer seemed genuinely happy with her lot in life. She was a fortunate woman, Cat thought. Few females of her acquaintance enjoyed true contentment. Cat herself was better situated than most, but even she had moments when she longed for a husband and children. She liked living with Lord and Lady Rutland, but she did not want to stay there forever.

The banquet found King Henry in a jovial mood. Throughout courses of fruits and cheeses and sweet wines and the dancing afterward, he laughed and joked. And he appeared to take special pleasure in part-nering Cat's sister. At the end of the last pavane, he lingered with Nan in a secluded corner, unaware that Cat stood close enough to overhear their conversation.

"Will you accompany me when I go hunting tomorrow?" King Henry asked.

"Alas, Your Grace, I cannot, for I have no horse."

"You may borrow one of mine."

"I have no saddle, either."

"That, too, will be supplied."

"You are most generous, Your Grace."

"You will lack for nothing, I promise you." King Henry raised Nan's hand—the one wearing the ruby ring—to his lips. He kissed each of her fingers in turn. "Until tomorrow, sweeting."

Cat watched him walk away, then looked at her sister. She could tell nothing from Nan's expression, but she had her suspicions. As soon as they were alone in the double lodgings they'd been assigned—two spacious rooms with fireplaces and a private privy—she drew in a deep breath and asked the obvious question: "Are you the king's mistress?"

"Not yet."

Something in Nan's tone made Cat look more closely at her sister. "Do you want to be?"

"I'd have influence. A good marriage at the end of it." She shrugged.

"What happened to Margaret Skipwith?"

"Married off to Lord Talboys."

Cat frowned. "Isn't he Lady Clinton's son?"

"He is." Nan grinned. "Appropriate, don't you think, marrying off one mistress to an earlier mistress's child?" Lady Clinton, previously Lady Talboys, had been born Bessie Blount. Prior to her first marriage, she'd given birth to the king's bastard, the late Henry FitzRoy.

"Will the king send for you tonight?" Cat asked as her sister began to undress for bed. Cat took over the duties of a tiring maid, since she saw no sign of Constance. She supposed Nan had dismissed her for the night.

"I do not think so." Nan gave a short, humorless laugh. "You see, Cat, His Grace is bent on *courting* me."

Cat did not know what to say to that. Surely Nan did not think the king would *marry* her.

"But what of you, Cat?" Free of her own garments, Nan unlaced Cat. "Have you any suitors? The last I heard, the Bayntons thought our dowries insufficient to make a match."

"I am certain Mother will tell me when she's found someone."

"Perhaps Ned Corbett?" Nan took a gold toothpick from a small, jeweled case and began to clean her teeth.

Cat could not stop the wave of heat that rushed into her face. She suspected that it was accompanied by a revealing wash of red.

"Oh ho!" Nan exclaimed, confirming it. "So he did show an interest."

"He was kind to me after Queen Jane died, but nothing came of it. The only times I see him now are when he brings me letters from Calais."

Nan did not look as if she believed it, but she did not pursue the subject. Instead she asked if there had been any more talk of sending Cat to the Duchess of Suffolk.

"None at all, and happily no more discussion about sending me to Lady Hertford, either. I prefer to remain where I am. Lady Rutland treats me like one of her own daughters. Lady Hertford, I am told, is almost as hard for her waiting gentlewomen to please as Mother is."

Nan washed her mouth with mint sodden in vinegar, then rubbed powder made of ashes of rosemary onto her teeth with a soft cloth and rinsed with plain water.

"I do not think the Hertfords were enthusiastic about having me join their household in any case." Cat mixed vinegar and chamomile with water and used the solution to cleanse her face, neck, and arms. "Mother's attempts to win their favor were unsuccessful, although that was not her fault."

"Why? What happened?" Finished with her own ablutions, Nan climbed into bed, leaving the curtains open while Cat cleaned her teeth and freshened her breath. Cat snuffed out the candle and joined her sister under the covers.

"Well?" Nan demanded. The darkness and close quarters were conducive to sharing secrets.

"I had the story from Master Husee. Mother sent two gifts to the Earl of Hertford."

Even after his sister's death, Queen Jane's brother was someone Lady Lisle wanted to cultivate. She'd begun corresponding with him the previous November, right after they'd both been part of the same company entertained by the king at court.

"One was a linnet in a cage," Cat said, "and the other a stool decorated with crewelwork. The ship on which they were sent sank off Margate. The cargo was rescued and there was no loss of life, but the stool was damaged by saltwater, and the colors of the crewelwork had faded. As for the bird, it was brought safely to shore and taken to a house in Billingsgate. Master Husee was only waiting for a convenient time to deliver it to Lord Hertford." A chuckle escaped Cat, hastily stifled. "It is *not* funny."

Nan poked her in the ribs. "Tell. Tell."

"The household contained a cat. The cat ate the linnet."

"Oh, dear." Silent mirth made Nan's shoulders shake. "Oh, my. So neither reached the earl?"

"Oh, in the end, he received a much better gift. Mother sent Arabella to replace the linnet that was lost."

"No! Not Arabella. She loves that bird."

"She loves finding favor with influential courtiers more. Master Husee said she told the earl, in a letter, that Arabella was the best linnet in all of Calais and that it would be a long time before she was mistress of such another."

"She is willing to sacrifice much for advancement," Nan murmured, yawning hugely.

She was not the only one, Cat thought, as her sister rolled over and pulled the covers up to her chin. And it was surely a mixed blessing to be favored by the king.

DURING THE MONTHS after Clement Philpott and Sir Gregory Botolph arrived in Calais, Ned Corbett formed the habit of spending most of his free time in their company. Gambling at the Rose, a tavern just outside the walls of Calais, was a favorite pastime. There they could talk almost as freely as the ale flowed, but there were limits.

The garrison in Calais was a dumping ground for troublesome younger sons, and many of them had bones to pick. On this particular June evening, a hotheaded soldier owed money by the Crown told his troubles to anyone who would listen, cursing all those responsible for holding back his pay.

"Were he in London, he'd be charged with treason for that tirade," Ned remarked.

"He'd be in greater trouble if he complained about changes in the liturgy," Philpott muttered, "and a dead man already if he had Plantagenet blood in his veins." He threw the dice and muttered an oath when he lost yet again.

"Did you hear that the old Countess of Salisbury has been taken to the Tower?" Botolph asked.

Ned had not, although he'd known that Margaret Plantagenet, Countess of Salisbury, Cardinal Pole's mother, had been under house arrest somewhere in the countryside since the previous November, even before her oldest son, Lord Montagu, was executed for treason.

Aloud he said only, "I doubt the king will execute a woman."

Botolph snorted. "He beheaded Anne Boleyn."

"That harlot got what she deserved," Philpott said.

"Did she?" Botolph's eyes glinted with deviltry. "Or did His Grace simply claim she did in order to rid himself of an encumbrance to his marriage with Jane Seymour?"

Ned stayed out of the debate. He doubted anyone would ever know the whole truth of the matter. Neither was he entirely comfortable discussing such things in a public place, even one like the Rose.

"Careless words are dangerous." With that warning, as he steered his two friends toward a table in a back corner where, noisy as the tavern was, there was less risk of being overheard. Ned signaled for the waiter to refill their flagons.

Calais was a breeding ground for dissension. Because the border with France lay close at hand on one side of the Pale, and that of Flanders, one of the Low Countries, on the other, there were many living in Calais whose sentiments veered toward extremes in both politics and religion. Some were papists. Others wanted radical reform within the English church—much more far-reaching changes than had already been made.

"Lady Salisbury's son was condemned for nothing more than writing letters," Philpott mumbled into his ale. "An outrage!"

"But they were letters to a man who has sworn to overthrow the rightful king of England," Ned reminded him.

"They were letters to his brother. And your *rightful* king has been excommunicated by the pope."

"God will sort things out." Botolph took a deep swallow of ale, then winked at Ned. "The real reason our friend here is so melancholy is that he has troubles closer to home. Note the long face, the sad eyes, the short temper."

"My luck is out," Philpott admitted.

"At cards, dice, or love?"

"All three. Mistress Philippa has refused my suit. I cannot understand it. I am a fine, upstanding gentleman."

"What is so difficult to comprehend? Philippa Bassett thinks she can do better." Botolph chuckled. "And Mary Bassett *knows* she can."

"Do you mean to say that sickly Mistress Mary has a lover?" Philpott sounded amazed.

"I cannot say. I am bound by the sanctity of the confessional."

Ned scowled at them both. "Have a care what you imply, lest you impugn a good woman's reputation."

"Oh ho! Listen to the chivalrous knight!"

Ned ignored Philpott's mockery, but Botolph's smirk bothered him. He wished Mary had chosen one of the older priests as her confessor. She was, at long last, free of her recurring bouts of fever, and the identity of her lover should be no one's business but her own.

Ned liked Sir Gregory Botolph. Everyone did. He was a stirring speaker and an engaging companion. He had acquired the nickname "Gregory Sweet-lips" since coming to Calais because he could so easily persuade others to his way of thinking. But in private, Botolph had none of the virtues of a man of God. He gambled and swore and drank to excess and even kept a mistress in the town.

"Perhaps you'll have better success with Lady Lisle's newest waiting gentlewoman," Botolph suggested to Philpott.

"She's comely enough, but has she a decent dowry? She's some kin to John Husee, is she not? He's a nobody, the son of a vintner."

"Mary Hussey is not related to John Husee at all," Ned said. "She is one of the daughters of Lord Hussey of Sleaford."

For a moment, Philpott brightened. Then, remembering, his face fell. "He was executed for rebellion against the Crown." Some two years earlier, there had been an uprising in Lincolnshire. Yet another ill-thought-out scheme to overthrow King Henry. It had been put down quickly and brutally. "What was Lady Lisle thinking, to take a traitor's get into her household?"

"Of the benefits of charity, no doubt." Botolph leaned back against the wall, cradling his flagon between his hands. "All of Lord Hussey's lands and goods and chattels were seized by the Crown, even clothing and jewelry."

"With Lord Hussey dead and his title forfeit," Philpott mused, "his daughters will have been left destitute. Why else would a baron's daughter enter the service of a mere viscountess?"

"Still," Botolph mused, "if the old order is ever restored to England, the man married to Mary Hussey would have a claim to her father's title."

Briefly, Ned wondered if Botolph imagined Cardinal Pole leading an army against King Henry. Then he decided that the priest was simply amusing himself by baiting their credulous friend. It would not be the first time Botolph had led Philpott into expressing seditious sentiments. Had one of Lord Cromwell's spies been present to overhear, they'd both have been under arrest for heresy. It was neither wise nor safe to speculate about the return of the Catholic Church to England.

"I do feel sorry for the girl," Philpott allowed. "Imagine being at Lady Lisle's beck and call!"

"Sorry enough to marry her?" Botolph asked.

Philpott looked tempted. He scratched his beard, took another swig of ale, and studied the stained and cracked boards of the table. Then he sighed. "So long as any taint of treason clings to her, there is too much risk that it will attach itself to whatever man she marries."

Botolph took a long swallow of ale and gave Philpott a considering look. Ned could tell he had some further deviltry in mind. "Ah, well," he said as the sounds of a scuffle reached them from the far side of the tavern, "without a dowry to attract a husband, I doubt she expects to be honorably wed. I wonder if she would accept a suitable gentleman as her protector? She'd make an excellent mistress, would she not?"

Philpott brightened at this suggestion. With Botolph egging him on, he began proposing schemes, each more preposterous than the last, to get Mary Hussey into his bed.

As if, Ned thought, any girl in her right mind would settle for

Clement Philpott as either lover or husband. Ned barely knew the girl, but he hoped, for her sake, that she had higher standards than that.

He was about to say so when what had merely been a noisy dispute over a reckoning suddenly erupted into a fistfight. When a stool sailed past Ned's head, nearly clipping his ear, he came to his feet with a bellow. His two companions beside him, he waded into the fray. He had no idea which side anyone was on. It did not matter. He threw punches with indiscriminate abandon. To Ned's mind, there was no better way to end a night at the Rose than a full-scale tavern brawl.

A FEW DAYS later, in the second week of June, Ned stood in front of the Mewtas house, staring at the overhanging upper stories. Sun glinted off dozens of clear windowpanes, proof of the owner's wealth and position. Still, it was a small place compared to Sussex House, and Peter Mewtas and his wife had pedigrees no more exalted than Ned's own. Why was Nan living with them? If John Husee had the right of it, her decision to stay on in Tower Street had caused a rift with the Countess of Sussex. What advantage had there been to Nan in alienating her greatest benefactor?

He'd never find out by standing in the street. Squaring his shoulders, Ned marched up to the door. He was admitted by a servant and shown into an upstairs room. He stopped short at the sight of Nan, seated in a Glastonbury chair, positioned so that the sun bathed her in light and picked out the golden highlights in her light brown hair.

"Mistress Nan," he said, inclining his head. "You look . . . radiant."

"Master Ned." A faint smile lifted her lips and her eyes were so merry that he suspected she'd watched his arrival through the window and arranged herself in that sunbeam on purpose to disconcert him.

She seemed more self-assured than when he'd last seen her, although she'd never lacked for confidence in herself. Her clothing was expensive, but not ostentatious. Only one gemstone glinted on her fingers, but it was a very fine ruby. He wondered who had given it to her.

"I have letters for you from Calais." He handed them over and watched her set them aside, along with her needlework.

"Have you already delivered messages to Cat?"

"Not yet. Shall I give her your regards?"

Nan's eyes abruptly narrowed. "She is not for you, Ned Corbett. Leave her alone."

"Jealous, Nan?" He took a step closer, trying to read her expression without success. "Cat has nothing to fear from me. You quite ruined me for lesser women, Nan. I tried. Believe me, I tried! But after being with you, I could not bring myself to court your sister." Resentment crept into his tone. "She is an admirable woman, I am sure, but I could not stop comparing her to you. She lacks your spirit, your vitality, your allure."

"What nonsense you talk!" But she looked pleased. She gestured toward a second chair. "Make yourself comfortable while I read these and decide if I must answer them today."

She'd want him to write for her, he supposed. Instead of sitting, he circled the room, taking a closer look at his surroundings, seeing chairs where stools and benches were more usual. Turkey carpets had been placed on the tops of tables, but also on the floor, a great extravagance. And an exquisite piece of arras work depicting the fall of Troy hung on one wall.

Sounds from the street drifted in—the cries of hawkers, the squeak of cartwheels, and the clatter of hooves—but the house itself was silent. "Where are your chaperones?" he asked abruptly. Aside from the servant who'd admitted him, there seemed to be no one else in residence.

"I do not have any. That is one of the reasons I enjoy living here."

"Not even the faithful Constance?"

Nan looked up from the letter she was reading. "Constance is somewhere about. I do not require someone in constant attendance upon me."

Ned examined an ornate clock given pride of place on a sideboard. "Whatever Master Mewtas does for the king, it pays well," he murmured.

Nan gave him a sharp look. "What do you mean by that?"

He shrugged and continued his perambulation, stopping to study a portrait hung atop a second, smaller tapestry. Master Holbein's work, he thought. "You know already," he said absently, admiring the realistic look of the sitter.

"If you mean that absurd story Mother told me, about Peter Mewtas being sent to assassinate Cardinal Pole—"

"Oh, it's quite true." Ned had heard the tale firsthand at the Rose.

"Even if it is, the plot failed. Cardinal Pole is still alive and very much a thorn in King Henry's side. You must not paint my friend's husband as a hired killer, Ned. He is a gentle, considerate man, and he is high in the king's favor."

"And that, as we both know, is all that matters." A trace of bitterness crept into his voice.

Nan caught his arm as he passed her chair. "Dear Ned. I am sorrier than you know that we have no future together, but it is far too late for me to change my course."

"Is it?" He was not entirely sure what she meant, but the reminder of what they'd once shared spurred him to action. He hauled her up out of the chair and into his arms and kissed her before she could protest.

At the first touch of his lips to hers, he realized he'd been deceiving himself to think he'd accepted her rejection and moved on. He should have known he still wanted Nan and no other. Why else would he have failed to pursue Nan's sisters?

As for Nan, she responded with all the fervor Ned remembered. But the first rush of passion did not last. He felt her lips compress under his mouth, firming into a thin, hard line. She squirmed, attempting to break his hold, and pushed at his chest with both hands. When he did not release her at once, she stomped on his foot.

As abruptly as he'd embraced her, Ned let her go. Nan stumbled backward a few steps, her French hood askew and the fine linen partlet at her throat rucked up where his fingers had been at it. Her hands shook as she hastily put herself to rights.

"We must never do that again," she whispered.

"Why not? You enjoyed it . . . until you remembered that I have neither wealth nor title." He reached for her.

She shied away. "Ned, stop. Please."

More than the words, the catch in her voice and the shimmer of incipient tears in her eyes kept him silent. He turned away from her, striding to the window to put some distance between them. His fist struck the casement hard enough to bruise his knuckles and he welcomed the pain. Anything to distract him from the fact that he'd just made a fool of himself.

Nothing had changed. She was still set on her path. His lips twisted into a wry smile. He'd probably not be so attracted to her if she'd been any different. He turned to find her watching him with wary eyes.

"There's something you should know, Ned."

"Go on."

"The king . . . the king has singled me out. Even if I wished to . . . be with you again, I would not dare show you any special favor. For your own safety. The king does not like to share."

"The king? King Henry?" He had not expected this.

Her lips twitched. "Have we some other king I do not know about? Yes, King Henry. He has had his eye on me since I first came to court." Defiant now, she tossed her head and stood with her arms folded across her chest, daring him to criticize.

"So, you are his mistress."

"Strangely, I am not. Not yet." She dropped her arms and her gaze, avoiding meeting his eyes.

"But you're willing." It was not a question. One did not refuse the king.

Nan drew in a deep breath. "There is much to be gained from being in the king's favor. He gave me this." She showed him the ruby and enamel ring she wore. "And this." From a velvet purse suspended from her belt, she withdrew a miniature portrait of the king. "And he presented me with a palfrey and a saddle because I had no horse of my own to ride with him to hunt."

"And where is the king now?" Ned demanded. "Why are you not at his side?" He knew part of the answer already. King Henry was off on his annual summer progress.

"I have encouraged His Grace to court me," Nan said, "but not to claim me." Again, she sighed.

"It is not like you to be indecisive." Ned was beginning to lose patience with her. Did she want to bed the king or not? And if she was not as ambitious as he'd supposed, then what did she want?

"You *want* me to become his mistress?" She sounded incredulous.

Ned forced himself to think logically. He had always been good at separating self-interest from sentiment. Ordinarily, Nan was, too. And although he had not realized it at the time, when they'd been together he'd treated her as a friend as well as a lover. It was the friend she needed now. It could not be easy waiting upon the whim of the most powerful—and most dangerous—man in England.

"I am willing to let His Grace have you for a little while." He grinned at her. "When he tires of you, I'll still be here."

He could tell she thought he was jesting. His declaration coaxed a smile from her. Let her believe what she would, Ned decided.

"Know I wish you well," he said, "whatever you do. And now, if you wish to dictate a letter to Calais, my pen is yours to command."

NAN DID NOT pretend to understand why Ned Corbett suddenly wanted to be her friend, but she was happy to make a place for him in her life. Although she doubted that she would ever trust him enough to tell him about his son, she could talk to him about everything else, from the foibles of her family in Calais to her desperate need to regain her place at the royal court.

He stopped in again the next time he was in London, the only bright spot in the long weeks while the king was on progress. He made no more attempts to kiss her. They simply talked. He told her of the rivalries and feuds that were a daily part of life in the lord deputy's household—particularly the animosity between Sir Gregory Botolph and the other chaplains—and somehow made it all seem lighthearted and amusing.

At last, in early August, Nan, together with Jane Mewtas and a great number of other ladies and gentlewomen, was invited to travel to Portsmouth to view the royal fleet. The expedition required four days of travel—London to Guildford, Guildford to Alton, Alton to Winchester, Winchester to Portsmouth. Nan spent the entire time in a state of nervous anticipation. She was sure of her goal now. She could not tolerate being away from court, ignored and forgotten. Just as soon as she could manage it, she meant to become King Henry's mistress.

But the king did not join his guests on their tour of several great warships. He was not even in Portsmouth. He had arranged the expedition as a "treat" for them.

"I do not understand why men are so fascinated by ships," Nan grumbled. "There are many things I would find far more interesting than boarding one great, lumbering vessel after another."

They stood at the rail of the *Harry Grace à Dieu*, the largest of the king's warships. At least the view was impressive. Across the Solent, the Isle of Wight rose up out of the water. Nan could make out fortifications, but most of the place appeared to be forested. She wondered what it would be like to live on an island that small.

A stiff breeze carried the scent of lavender along with the smells of the sea and ships, warning Nan of the approach of King Henry's former mistress. Margaret Skipwith, Lady Talboys, was wont to drench herself in that perfume, one Nan had once been fond of herself. Jane glanced over her shoulder, saw Margaret, and quickly ceded her place at the rail.

"I suppose you think it a great honor," Margaret said in a low voice that reached no farther than Nan's ear.

Nan kept her gaze on the distant shoreline. "It was kind of His Grace to arrange this outing for us." Out of the corner of her eye, she saw fury race across Margaret's face as Nan deliberately misinterpreted her

comment. Just in case the other woman contemplated pushing her over-
board, Nan tightened her grip on the rail.

"You will not suit him at all. He does not like women who are too
tall." Margaret was several inches shorter than Nan.

"From what I have observed, he likes women of all sizes and shapes."

"He prefers golden hair." What showed of Margaret's hair at the
front of her French hood was fair, but more like ripened wheat than
gold. Her eyes were narrow slits, green in color and green with envy,
too.

Nan smiled serenely. "I can always achieve that color with the help of
yellow powder, but I believe he likes me just the way I am."

Margaret's fingers dug into Nan's forearm with painful force. Nan
tried to shake her off, but her grip was too strong. "You were well compensated, *Lady Talboys*," Nan said through gritted teeth. "It is my turn
now."

"Compensated? I was married off to a boy of sixteen." Margaret's disgust was plain in her voice and in her face, only inches from Nan's.

A boy who then took immediate control of his inheritance, Nan
thought, five years earlier than he would otherwise have been able to. She
had heard all the details from Anne Herbert and had no sympathy for
Margaret. She'd gotten a wealthy, titled husband and the age difference
was trifling. Margaret was only a few years older than her spouse. "Most
women would be well pleased with such an arrangement," she said. "I
would be myself."

"Then you are a fool!" Margaret released her and was about to stalk
off in high dudgeon when Nan turned the tables and caught her arm. "Is
the king such a wonderful lover that you cannot bear to lose him?"

Margaret's eyes widened at the blunt question. A series of emotions
played across her face—anger, disdain, and, finally, what looked like fear.
Belatedly, she seemed to realize that confronting Nan in a public place
had been unwise. They were standing apart from the others, but a stray
breeze could easily carry their words, and no one watching was in any
doubt as to the subject of their quarrel.

"He does not need you," Margaret said in a harsh whisper. "He has me." And with that, she walked rapidly away.

Nan stared after her, absently rubbing her arm. *Was* Henry Tudor that good in bed? Or was it only her influence with him that Margaret sought to keep? Nan's hands clenched into fists as another possibility struck her. She stared, unseeing, at the colorful bevy of gentlewomen on the deck of the ship. Could it be that Margaret Talboys had fallen in love with the king? Poor creature. If that were so, now that His Grace had found her a husband, she had no chance at all of keeping him to herself.

"Nan Bassett!" Joan Denny, wife of the chief gentleman of the king's privy chamber, trotted toward her. "There you are, Nan. Come along. We are to be taken ashore now."

Nan complied, dismissing Margaret Skipwith from her thoughts. Joan's conversation ran in domestic channels. She chattered for the most part about her newly acquired house in Westminster. "It is almost like living in the country," she boasted. "The air is fresh and there is room to take long walks. And yet we are hard by Whitehall, convenient to wait upon the king."

Nan had no desire to rusticate and little interest in gardens, but she nodded politely at all the right moments. Joan's husband, Anthony Denny, owned a goodly number of properties now, a direct result of the dissolution of the monasteries.

"Still, I am fond of our London house," Joan said. "Aldgate is a prosperous part of the city and we have interesting neighbors. One of them is Hans Holbein, the portrait painter. Did you know he has been sent to Cleves? The king will not make the final decision to marry the Lady Anna until he has seen for himself what she looks like. Master Holbein is expected back at the end of the month with her likeness."

It had been Master Holbein's portrait of Christina of Milan that had so delighted the king after an earlier mission to paint prospective brides, and Nan had a sample of his work herself, the miniature the king had given her.

"Have you ever had your portrait painted?" Joan asked.

Nan shook her head.

"You should consider it. A likeness in small makes an excellent gift. It keeps the giver always in the recipient's thoughts."

EARLY THE NEXT morning, in company with Jane Mewtas, Nan set off on the return journey to London. At Guildford, a letter from Lady Lisle caught up with them.

"She thinks I am at court," Nan said when she had read the missive. "She wants me to ask the king to pardon some man from the West Country, although she does not say what crime he committed or why he has prevailed upon her to intervene." She barely managed to keep the irritation out of her voice. She'd never heard of the fellow and had no idea whether or not he deserved a pardon.

"Well, you are not at court, and there's the end of it," Jane said. "Write to your mother and tell her that you cannot help."

"She will be furious with me."

"She is in Calais and you are here. You will not be able to hear her curses."

"True enough, but I cannot simply refuse. I must give her some reason or she will hound me about it for weeks." Lady Lisle was an indefatigable letter writer.

"Tell her you do not expect to see the king again until His Grace comes to Grafton or to Ampthill and that you are in doubt whether you will see him then."

Nan cocked a brow at the other woman. "*Am* I in doubt? I thought we were going to Grafton." The king's summer progress would stop there and, although that meant accommodations in the neighborhood would be hard to come by, Peter Mewtas had friends who lived nearby.

"I may decide not to make the journey, and you cannot go without me. I am tired of all this rushing about. And I think I may be breeding."

"But—"

"If you are looking for excuses to give to your mother, Nan, then that one will do nicely."

"You truly mean to stay in London?" Nan was taken aback by the idea. Even when the king was at Whitehall, visiting the court would be difficult without a respectable gentlewoman for company. Nan would be obliged to wait for the king to come to her. In the meantime, as a married noblewoman, Lady Talboys could visit the court and keep her own rooms there, too.

The prospect was intolerable. She had come so far. She would not abandon hope now. Nan set her mind to finding a way around this newest obstacle to her ambition.

Mistress Mewtas and I are now at Guildford, going to London; and I
think we shall not see the King again till his Grace come to Grafton and
to Ampthill; and that I am in doubt whether I shall see his Grace then
or not, for Mistress Mewtas is in a doubt whether she go or not. Your
ladyship knows well, being with her, except she go I cannot go; for I have
nor horse nor man except the nag that the King's Grace gave me for
myself and a saddle withal.

—Anne Bassett to her mother, 8 August 1539

I am now with my Cousin Denny, at the King's Grace's commandment:
for whereas Mistress Mewtas doth lie in London there are no walks, but
a little garden, wherefore it was the King's Grace's pleasure that I should
be with my Cousin Denny; for where as she lieth there are fair walks and
good open air.

—Anne Bassett to her mother, 5 October 1539

9

It was the first of October before Nan was summoned back to
court, and the invitation did not come from the king. Her stepfather, Lord Lisle, was at Whitehall.

Lisle greeted Nan warmly when she and Constance arrived at the
lodgings assigned to him. He had arranged for her to have her own small
chamber in the suite of rooms.

"You see how well I am regarded." With a sweep of his hand, Lisle
indicated the luxurious surroundings. A series of tapestries graced the
walls, depicting scenes of sylvan glades and dancing nymphs. Both the
ceiling and the floor had been plastered, the former shaped into geomet-
ric patterns and flowers and the latter painted to resemble marble. The

furniture was heavy and elaborately carved. The hangings around the bed and at the windows were of expensive fabrics, embroidered with vines and fruits.

"Very grand," Nan agreed, crossing a section of rush matting put down to protect the plaster. She gave him a peck on one leathery cheek. "You look well, sir."

He preened a bit. "Not too bad for an old man, eh?" Although he was just entering his seventy-eighth year, Lisle had kept himself in excellent physical shape. If not for the deep lines around his mouth and eyes, he could have passed for sixty. "I owe it all to your mother," he said. "Honor keeps me young."

Honor kept him hopping, Nan thought, although the welcoming smile on her face never wavered. She wondered what had brought her stepfather to England.

"I have had no news from Calais in over a week," Lisle lamented. "The weather has been so bad that no one has been able to cross the Narrow Seas."

"Then you will receive all her letters at once." Nan took a sip of the French wine with which her stepfather was always well supplied and waited for his next conversational gambit. She doubted he'd invited her to stay with him solely for the pleasure of her company.

"The king entertained me most lovingly at Windsor and Hampton Court and now here," Lisle said. "And he has granted me the commission to suppress the White Friars of Calais."

Nan was not sure what to say to that. There was considerable profit to be made from such an undertaking, but it must go against the grain for Lord Lisle to shut down a religious house. Nan's mother would have even more qualms, being the most devout member of the family and the most reluctant to abandon the old ways.

"I was less successful in another endeavor." Lisle sent her a slightly embarrassed look.

"Indeed?" Had he tried to make a match for her with some elderly knight? Or negotiate her return to the Earl of Sussex's household? Or find a place for her in that of some other nobleman? She imagined the king would have put a stop to any of those plans. If His Grace had not forgotten her entirely.

"I wished to become governor of the Lady Elizabeth's household."

Caught off guard, Nan had difficulty hiding her astonishment. "Do you mean to say that you would leave your post in Calais to take charge of the king's bastard daughter?"

He winced at her sharp tone. "She was not always a bastard and I suspect she will not remain one forever. You may not know this, but we tried last year to place your sister Mary in her service. In any case, I would welcome the chance to leave Calais." He lowered himself into a chair near the bench where Nan sat and reached over to pat her knee. "You have not been back for more than two years. You do not know what it is like there now."

Nan stared at his hand. There were liver spots on the wrinkled skin and his bones had a brittle look, reminding her again of just how old he was.

"I have been most concerned, since Easter and before," Lisle continued, "about the growing number of soldiers and townsmen in Calais who maintain erroneous opinions in matters of religion."

"It is scarcely your fault if there are heretics about."

"Ever since King Henry broke with Rome, there has been considerable confusion among people in all walks of life about how to celebrate Mass, and whether or not one should pray to Our Lady, and dozens of other matters to do with religion. I have no authority to enforce obedience to the tenets of the Church of England, nor even proper guidelines as to what is and is not acceptable. I fear that if I cannot stamp out heresy, I will be accused of abetting it."

Nan put her hand over his and gave it a comforting squeeze. "No one would ever think such a thing of you, sir. You are too well known for your devotion to king and country."

"Lord Cromwell has been most critical of my stewardship." He sounded more sad than angry.

Nan said nothing. Cromwell had made no secret of his opinion. He thought her stepfather was incompetent.

"I had hoped to speak privily with the king about my concerns, but Cromwell was always at His Grace's side. And now that he has finally left court for his own house in London, the king is suffering from a cold. He will see no one." He hesitated. "I have heard that you have the king's . . . favor. That he gave you a horse."

"A nag," Nan said dismissively. She wondered how much Ned Corbett had told him, then chided herself for her lack of trust.

Ned would never betray her. In the course of the last few months, he had paid several visits to Tower Street. He'd gone out of his way to lift her spirits with amusing stories about his friends in Calais—not the most admirable of men, but diverting. He'd bolstered her self-confidence with his compliments to her beauty, her gracefulness, and her skill on the lute and with a needle. To their mutual surprise, they rubbed along very well together, so long as they did not speak of love, marriage, or coupling.

"Well, do what you can," Lisle said. "That is all anyone can ask of you."

Nan considered his request in light of her own situation. She'd had no personal message from His Grace in all the weeks since her return from Portsmouth. It was past time to take some action. But if His Grace was ill, how—?

"Ah!" The solution was so obvious that she laughed aloud. She turned to her stepfather, who was staring at her in bewilderment. "Have you any of Mother's conserves with you?"

Lisle blinked at the unexpected question, then nodded. "A codiniac."

"Quince marmalade? Excellent. We will send it to Anthony Denny to give to His Grace. I will compose a note to go with it."

THREE DAYS PASSED without any response from the king. While her stepfather waited on Lord Cromwell, who handled all the paperwork for commissions to suppress religious houses, Nan threw herself into the activities of the court. There was no point in sulking, and at Whitehall, even when the king was indisposed, there were any number of enjoyable pursuits available.

On the third night there was dancing. Nan had no shortage of partners. Sir Edmund Knyvett, a dark-haired, blue-eyed man in his prime, was particularly attentive. A pity he was married. There was also Master Walter Hungerford. He had no wife, and was the heir to a barony, but he was nearly four years younger than she was, a tall, thin, gangly lad of fourteen.

In spite of what she'd told Margaret Skipwith, she had a hard time imagining herself marrying a gawky, pimple-faced boy. He was a good dancer, though, and as they executed the movements of a pavane, she tried her hand at coaxing information out of him about his master, Lord Cromwell. She hoped to learn something that would help her stepfather.

"He does not like his men to speak of his business, mistress." Color crept up the boy's neck and into his face. A lock of dark, curly hair slipped out from under his bonnet to hang over his forehead. She had to fight the urge to tuck it back into place. She might not be interested in being his wife, but she certainly was not desirous of acting like his mother!

"Have you heard him speak of my stepfather, Lord Lisle?" They moved apart with the steps of the dance and came together again a moment later.

"He is no friend to Lord Lisle," Hungerford admitted.

"I know that much." Impatient, Nan threw more questions at him, trying to persuade him to say more. She only succeeded in making him more nervous. She read growing panic in his eyes as the dance progressed, and something else that she could not identify.

When the music stopped, he bowed, then stood gaping at her, mouth moving but no words coming out.

"Well? Speak your mind, sir, or begone."

"Keep your opinions close, mistress. That is all I can say. Remember that it was Lord Cromwell who convinced the king to burn heretics—those who do not agree with His Grace on matters of religion. Anyone can be accused of holding the wrong view, especially when the right one keeps changing."

Nan shivered even though the room was well warmed by a fire in the hearth. Young Hungerford, as if regretting he'd said even that much, rushed away. Nan stared after him. His words of warning suggested a mature understanding of the dangers of life at court. There was more to the youth than she'd suspected. Intrigued, she was about to go after him when Anthony Denny appeared at her elbow.

"I have been sent to fetch you to the king," Denny said.

Nan's breath caught in her throat. At last!

As she followed Denny from the hall, they passed Sir Edmund Knyvett. He winked at her in a manner that was frankly salacious. Truly, there were no secrets at court!

Denny led her through a series of small rooms into what were known as the king's secret lodgings, tucked away behind his privy chamber. Nan's heart pounded harder when he opened a door and stepped back to let her pass through, but she found herself in a library, not a bedchamber. The king, fully dressed, awaited her with a book in his hands.

Nan hastily dropped into a curtsy, as much to hide her reaction as because protocol demanded it. Her first good look at King Henry in many months shocked her. His appearance was greatly altered, and none of the changes could be attributed to his recent illness. He had gained a great deal of weight since Queen Jane's death, but that was not the worst of it. His hair was now liberally streaked with gray and was thinning in several places. He looked *old*.

"Your Grace," Nan murmured, hoping none of her dismay leaked into her voice.

"Rise, Nan, and give me your opinion of this." He thrust a book of hours into her hands.

Nan caught her breath in pure pleasure as she turned the pages. It was beautifully illuminated in brilliant colors. "What a lovely thing."

The king's tone was repressive. "It represents all I would overturn."

Nan felt herself blanch. Was this some sort of test of her loyalty?

The purpose of a book of hours was to provide readings for each of the canonical hours. It contained, in particular, prayers to the Virgin Mary, seeking her intercession. Was that heresy now?

In response to Nan's stricken expression, His Grace managed a grim smile. It did nothing to reassure her. "You see my dilemma."

"Yes, Your Grace." She swallowed hard, remembering what Sir Gregory Botolph had said about the actions of the king's men when they closed down a monastery or a cathedral. They removed the precious gems from chalices and reliquaries, then melted them down for the gold. Heretical books were thrown into bonfires. She did not even want to think about what might be done with saints' bones and other relics. "Will you destroy it, Your Grace?"

"No." He took the book back from her and closed it with an audible thump before placing it in a nearby chest. "A few such things are to be spared. Why even Lord Cromwell, who is most strict in these matters, has added a number of books from the libraries of dissolved monasteries to his own collection. With my permission," he added, lest she think otherwise.

"That is most generous of you, Your Grace."

He regarded her intently, then caught her hand and tugged. A moment later he was seated in a generously proportioned chair, Nan was in his lap, and the king was kissing her. His fingers found her breast and squeezed.

"Your Grace!" she gasped.

"Hush, Nan." He kissed her into silence. She began to tremble as he fondled her, running one hand up under her skirts.

Nan moaned softly. She'd intended the sound to be encouraging, but it came out laced with pain. Instantly, he released her.

"Once upon a time, you liked my kisses." Accusation tinged his words and temper was brewing in his stormy expression.

For a moment Nan's wits deserted her. Tears sprang into her eyes.

"Nan?" Beneath King Henry's irritation, there was concern.

"I beg your pardon, Your Grace. It is just that . . . I fear . . . I—"

Inspiration struck. "It is the megrim, Your Majesty. I suffer terribly from such headaches and I have sensed one coming on all day."

Instantly, he was solicitous. "My poor Nan. I, too, suffer from megrims, an affliction I have endured ever since a fall I took during a tournament three years ago."

Nan's mind raced. The king hated being around sick people. He was supposed to send her away, not commiserate with her. And yet, she did not want him to lose interest in her. She had not intended to plead a headache. She'd meant to give herself to him, to become his mistress. If only he were not so old and so fat!

Awkward, nerve-racking seconds passed. If the king suffered from megrims himself, would he see through her ruse? Should he realize she was only pretending to be incapacitated by a severe headache, he would be furious with her. He might even banish her from court.

At last he spoke: "You must lie abed with the hangings pulled tightly closed against the light. That will ease the pain, even if it will not vanquish it."

Nan forced a weak smile. She began to think rationally once more. "Darkness does help, Your Grace. But I have found that once the throbbing begins to die away, a walk alone in the open air is effective to complete the cure."

He shifted her on his lap so that her head rested on his broad shoulder. The gold braid and the gemstones studding the brocade bit into her cheek. She ignored them. His gesture was well meant. The king—the king of England!—was concerned about her health.

"I suppose that could have a positive effect," he mused. "I would not know. I am almost never alone."

"Mistress Mewtas has but a small garden," Nan ventured. "As I lodge with her, I have few opportunities to walk far, or to find fresh air."

Apparently lost in thought, King Henry said nothing. Nan shifted in his lap, trying to make herself more comfortable. Beneath her rump she felt the shape of his codpiece, and abruptly stilled. It was heavily padded and elaborately decorated, as was the fashion. The size of the bulge had decreased once he'd stopped fondling her. The last thing she wanted was to induce it to grow larger again.

Nan frowned. She had little basis for comparison, having taken only one lover, but it seemed to her that the king was not nearly so well endowed in that area as Ned Corbett. Now that she considered the matter, she was certain her kisses should have provoked a more pronounced effect.

"I should send you to your bed," the king murmured. "You need to rest and recover your health."

"Your Grace is most kind and understanding."

"I want you well."

Reminding herself of her goal, Nan broached a possibility she had been considering of late. "My cousin Denny has a fine house in Westminster. Near at hand are open meadows that stretch clear down to the Thames. Such a place would be most healthful to live in."

Whitehall Palace was also near at hand.

The king rose and set her on her feet without taking the hint. "There is something I would show you before you go, if you are not too ill to stay a few minutes longer."

She assured him she could manage and he led her to an easel covered with a velvet cloth. He lifted it to reveal a portrait of a woman.

Nan gasped. "She is beautiful."

"Anna of Cleves. Master Holbein returned with this likeness at the end of August. I have no doubt that she will be even more attractive in person."

"The new queen." It was not a question.

"The treaty is already drawn up."

Staring at the portrait, Nan wondered that His Grace still had any interest in mistresses. She fled back to Lord Lisle's lodgings convinced that her chance had passed her by. She was both disappointed and relieved.

The next day, Nan received an invitation to move into Anthony Denny's house in Westminster. The offer confused her, but she lost no time in accepting. After that, she was often at court. She danced with the king and flirted with him. If he had pressed her to come to his bed, she would have yielded. He did not. To her delight, Nan enjoyed all the benefits of His Grace's favor with none of the drawbacks.

Meanwhile, plans commenced to welcome Anna of Cleves to England. The queen's apartments were repaired and redecorated at all the royal residences. The marriage was to take place at Greenwich at the start of Yuletide, followed by twelve days of revelry before Anna made her state entry into London. Her coronation would take place on Candlemas Day, the second of February, in Westminster Abbey.

"The Earl of Rutland will be lord chamberlain of Queen Anna's household," the king told Nan. His leg, propped up on a stool, had been bothering him and he'd sent for Nan to distract him from the pain. "Sir Edward Baynton will be vice chamberlain. And you will be one of the maids of honor, as I promised long ago."

"I look forward to my new duties," Nan replied, and began to strum the lute she'd brought with her to the king's privy chamber.

As she played, seated on a cushion at King Henry's feet, she stole glances at the bulky wrapping of linen bandages beneath His Grace's hose. He suffered from gout, but the padding hid an ulcer that would not heal. She tried not to wrinkle her nose in distaste when she caught a whiff of a strong, unpleasant stench.

"Have you decided who the other maids of honor will be?" Nan asked when she finished the first song. She had not forgotten that her mother expected her to find a place at court for at least one of her sisters. Cat was still with Lady Rutland. Mary and Philippa remained in Calais.

"I have received requests from many quarters," King Henry said.

Some of those originally named to serve Queen Jane's successor had married since her death. Others, like Jane Arundell, had decided they preferred to remain where they were.

"It is not easy to be king, Nan." His Grace winced as he shifted in his oversize chair. "Everyone expects favors of me."

"And yet, I suspect, Your Grace has already decided." She smiled up at him. "Will you not tell me who my companions will be?"

"The first is Catherine Carey, Lady Stafford's daughter."

Nan hoped she hid her surprise. Lady Stafford was Mary Boleyn. Rumor had it that Catherine Carey's father was King Henry himself. Certainly Mary Boleyn had been his mistress before His Grace fell in love with Mary's sister, Anne.

"Then there is Lucy Somerset," His Grace said. "She is the Earl of Worcester's sister. And you already know Mary Norris, for she was one of Queen Jane's maids, as you were. There is also a Howard girl, one of the Duke of Norfolk's many nieces."

"And the sixth name?" She'd heard several possibilities mentioned, including Lord Bray's sister and Lord Cobham's daughter.

"A young woman who, like yourself, is kin to the Countess of Sussex. Her name is Katherine—"

Nan felt an explosion of joy, certain he'd chosen her sister to please her. And that, in turn, would please their mother.

"—Stradling."

Stunned, Nan stared at him. Katherine *Stradling*? Cousin *Kate*?

Nan had not given Kate Stradling a single thought since leaving Cousin Mary's service. Kate's selection as a maid of honor made no sense. She was not the sister or daughter or niece or stepdaughter of anyone important.

The only explanation was that the Earl and Countess of Sussex had sponsored her. What dark secret, Nan wondered, did Kate know about one of them? Aloud she said only, "How delightful," and began to strum another tune.

Her thoughts raced in time to the music. Cousin Kate would have returned to court in any case when the new queen came, since Cousin Mary was one of the six "great ladies of the household" and Kate was one of Mary's waiting gentlewomen. But in that post she'd have had only occasional contact with Nan.

That Kate was to be a maid of honor changed everything. Nan would see her every day. She might even have to share a bed with her again. That was far too close for comfort, but there was not a thing Nan could do about it.

She told herself she could deal with Kate. If her cousin asked for gifts to keep silent about Nan's liaison with Ned and the resulting child, then Nan would give her whatever she asked for. She'd have no choice.

As always, the reminder that she had a son made Nan sad. She had managed to pay a few visits to the silversmith's shop while living in London, but none since she'd moved in with Anthony and Joan Denny in Westminster. She doubted she'd be able to see him at all when she was living at court as a maid of honor.

Nan reined in her regrets, resolving that she would not dwell on the things she could not change. She set aside her lute. She was all but alone with the king. She had his undivided attention and her playing seemed to have soothed him. She would never have a better opportunity.

"My mother writes that all is in readiness to receive Queen Anna at Calais."

King Henry shifted in his chair. "Lady Lisle's conserves are the best I have ever tasted. I pray you bid her send me more of the codiniac and some of the conserve of damsons, too."

"She will be pleased to do so, Your Grace." Conserves were far easier to come by than quails. "I wonder, Your Grace, if there might be a post in the new queen's household for my sister, perhaps as a chamberer, or—"

She broke off when the king suddenly turned a ghastly shade of white and clutched at his leg.

"Your Grace?" She scrambled to her feet, reaching out, then pulling back as Tom Culpepper, one of the gentlemen of the bedchamber, rushed to the king's aid.

"Best leave me now, Nan." King Henry spoke through clenched teeth. Beads of sweat popped out on his brow. "When these cramps start, they can continue for hours."

Nan curtsyed and hastily backed out of the room, grateful she was not the one who had to tend that gross and misshapen ulcerated leg.

ON THURSDAY, THE eleventh day of December, Lord Lisle led the Calais Spears and the members of his own retinue to the boundary of the

Pale of Calais. Queen Anna was on her way from Gravelines, just across the border in Flanders, to Calais. She was said to be traveling with a train of 263 attendants and 228 horses, which no doubt accounted for the extreme slowness of her progress from Cleves.

The Spears were all in velvet coats with gold chains. Members of Lord Lisle's household wore livery of red and blue. As Ned trudged along, he tugged on the hem of his coat. It had been made in haste and did not quite fit. He did not know why he cared. He'd be covered with dust before they reached the meeting place. What bothered him more was that he did not have a horse to ride. After all, he *was* a gentleman.

Clement Philpott marched next to him, a martyred expression on his long, thin face. But neither sore feet nor an ill-fitting coat were responsible for Philpott's grim demeanor. Sir Gregory Botolph, out of pure deviltry, had convinced him that Lord Lisle planned to arrange a marriage for him with a gentlewoman of Cleves. Philpott, who had never given up "the true religion," was appalled by the thought of being joined for life with a Lutheran, even if she was a member of the new queen's retinue.

At last they caught sight of Queen Anna's device, two white swans. A short time later, Ned got his first good look at Anna of Cleves. She was not at all what he'd expected. She was reputed to be twenty-four years old, but she looked older. Beneath a pearl-embroidered caul and bonnet, her cream-colored skin was pitted with smallpox scars.

Those were only the first marks against her. By court standards, her complexion was nowhere near pale enough. To make matters worse, she had a high forehead, heavy-lidded eyes that were too far apart for true beauty, an extremely long and slightly bulbous nose, and a pointed chin. That she did not smile made Ned wonder about the condition of her teeth.

"I thought she was supposed to be a great beauty," he whispered to Philpott. "If that is what the king is expecting, he's in for a disappointment."

Philpott said nothing. He was staring in horror at Queen Anna's attendants. They all wore heavy, unflattering gowns cut in the Dutch fashion, apparel that would have made them look dowdy even if they'd been beautiful. They were not.

After a series of short speeches, Lord Lisle signaled for the start of the return journey to Calais. About a mile from town, they encountered the special delegation sent by the king to escort his bride across the Narrow Seas. There were nearly four hundred people in all. The noblemen were attired in cloth-of-gold and purple velvet. Gentlemen wore coats of satin damask and velvet and some two hundred yeomen were in the king's colors.

Following more speeches, the company marched into Calais, all except Ned and Philpott. They veered off just outside the walls and entered the Rose Tavern.

Ned spent the next few hours watching Philpott get prodigiously drunk and trying in vain to convince his friend that Botolph had only been jesting about a betrothal to one of the ugly Dutch maids.

THREE DAYS BEFORE Christmas, Nan was at Whitehall. She had expected to be at Greenwich, part of the household of the new queen of England. Anna of Cleves, however, was still in Calais, although small boats continued to make the crossing, bringing letters and a scattering of less-important passengers. The queen and her retinue and the English dignitaries sent to escort them were unable to embark for England until the weather cooperated.

John Husee had brought a letter from Nan's mother and stood ready to write down her reply. Nan still had not bothered to learn to write in English. The important things could not be put into letters anyway.

"I humbly thank your ladyship for the news of Her Grace," Nan dictated, "that she is so good and gentle to serve and please."

But Nan had already heard the rumors. Anna of Cleves was not quite as she had been represented. She continued for a few more sentences, allowed Husee to suggest a change of wording, and considered carefully what to say next. Lady Lisle, as always, had been generous with both advice and admonitions. She clearly suspected that Nan's association with the king had become more intimate. She did not approve, but neither was she above using her daughter's influence.

"Thank her for her good and motherly counsel," Nan instructed Husee, "concerning my continuance in the king's favor, but tell her that I must be careful not to offend His Grace."

Husee scribbled away. By the number of words he put down, she knew he was elaborating on what she'd told him to say.

"Inform her that King Henry enjoyed the conserves she sent him so much that he has commanded me to ask for more. She should send them as soon as may be."

The scratch of quill on paper sounded loud in the quiet room, a small antechamber near the dormitory Nan shared with the other maids of honor.

"That is all I have to say at this time."

Husee finished the letter and handed it over. Nan read what he had written, nodding her approval. Beneath the words "Your humble and obedient daughter," she signed her name with a flourish.

Duty done, she dismissed Husee and went in search of amusement. So far the traditional Christmas festivities had been subdued, but an air of anticipation pervaded the court. Every courtier in the land seemed to have crowded into lodgings in the vicinity, ready, willing, and eager to celebrate the arrival of the new queen.

In all the confusion, Nan had managed to slip away on two occasions to visit her son in London. He was growing fast, and she still felt regret that she'd had to give him away, but she took comfort in knowing that the Carvers, who indulged her as a well-meaning acquaintance, loved him. He was happy and safe.

NEW YEAR'S DAY was the traditional time to exchange gifts. After the king had received all his subjects' offerings, he summoned Nan to keep him company. He was in a jubilant mood. Anna of Cleves had landed safely at Deal. After a delay of fifteen days in Calais, waiting on the wind and tide, the crossing had taken seventeen harrowing hours. Her Grace had been met by the Duke and Duchess of Suffolk and escorted to Dover Castle for the night. In spite of bitter weather—high winds, hail, and sleet—she had set out for Canterbury the next day and would soon arrive at Greenwich.

But that was not the only reason for the king's delight. Master Hans Holbein had given him a New Year's gift that pleased him enormously. King Henry removed a portrait of two-year-old Prince Edward from its coffer of dark red velvet plated with copper and showed it to Nan.

"Is he not magnificent?" King Henry demanded.

"He is," Nan agreed, uncertain whether the king meant the boy in the portrait or the genius who had painted him. The word described both.

The child's likeness stared back at her with serious eyes. He was gorgeously, richly dressed. His face, shaded by a wide-brimmed hat with a feather, looked solemn, as befit a future king, but in one hand he held a golden rattle. Perhaps, Nan thought, she could suggest to Mistress Carver that they commission Master Holbein to paint a portrait of young Jamie. Then, in secret, she could obtain a copy for herself.

She was still considering the possibilities when a messenger arrived from Rochester. The queen had reached the last stop on her journey to Greenwich.

"You will see her soon, Your Grace," Nan said. "At the formal reception."

"I cannot wait that long," the king declared. "I will go to her this very day."

"The Lady Anna will be tired from her journey, Your Grace." Anthony Denny's brow was furrowed with a concern Nan shared. Surprising the bride was not a good idea, but neither was it wise to argue with the king. "By the time you reach Rochester, she may be abed."

"Then I will wake her!" King Henry laughed, his enthusiasm not a whit diminished by the prospect. "Indeed, I will show her what an English welcome is like. I will go to her in disguise."

Appalled, Nan started to protest, then caught herself. Neither she nor any of the king's gentlemen dared dissuade His Grace from one of his favorite jests. From the very beginning of his reign, King Henry had delighted in wearing masks and costumes. Although everyone recognized him immediately—his height alone gave him away—he continued to believe he kept his identity secret until he unmasked.

Members of the court went along with the ruse. When he revealed himself, they obligingly feigned surprise. No one wanted to disappoint the king—or worse, make him angry—by admitting that they knew who he was all along.

"We will all dress alike," King Henry instructed his minions. "Those multicolored cloaks and hoods from last night's masque will do. I will tell the queen that I am a messenger sent with gifts from the king."

While the five gentlemen he selected to accompany him rushed off to assume their costumes and arrange for horses, the king turned to Nan. "I need a suitable gift. Something to nourish love. Help me select some bauble Her Grace will like."

"Not jewelry, Sire," Nan replied. "At this time of year and after the wretched weather Her Grace has endured to come to you, make her a gift of furs."

"An excellent notion!" Without warning, King Henry picked Nan up and whirled her around, ending the embrace with an enthusiastic kiss as he set her on her feet again. "Ah, Nan," the king asked, "what would I do without you?"

I have left her as good a maid as I found her.

—Henry VIII to Thomas Cromwell, 7 January 1540 (the morning after his
wedding night)

is Majesty returned to Whitehall very late and very angry.
The maids of honor could hear him from their dormitory,
crashing about in the queen's apartments and bellowing in rage. They
could not make out his words, but no one was under any illusions about
His Grace's state of mind. Something had gone horribly wrong at Rochester. Left to her own devices, Nan would not have ventured out from behind
the bed curtains. But the king sent Anthony Denny to fetch her.

"The king wants you, Nan." Denny did not meet her eyes.

Nan took a step back. The cold tiles beneath her bare feet felt like ice,
but that was not what made her shiver. "It is the middle of the night,"
was the only faint protest she could think of to make.

"His Grace . . . needs you. Now." His words carried the force of a command.

Nan drew in a steadying breath, wrapped her black satin night-gown—a robe the king himself had given her—more tightly around her, and followed Denny to one of the small, private rooms, newly decorated, that were part of the queen's privy lodgings.

A fire burned in the hearth. Someone had brought bread and cheese and wine, which were laid out on a small table beside a chair. His Grace had not touched the food, but he had clearly been drinking, and heavily, too.

A few paces into the candlelit chamber, Nan tripped over one of the furs the king had taken as an offering to his bride. It was a richly garnished partlet of sable skins to be worn around the neck and throat. A furred muffler and cap also littered the floor, as if they'd been hurled down in a fit of temper. Nan wondered if His Grace blamed her for selecting the wrong gifts. Was that why he'd sent for her?

She dropped into a curtsy. Behind her, she heard the door close with an ominous thump. Anthony Denny had left her alone with the king.

Keeping her head bowed, Nan struggled to slow the frantic beating of her heart. Only by clasping her hands tightly together could she stop them from shaking.

"Rise, Nan, and come to me." King Henry's voice was hoarse with emotion. He stood at a window with his back to her. The renovated queen's lodgings boasted a spectacular river view, even at night. "I did all this for her. Beauty and comfort."

"Yes, Your Grace. These rooms are surpassing beautiful." Desperate to divert and calm the king, she said the first thing that popped into her head: "And the décor is practical, too."

"Practical?"

"Why, yes, Your Grace. While it is lovely to have plastered wooden floors, they are very cold at this time of year, but you have provided not just rushes, but rush matting woven in strips." And sables, she thought on a bubble of hysteria. One bare foot still crushed soft, silky fur.

The king considered the floor beneath their feet. Sections three strips wide, sewn together with twine, covered the entire room. "These are made in Southwark. I granted John Cradocke the monopoly for life. But I intended to put carpets on top of the mats for special occasions and there is nothing special—"

He broke off, shaking his head.

So much for trying to distract him. "Your Grace?"

He turned to her with almost pathetic eagerness, his eyes haunted. "She is not what I was promised, Nan. Nothing like. She is badly dressed and she speaks no English. Her face, far from being beautiful, is very brown in color and pitted with smallpox scars. And she has no charm of manner to make up for her want of beauty."

This was bad. Very bad. Nan did the only thing she could think of. She moved closer to the king, put one hand on his velvet sleeve, and leaned against him so that her head rested on his shoulder. His arm came around her shoulders, clamping down so tightly that she winced. He did not notice.

"I carried on. What else could I do? As I'd planned, I did not identify myself, but embraced Anna and told her I had been sent by the king. She did not know me, Nan. Not at all, even though she'd been sent my likeness."

Nan made a sympathetic murmur of sound. She dared not speak for fear she would say the wrong thing.

"She seemed bored!" The king's voice rose in outrage. "She had been watching a bullbaiting from her window when I arrived. She spoke a few words in Dutch or German. I know not which, but the sound of it grated on my ears. Then she returned to the window."

Greatly daring, Nan slid her arms around the king and gave him a tentative hug. He might be king, but he was a man, too, and he had received a terrible shock. The bride he had longed for was nothing like her portrait. And to add insult to injury, she had ignored him, thinking him a mere messenger. Had she treated him with proper deference, he might have looked more kindly on her lack of physical beauty. There was no hope of that now.

"I left the room to assume the purple velvet coat I had brought with me." He was still wearing it. "When I returned, everyone bowed, and Anna seemed to recognize me at last. She realized her error and curtsied, but we still could not converse." The king expelled a shuddering sigh. "I like her not, Nan. How can I marry her?"

Nan bit her lip. It was not her place to remind him that he'd already signed the marriage contract. All that remained to seal the treaty was consummation.

The king heaved another great sigh and kissed Nan's cheek. "I'd have done better to marry you, Nan."

Her heart stuttered. "That is kind of Your Grace to say, but I am only a humble gentlewoman. I am not worthy to be queen."

"You are a woman of great beauty and you always smell sweet." He turned her in his arms. "She has a very evil smell about her. How am I to take such a one into my bed?"

He did not expect an answer, and even if Nan had wished to give him one, she was prevented. His lips found hers. His hands slid to her waist and gripped her tightly, molding her body to his.

She did not resist. She did not dare. He was already in a volatile mood and the least resistance would turn him against her as easily as his reception by Anna of Cleves had changed his mind about her. Feigning eagerness, she kissed him back. She thought of Ned in the hope that it would make what was to come more bearable. If she pleased the king, if she eased his acceptance of a marriage he disliked, she would have influence. Prestige. Power. And a baron, at the least, to marry when the king tired of her.

His fingers were clumsy as he unlaced his codpiece. In his eagerness, he tumbled her to the floor. Nan found herself lying on a bed of rush matting and furs with the skirt of her black satin gown shoved up to her waist. The king engaged in a few minutes of frantic pawing and fumbling before he tried to push himself into her body. He'd barely entered her before he spilled his seed. A moment later, he collapsed on top of her and began to snore.

Stunned, nearly crushed by his great weight, Nan struggled to breathe. She pushed at the king's massive shoulders. He grunted and rolled aside. He did not wake as Nan freed herself and sat up.

In the candlelight, his features slack, King Henry was an appalling sight. He was nearly bald. Even his beard was sparse, and there was far more gray in it than red. His face was deeply lined, with pouches under his eyes and sagging jowls. The rest of him was even worse—a great belly straining against his doublet; a pathetic little male organ, spent, dangling inside the opened codpiece; and, not quite hidden by his hose, the bulge of bandages.

As quickly as she could, shaking all over, Nan stumbled to her feet and straightened her nightgown. She was careful not to wake the king. Her first thought was to run away, to escape, but she stopped herself in time. Her jumbled thoughts cleared. What was done was done. It was up to her to make the best of the situation.

She was the king's mistress now. He was already married by proxy, but he despised his new queen. He had said that he'd have done better to wed her. There was food for thought. After all, he'd rid himself of his first two wives by having those marriages annulled. Who was to say he might not annul a third?

As Nan stared down at the damp spot on the rush matting, an idea came to her. Perhaps nothing so grand would come of this night's debacle, but as long as there was a chance . . .

Moving quietly, her eyes on the king lest he should wake, Nan seized the cheese knife and cut through the twine that held the stained section to those on either side. Slicing through solid matting was more difficult, but she managed it. The knife was very sharp. Carrying the rectangular piece she'd detached to the hearth, she stirred the fire with a poker until the flames were sufficiently high, then tossed in the tightly woven rushes. The material caught instantly and was consumed in moments. Satisfied,

Nan returned to the king and lay down beside him to wait until he awoke.

A short time later, His Grace's puffy eyes opened. He stared at Nan in bleary confusion. She wondered if he recognized her. She'd seen him use spectacles in private. It was possible his eyesight was failing him along with the rest of his body.

"Nan," he said at last. She could see his struggle to recall where they were and what had happened between them. When he reached for her, she scooted away.

"Your Grace." She gave him what she hoped would be taken for a shy smile. "I fear I am too sore for more of your lovemaking." She ducked her head, averting her eyes. "It was my first time, as Your Grace knows."

She sensed rather than saw the slight start he gave upon noticing the missing piece of matting.

"I . . . I burned that section. It was stained with my blood. I . . . I did not think . . . I did not want everyone to . . ."

A low chuckle cut short her stumbling explanation. Nan did not dare glance up. She was afraid the king would see the elation in her eyes.

"My sweet Nan," he murmured, "a virgin no longer." He sounded well pleased with himself.

"It is not that I am not proud to be your mistress, Your Grace. Never that. You are a most wonderful lover. I never knew . . . I never—"

"Never mind, sweeting," the king said. "A foot carpet will cover the hole and it will be our secret."

Bracing his weight on the chair, he heaved himself to his feet. Nan pretended not to notice how difficult the process was for him. She waited to rise until he offered her a hand, then went up on tiptoe to kiss his cheek. Whether he really believed her or simply thought her too innocent to realize that he was not much of a lover, he was willing to accept that he had taken her virginity. He would demand no further proof of her innocence. He would never know that she had deceived him. And if he did decide to annul his marriage to Anna of Cleves—well, that remained to be seen.

*   *   *

QUEEN ANNA BROUGHT with her a hundred personal servants, including a physician, a secretary, and twelve maids of honor. When the king rode out of Whitehall toward Greenwich, this time taking with him most of the court—by some estimates as many as six thousand persons—he left Nan behind.

She had hoped to witness the new queen's official reception. She had expected to enter Anna's service before the wedding ceremony, which was now scheduled for the sixth of January. Instead, she and the other five English maids of honor selected by King Henry were told to wait at Whitehall until they were summoned.

"It is not fair," Mary Norris complained that evening. The tall, thin maid of honor had changed little since Queen Jane's death. At twenty-two, she was now the oldest of the group. She was also the plainest. "Everyone else is at Greenwich, set to enjoy banquets and masques and merry disports while here we sit, miserable and alone."

"We could disguise ourselves and go," Catherine Howard suggested. "Hire a wherry to take us to Greenwich. My silkwoman tells me that the London guilds have all procured barges and decorated them with flowers and banners. They mean to row down the river to the palace. There will be musicians onboard, and singers, too."

Catherine was eighteen, a tiny but voluptuous girl with dark blond hair, hazel green eyes, and an effervescent nature. Nan had not met her until Catherine came to court, but she had known Catherine's father, who had died the previous year. Lord Edmund had been comptroller of Calais until his death and a good friend to Nan's mother and stepfather. He'd even consulted Honor Lisle a time or two for her home remedies. Nan felt her lips curve into a smile. Once, when Lady Lisle had given Lord Edmund a mixture to cure the stone, the concoction had caused him to bepiss his bed. His wife, who had been sharing it at the time, had beaten him soundly.

"We were told to stay here," said dark-haired, brown-eyed Lucy

Somerset, the most demure of the group. "I do not think we should dis-obey the king."

Nan was not sure what to make of Lucy. She was barely sixteen, but she carried herself with a dignity that made her seem older. Perhaps it was because her father was the Earl of Worcester, which gave her prece-dence over the rest of them. She lived in the maids' dormitory and asked for no special favors, but her clothes were much finer than Nan's and her jewels more expensive.

"No one would know." Catherine's wide green eyes sparkled with mischief. "That is the point of being in disguise."

"But what if we are caught," Kate Stradling objected. "We might lose our positions."

Catherine's giggle was infectious. "We will not be. I am skilled at creeping in and out of places after dark. And good at smuggling people in, too."

"What people?" The third Catherine, Catherine Carey, a plump girl of seventeen, plainly failed to understand the implications.

"Men," Catherine Howard said. "What would be the point of secrecy if we only brought other women into the dormitory?"

"I would not boast of such things if I were you," Mary Norris said. "Not if you hope to catch a husband while you are at court."

Catherine Howard tossed her head, unconcerned. "Men like a girl who is eager to please."

"Not if she is eager to please *everyone*," Mary shot back.

Nan frowned. Until Catherine Howard came to court, she had lived in the household of the old Dowager Duchess of Norfolk, who had houses at Lambeth, across the river from Westminster, and at Horsham, in the country. Nan had pictured an environment that was dignified and cultured, where young women connected to the powerful Howard family received lessons in music and dancing and other social skills. It appeared that, in truth, those girls had learned very different skills.

"I mean to disguise myself and go," Catherine announced. "Who will come with me?"

"The last time someone visited Anna of Cleves in disguise, matters did not go well."

All eyes turned toward Nan.

"You left the dormitory that night." Cousin Kate made the statement sound like an accusation. "Were you with the king?"

Lucy's eyes grew round as saucers. Catherine Carey gasped. The look Catherine Howard sent Nan's way was one of grudging respect.

Nan sighed. "His Grace sent for me," she admitted. She had not expected to keep that much secret. "It was just after he returned from Rochester. He needed a sympathetic ear."

"What did he tell you about the new queen?" Kate asked. Rumors had already spread that Anna of Cleves was not quite what the king had expected.

Thinking quickly, Nan chose the lie most likely to divert attention away from the night she'd spent in the queen's apartments with the king. "His Grace told me that Queen Anna brought her own maids of honor with her and that she meant to keep them."

"Twelve of them," Catherine Howard muttered, as if the sheer number offended her.

"You know already that this was the reason we were left behind," Nan said, "and it follows that we must not go to Greenwich on our own, not even in disguise. We must wait patiently for the king to act."

Nan did not tell the other maids how the king really felt about his new bride, or of her suspicion that he would try his best to find a way out of the marriage. She doubted he would succeed. If he refused to go through with the wedding ceremony, there would be international repercussions. Likely he would honor the treaty he'd signed and Nan would have to make the best of it. She could be certain of one thing, however—His Grace fully intended to send the twelve ugly Dutch maids home and put six pretty English girls in their place.

ON THE SIXTH of January, King Henry married Anna of Cleves at Greenwich Palace. At the end of January, when the court returned to

Whitehall, the Dutch maids were still in place. Two weeks later, Nan was still waiting to be summoned to wait upon the queen. She and Cousin Kate had been moved into Cousin Mary's chambers, crowding Isabel and Jane. Mary, Lucy, and Catherine Carey were billeted with convenient relatives of their own at court. Only Catherine Howard had left Whitehall entirely, returning to the Dowager Duchess of Norfolk's mansion just across the river in Lambeth.

"What I mind most," Cousin Kate complained when she and Nan were alone in the Countess of Sussex's apartments save for Constance and Kate's maid, "aside from the loss of income, is the loss of all the privileges to which a maid of honor is entitled."

"You still have a servant and bed and board."

"I had my heart set on a spaniel." The sulky expression on Kate's face did nothing to improve her appearance as she primped before Mary's looking glass. It had been a New Year's gift from the earl to the countess and was garnished with two blue sapphires, two rubies, and twenty-six pearls, and had a small pointed diamond at the top.

"We will probably be paid our ten pounds for the year whether we serve or not." Nan hoped so. She had very little ready money.

"But we have lost other privileges. Why, just my share of supplies for the six of us comes to more than twenty-four pounds a year."

"Trust you to know the amount."

Kate turned away from her reflection to tick off items on her fingers. "A daily ration of two loaves of coarse bread and three of white, four gallons of ale, a half pitcher of wine, and six candles; three torches every week; and from the last day of October until the first day of April, six talshides of wood and six bundles of faggots to keep the dormitory warm. And then there is the matter of getting husbands. I have met a gentleman I fancy and I warrant he'd consider marrying one of the queen's maids of honor. An impoverished gentlewoman dependent upon a kinswoman for everything she has is another matter entirely."

Nan could not help but sympathize, and she was as tired of waiting as Kate was, but she said nothing and only half-listened as Kate began to ramble on about a fellow named Parker or Palmer or some such. Nan's thoughts drifted to King Henry.

The king had been gracious the few times she'd seen him since his return from Greenwich, but he had not sent for her again. She did not believe it was because he was happy with his new bride, or because he wished to avoid being importuned to get rid of the Dutch maids. She suspected he wished to avoid temptation. She smiled to herself, liking that explanation. It fit the fact that His Grace seemed bent on a public display of harmony between himself and Queen Anna.

"Nan?"

She gave a start. From the look on Kate's face, it was not the first time her cousin had called her name. "I beg your pardon, coz. My mind wandered."

"Thinking about your son, I warrant."

Nan felt her cheeks grow warm. Nervously, she glanced toward Constance and the other maidservants, but they were on the far side of the chamber, busy with the mending. Constance was darning the heel of one of Nan's stockings. Kate's maid was repairing a tear in a kirtle.

"Have you seen him since you gave him away?" Kate's sudden interest in Jamie set off alarm bells.

"No," Nan lied. "That part of my life never happened."

"That is as it should be."

Nan did not like her cousin's sly smile. With regret, she abandoned her plan to pay another visit to the silversmith's shop. She would wait until Kate lost interest. Another week. Or perhaps two. There was, she supposed, no great rush.

IN EARLY MARCH, Ned met John Husee at the Red Lion in Southwark, the inn Husee had often used as his headquarters before he'd acquired lodgings of his own in London. It was a hospitable place, but at this hour of the day the common room was nearly deserted. Their only companions were an old man half asleep on a bench along one wall and a blue-coated servant distracted by a fight between two urchins in the street outside the inn.

"It is quiet these days in Calais," Ned remarked, "what with Botolph and Philpott still here in England." He coughed when he inhaled a wisp of smoke from the fire in the hearth, then took a long pull of ale to soothe his throat.

"Sir Gregory Botolph did not come to England," Husee said. Ordinarily calm and matter-of-fact, he suddenly seemed agitated, scrubbing at his short brown beard with the back of one hand.

"Are you certain? Lord Lisle gave both Boltolph and Philpott leave to travel to England more than a month ago, to attend to personal business. Botolph was planning to visit his brothers."

Husee continued worrying his beard. "When I saw Philpott, he told me he was on his way to Leystocke, John Botolph's country house, on Sir Gregory's behalf. He was to collect some money owed to Sir Gregory, then travel on to Suffolk to see the third Botolph brother, Sir William, who has a small living as parson of Hofton."

Ned shifted uneasily on his stool. Something was not right. When he'd last seen Botolph, the priest had meant to catch the tide at two in the morning. He'd left Calais with Philpott before the gates were shut for the night and had planned to pass the time at the Rose until they sailed.

"If Botolph never planned to come to England at all, then where did he go?"

"Catholic lands surround the Pale of Calais. Botolph may have decided to join other English priests who have followed the example of Cardinal Pole."

"Live in exile?" Botolph, for all that he detested seeing religious houses shut down, had never struck Ned as one who wished to live the monastic life.

"There is another possibility." Husee had both hands clasped around his flagon and stared disconsolately into his ale. "I have heard a most distressing rumor," he confessed. "A matter of some valuable gold plate that disappeared from the religious house where Sir Gregory was once a canon."

Ned's eyes narrowed. The implication was clear, but he wanted to be sure he understood what Husee was telling him. "Do you mean to say that you recommended a suspected thief to Lord Lisle?"

"I did not know anything about the missing plate then. And, indeed, Sir Gregory came to me most highly recommended."

"By whom?"

"A number of men. Good men."

"And how did they know him?"

"I . . . I do not know. Perhaps a third party . . ." His voice trailed off. He looked unhappy.

Someone powerful, then. Archbishop Cranmer? Lord Cromwell?

"If Botolph committed a crime in England," Ned mused aloud, "it follows that he would wish to avoid returning here. The theft of such valuable goods is a hanging matter." Unless, of course, it was the king who seized religious property for his own use when he dissolved a monastery or convent.

"Speculation is useless," Husee said abruptly. "The fellow will turn up again or he will not. We have more important matters to deal with."

Clearly Husee wished he'd never broached the subject of Sir Gregory Botolph. He did not mention him again, but rather spent the next hour discussing Lord Lisle's business. When they were done, they had a last drink in the dimly lit common room and Husee relayed the latest news of Lady Lisle's daughters.

BEFORE HE RETURNED to Calais, Ned went to court. He found Nan in the queen's presence chamber, for in the middle of the previous month, the Dutch maids of honor had been dismissed and the English maids of honor recalled.

Nan took his breath away. She was attired in a new gown of soft tawny velvet with a bonnet in the latest style that showed a great deal of her beautiful brown hair and flattered her pretty face. That face, however, was marred by an expression of alarm when he asked for a word with her in private.

"We have nothing to say to each other that cannot be spoken of before witnesses."

"Not so, Nan. There is a delicate matter concerning your youngest sister that I have been ordered to discuss with you in strictest confidence." He had been given no such commission, but it was as good an excuse as any to get Nan alone.

"Mary? Is she ill again?"

"She is in love."

"Go, Nan," Kate Stradling said, giving her a shove, "but be prepared to tell all when you return."

Her laughter followed them out of the queen's apartments. Nan led the way through a maze of rooms and corridors until they came to a window embrasure that overlooked a garden. Even in winter, it was a stunning sight, filled with topiary beasts and beds set out in patterns.

"Well?" she demanded.

"I lied."

"Mary is not in love?"

"Oh, she is, but she did not ask me to share that intelligence with you."

"Who?"

Ned shrugged. He saw no harm in telling her. "The young seigneur de Bours, Gabriel de Montmorency."

"He's a child."

"So was Mary when you last saw her. She has grown up into a beauty." He reached out to run the back of his hand down Nan's cheek. "As pretty as you are, my love."

She jerked her head away. "If that is all you had to tell me, then I will return to my duties. The queen—"

"The queen will not even notice you are missing. She was nowhere in sight when I found you and Kate. What is the matter, Nan? Why does it make you so nervous to be alone with me?"

"I am reluctant to be *seen* alone with you."

"Still afraid someone will guess that we were once lovers?"

"I would deny it if any dared suggest such a thing." Anger flashed across her features, sparking the same emotion in him.

"Have you finally caught the eye of some poor fool of a nobleman?" The thought was more unsettling than he'd anticipated.

"A nobleman?" she scoffed. "Oh, no, Ned. I have done better than a mere nobleman."

Ned's stomach twisted. She'd told him of the king's interest in her. Warned him off. He'd joked that he'd be willing to take King Henry's leavings. But back then, Nan had not been the king's mistress. Ned had convinced himself she never would be. The image of them together, his Nan with that fat and diseased old man, repulsed him. "So, you've won the prize."

"And hope for even more. Please, Ned. Do not cause trouble. He believes he was the first."

He had no difficulty in understanding her. "And to think I once admired your ambition! This is madness, Nan. Remember what happened to the others."

One divorced. One beheaded. One dead of childbirth. Even if she wouldn't have him, Ned wanted better than that for Nan. He wanted her to be safe as well as happy.

Nan stamped her foot in frustration. "You're just jealous and you have no right to be. Go away, Ned. Leave me be. I know what I'm doing." With a final glare to make her point, she turned on her heel and strode rapidly away from him.

Ned stared after her, his emotions in turmoil. Why was he so upset? *Was* he jealous of the king? No, that wasn't it. Not entirely. And he should never have lashed out at Nan the way he had. She could not change her nature any more than he could change his. He should be pleased for her. Instead, he was worried that if she attained her goal, she would pay a terrible price for it.

NED'S VISIT PUSHED Nan into taking action. Because she'd found the king such an unappealing lover the one time they'd coupled, she'd made no particular effort to attract his attention since. But if she was to have the ultimate prize, if she was to be queen, she could not afford to delay any longer.

Henry Tudor was unhappy in his marriage to Anna of Cleves. Everyone knew that. There were rumors that the king had been unable to force himself to consummate the marriage. And Nan had heard there were grounds for annulment—an earlier betrothal between Anna and some minor German prince. If the king decided to pursue that course, he would soon be in the market for a fifth wife.

Nan had dreaded being summoned to the king's bed as his mistress. But if she could be queen . . . that was entirely different. The privileges, the power, the beautiful clothes—all those things would compensate for the distasteful aspects of intimate relations with the king.

King Henry believed he was the one who had deflowered her. That meant he would not expect a virgin on their wedding night. There did remain one problem. If His Grace ever found out that she had a child, he would know she'd deceived him.

Nan sighed. If she was to succeed in winning the king, she would never be able to see Jamie again. On the other hand, as queen, she would be in a position to advance anyone she chose. Members of her family, acknowledged and unacknowledged, would profit from her position. When Jamie Carver was a little older, perhaps she could bring him to court as a page.

Nan trusted Constance not to betray her secret. Cousin Kate would expect some material gain for her silence, but that could be arranged. Once she was queen, she would have the means to give Kate many "tokens" to keep her sweet.

The first step was to seduce the king. Nan chose her time with care. There were occasions when Queen Anna did not wish to have an entire retinue following at her heels. When she went to walk in her gallery for exercise, she took only four maids of honor with her, leaving the other two to their own devices.

Freed from her duties on the afternoon following Ned's visit, Nan hurried to the maids' dormitory. She washed with perfumed water and changed into clean linen. Constance, summoned from whatever place maidservants to maids of honor went when they were not needed, appeared in time to tie her laces and assure her that her headdress was on straight and her hair, what little showed of it, looked clean and neat.

"Are you certain about this, Mistress Nan?" Constance's lips pursed with disapproval as she made one last adjustment to Nan's skirts.

The fluttering in Nan's stomach intensified. "About what, Constance?"

The maidservant sighed. "There is only one reason you'd be primping in the middle of the day. The mouse is off to play while the cat walks in the gallery."

Nan had to smile at Constance's odd turn of phrase. "His Grace means to discard the queen and marry again," she said. "You have heard the rumors."

"The wagering belowstairs favors it," Constance agreed.

That surprised Nan, though when she thought about it she realized it should not have. Servants heard all kinds of things while waiting on their betters. "His Grace told me once that if he were not obliged to marry the princess of Cleves, he'd take me to wife. Once he rids himself of this woman he cannot abide, there will be no barrier to keep him from putting me in her place."

Constance's eyes widened. "But if he finds out—"

"He will not."

"But you are no—"

"His Grace believes himself to be . . . responsible. Now say no more of this, Constance. If you love me at all, never speak of it again."

Constance's expression remained grim but she nodded. "God go with you, mistress."

Nan sallied forth from the maidens' chamber in search of the king. She knew his routine. At this time of day he was most often in his own gallery. He was unlikely to be alone. She was prepared for that. But unless someone important, like Lord Cromwell, walked with him to discuss serious matters of state, she was certain he would be happy to send the others away.

She'd smile and tell him how much she had missed him. Flirt with and flatter him. Let him know she wished to be sent for when His Grace retired for the night. How could he resist? If all she'd heard was true, he had not made love to a woman since the night he'd taken her on the rush matting.

The king was indeed in his gallery, but his companion was not the Lord Privy Seal or the groom of the stole or any of his gentlemen attendants. It was Catherine Howard who walked beside him. She was so tiny that she only came up to the king's shoulder. He had to bend down to speak with her, but this seemed to please him. A broad grin split his face at her answer.

King Henry's attention was so fixed on the pretty young woman attached to his arm that he failed to notice Nan's presence in the gallery. Shaken and dismayed, Nan watched the king and his companion. How, she wondered, could she have missed the signs? Catherine Howard had returned to court dressed in the latest French fashions, and yet Nan knew the young woman had no fortune. Her parents were dead. She had numerous brothers and sisters and half brothers and half sisters, all with a claim on what little Lord Edmund Howard had left. A stepmother, too. So those clothes had been gifts from someone else.

Not the king. He'd had no opportunity to catch more than a glimpse of Catherine Howard before he wed Anna of Cleves. The Duke of Norfolk was more likely. He'd already helped put one niece, Anne Boleyn, on the throne of England. It was reasonable to assume that he'd provided pretty little Catherine with beautiful clothing in the hope that she would catch the king's eye. And she had.

Belatedly, Nan saw Catherine's sojourn with the dowager Duchess of Norfolk in a new light. She recalled several occasions, during the weeks before the Dutch maids of honor were dismissed, when King Henry had crossed the Thames with only a few of his gentlemen and spent the day in Lambeth.

Then there were the gifts Catherine had received. Nan had seen them in the maiden's chamber. Small things—quilted sleeves, a painted brooch—but Catherine had never said who'd sent them. No doubt there had been other presents—jewels, perhaps a painted miniature of King Henry, maybe even a horse.

When Catherine laughed and the king joined in, Nan turned and fled back toward the maiden's chamber. She had left it too late. The king had found someone else to ease his disappointment in the queen.

The dormitory was deserted when Nan reached it. Grateful for the solitude, she flung herself onto the window seat and stared out at the winter-brown landscape. March was not yet half gone. She shivered and thought about stirring the embers in the hearth and adding wood to the fire, but suddenly lacked the energy to get up and do so.

Was the king's interest in Catherine Howard a passing fancy, or was Catherine's goal the same as her own, to marry the king? That girl was no innocent. Nan was sure of it. And she doubted that the king would offer marriage without first sampling the wares. When he discovered she was not a virgin, he was unlikely to make her his queen.

So, Nan decided, it was only a matter of time before he tired of his new love. And then what? Nan was no longer so certain she could re-kindle his interest in her. Even if she did, it might not lead to marriage.

Nan had never been given to introspection, but she forced herself to examine her reaction to discovering Catherine Howard with the king. Now that the shock had worn off, she knew that what she was feeling was not jealousy. Rather, it was a sort of rueful relief.

It was a pity that her opportunity had been lost, but she was no worse off than she had been and she'd been spared the onerous task of pretend-ing, night after night, perhaps for years, that the king was a wonderful lover.

Perhaps she'd had a lucky escape. Tom Culpepper, whose duties included changing the king's dressing, had told her that the ulcer it covered never healed. In fact, His Grace's doctors advised him to keep it open beneath the bandages. Nan shuddered, remembering the nauseating odor she'd caught a whiff of once or twice.

"The king is still fond of me," she murmured. "I am still a maid of honor, still at court. And so long as those things are true, I can still hope to catch the eye of a wealthy and eligible nobleman."

Whereas I desired you in my last letters to send and provide me my money in English groats, I now pray you provide it in Flemish money if ye can—that is, in Parmesan ducats or French crowns.

—Sir Gregory Botolph to Edward Corbett, 26 March 1540

11

On the seventeenth of March, Sir Gregory Botolph returned to Calais. When he'd paid his respects to Lord and Lady Lisle, he sought Ned out. "What a journey!" he exclaimed. "The ship from England was wind-driven onto the French coast and I was obliged to make the twelve-mile journey from Boulogne on a borrowed horse."

Ned hesitated. Boats bound for Calais could not control the direction of the wind. It was not uncommon to put ashore in France or Flanders instead. But if John Husee was right, Botolph had never been in England at all.

"Did you see the French king in Boulogne?" he asked. "I've been told he and his court are to celebrate Palm Sunday there."

"Are they? That explains why the town was so crowded. I did not linger. Nor have I had a proper meal in days. Praise God it is almost time for dinner." Leaving Ned with the distinct impression that he wished to avoid talking about his journey, he trotted off toward the dining chamber.

The noonday meal was a formal affair under Lady Lisle's regime. Places were assigned by rank, above and below the salt. Sir Gregory Botolph's customary seat at table had no particular advantage over those given to the other two chaplains, except that it was better protected from drafts by a tapestry showing scenes from the story of Holofernes that hung on the wall behind. For that reason, one of the other priests had appropriated it during Botolph's absence.

With Botolph glaring at him, Sir Richard started to rise. Sir Oliver, the senior chaplain, stopped him with a gesture and spoke to Botolph. "Have you returned only to disrupt good order, Sir Gregory?"

"Not *only* for that reason, Sir Oliver." Botolph swung one leg over the bench and nudged Sir Richard out of his way.

"You are the most mischievous knave that ever was born," Sir Oliver declared.

"It is a gift from God."

"You have a glib tongue," Sir Oliver complained.

"The better to lead men on a righteous path," Botolph answered. Not without reason he was known as Gregory Sweet-lips.

"If you go on as you have been," Sir Oliver warned, "you will surely be hanged."

"Hanged, you say?" Botolph looked startled. "On what charge? If it is my orthodoxy you question, I believe burning is the fate of martyrs."

"You know well enough what charge."

Ned stared at Sir Oliver. It sounded to him as if Husee was not the only one who knew about the plate Botolph had allegedly stolen when he was a canon in Canterbury. Hanging was the punishment for the theft of items worth more than twelvepence.

Sir Oliver's glower was intended to intimidate, but Botolph only laughed and, apparently unperturbed by the other man's hostility, ate with a hearty appetite.

It was Ned who brooded throughout the meal.

Ned thought it even more peculiar when, the next day at dinner, Botolph entered the dining chamber to find Sir Oliver in his place and Sir Richard seated where Sir Oliver usually sat and, instead of making some flippant remark or rude comment, simply took Sir Richard's regular seat on the long bench and ate his meal in silence.

The following day, a Saturday, at nine in the morning, Mary Bassett's Gabriel, the young seigneur de Bours, arrived in Calais, ostensibly to deliver a letter to Lord Lisle from the constable of France. He was a good-looking lad with an aquiline nose and vivid blue eyes. He had visited Calais once before, in mid-Lent, but on that occasion he'd stayed only long enough to dine. This time he planned to spend the night.

De Bours went with the family to morning services—Lady Lisle heard Mass every day, not just on Sunday. Afterward, as the congregation was leaving the lord deputy's private chapel, Ned saw Sir Gregory Botolph take Lady Lisle aside. Curious, he moved close enough to over-hear what they were saying.

"My lord husband is content that you depart," Lady Lisle said, "and you have my blessing to go."

"I will remember you both in my prayers." Botolph's voice and bear-ing were somber, but only until Lady Lisle walked away. Then his face split into a jubilant grin.

"So, you are leaving again," Ned said.

"Escaping. I have permission to travel to the Low Countries and at-tend the University of Louvain."

"Is that wise? You'll be branded a papist if you study at Louvain."

"There are worse things, my friend."

Perhaps it would be best if Botolph left Calais, Ned thought, but did he really intend to matriculate? "How do you mean to reach Lou-vain?"

"I traded a bolt of tawny damask for a nag and a saddle. It was a good bargain. I bought the cloth cheap and I am owed thirteen shillings and fourpence on the exchange, to be paid in coin at a later date."

"When do you leave?"

"Now that I have both a horse and my lord's permission, I am of a mind to set out at once. If I stay, I will be obliged to eat another meal with Sir Oliver and Sir Richard. Unfortunately, I must delay until Philpott's return from England."

"Take your meals in town," Ned suggested.

Botolph laughed. "But then folk would reckon Lord Lisle was displeased with me. I believe I will go to Gravelines and wait for Philpott there. The only drawback is that if I keep my nag there, I will have to pay for stabling, and I have little ready money."

That was a difficulty Ned could appreciate. "Leave the horse in Lord Lisle's stable till such time as you depart for Louvain. Gravelines is only ten miles distant, just over the Flemish border. A man does not require more than sturdy shoes and a passport to take himself there. I will send the horse to you when you have need of him."

"That's settled then. I will go at once and pack." He clapped Ned on the back. "And you, my friend, must go in and dine and tell me later how my absence is taken."

"They will be too busy gawking at Mistress Mary's suitor to notice."

Botolph caught Ned's arm when he would have started toward the dining chamber and pulled him back inside the deserted chapel. It was cold out of doors but more frigid still within the stone walls. Ned shivered and wrinkled his nose. With the scented candles snuffed out, the place had a dank, unpleasant odor.

"I would have one more favor of you, in strictest confidence." From inside his doublet, Botolph withdrew a packet wrapped in paper and bound with thread. By the sound it made when he hefted it, there were coins within.

"I thought you said you had no money."

"None I can spend. These coins are broken, ready to be melted down. You must swear not to show them to anyone but Philpott. When he returns, give them to him."

"And what is he to do with them?" Broken coins still had value, but those who tried to spend them were looked upon with suspicion.

"Philpott will have the gold made into three rings. One of them will be yours, for your trouble."

Greed overcame caution. Ned slipped the small package into a pocket. It was not until that evening, after Botolph had left Calais, that he unwrapped it for a closer look. Inside were papal crowns issued in Rome. Possessing such money was dangerous, and the coins, even if they had not been broken, could not be spent in England or in Calais. Ned hastily rewrapped them. When it was full dark, he hid the packet beneath a floorboard in the stall occupied by Botolph's nag.

The next day was Palm Sunday. Mary Bassett's French suitor stayed until after dinner. Soon after he left, Mary came searching for Ned. She looked so radiant that he could not help but smile. "All went well, I trust, Mistress Mary?"

"Very well." She blushed becomingly. "I will burst if I do not tell someone. We have agreed to marry. When Gabriel returns he will bring a formal request for my hand from the head of his family."

"Then, surely, you do not need to keep your secret any longer. You should prepare your mother and stepfather for what is to come."

"Not yet. And you know I would not have confided in you, except that you already know how much I hoped this day would come." She blushed prettily.

"I will not betray you," Ned promised. He'd do his best not to betray anyone's secrets.

ON THAT SAME Palm Sunday, in London, Wat Hungerford was sent on an errand by Lord Cromwell. He approached the house of John Husee without any particular sense of foreboding. Husee himself proved to be a nondescript sort of man and he seemed only mildly surprised to receive a letter from Wat's master.

"Wait, in case I wish you to take a reply." Husee broke the seal and began to read. His eyes had gone wide before he was halfway down the page. By the time he came to Cromwell's signature, his face was beet red and his hands were shaking so hard that he dropped the letter.

Wat bent to retrieve it. He could not help but see a few lines when he picked it up, enough to tell him that Husee was Lord Lisle's factor in London and that Cromwell had written to suggest that he leave Lisle's employment at once.

Husee seized the page before Wat could read more. "There will be no reply!"

Wat prudently retreated. Out in the street again, he took his time walking back to Lord Cromwell's house. He knew Cromwell thought Lord Lisle should be removed as lord deputy of Calais, and that he had his own man in mind to replace the viscount, but why would Cromwell want John Husee to resign from his post? He mulled that over for a while and decided that Husee, as Lisle's man of business, was likely responsible for keeping his irresponsible master out of financial difficulties. Yes, that made sense. Deprive Lisle of sensible advice, and his position would be that much weaker.

Lord Cromwell was good at exploiting weaknesses. Time and time again, Wat had seen that firsthand. In Lord Lisle's case, however, it bothered Wat a great deal to know in advance of that nobleman's impending downfall.

He detoured around a steaming pile of horse dung in the street and continued on, his thoughts shifting to the reason he had always taken a particular interest in anything connected to Arthur Plantagenet, Viscount Lisle—Mistress Anne Bassett.

She was the most beautiful girl he'd ever seen. Wat had thought so from the first moment he'd seen her—the day of Prince Edward's christening. He'd decided on the spot that he was going to marry her someday.

The fact that he was four years younger than she was did not strike him as a serious obstacle, and since she had not married anyone else in the interim, he was optimistic that he would, in time, make his dream a reality.

She'd danced with him once. He treasured the memory.

Because Lord Lisle was Mistress Anne's stepfather, Wat resolved to keep his ears open and his eyes peeled for any further machinations on Lord Cromwell's part. If his master moved against the viscount, Wat would warn Mistress Anne. Even if he lost his place with Lord Cromwell as a result, it would be worth it. He'd save her family. She would see that he was just like the chivalrous knights in the stories. He would be her champion.

WHEN CATHERINE CAREY left the ranks of the maids of honor to marry, she was replaced by Lord Bray's sister, Dorothy, a pretty, dark-haired girl with a turned-up nose. Within a week, Dorothy had discovered the spiral staircase that linked the ground and first floors of the queen's apartments. They were there so that food and other goods could be delivered without intruding upon the queen's privacy, but they also provided a way for members of the household to leave without being seen. Within two weeks, Dorothy had put them to use to sneak out to meet her lover—Anne Herbert's brother, Will Parr. Nan glanced up from her embroidery late on Palm Sunday afternoon and was just in time to see Dorothy slip away.

Beside Nan on the padded bench, another of Queen Anna's maids of honor sat and stitched. Like Nan, Catherine Howard had noticed Dorothy's stealthy departure. When her eyes met Nan's, they shared a look that said Dorothy Bray was a foolish girl.

Abruptly, Catherine's expression changed to one of intense dislike. Startled, Nan broke contact and fixed her gaze on the needle in her hand, but she could still feel Catherine staring at her.

"Dorothy Bray has made a poor choice," Catherine said after a moment. Nothing in her voice betrayed strong emotion.

Nan kept her own tone light. "Lord Parr seems pleasant enough."

"He has two counts against him. He has no great fortune and he already has a wife."

"Becoming the mistress of a married man is never wise." Nan wondered where this conversation was headed. Did Catherine know Nan had seen her with the king?

"His Grace is fond of you, Mistress Bassett." The sibilance of Catherine's whisper made Nan think of snakes hissing.

"So I would hope, Mistress Howard. I should not like King Henry to think ill of me."

"In that case, you should be careful how you behave in his presence."

"I do not understand you." Nan's hand paused over her needlework.

"I should take it very badly indeed should I hear you had returned to his bed."

Forcing herself to continue stitching, Nan slowly turned her head to look at the other woman. "I am the king's to command, Catherine. If he sends for me, I must obey."

"I will turn him against you if you try to usurp my place."

Surely, Nan thought, it was the other way around. Catherine Howard had been much in King Henry's company this past month, while Nan had received little more than casual greetings from His Grace. Catherine's threat did not make sense . . . unless she had not yet become the king's mistress.

Why would she withhold her favors? The moment Nan asked herself that question, she knew the answer. Catherine Howard was angling to be queen.

Slanting another glance at her fellow maid of honor, Nan saw that Catherine was pouting, like a toddler deprived of a toy. She was childlike in other ways, too—impulsive, self-centered, set on having her own way regardless of the consequences.

Nan did not like Mistress Catherine Howard. She gave herself airs. She snubbed the other maids of honor when they invited her to play cards with them or go to listen to the king's musicians practice the latest songs. Catherine spent most of her free time, when she was not with the king, in the company of Lady Rochford.

The older woman seemed an odd choice to Nan. Lady Rochford was reputed to have brought about the downfall of Queen Anne Boleyn by telling Lord Cromwell that the queen had committed incest with her brother, George Boleyn—Lady Rochford's husband. That Lady Rochford had not shared in the Boleyns' disgrace gave credence to the tale. She had been one of Queen Jane's ladies and now served Queen Anna. Perhaps, Nan thought, Catherine saw her as a source of privileged information about the queen's intimate relations—or lack of them—with the king.

A sharp pain in her shoulder made Nan jump. Catherine Howard had stabbed her with a needle!

"Pay attention to me, you stupid cow," Catherine hissed. "The king is mine. I will not tolerate any interference in my plans."

"You are welcome to him," Nan whispered back, sliding to the far end of the bench as she clapped one hand protectively over her wounded arm. "I am content with my place as a maid of honor to the queen of England."

She glared at the other woman. Catherine was not a clever girl, nor had she been well educated, but she had a kind of animal cunning. She was ambitious and determined. Nan suspected it had not taken much effort for the Duke of Norfolk to convince her to set her cap for the king.

"Do you swear that is true? You do not want him for yourself?"

"You have my word on it. If you succeed in your quest, I will serve you every bit as loyally as I do our current mistress."

The irony in that statement seemed to elude Catherine Howard. "See that you do, Nan Bassett." Rising in as regal a manner as someone of Catherine's tiny stature could manage, she swept out of the room.

Nan went back to her embroidery, glad that it was the king's favor she needed to keep and not the queen's.

*   *   *

ON THE TUESDAY after Palm Sunday, Ned faced Lord Lisle in the latter's study. "I have come to request a license to go to Gravelines on the
morrow," he said.

"What business do you have in Flanders?" Lisle was already reaching
for the form used for passports.

"Sir Gregory Botolph has asked me to take certain of his possessions
to him there." Botolph wanted his nag and some other belongings he had
left behind.

Quill poised over paper, Lisle looked up in surprise. "Do you mean to
say that Sir Gregory has traveled no farther than Gravelines? He should
be halfway to Louvain by now."

"He has been awaiting Clement Philpott's return from England."

"Then the man's a fool. Why waste money on lodgings in Gravelines
when he might as easily have stayed here?"

"I believe he wished to avoid Sir Oliver," Ned said.

As Lord Lisle wrote out the passport Ned needed to cross the border,
Ned steeled himself to broach another subject. "My lord, I understand
that Master Husee has left your service."

"Bad news travels quickly. I only received his resignation this morning."

"I wondered, my lord, if you have someone in mind as his replacement?
You will recall that I have served in London in Master Husee's place on
occasion and that I am familiar with your business dealings in England."

As if he wished to avoid meeting Ned's gaze, the lord deputy bent
over the passport to sign his name. "I need you here," he mumbled.

Ned swallowed his disappointment and asked for the loan of a horse
for the trip to Gravelines. Bright and early the next morning, he and
Browne rode out of Calais, Ned on the gelding he'd borrowed from Lord
Lisle's stable and his servant on Botolph's nag.

Two hours and ten miles later, they located Botolph at the Sign of the
Checker in Gravelines. Ned had planned to turn right around and return
to Calais, as he was on duty in the marketplace early the next morning,
but Botolph forced a delay by sending Browne on an errand.

When he'd gone, leaving Ned and Botolph alone in the latter's well-appointed chamber, Ned sent the other man a speculative look. "Do you intend to explain why you got rid of my manservant?"

"I have a confession to make." He poured wine into goblets and handed one to Ned, gesturing for him to sit.

"Hearing confessions is your profession, not mine." But Ned took the bench by the window.

Botolph dropped into a Glastonbury chair and stretched his legs out toward the hearth. "I did not go to England."

Ned tasted the wine before he spoke—hippocras, richly spiced. "I suspected as much after talking to John Husee some weeks ago." He felt a brief surge of resentment that Lord Lisle did not consider him worthy to be Husee's replacement. "Where did you go, then?"

"First to the French court, which was then at Amiens. There I was given money for my journey by the pope's ambassador to France. I was able to hire good horses all the way to Rome."

Ned did not believe him. "You were not gone long enough to make a trip to Rome and back, especially at this time of year."

"The weather was in my favor."

Ned frowned into his goblet. The gold crowns Botolph had given him in Calais did lend credence to the claim, but Botolph was skilled at spinning elaborate fabrications. Look at how he'd had poor Philpott convinced that he was about to be married to a Lutheran lass. "Why would you want to go to Rome?"

"To see Cardinal Pole. I offered him my services."

Ned began to have the uncomfortable feeling that Botolph was serious. He should walk out now, before he heard any more.

But in the next moment, Ned realized he was already in too deep to escape. Cardinal Pole was a traitor to England. If Botolph was telling the truth, he'd committed treason by treating with Pole. And Ned, now that he knew that much, was guilty by association. He might as well satisfy his curiosity.

"If you went to Rome, why didn't you stay there?" He took another swallow of wine.

"Because Cardinal Pole and Pope Paul need me here. I met with them in the Holy Father's own chamber and I have been given a mission by His Holiness, as well as two hundred crowns with which to accomplish it. In herring time, when Calais is crowded with fishermen bringing their catch to market, we will return the English Pale to the true church."

The fanatic gleam in Botolph's eyes, the fervor with which he spoke, almost convinced Ned that it could work. But what few details Botolph provided revealed that the scheme hinged on subverting men of the garrison. Although there was some discontent over matters of religion, those men were loyal to king and country. They would never open the gates to England's enemies. Precisely who would take control of Calais, Botolph would not say.

"By herring time all will be in readiness." Botolph sat back, a satisfied look on his face, and polished off his goblet of wine.

"Herring time is six months away," Ned objected. The Calais herring mart ran for two months, from Michaelmas, at the end of September, until St. Andrew's tide. During that time, over three hundred herring boats brought their catch into port. "You will be hard pressed to keep your plans secret for that long. You've already risked both the plot and your own neck by talking so freely to me."

This scheme was every bit as foolish as those that cropped up at regular intervals to restore the Catholic Church to England by overthrowing King Henry. He'd heard enough. Too much. Ned rose and started for the door.

"You will not betray me, my friend. You are loyal," Botolph called after him. "Besides, you know what will happen to you if you tell anyone."

Ned stopped, his hand on the latch. He'd be charged with treason because he knew of the plot. Warning Lord Lisle would accomplish nothing except putting himself in prison right alongside Botolph. He turned back. "Listen to reason, *friend*. This scheme has no chance of success. If you persist, you'll end up burnt for a heretic, or hanged, drawn, and quartered as a traitor."

"Only if you betray me. My death would be on your conscience, Ned."

Ned began to pace. "You will betray yourself when you return to Calais and try to bribe members of the spears."

"That is why I will not go back, nor ever into England again so long as King Henry sits on the throne. I will send others in my place while I remain safe in the emperor's dominions."

Ned stared at Botolph in disbelief as the other man rose from his chair and refilled his goblet. "You intend to sacrifice your friends? That is monstrous."

Botolph turned, the wine in his hand. He gave Ned a considering look. Then he laughed. "Did you truly believe me? I thought surely the plot was so far-fetched that you would see right through the jest."

Anger rippled through Ned. His fists came up and he took a step toward Botolph. "A joke? What if someone had overheard? We'd both be in prison for plotting against the Crown."

"Where is your sense of humor, Ned? You'd be laughing right along with me if it were Philpott I'd cozened with my tale."

Ned didn't know what to believe, although it was true Botolph took unholy pleasure from playing just this sort of trick on his friends. Slowly, he unclenched his fists and reached for his wine goblet. "If you did not go to Rome, where were you?"

Botolph's expression turned serious again. "This is the true confession. When I was a canon in Canterbury, I did something . . . ill-advised. Sir Oliver learned of it, and for the enmity he bears me, would see me hanged if he could."

Ned took a long swallow of wine. This, at least, he could believe, but Botolph had not answered his question. "Where did you go?"

"Louvain, to make arrangements for my studies there. And now, Ned, I would think it a great kindness if you would collect the debts owed to me, and a few more things that I left behind in Calais and send them to me here."

Ned couldn't believe his ears. "After such a trick, why should I do you more favors?"

Botolph smiled engagingly and exerted the full force of his personality. "Because we are friends, you and I and Clement Philpott. Friends help each other."

CLEMENT PHILPOTT HAD returned to Calais while Ned was in Gravelines. At his first opportunity, Ned gave Philpott a condensed account of Botolph's return to Calais, his quarrel with the other chaplains, his departure for Gravelines, and Ned's own journey there with Botolph's nag. He left out the wild tale of rebellion in herring time. He told himself he'd been a fool to fall for such a fantastic story.

Philpott set off into Flanders to take Botolph the money Botolph's brother had sent. Botolph, meanwhile, had sent Ned a letter telling him he was about to leave and asking Ned to retrieve a shirt he'd sent out to be laundered and to collect his blue livery cloak, his pillow, his ring, his sarcenet tippet, the good scabbard for his sword, and his knife, as well as the money he was still owed in the exchange of cloth for nag and saddle. Ned was shaking his head in disbelief by the time he got to the list of other debts Botolph was owed. He wanted Ned to send the money to him in groats, but only after using some of the coins to buy him an ell of the finest colored kersey.

When Philpott returned to Calais the next morning, he brought another missive from Botolph. In this one, Botolph requested that his debts be repaid in ducats from Parma or in French crowns. He also wanted Ned to send him the books he'd left behind.

"And he asked to borrow your servant," Philpott added. "He wants Browne to go with him as far as Bruges, as it is unwise for a gentleman to travel alone."

Since Ned was already planning to send Browne as far as Gravelines to deliver Botolph's money and the other items, he agreed. It hardly mattered if his man rode on a little farther.

"And he said you had some coins for me," Philpott added.

Belatedly, Ned remembered the broken papal crowns. After that, try as he might, he could not quite shake the niggling fear that Botolph might have been serious about herring time.

As March turned into April and April advanced, it became abundantly clear to Nan that Catherine Howard would succeed in pushing out Queen Anna. The king rarely left Catherine's side and was clearly besotted with her.

On the twenty-third of April, Lord Lisle arrived at court. He paid his respects to the king, but then he retreated to his lodgings, pleading the sudden onset of illness. Nan, worried about him, visited him the following evening. Her stepfather was the oldest man she knew and, in spite of his usual robust good health, he could not live forever.

She was relieved to find him in good spirits in spite of being propped up in bed and wrapped in furs. He greeted her with a thunderous sneeze. His eyes were red and watery. He'd rubbed his nose raw and used handkerchiefs littered the counterpane. Nan kissed his cheek in greeting, then stepped back a prudent distance.

"I sound worse than I feel." Lisle swabbed his dripping nose. "This is only a nasty catarrh. A few days' rest and I will be back to my old self."

"I devoutly hope so, my lord." When he fell into a fit of coughing, she found a pitcher of spiced ale on the sideboard, filled two cups, and handed him one of them.

"I have incentive to recover quickly." He sipped and gave a contented sigh. "I have every expectation of being elevated in the peerage during this visit to court. An earldom, Nan—what do you think of that?"

"That you have served the Tudors long and well and deserve a sign of royal favor." Nan perched near Lord Lisle's feet, sinking down into the soft feather bed.

"Honor will be pleased. She and your sisters are in good health. So is my daughter, Frances, and the child she gave birth to last May."

The baby, Nan recalled, had been christened Honor Bassett. Mother and child remained in Calais while Nan's brother continued to study law at Lincoln's Inn. It was a sensible arrangement, as the marriage had been. Frances's union with her stepbrother kept her inheritance in the family. According to Ned Corbett, the two got along as well as any married couple.

That reminded Nan that she had not seen Ned for some time and that, during his last visit, they'd quarreled. When she'd heard that John Husee had left Lord Lisle's employ, she'd half expected that Ned would be appointed to fill his place, but the post was still vacant.

Thinking of Ned—to be honest, missing Ned—inevitably reminded Nan of the son she had borne him. It had been even longer since she'd seen young Jamie. With both Cousin Kate and Catherine Howard suspicious of her, she'd not dared risk a trip into London. She'd consoled herself with the knowledge that even if Jamie were her legitimate child and his father some wealthy nobleman, she'd not be able to spend much time with him. Cousin Mary rarely saw her boy. Even the Countess of Rutland, who regularly journeyed to Belvoir Castle with Cat in tow, had a limited amount of time to spend with her children.

"The young seigneur de Bours has been to visit," Lord Lisle said when he'd recovered from another bout of coughing. He frowned. "That is a matter I must broach with the king as soon as I recover. The lad wants to marry your sister. A letter from his uncle, as head of the family, formally proposing to open negotiations, arrived just after I left Calais. Your mother sent it on to me in Dover. I must have the king's approval before I can go forward in the matter."

"I cannot think why His Grace should object to Mary's betrothal. She has no Plantagenet blood in her veins."

"True. Perhaps I can leave the business until later. I have a great deal more to speak about with His Grace. These are difficult times in Calais." His fingers fumbled with the fur he kept wrapped around himself. His brow furrowed, adding new creases to a face already deeply lined with age.

"Has something in particular happened?" Nan sipped the spiced ale, untroubled by any premonition of disaster. There was always unrest in the Pale.

"A most nefarious plot against the Crown," her stepfather said.

"Treason?" That, too, was all too common. Someone always seemed to be fomenting rebellion or preaching sedition.

"Of the worst sort—betrayal by members of my own retinue."

Suddenly uneasy, Nan slid off the foot of the bed and set her cup on the sideboard. "Who has betrayed you, my lord?"

Lisle rattled off a list of names, but Nan heard only one—Corbett.

Her heart stuttered and she couldn't remember how to breathe. Ned . . . and treason?

"Sir Gregory Botolph conceived the dastardly plan. The depositions contradict each other on numerous points, but it seems certain that Botolph went to Rome, met with Cardinal Pole, and conspired with him to open the gates of Calais to England's enemies during herring time, when the town is crowded with strangers."

"Enemies?" Nan echoed in a choked whisper.

Lisle's lips twisted into a wry smile. "No one was too clear about what army would come. The French, perhaps. Or the emperor's men. Someone allied with the pope, that much is certain. When Clement Philpott first came to me with his story, I did not believe him. But when those he accused were questioned, they confirmed everything he told me."

"Where is . . . Philpott now?" Nan did not dare ask after Ned. If she spoke his name, the tremor in her voice would betray the depth of her concern for him. She clasped her hands together to hide their trembling.

"Philpott, Corbett, and the rest are in the Tower of London. After they were examined in Calais and gave their depositions, they were brought over to England in the greatest secrecy. I suppose the torturer will have a go at them now, although I suspect they have already confessed everything they know."

Nan squeezed her eyes shut, but nothing could block out the horrible images crowding into her mind. She had heard terrifying stories about men stretched on the rack until they would admit to anything just to put an end to the pain. She breathed deeply, trying to calm herself. It would not do to let the extent of her agitation show. Any association with a traitor could put a man, or a woman, at risk of being accused of that same crime.

When she had regained a measure of control, she asked, "Are all those arrested equally guilty?"

Lisle blew his nose before answering. "Corbett admits to no more than a single meeting with Botolph in Gravelines and to helping the fellow retrieve money owed him and a few belongings he left behind in Calais. But Corbett did not just convey those things to Botolph. He ordered his manservant to accompany the villain partway to Louvain. He helped Botolph escape the king's justice."

Nan blinked at him, and only with difficulty grasped his meaning. "Do you mean to say that all these men are imprisoned in the Tower of London while Sir Gregory, who devised the scheme, remains free?"

"Exactly so. He is at large somewhere in the Low Countries. Flanders, perhaps. No one knows. The king's agents are trying to track him down. In the meantime, because I brought this treasonous plot to light, Lord Cromwell assures me that I will remain high in royal favor. As soon as I am well again—for you know how His Grace abhors sickness!—I will present myself to King Henry. An earldom is in the offing as my reward for diligence. I am sure of it."

Nan tried to match his smile, but she was glad the light was dim in the bedchamber. She had a feeling the expression on her face was closer to a grimace. If Lord Lisle did not see the flaw in his logic, she was not about to point it out to him. She had no doubt that Clement Philpott had also expected to benefit from exposing the plot.

Nan suspected that her stepfather would return to Calais with no greater honors than he already possessed. That the plot had been conceived on his watch would count against him in the king's eyes, and Cromwell would likely use the debacle to have him replaced as lord deputy.

She felt pity for her stepfather, but she did not fear he'd come to any real harm. What Ned Corbett faced, however, terrified her. When she had coaxed Lord Lisle into telling her all he knew of the prisoners, she made her excuses and returned to the maidens' chamber.

Her eyes blurred, blinding her as she fumbled her way out of her clothing and into her bed. Her heart felt as if it had been rent in two. She wanted to wail and tear at her hair, but she was not alone in the dormitory. She could only lie still, silent tears coursing down her cheeks, until she finally fell asleep from sheer exhaustion.

One of her lover's letters was carried in her bosom when she was found by Lord Sussex . . . and this, with various others, she threw down the garderobe on the advice of the daughter of Lord Hussey of Lincolnshire.

—Elis Gruffudd of the Calais retinue, *Chronicle* (translated from the Welsh Mostyn MS)

Mary Bassett hath written with her own hand as much of the effect of the letters cast into the jakes as she can call to her remembrance, as she saith, which we send you here enclosed, with certain other French letters found in the house.

—the Earl of Sussex and Sir John Gage to Lord Cromwell, 5 June 1540

*N*ed Corbett woke from a nightmare, the scream of agony lodged in his throat. Sweat covered his body in spite of the chill of the stone walls and floor. He wrapped the single blanket he'd been given more tightly around his shoulders and fought the urge to squeeze his eyes shut and curl himself into a ball.

He was still in a bad dream, but he was not going to wake up from this one. Hiding from the truth would do no good, either. He lay on his back on a straw-filled pallet and stared at the bars on the nearest window. He was a prisoner in the Tower of London, charged with treason. He had not been tortured yet, but it was only a matter of time. His imagination had already supplied the gruesome details.

Afterward, as a confessed traitor, he'd be taken out of his cell, marched under guard across the bridge over the moat, past the Lion Tower and through the gate. They'd deliver him to the Guildhall for trial, but the verdict would already be a given and the punishment, too. Then it would be back to the Tower until it was time for one last journey, this time to Tyburn.

Hanged, drawn, and quartered.

That was the fate of traitors.

Ned swallowed hard and swiped at the sweat on his face with one dirty sleeve. No. He must not give up. All he had to do was stick to the story he'd already told, the one that left out all the details Botolph had given him in Gravelines.

Ned had admitted he'd taken personal belongings to Botolph. He'd even confessed to having possession, briefly, of the ten broken crowns, although he'd claimed he'd never opened the packet. But he'd steadfastly insisted he knew nothing about any plot to overthrow Calais. The only one who could say that was a lie was Botolph himself. As far as Ned knew, the villainous priest was still at large on the Continent. Ned sent up a silent prayer for the other man's safety. His own life might depend upon the priest's continued freedom.

In all honesty, he *was* guilty of treason.

He should have reported Botolph directly to Lord Lisle as soon as he returned from Gravelines. He should have turned on his friends. That might have saved him. Then again, it might not have.

Ned stared at the cold, damp stones hemming him in. His cell was separate from the one where the others were being held, the men arrested because Philpott had done exactly what Ned should have. Philpott's mistake had been to wait several weeks after his return to Calais before he succumbed to panic. Then the fool had told the truth, admitting to even the parts that were certain to condemn him to death.

Ned covered his face with one arm. There was no hope for any of them. He'd known that as soon as they'd been taken from Calais and put aboard a ship in the middle of the night to be brought to England.

A muffled groan escaped him. His servant, Browne, had also been arrested. Ned had no idea how involved Browne had been in Botolph's scheme. It was possible the priest had subverted Browne's loyalty and sweet-talked him into joining the conspiracy. Or Browne could have been an innocent bystander. Ned was not worried that Browne could testify against him in regard to the Botolph plot, but Browne did know Ned's other secrets.

He knew Nan Bassett had been Ned's mistress before she was the king's.

AFTER THE MAY Day tournament at Whitehall, the court moved to Greenwich for Whitsuntide. Nan carried out her duties as a maid of honor with an outward appearance of calm, but her heart ached and her mind was always in turmoil. She'd heard nothing more about Ned since her stepfather's announcement that he was in the Tower. Her imagination painted terrible pictures: Ned being tortured; Ned dying; Ned executed in the horrifying way traitors were put to death. She had never felt so helpless, not even when she had first discovered that she was with child.

She tried to take heart from her stepfather's continued presence at court. The king seemed well disposed toward him, but although King Henry had elevated Thomas Cromwell in the peerage to Earl of Essex— the title Lord Parr had expected to be granted in his much-despised wife's name—His Grace had not advanced Lord Lisle. Nan thought it unlikely that King Henry's benevolence would extend to a pardon for any of the men in Lord Lisle's retinue, not even at the request of a pretty maid of honor.

Word of the arrests eventually leaked out. Constance dissolved into tears when she heard that John Browne was in the Tower. Nan's sister Cat, at court as one of the Countess of Rutland's waiting gentlewomen, denounced Ned in no uncertain terms, both as a traitor and because he had been disloyal to Lord Lisle.

No one else at court seemed much interested in an insignificant and

unsuccessful treason plot in an outpost across the Narrow Seas. A far
more fascinating scandal had erupted closer to hand. Lord Hungerford
of Heytesbury was also in the Tower of London. He was to be tried for
sorcery and buggery as well as for heresy and treason.

Nan paid little attention to the details of the case, although she did
spare a moment's pity for Lord Hungerford's son. When young Wat
Hungerford sent word that he wanted to speak to her, Nan set aside her
needlework, prepared to meet with him.

Her cousin, the Countess of Sussex, stopped her. "Best you have
nothing to do with the lad," Mary advised.

"The son is not in disgrace, only the father." And Wat was still in
Cromwell's service. Nan had seen him at a distance, resplendent in the
new Earl of Essex's livery. Wat's arms and chest had filled out and he'd
grown taller. She did not think he would be referred to as a lad for much
longer.

"Lord Hungerford is worse than a traitor, Nan. You do not want your
name linked with him, even indirectly."

Nan frowned, trying to recall what she'd heard. Something about cast-
ing a horoscope to know when the king would die. And another charge:
Lord Hungerford was supposed to have taken another man as his lover.
Under a newly passed law, the penalty for that unnatural act was death.

Nan supposed Cousin Mary was right. It was best to have nothing to
do with Wat Hungerford. She barely knew him, after all. She sent him
away without hearing what he had to say.

NAN SUPPED WITH her stepfather in his chamber on the evening of the
seventeenth of May and stayed late because Lord Lisle was in an expan-
sive mood. He had plans to take a more active role in Parliament and
at court. His continued belief that he would soon be honored with an
earldom gave him new vitality, and his enthusiasm was infectious. When
Nan was with him, she could almost believe it would happen. She hoped
it would. A highly favored earl would be in an ideal position to ask the
king to pardon one of his gentlemen servitors.

"Have you broached the subject of Mary's betrothal with the king?" she asked. "I've had a letter from Mother asking me to sing Gabriel's praises to His Grace."

"I will wait until I have my earldom to discuss the matter with King Henry." Lord Lisle bit into a tart.

"Is it wise to delay? You would not want to be accused of keeping their liaison secret."

"Do not worry your pretty little head about it, my dear. I will know when the time is right."

Nan made no further protest, but she felt uneasy. The king had a limited supply of goodwill.

"You seem agitated, Nan." Lord Lisle reached for another tart.

Someone began pounding on the door before Nan could deny it.

"Send them away, whoever they are," Lisle shouted to his manservant.

But the men on the other side of the door did not wait to be admitted. Several yeomen of the guard in royal livery and carrying halberds burst into the chamber. Nan recognized their leader. He was Lady Kingston's husband, Sir William—the constable of the Tower of London.

"What is the meaning of this intrusion?" Lisle rose to his feet so quickly that his chair toppled over with a crash.

Nan jumped up and ran to his side. A terrible tightness constricted her breathing. When the edges of her vision narrowed, she was afraid she might faint. She forced herself to drag in a great gulp of air. Even before Sir William spoke, she knew he had come to arrest her stepfather.

IT WAS TWILIGHT when the Earl of Sussex entered the great parlor of the lord deputy's residence in Calais. Mary Bassett, perched on a stool near a wicker screen and picking out a tune on her lute, saw him first. Her mother caught sight of him a moment later, as did Frances and Philippa, who were comfortably ensconced on large cushions on the floor to engage in a game of cards.

The earl's gaze roved over the domestic scene. His expression revealed nothing, but Mary saw a flash of panic in her mother's eyes. Had something happened to Lord Lisle? Her stepfather had written of falling ill shortly after his arrival in England, but that had been almost a month ago.

Honor Lisle remained seated in the room's only chair, her embroidery hoop clasped in both hands. "My Lord Sussex, this visit is unexpected."

Sussex moved toward her. Behind him came three men Mary recognized as members of the Calais Council.

"Gentlemen?" Mary heard the note of alarm in her mother's voice, but Lady Lisle, elegantly dressed in a kirtle of black velvet and one of her best taffeta gowns, assumed a regal hauteur as she waited for an explanation.

"Madam, I am sorry to have to tell you this," the earl said, "but your husband has been arrested and charged with treason."

Mary bit back an exclamation of dismay.

Her mother dropped her needlework to grip the arms of her chair. "No. That is not possible. My husband has done nothing wrong."

But Sussex was still talking. "By the king's command, I am ordered to seize and inventory all of Lord Lisle's possessions, most especially all correspondence, and to question everyone in this household. You, madam, are to be confined to your chamber." At his signal, one of the Calais Spears entered the room. "Take Lady Lisle away and stand guard outside her door."

While her mother raged against such treatment, drawing everyone's attention to her, Mary set her lute on the floor and slowly, quietly, rose from her stool. In a few furtive steps she was hidden by the wicker screen that shielded the room from drafts. Seconds later, she was through the small door behind it and on her way to her bedchamber.

They were going to confiscate letters. They were looking for treasonous correspondence. They probably thought her stepfather had been writing to Cardinal Pole. Mary did not care about that. She had other letters to hide from prying eyes. Personal letters. Private letters. Love letters.

She kept everything Gabriel had ever written to her in a coffer near her bed, tied up with a red ribbon. Retrieving the thick packet, Mary hugged it to her breast. She could not bear to think of strangers reading words meant only for her.

There was no fire in the hearth, not on the twentieth day of May. Mary reached for the tinder box to start one, then had a better idea.

She encountered one of her mother's waiting gentlewomen as she left the bedchamber. "What has happened?" Mistress Hussey asked. "There are soldiers everywhere." She was a young woman only a few years Mary's senior and she was pale with fright.

"Lord Lisle has been arrested. The king's men are looking for damning documents to use against him."

Mistress Hussey's dark brown eyes went wide. Her face turned the color of whey. She hastily crossed herself.

"For God's sake, do not do that! They'll take you for a papist."

"It is happening all over again. Is nowhere safe?" Frantic, Mistress Hussey craned her neck in every direction, as if searching for a place to hide.

Belatedly, Mary remembered that Lord Hussey of Sleaford had been executed for treason. "Your father took part in a rebellion against King Henry," she murmured. "This is not at all the same."

Still gripping the packet of letters, Mary ignored the silent tears running down the other woman's cheeks and pushed past her, heading for the nearest garderobe.

The tiny room was cut into the outer wall. A wooden seat rested atop a shaft that emptied into a cesspit far below. Mary's stomach twisted, but she had no choice. No one must ever read what Gabriel had written to her. Before she could lose her nerve, she untied the ribbon and ripped the first letter in two, then tore it again before she let the pieces fall from her hand and flutter into the abyss.

"Let me help." Mistress Hussey appeared at her side.

Mary thrust half the letters into the other woman's hands and went back to tearing those that remained into tiny bits. She kept back only one, the letter in which Gabriel had first said that he loved her.

This she tucked into her bodice, certain no one would dare search her person.

"What now?" Mistress Hussey asked.

"Now we join my sisters in the parlor and pretend that we have only just heard of the arrival of the Earl of Sussex."

NAN SPENT TWO weeks in daily anticipation of more bad news. Her stepfather was suspected of conspiring with Sir Gregory Botolph. He was a prisoner in the Tower. In Calais, Nan's mother and sisters had also been arrested. Nan had no idea what the accusations against them were. She only knew that the king's men had seized and inventoried everything in their house—clothing, books, papers, and even an old piece of tapestry too moth eaten to hang.

It was the fifth of June before Nan herself was summoned to be questioned. She dreaded the interrogation, expecting it to be conducted by Thomas Cromwell. Instead, Anthony Denny joined her in a small, stuffy room, accompanied by a clerk who would take down everything she said.

"Of what are my mother and sisters accused?" she asked before Denny could begin. "Surely they had no part in Sir Gregory Botolph's mad plan."

"They tried to conceal your sister's trothplight to a Frenchman."

Nan gasped. "She was already *betrothed* to him?"

Denny's eyes narrowed. "What do you know of this matter, Mistress Bassett?"

Not "Nan," she thought, as she had been when she lived in "Cousin Denny's" household, but "Mistress Bassett." Like everyone else, Denny would try to distance himself from the contagion of treason, as if it were something that could be contracted by breathing the same air.

"I know very little," Nan said. "Only that a formal proposal of marriage from the young man's uncle, the head of his family, was delivered to Calais just after my stepfather left for England. Mother, very properly, replied that he must wait for an answer until her husband came home.

Then she wrote to Lord Lisle, telling him of the offer. Later, she sent me a letter, asking that I tell the king what I know of the seigneur de Bours, should His Grace question me about him."

"And what *do* you know?"

"Only that my sister was brought up in the de Bours household and that a very natural affection grew up between them."

"Marriage to a foreigner is not permitted without the king's approval."

"My stepfather intended to ask for King Henry's blessing as soon as he arrived at court, but, if you recall, he fell ill shortly afterward."

"And it slipped his mind thereafter?"

Nan ignored Denny's sarcasm. "There was no formal betrothal, only a first step toward opening negotiations."

"Certain depositions that were taken in Calais say otherwise. Your sister secretly married the Frenchman when he visited Calais on Palm Sunday last."

"How is that possible?"

"They spoke legally binding words to each other. In such cases, neither witnesses nor ceremony are required, only consummation."

"The words," Nan interrupted. "My sister admitted that she pledged herself *per verba de praesenti*? Not *per verba de futuro*?" The latter was not binding; the former was.

Denny nodded.

Nan closed her eyes to hide her distress. Mary had entered into a clandestine marriage. Ned Corbett had once asked Nan to do the same.

"She compounded her crime by trying to destroy the letters de Bours had sent her. She threw them down the jakes. My lord of Sussex's men retrieved a few fragments, enough to piece together the story. And enough to make them suspicious that more than love words were contained in those letters."

"You think *Mary* was plotting to overthrow Calais?"

"The entire situation is suspicious."

"The entire situation is ludicrous."

Denny's face remained set in grim lines. For a moment, the scratch of the clerk's quill was the only sound in the quiet room. Nan forced herself to relax her clenched hands, to breathe evenly. Panic would avail her nothing.

"Why is my mother being held?"

"Your mother and sisters and several of the waiting gentlewomen at first denied any knowledge of the plighttroth. Some changed their stories when they were questioned a second time."

"But Mother would not have known. Not if it was a secret marriage." Philippa likely had. And Frances. "Where is my brother's wife?" she blurted out, suddenly alarmed.

"Your brother went to Calais and took his wife and daughter back to England. They could not remain there. The household has been disbanded."

"Then where—?"

"Your sisters have been placed under house arrest with families in Calais. They are well treated, I assure you. Your mother is likewise confined in the residence of a gentleman of the town. She has been permitted to keep with her a waiting gentlewoman, two other servants, and a priest."

From her own household, Nan wondered, or spies appointed by the Crown?

Nan's mind raced. On top of the charge that her stepfather had known about Sir Gregory Botolph's plans, the suspicion that he'd arranged a secret alliance with a Frenchman could seal his fate, and perhaps her mother's, too. How could Mary have been so foolish? Unless there really had been something treasonous in Gabriel's letters, she had made matters far worse by destroying them.

"What now?" she asked after a long silence. "Am I to be arrested, too?"

Denny reached across the table and patted her hand. "You have done nothing wrong. You had no part in any of this. Keep your thoughts and opinions to yourself and be patient. There are other changes coming, but most will do you more good than harm."

It was excellent, if enigmatic, advice, but difficult to follow. Nan was worried about her stepfather, about her mother and sisters, and about Ned Corbett, too. And she could not help but fear for her own future. If she tried to help any of those she cared about, she might also be accused of treason.

FIVE DAYS AFTER Nan's interview with Anthony Denny, on the tenth of June, she heard of the arrest of Thomas Cromwell, Earl of Essex. No one was quite sure what he had done to incur the king's wrath, except that he had been instrumental in arranging His Grace's marriage to Anna of Cleves.

The news made Nan think of young Wat Hungerford. He had wanted to speak with her shortly before her stepfather's arrest. She wondered what he'd wanted, and what had happened to him now that both his master and his father were in the Tower. She knew Lord Hungerford's lands had been seized. Wat had no home to retreat to.

One more person to worry about, she thought, when fretting did no one any good. She was glad she had her duties as a maid of honor to keep her busy. But only two weeks later, Queen Anna and her entire household were abruptly banished from court, sent to live at Richmond Palace while the king stayed behind.

Stout yeomen hauled traveling trunks into the maidens' chamber, setting off a flurry of activity. Constance at once began to pack Nan's belongings. She had outgrown her youthful awkwardness in the last year and developed into a sturdy young woman accustomed to physical labor. She did everything from beating the dust out of her mistress's clothing to hauling water to the maids' dormitory for baths.

"I am not going to Richmond," Kate Stradling announced.

"But you must," Nan said. "All the maids of hon—"

"Not Catherine Howard. She has already left for the old dowager Duchess of Norfolk's house at Lambeth."

Nan folded a pair of sleeves to give herself something to do with her hands. As impossible as it had seemed a few months earlier, the king was going to rid himself of his wife in order to marry Mistress Howard. "We know why Catherine has abandoned Queen Anna," she said to her cousin, "but what incentive have you to stay behind? You'll have no place at court."

"My place will be with my husband."

"You've married Sir Thomas Palmer?" Lucy Somerset exclaimed in surprise. Along with every other woman in the room, her gaze fixed on Kate. Sir Thomas Palmer had been courting Kate for some time, but Nan had always suspected that her cousin thought she could do better. Sir Thomas had a goodly estate but was also fourteen years Kate's senior and had several grown children from an earlier marriage.

"I will be his wife just as soon as Thomas can obtain a special license." Kate looked well pleased with herself. At twenty-eight, she could no longer afford to be choosy, especially now that it was obvious Queen Anna was to be put aside.

"I wish you well," Nan said, embracing her cousin. But what she felt most strongly was a sense of relief. Kate knew too many of Nan's secrets.

"Everything is packed," Constance said, closing the heavy trunk lid with a thunk. The finality of the sound made Nan shiver. So much seemed uncertain. Richmond Palace was a beautiful place, but she had no desire to spend the rest of her life entombed there.

"POOR QUEEN ANNA," Cat Bassett said, fanning herself. In spite of the breeze that occasionally blew up off the Thames, Richmond Palace was stifling. "She refuses to believe that the king will annul their marriage. Lady Rutland says Her Grace is convinced there are no grounds to dissolve their union."

Nan was too hot and uncomfortable to twit her sister for quoting

Lady Rutland. The weather had been abnormally warm and dry since the beginning of June and it was now the tenth of July. Even the most accommodating of individuals felt irritable. Those with little self-control lost their tempers at the drop of a hat.

"Lady Rutland fears for the queen's life," Cat continued. "If she opposes the king's wishes—"

"She could end up like the last Queen Anne!" Nan snapped. "If she cannot see the way the wind blows, she deserves that fate."

"How can you be so hard hearted?" Cat took a handful of caraway seeds dipped in sugar from an ornate little box and nibbled them.

"I feel sorry for the woman, just as you do. But if the queen fights to hold her place, as Catherine of Aragon did when King Henry put her aside, she will be fortunate to keep her head."

"It is not her fault that neither her mother nor any of her senior ladies explained to her what constitutes the duties of a wife. She went to her marriage bed in total ignorance. She truly believed, until Lady Rochford bluntly told her otherwise, that the king had consummated their marriage simply by kissing her and spending part of the night in her bed." The king, by common report, had never been able to force himself to couple with the queen.

"There is nothing you or I can do for her," Nan said. "There is nothing we can do for anyone, not even our own kin." She had never felt so helpless. She turned away from her sister to stare out the nearest window. The view might have been soothing had the drought not turned the grass brown and withered the leaves on vines and flowers.

When Nan looked her sister's way again, Cat was calmly embroidering a sleeve with tiny rosebuds. Nan was too restless to settle. She prowled Lady Rutland's chamber, picking up various of the countess's possessions and putting them down again without registering what they were.

"Everything is Mary's fault." Nan knew the accusation was unfair as soon as she muttered the words, since Mary had nothing to do with King Henry's dislike of his queen.

"She fell in love," Cat said.

"That is no excuse for behaving like a fool. Her actions made every-thing worse. His Grace believes she knowingly destroyed evidence of treason."

"And so she did, since her betrothal was exactly that, but it was clever of her to think of throwing those love letters into the privy. They should have been lost forever. Who would have thought that the Earl of Sussex would order his men to search through the offal and pick out all the bits that could still be read?"

"Go on," Nan said irritably. She was perspiring again. She hated to sweat. "Take her side. What do you care? You will continue just as you are, in service as Lady Rutland's lapdog."

Cat refused to quarrel. "You can always return to Cousin Mary's household."

"She pretends she has forgiven me for moving out, but she will never invite me back."

"Then go to Jane Mewtas or Joan Denny."

"They only took me in to please the king. What advantage can I bring them now? And do not suggest that I return to Calais, or to France! If Queen Anna's household is dispersed, I'll have nowhere to go."

Cat kept stitching. "John and Frances have property in the West Country."

"The ends of the earth!" Nan stopped in front of Lady Rutland's looking glass. She stared at her regular features, her blue eyes, her flaw-less skin. She was pretty, but who was here to see? Her hopes of finding a wealthy nobleman to marry grew dimmer by the day.

"Nan?" Cat's voice was tentative. "Did you ever meet Sir Gregory Botolph?"

"Why?"

Cat kept her head down. "I heard a rumor. It is terrible the things people will say. Vicious, untrue things."

"What did you hear?"

"That Mother was Botolph's mistress. And that she turned traitor for his sake."

The idea was so preposterous that Nan laughed aloud. "What non-sense. I know people call him Gregory Sweet-lips, but Mother would never be taken in by honeyed words. Neither she nor our stepfather had any part in the conspiracy."

Nan was also sure Ned Corbett was innocent.

Always, just at the back of her mind, ready to leap out and squeeze her heart if she let down her guard, was her anguish at Ned's peril. She did not believe he had been involved in Botolph's scheme, but these days a careless word or a thoughtless act was enough to condemn a man.

A fearful image suddenly filled her mind: Ned hanged, drawn, and quartered—a traitor's death. She jumped, a shriek caught in her throat, when the door suddenly creaked open.

The Earl of Rutland stood in the opening, his attention on Cat. "Where is my wife?"

"With the queen, my lord. In Her Grace's presence chamber."

"Good." His gaze shifted to Nan. "What are you doing here? You should be in attendance on Her Grace, as well."

"Queen Anna prefers the company of the two young women she brought with her from Cleves, especially Gertrude. She scarce notices what the rest of us do."

"Come with me, Mistress Nan. All the queen's ladies and maids of honor must stand witness to what I have to say." Shooing Nan in front of him, he set off for the presence chamber at a brisk pace.

Nan did not argue. As the queen's lord chamberlain, Rutland was responsible for dealing with all the details of daily life in her household.

When they reached the presence chamber, Nan went to stand with Lucy Somerset, Mary Norris, Dorothy Bray, and the two maids of honor from Cleves. Sensing that something important was about to happen, Nan toyed nervously with her pomander ball.

"My lord of Rutland—you have something to say to me?" Queen Anna spoke English but it was heavily accented.

"Your Grace," Rutland said in a carrying voice, "you have been or-dered to sign your consent to the annulment of your marriage to the king." He produced a sheaf of papers and presented it to her with a flourish.

A secretary translated his words, although Nan suspected that Queen Anna understood precisely what was afoot. Her Grace took the pages, which she could not read, and stared at them for a long moment. Without warning, she burst into tears.

No one seemed to know what to do. Impatient with protocol, Nan stepped forward and offered the queen a handkerchief. For just an instant, their eyes met. The queen's conveyed gratitude, but Nan saw something else in them, as well. Calculation?

When more senior ladies took over, Nan was glad to step back. The Earl of Rutland, through his interpreter, attempted to calm the queen. The murmuring went on for some time, but in the end the earl went away without the queen's signature.

The next morning, the Earl of Rutland made another attempt to persuade the queen to end her marriage. This time he offered a much better bargain. Anna of Cleves would be allowed to remain in England. If she would agree to become the king's "sister," she would have an income of £4,000 a year. Richmond Palace and other properties would be given to her. All she had to do was admit that there had been an irregularity in the marriage—that she had been betrothed to someone else before she wed King Henry and that this precontract, although Anna herself had not, at the time, been aware of it, had been binding.

Even Nan could see gaps in the logic of this explanation, but she was not foolish enough to point them out. No one else did, either. Anna of Cleves signed the papers and freed King Henry to marry for the fifth time.

"Lord Cromwell and Lord Hungerford were executed last Wednesday," Cat Bassett told her sister on Saturday, the thirty-first day of July.

Nan was in the maid's dormitory at Richmond, once again staring out a window at the bleak landscape. The heat wave continued unabated.

There had been no rain for weeks. Nan had her partlet open at the throat and her skirts kilted up. Neither measure did much good. Sweat pooled between her breasts where her bodice shoved them up and together.

As Cat's words sank in, Nan turned to face her sister. "Were there . . . others who were executed?"

"No one we know. But on the same day, so Lord Rutland says, the king married Catherine Howard. They will not make an official announcement yet. Lady Rutland says they first plan to remain at Oatlands in Surrey for another week."

"Are more executions scheduled?" Nan asked.

"None that I've heard about, but the general pardon the king issued after Parliament adjourned specifically exempted Mother and Lord Lisle and those men from Calais who were charged with treason." Cat frowned. "And yet, the Calais men who were being held in the Fleet have been released by the lord chancellor."

Nan had not known there were Calais men confined in that London prison. "Were they accused of conspiring with Botolph?"

"No, only of heresy." She shrugged. "According to the Earl of Rutland, the lord chancellor told them they were free at His Grace's pleasure. A pity that pleasure does not extend to members of our family." She gave Nan a pointed look.

"These days His Grace's pleasure is Catherine Howard. I doubt he remembers that any other woman exists."

Long after Cat had returned to Lady Rutland's chamber, Nan stayed where she was, mulling over what her sister had said. If the king had no objection to letting some prisoners go free, even some of those who had been exempted from the general pardon, then he might not object to freeing more of them.

An audacious idea occurred to her. At first she told herself it would never work. She'd end up in prison herself if she attempted it. But she could not stop thinking about it.

She did not want Ned Corbett to die. He had done nothing worse than befriend a deceitful priest. Ned, who had been her first lover, who was the father of her child, even if he did not know Jamie existed, deserved his freedom just as much as those men in the Fleet did.

For another week, the king would not be interested in anything but Catherine Howard. And while His Grace was occupied with his new bride, he would pay no attention to what Nan Bassett did. If she was very careful and very clever, she should have just time enough to save Ned's life.

13

"My lord of Rutland," Nan said, dipping her head, "a word with you?"

His frown told her she'd caught him in the middle of some important business. "Be brief, if you will, Mistress Nan."

"The queen . . . the Lady Anna has little need of my services, my lord."

"You wish to leave her household?"

"No, my lord. I beg leave to travel to London to visit my stepfather."

"Ah. Hmmm." He tugged at his beard as he considered her request. "I suppose there is no harm in it. Did you wish to take your sister with you?"

"I would not dream of depriving Lady Rutland of Cat's company. My maid will accompany me. I will not be away long. A week at the most."

One of Rutland's secretaries approached carrying several letters. Rutland ignored him. "Will you make the journey by water or by road?"

Nan had brought the horse the king had given her to Richmond. "I will ride, with Constance on a pillion behind me."

"My lord," murmured the secretary, "it is a matter of some urgency."

Even rushed, Rutland was conscientious. "You may leave in the morning, but I will send two of my own men with you. They will escort you to my house in Shoreditch. You will reside there during your visit." It was less an invitation than a condition. "There is plague in London again this summer. The number of deaths there reached nearly three hundred last week. Once you pass through Bishopsgate, ride straight to the Tower. Keep your pomander ball to your nose at all times to avoid breathing in the contagion."

Nan was not much concerned about the plague. There were outbreaks every summer, particularly in heavily populated areas like London. That was why the court usually spent the hottest months of the year in the countryside. She thanked the earl effusively and was at Rutland House by evening the following day.

The next morning, Nan explored the premises. It did not take her long to discover a way to leave without being seen by the small staff left behind by the earl and countess. A short time later, Nan's old friend the megrim provided her with an excuse to retire to her bedchamber. She was out again within an hour.

They walked to the Tower of London, where Nan approached one of the warders, unmistakable in the king's livery, and demanded to be taken to her stepfather. As she'd expected, she was escorted instead to the constable of the Tower. Or rather, to his lodgings, where Lady Kingston greeted her and offered her a choice of barley water or ale while they waited for a servant to fetch Sir William.

"Lord Lisle is in excellent health," Lady Kingston said.

"I am relieved to hear it, but I wish to see for myself that he is well and has everything he needs."

"I assure you, he lacks for nothing. High-born prisoners' expenses are paid out of their confiscated estates. He has two servants, a comfortable apartment in the Bell Tower, and a goodly supply of coals, wood, and candles."

Nan suppressed a smile at Lady Kingston's defensive attitude. She kept her expression somber and lowered her voice. "That is all very well, but others who were once lodged here in similar comfort have since been executed." She did not have to name them. Lady Kingston had known the Marquis of Exeter and Lord Montagu and their friends from her days at court, and Thomas Cromwell, too.

The two women politely exchanged news of mutual acquaintances until Sir William appeared. Already briefed, he offered to escort Nan to Lord Lisle's rooms himself.

To reach the Bell Tower, which stood sixty feet high and housed a bell in the wooden turret at its summit, they had to pass through the lord lieutenant's lodgings. These were in the process of being rebuilt. The noise and confusion of the construction project was so great that Nan was surprised her stepfather had not slipped away under its cover. She understood why he had not when she saw the two burly guards posted just outside the door to his rooms. Sir William left Nan there, promising to return for her in an hour.

Lord Lisle's appearance filled Nan with dismay. He had lost weight and more than ever looked his age.

"My dear," he said when he'd kissed her, "it is good to see you. But how does your mother fare? They will not let me write to her."

"The same restriction must apply to her," Nan said, "for I've heard nothing from her directly. But I am certain she is well treated. And neither of you has been put on trial. That has to be a good sign."

Lord Lisle's shoulders slumped. "Reason for optimism? Ah, Nan, I wish I could believe it."

"Is there anything you need, my lord?"

"Aside from the king's pardon?" He managed a small smile.

"Aside from that." As a last resort, she would plead with His Grace for her stepfather's life. She would ask for a pardon for him and for the release of her family in Calais. But, for the moment, all her kin seemed safe enough. Ned Corbett was another matter.

"I have creature comforts," Lord Lisle said. "And I am allowed to walk on the leads for exercise. In time, I may be granted what they call 'the liberty of the Tower'—the freedom to wander anywhere in the precinct."

Nan spent the full hour with her stepfather. By the time Sir William came for her, she knew considerably more about daily life in the Tower of London. She also knew that Ned, as a gentleman, had a cell to himself, and that his manservant, Browne, had been allowed to move in with him to see to his needs. The plan she'd conceived at Richmond could work. Its success or failure now depended upon the character of the constable.

The bell in the Bell Tower began to ring as she and Sir William crossed Tower Green. "That is the signal that it is five o'clock and time for all the gates to be shut and locked for the night," he said. "All prisoners are required to withdraw into their chambers. Have you a place to stay in London?"

"I thought perhaps an inn . . ."

The rules of hospitality obligated Sir William to invite her to spend the night in his lodgings. Over supper, Nan flattered her host by asking questions about his duties and listening carefully to his answers. But she waited until Lady Kingston excused herself to use the privy to broach the subject of the men who had been released from prison following Lord Cromwell's death.

"I have heard that His Grace took pity on them, even though they had been exempted from the general pardon."

Sir William discarded a well-gnawed chicken bone. Relaxed by good food and wine and relishing the attention of a pretty maid of honor, he had no qualms about trying to impress her with his special knowledge of the matter. "Do you want to know a secret?"

Nan sent him an eager look. "About those men from Calais?"

The constable nodded. "The king did not order their release. The lord chancellor took it upon himself to let them go. They were misguided in matters of religion, but not guilty of doing any real harm."

"And there was no trouble over it?" Sir William's attitude was unexpected but most welcome—if he meant what he said. Nan chewed and swallowed but had no idea what she was eating.

Sir William chuckled. "The king was, and is, preoccupied."

"Yes. He is. I wonder . . . if you had someone in your charge who had done no real harm, might you be inclined to extend the same mercy to him?"

A look of alarm raced across his face. "I cannot free your stepfather. His absence would be noticed."

"I can see that. He is too important."

"Yes. A nobleman. I could no more let him go free than I could release the old Countess of Salisbury."

Nan had forgotten that Lord Montagu's mother was still a prisoner in the Tower. She'd been charged with treason for nothing more than corresponding with another of her sons. Unfortunately for her, that son was Reginald, Cardinal Pole.

Nan bit delicately into a piece of manchet bread. "What if the prisoner were someone of no importance?"

He chuckled indulgently. Clearly, he did not think she was seriously proposing that he do such a thing. "I suppose it would depend upon the crime, and upon the man."

"And whether anyone would notice he was gone?"

"Indeed."

Nan hesitated. There would be no going back once she mentioned Ned's name. On the other hand, what she'd already said was probably enough to condemn her, even if the constable did think she was jesting.

"Sir William, I am in earnest. If you truly believe a man innocent, and if no one would notice he'd gone, then surely—"

"Who would you have me release?" His voice hardened but he made no move to call the guards.

At the last moment, Nan lost her nerve. "There is a servant. A man named Browne. He is unimportant, save to my tiring maid. Constance has an attachment to the fellow."

"Ned Corbett's man?"

"Yes. I know Browne was exempted from the king's pardon, but so were those men in the Fleet." Nan took a deep breath and added, "So was Master Corbett himself." Her heart was in her throat but she managed a little trill of laughter. "He is not very important, either."

Sir William ran a finger under his collar, as if it suddenly felt too tight. "I agree that neither man deserves to die. I've read their depositions. Corbett did nothing more than assist a friend, but that friend turned out to be a foul traitor."

"So he knew nothing of the plot to overthrow Calais?"

"So he says, but that will not save him. He'll be executed along with the rest of the conspirators."

Except for Sir Gregory Botolph, Nan thought bitterly. The king's men had found no trace of him. Aloud, but softly, she said, "Corbett and Browne need not die. You could save them."

"Not without considerable risk to myself." He picked another piece of chicken off the platter.

With Lady Kingston likely to return at any moment, Nan proceeded with the plan she'd conceived before leaving Richmond Palace. It might have a better chance of success than she'd originally thought, given Sir William's avowed sympathy for Ned.

"Would clear title to Painswick Manor make the risk more bearable?"

Sir William froze with a chicken leg halfway to his mouth. "Painswick? I already own it. I purchased the property from Lord Cromwell after he obtained it from your mother and stepfather. True, the transaction was only half complete at the time of Cromwell's arrest, and his lands were forfeit to the Crown, but I have sued out a special grant. I expect to have clear title to the property any day now."

"Painswick," Nan said, telling the bold lie without a flicker of hesitation, "was not my mother's to sell. It belongs to my brother John

Bassett, who is not attainted and is therefore free to challenge your ownership."

"But Painswick cost me fourteen hundred pounds."

Nan said nothing for several minutes, letting Sir William jump to the conclusion that he would never get his money back if John pressed his claim and won.

"Sir William," Nan said softly when she thought he'd stewed long enough, "Ned Corbett and my brother are great friends. If Corbett and his man Browne are released, John will leave matters as they are with regard to Painswick."

Nan's fate, as well as Ned's, hung in the balance while Sir William considered what she'd said. She thanked God he was already inclined to help, that he'd approved of the lord chancellor's action at the Fleet. She only hoped that her threat—or perhaps it was a bribe—would be enough to convince him to do as she asked.

At the sound of approaching footsteps, the constable's eyes narrowed. Had he seen through her fabrication? Was he about to arrest her?

"Have a boat waiting in the shallows of St. Katherine's Dock at midnight tomorrow."

Nan had only enough time to nod before Lady Kingston entered the room.

NAN AND CONSTANCE left the Tower early the next morning.

"Do you think he will let them go?" Constance's anxiety echoed Nan's.

"I pray he will, but it is up to us to procure a small boat."

"I can steal one," Constance offered as they fought their way through the usual crowds that clogged London's streets.

"Can you also steal a ship bound for foreign parts? They will need to leave England as soon as possible. Otherwise, they could be arrested again, and us along with them."

Ned was too well known among Lord Lisle's acquaintances. All it would take would be for one of them to see him and there would be an inquiry into his release from the Tower. Even if Ned tried to shield her, Nan had no illusions about Sir William Kingston. He'd throw her to the wolves to save himself.

"This is Master Husee's house," Constance said in surprise when Nan stopped before the familiar edifice.

"It is," Nan agreed, and marched up to the door.

Ten minutes later, she was alone with John Husee in his counting house, what had once been a parlor. "I left Lord Lisle's employ some time ago," he reminded her.

"Why?"

"To serve other clients in the same manner but for better profit. I have turned part of this house into business premises."

"Did you know of Botolph's plot? Is that why you abandoned my stepfather?"

Husee could not meet her eyes. "I was uneasy about the fellow," he admitted, "and I was . . . advised to look elsewhere for employment."

Nan's eyebrows shot up in astonishment. "Someone *warned* you? Who?"

"I . . . I would rather not say."

Nan leaned across Husee's worktable, staring at him until he looked up. "I did not come here to cause you trouble, Master Husee. But I could. If you had suspicions of Sir Gregory Botolph, it was remiss of you not to warn Lord Lisle."

Husee sent her a rueful look. "An unfortunate oversight. Is there some small way I can make it up to you, Mistress Nan?"

"You can arrange passage for two men on a ship bound for the Continent. It should sail on tomorrow's tide."

"Do these men have passports to travel out of England?"

"Passports? I did not need one when I left England for Calais."

"That is because you were a member of the lord deputy's family. Everyone else requires the proper documents to travel abroad."

Dismayed, Nan soldiered on. "How . . . who issues such papers?"

"Any number of people." Husee regarded her steadily for a long moment. His fingers drummed on the tabletop in front of him. "I might be able to obtain something that will do, without going through the usual channels, but it will be expensive."

Forged documents would be better than nothing. Nan tugged off her glove and removed the ruby ring from her finger. "The king himself gave me this. I do not know its value, but it should be worth enough to cover your expenses."

By the way Husee's eyes widened, Nan guessed the ring would sell for enough to leave him with a profit. "It will do. I need your friends' names."

Nan thought quickly. "John Browne." His name was too common to present any problems, but there was no way Ned could travel as himself. "And Martin Rogers." She chose the alias on the spur of the moment, but it was a good, steady, English name.

"Where can I find you when I have made the arrangements?"

"I will wait here."

Husee looked as if he wanted to object. Then he opened his hand and took another look at the ruby. "I will return in a few hours. Make yourself at home."

NED CORBETT'S CELL was in the Beauchamp Tower on the western curtain wall. Three floors high with a lead roof, brick floors, and whitewashed walls, it was used to hold prisoners of middling status who had been accused of treason. There were seven men currently lodged on the middle floor.

The conditions of Ned's captivity had improved since he'd first been brought to the Tower. After he'd been allowed to send to the London goldsmith who held his money for him, he had paid to be unshackled and for a camp bed, bedding, candles, food, and drink. There had been no need to buy firewood or coals for a brazier. This was the hottest summer anyone could remember and it was warm, if damp, even within the thick stone walls of the Tower.

He was rousted from his bed in the middle of the night when the door to his cell was suddenly flung open. A man entered, carrying a lantern. It took Ned a moment to recognize him as the constable of the Tower.

On his pallet on the floor, John Browne grunted and sat up. He blinked warily at Sir William Kingston, then looked to his employer for guidance.

Kingston cleared his throat. "Get up, dress, gather your belongings, and come with me. You are both to be released at the king's pleasure."

Ned opened his mouth, then closed it again, sensing that there was something peculiar about this turn of events but reluctant to miss a chance at freedom. The feeling of wrongness increased when he stepped out of the cell. There were no guards in sight, nor did he see any as Kingston led them down the stairs and out of the Beauchamp Tower. As soon as they were through the outer door, Kingston closed the lantern and relied on the moon and the light from nearby buildings to guide them.

They followed the wall south toward the lord lieutenant's lodgings. Ned recognized that building as the place where he had been questioned when he was first brought to the Tower. The kitchens there provided food for all the prisoners. Those with sufficient rank were sometimes invited to dine with Sir Edward Walsingham, the lord lieutenant. A few were even lodged in his house.

Did Walsingham know what Kingston was up to? When the constable continued to keep to the shadows, Ned decided he did not. Kingston was not releasing them. He was helping them escape.

A sense of elation filled him. He'd had no real hope of a pardon. He had nothing to lose by attempting an escape. His heart pounded with anticipation, not fear, as they went through the Byward Arch and passed the large, semicircular barbican where the royal menagerie was kept. Ned remembered visiting it years before to view four lions and two leopards in wooden cages.

Kingston proceeded along a path that looped around the Middle Tower and led to a gate. It was closed and locked and guarded by two warders, but to one side there was a little wicket. As soon as the guards were looking the other way, Kingston ushered Ned and Browne through.

Ned inhaled a deep breath of salty, sewage-filled Thames air. Freedom!

But they were still not safe. The path wound back, taking them close under the outer wall. Should anyone chance to look out a window, they'd be plainly visible in the moonlight.

They continued on until Kingston stopped and pointed. "There the moat is so narrow and the water level so low that you can climb down the bank and cross on foot. Continue on to St. Katherine's Dock."

By the time Ned and Browne reached the other side, Kingston had disappeared back inside the fortress.

"I'll look for a boat," Browne said.

"Here," a soft voice called.

Ned stood stock still. Impossible! But that had sounded like—"Nan?"

"Hurry!"

It *was* Nan. She was one of two cloaked and hooded figures waiting for them in a little rowing boat. In haste, he and Browne lowered themselves into the small craft. Browne gave a strangled cry when he recognized the other person as Constance, Nan's maid.

Suddenly Ned felt like laughing. He might have, and hauled Nan into his arms and kissed her soundly, too, but she held a finger to her lips, reminding him that they were not yet out of danger.

"Take the oars from Constance," Nan whispered to Browne, "and row downriver. Hurry." She shifted on the passenger seat to make room for Ned.

She kept her eyes on the wharf as they pulled away. Ned followed her gaze. He saw two cranes, used to lift goods from boats, but not a single sign of man nor beast between Petty Wales and St. Katherine's. No one pursued them. No one even knew they were gone.

"How did you manage it?" he whispered.

"Luck, lies, a few threats, and a little judicious bribery." She laughed softly.

Browne grunted as he bent his back to the oars. Downriver was against the tide. "How far, mistress?"

"Put in on the opposite shore," Ned said. "We can walk back to the Red Lion in Southwark."

"No." Nan grabbed his arm and gestured for Browne to row on. "If you are recognized, you will be taken back to the Tower."

"I thought we'd been pardoned," Browne said.

"Not quite. You will have to leave the country."

"Exile?" Ned's jubilant mood evaporated.

"Would you rather be dead?" Nan leaned toward Browne, pointing to a small merchant ship anchored just ahead. "There. You'll sail as soon as the tide turns. Your passage to the Low Countries has been paid."

"And once we arrive? We have no money. No passports. No friends." Ned gave a bitter laugh. "Better to put us ashore in Southwark and let us hide out in one of the brothels."

Nan and Constance stared at him. Browne stopped rowing.

"I can take myself off to Winchester. Or York. Someplace where no one knows me. I'll still have no money or gainful employment, but at least I will not need a passport."

Nan pressed a purse made of leather into his hands. He heard the clink of coins. "I am sorry I could not manage more, but there is nearly five pounds here. And I have also procured these." She produced two passports from the folds of her cloak.

"How—?"

She pressed her fingers to his lips. "Do not ask questions. Go to the Low Countries and do not look back. That passport gives you a new name. Use it to build a new life for yourself."

Browne resumed rowing and brought them alongside the ship. Crewmen, expecting them, threw a rope ladder over the side. After a momentary hesitation, Browne climbed aboard.

Ned seized Nan's hand. "Come with me. We would not have much, God knows, but all I have I will share with you."

She ducked her head so that he could not have read her expression even if there had been enough light, but a tiny, choked sob reached him. "I cannot."

"Why not? With your stepfather under arrest, you cannot expect to make a great marriage. Have you even retained your post at court?"

Nan jerked her hand free. "I have lost nothing, and I will not, so long as you leave now. If you care for me at all, Ned Corbett, then go."

"Nan—"

"I must return to Queen Anna. To do otherwise will ruin everything. We will be pursued. Captured. Imprisoned. All of us. I cannot go with you."

"No," Ned said bitterly. "You do not *want* to." She was unwilling to give up her post as a maid of honor. He should have known better than to think that, just because she'd risked so much to save his life, she would ever put his desires above her own.

He reached for the rope ladder and began to climb. From the deck of the ship, he looked back. Constance was already rowing away. The incoming tide carried the small boat swiftly out of sight.

CONSTANCE STARTED TO cry as soon as she and Nan abandoned the rowing boat they'd stolen and set off on foot. Her tears continued to flow all the way back to Rutland House. By the time they reached the small door hidden in the garden wall, racking sobs made Constance's entire body shudder.

"Stop that noise at once," Nan hissed at Constance.

The maid sniffed, gulped, and finally subsided, although anyone who noticed her puffy eyes and reddened nose would know she had been weeping.

"Control yourself," Nan warned.

"If John Browne had asked me to go with him," Constance said in a broken whisper, "I'd have been on that ship in a flash."

Nan pretended not to have heard. For just an instant, she *had* been tempted to accept Ned's invitation, but aside from the reasons she'd given him, there was one more thing keeping her in England. Jamie was here. She did not see him often, but she was loath to put even more dis-tance between them.

Nan slipped back into Rutland House unseen, and into her chamber. "To bed, Constance. A few hours of sleep, and then we will pay a visit to Cheapside."

They set out on foot at midmorning. Nan had intended all along to visit her son on this trip to London . . . if she managed to avoid arrest. He'd have grown since she'd last seen him. She hoped she would recog-nize him.

Her anticipation built as they neared Cheapside. Nan stopped to buy a poppet from a street vendor to take as a gift. She clutched it tighter when Master Carver's shop came in sight, an excited smile on her face. It was only when she reached the door that she realized the establishment was closed. All the doors and windows were boarded up and an air of neglect hung over the building like a pall.

A cold dread began in the pit of her stomach and traveled throughout Nan's body. She could feel the heat leach from her face. Something was terribly wrong.

Constance caught Nan's arm to support her. "I will ask the neighbors where Master Carver has gone."

Nan continued to stare at the empty shop, fighting to stave off the most obvious answer. But once Constance returned, there was no escape.

"It was the plague." Nan heard her maidservant's words through a buzzing in her ears. "The whole family died of it."

In the back of her mind, Lord Rutland's matter-of-fact voice echoed, reporting almost three hundred plague deaths in London the previous week.

She did not faint, but her body shut down. Unable to bear thinking, she blanked out everything. Afterward, Nan was never sure how Con-stance got her away from the silversmith's shop. By the time she came back to herself and into the worst anguish she had ever known, they had returned to Shoreditch.

Devastated by the loss of her son, guilt ridden because she had not visited him more often, tormented by the thought that if she had married Ned and kept the boy, he might still be alive, Nan was barely aware of where she was or what those around her were doing.

Constance took her back to Richmond, back to the maids' dormitory. Nan went through the motions of a normal life, but for a long time, nothing seemed real.

A small kernel of self-preservation kept Nan functioning day after day. She did not cry for all she had lost except late at night, when she was safely closed in behind the bed curtains. Even then, she was careful not to let any sound escape. She grieved in silence, despaired in solitude.

THE DAYS AT Richmond passed with such sameness that Nan scarcely noticed them slipping by. She felt only half alive, and took refuge in sleep whenever she could. She knew that Constance looked out for her and was grateful, but nothing shook her out of the darkness until the day the king paid a surprise visit.

"Why is His Grace here?" Nan whispered to Dorothy Bray. And where was his new bride?

The other maid of honor, wide eyed and tense, only shook her head. Her nervousness communicated itself to Nan—the first real emotion she'd felt in days. Hands twisted together, she waited for His Grace to enter the presence chamber of Anna of Cleves, now officially his "sister."

The former queen received King Henry with polite affection. He kissed her cheek and presented her with a small gift. When they stepped aside to speak together in private, Anthony Denny approached Nan.

"Do you wish to remain here or join Queen Catherine's household?" he asked after they'd exchanged pleasantries.

"I prefer to wait on the queen." The words came out without hesitation. More than anything, Nan wanted the distraction of life at court.

"Then make preparations to leave at once for Windsor Castle. In a little more than a week, the king and queen will leave there to go on progress through Oxfordshire."

Denny started to move on to Dorothy Bray, then turned back. "You may not have heard. The men who conspired with Sir Gregory Botolph to betray Calais were executed at Tyburn two days ago. Not your step-father," he hastened to add when she swayed. "I mean Clement Philpott and several others whose names I do not recall."

With an effort, Nan regained her poise. "So should all traitors die," she murmured.

And so Ned would have, if she had not acted when she did. She waited for Denny to mention the disappearance of two of the conspirators, but he said nothing more. Their absence on the scaffold had apparently gone unnoticed. Nan wished she could be sure, but she dared not risk reminding Anthony Denny or anyone else that Ned Corbett had once been a prisoner in the Tower of London.

The King is so amorous of her that he cannot treat her well enough, and caresses her more than he did the others. The new Queen is a lady of moderate beauty but superlative grace. In stature she is small and slender. Her countenance is very delightful, of which the King is greatly enamored, and he knows not how to make sufficient demonstrations of his affection for her.

—Charles de Marillac, French ambassador to England, to the king of France,
29 August 1540

14

Cat swept into the maidens' chamber the next morning as Nan was packing. She was so agitated that she could barely speak. "So, you are leaving."

Nan stared at her sister. "What ails you, Cat? You are remarkably flushed."

"I am to have a new post. As maid of honor."

"To Queen Catherine?" Nan sounded surprised. "I knew there were two vacancies. Dorothy, Lucy, Mary, and I are leaving Anna of Cleves to go to the new queen, but her two foreign-born maids will remain here at Richmond." She returned a pair of silver tweezers, used to pluck her eyebrows, to a small embroidered case and slipped it into a side pocket of her trunk.

"I am to take *your* place, sister dear. I will stay here and wait upon the princess of Cleves. Should I be grateful, do you suppose?"

"I have little to do with deciding who goes where," Nan protested. A small, jeweled box went into the trunk next. Cat knew it contained lozenges flavored with licorice. She preferred cinnamon herself.

"The king asked for you, I warrant."

"The king is entirely satisfied with his new wife."

Cat snorted. "I wonder how long that will last."

"Hush, Cat. It is treason to disparage Catherine Howard's character now that she has married the king."

Cat's gaze sharpened. "What do you know?"

"Nothing. I thought you—" Nan smiled and shook her head. "Never mind. The important thing is that you are to be a maid of honor to a royal lady. And yes, you should be grateful. Anna of Cleves is a kind and decent woman who will treat you well. Help her with her English and she will be beholden to you."

"But powerless to grant favors," Cat pointed out. "You are the one who will be close to the king. Do you mean to use your influence to help Mother and our sisters?" That was why Cat was so upset. She had counted on being at court herself, with Lady Rutland, able to use what little favor she'd found with the earl and countess to advance her family's cause.

"I will if I can, but you know how cautious one has to be with the king. I must choose my time with care."

"They are prisoners, Nan. Locked up in Calais. They do not even have the comfort of each other's company."

"How do you know they are still separated? I have heard no details since shortly after their arrest."

"Frances wrote to me," Cat said. "She gave me the names of the citizens of Calais charged with keeping Mother and Philippa and Mary."

"A pity Mary did not just elope with Gabriel," Nan grumbled.

"Matters would have been no worse and at least one of us would have been happy."

Nan continued packing but, to Cat's surprise, there were tears in her eyes. Cat frowned. Nan had been in a strange frame of mind for weeks. Only three days earlier, she'd walked right past Cat in the garden without seeing her.

"Nan—"

"Oh, just leave me be! I will do what I can for Mother and our sisters. I will!"

One glance at the wild look in her sister's eyes had Cat backing rapidly away from her. She'd seen that expression before—on their mother's face. It would do no good to talk to her now, and tomorrow she would be gone. Dissatisfied, but with no idea what else she could do, Cat went away.

NAN THREW HERSELF into the pleasures of life at court. With each passing day, more time elapsed between thoughts of Ned or Jamie or her stepfather or her mother or her sisters. The long journeys between houses on the royal progress were difficult to endure, but even on the road there was constant chatter about clothes and other trivialities to distract her. Once the progress reached a destination, another round of entertainments began. When Nan filled every waking hour with frivolity, she could almost forget how much she'd lost.

The new queen's household was very different from those of her predecessors. Unlike Jane, Catherine was not heavily pregnant or dying. Unlike Anna, she knew how to please her husband . . . and herself. The court had a frenzied quality, as if the new queen sought to live every moment to the fullest. As for the king, he was plainly smitten with his bride. He was at her side every moment he could manage, touching her upon the least provocation.

Face flushed, spirits artificially high, Nan spun round the dance floor with Sir Edmund Knyvett as her partner. He had been one of her admirers for a long time, but now, since he was one of the new queen's cousins, he was high in the king's favor. What a great pity that he already had a wife!

Sir Edmund caught Nan by the waist and lifted her. He was an excellent dancer. They moved easily in the intricate pattern of steps. When they touched hands and walked together before moving apart again, they were able to exchange a few words.

"I vow, Mistress Bassett," he declared, placing his hand over his heart, "you are the most beautiful woman at court."

"Excepting only the queen," she reminded him with a grin.

He had a wonderful laugh. In truth, he was a most appealing gentleman, dark haired and blue eyed. She guessed his age at thirty or so, but he regularly engaged in jousting and other sports and had a muscular build to show for it.

"Will you come and watch me shoot tomorrow?" he asked when the music ended.

"Gladly, Sir Edmund. I will even wager that you best all comers."

And so, in the morning, on a bright, early September day, Nan made her way to the archery range where gentlemen of the court practiced with the longbow. The butts, tall mounds surmounted by a target, were set up at one end of the field while the shooters ranged themselves at the other. Nan recognized all of the competitors, gentlemen of the court and knights like Sir Edmund himself.

She settled herself on a little knoll, seated on the blanket Constance had carried there for her, and prepared to be entertained. Constance sat at the very edge of the blanket, tailor fashion, her needlework in her lap. Several gentlewomen and ladies also came to watch the contest, but none of them joined Nan. She did not expect them to. So long as Lord Lisle remained in the Tower, the taint of treason also clung to her. She tried not to think about that.

The air was so balmy, the match so uneventful, that Nan was soon struggling to stay awake. She rearranged the pillows Constance had insisted on bringing to support her back and let her eyes drift closed.

Men's voices near at hand brought Nan out of a doze. She peered through her lowered lids and saw two of the king's yeomen of the guard walking by. Her eyes popped open when she heard what they were saying.

Sir William Kingston dead? A giddy sense of relief swept over her, quickly followed by a wave of guilt. She had not wished Sir William harm, but so long as he had been constable of the Tower, there had been a chance that her involvement in Ned Corbett's escape would come to light.

Her feeling of euphoria lasted through the end of the competition. Sir Edmund, having triumphed over the competition, was in high good humor when he joined her on her blanket.

"I trust you won a goodly sum with your wager, Nan. I vow I have never shot so well as I did knowing you were watching."

"Only a modest sum." She did not have much money with which to gamble.

"We both deserve a treat."

She tilted her head inquiringly, having no notion what he had in mind.

Sir Edmund took her hand in his. "Lie with me, my sweet. Be my love. I have desired you ever since I first saw you."

Nan blinked at him in confusion. "But . . . but you already have a wife!"

"I do not have a mistress." He leaned in, intending to kiss her.

Nan flung herself backward across the blanket, nearly bowling Constance over in her haste.

Sir Edmund rocked back on his heels, a broad grin on his handsome face. "Nan, Nan, I mean you no disrespect, but it is not as if you have any hope of an honorable marriage."

Scrambling to her feet, she glared at him. "I have every right to expect precisely that!"

He had the nerve to laugh. "Who is it you think will wed you? You are a traitor's daughter!"

"Stepdaughter! And Lord Lisle is no traitor."

"I was speaking of *Lady* Lisle."

"My mother did nothing wrong."

"Then why is she still confined in Calais?" With a sound of disgust, Sir Edmund levered himself off the blanket and stalked off.

As Nan watched him go, her hands began to tremble. The brutal truth was that he was right. She had no hope now of catching a wealthy and noble husband. Not even a mere gentleman, let alone a knight or a nobleman, would wish to be burdened with a wife whose mother and stepfather were in disgrace. She had little chance of making any marriage at all until the king pardoned Lord and Lady Lisle.

Soon, she decided. Soon she would force herself to speak to the king. But not yet. She could not compete with Catherine Howard and did not want to incur the new queen's jealousy. She would have to wait until the king was less besotted with his bride, more amenable to a request from someone else.

Nan gestured for Constance to gather up the blanket and pillows and began the long walk past the courtiers who had witnessed her exchange with Sir Edmund. Head high, she ignored the whispers of speculation. She was still a maid of honor to the queen, still at court. She was young and pretty and she had her whole life ahead of her. Her situation would improve. It had to.

WITH THE KING and queen so often in each other's company, the members of their households were encouraged to mingle. At Ampthill, in Bedfordshire, where they were to spend a fortnight on progress, from mid- to late September, their numbers were swelled by members of the local gentry.

Nan was watching several grooms of the king's privy chamber play at Hazard when one of them, Tom Culpepper, suddenly slanted his sparkling green eyes her way. "Have you noticed that you have an admirer?" he asked.

"Do I?" She thought at first that he was referring to himself. Culpepper was as much a nobody as Nan was, but he was pleasant company and with his fair hair and those beautiful eyes he was also one of the most at-tractive young men at court. King Henry was especially fond of him, but that was because Tom had a gentle touch when it came to dressing the ulcer on the king's leg.

Tom jerked his head to the left, indicating a young man who stood in front of a tapestry. The fellow was staring at them with an intensity that surprised Nan. No—he was staring at her.

She could not see his face clearly at this distance, but he was tall and broad shouldered, with well-formed legs. She did admire an attrac-tive physique. His clothes seemed very plain for court dress, but by his bearing he was a gentleman. She could not help but be flattered that he seemed to be fascinated by her. But she also found his intense interest a trifle disconcerting.

"Who is he?" she asked.

Tom did not answer. It was his turn to throw the two ivory dice. He kept throwing until he got a "main," any number between five and nine. In this case, it was a six. On the next roll of the dice, he'd need either a six or an eleven—a "nick"—to win. If he threw a two, a three, or a twelve, it would be the next player's turn.

Tom muttered darkly as a four came up, a "mark," as any number but two, three, six, eleven, or twelve was called. This obliged him to throw again until he rolled either another mark, for the win, or another main, which would now mean he'd lost. Nan waited impatiently, hoping for the main, and hid a smile when he rolled a six. With ill grace, Tom passed the dice to the player on his left.

"Who is he?" Nan repeated, gesturing toward the young man.

"Wat."

"I said who—"

"Not what, Wat. That's Wat Hungerford." Tom grinned at the play on words.

"Oh." She remembered him then. In the many months since she'd last seen him, he had gone from boy to man, at least in size. Although he could be no older than sixteen, he stood a head taller than anyone around him. Because he was so pleasing to the eye, Nan stole another glance at him as the game of Hazard continued. He was still watching her. For the first time since she'd sent Ned Corbett away, Nan felt the telltale flutter in her belly that signaled true physical attraction. The sensation had been notably absent during her flirtation with Sir Edmund Knyvett.

Nan went back to watching the game, but she was aware of the young man's gaze upon her. A few minutes later, she felt a touch at her elbow. Wat Hungerford stood beside her.

"A word with you, Mistress Bassett?" His voice was deep, making it difficult to remember that he was still a boy.

"We might walk awhile. It is very warm in here. I would not mind a breath of air."

The gardens at Ampthill featured low brick walls along the alley paths, secluded arbors, and turf-covered benches, as well as fragrant flowers. When they were well away from anyone who might overhear, Wat turned Nan to face him and, in almost defiant tones, blurted out the reason he'd been watching her: "I have admired you for many years, Mistress Bassett. You are the most beautiful of all the maids of honor."

Nan hid her astonishment. "*Many* years?"

"I attended Prince Edward's christening. Even then, I thought you were the most beautiful girl I'd ever seen."

Nan paused by a rosebush and bent to smell the flower. She loved roses, finding their scent both sweet and calming.

She was flattered by the young man's interest, but she knew better than to encourage him. Were he still Lord Hungerford's heir, it might have been possible to discount his youth, but he was the son of an attainted nobleman, stripped of lands and title and then executed. He had likely come to court to beg the king to restore some of the Hungerford inheritance. She doubted he'd have any success. His Grace disliked letting go of anything once it became his. And that meant, Nan knew, that she could not allow herself to consider Wat Hungerford as a potential suitor any more than she could have accepted Ned Corbett as a husband.

When she glanced up from the roses, their eyes met. "I would ask for your hand if I could. It should not matter that I am a few years younger than you are."

Nan did not doubt his sincerity, but what he wanted was impossible. She chose her words carefully, unwilling to hurt his feelings more than she had to. She was careful not to touch him. She told herself that he really was very sweet, in an adoring-puppy sort of way, and that it was only because he smelled most enticingly of mint that she felt the tug of physical attraction.

"Neither your desires nor mine count for anything, not when you are not old enough to wed without permission." Upon his father's execution, he'd have become a ward of the Crown. Either the king, or some person who had purchased Wat's wardship, had the responsibility for arranging his marriage. Until he was of full age, at twenty-one, he could not make that decision for himself.

Wat caught her hand in a surprisingly firm grip. Her fingers tingled in reaction. "We have much in common, Mistress Bassett. The king's justice has stolen our prospects. But together—"

"Our situations are very different," she protested, pulling free. There were other couples strolling in the garden, though at a distance. She began to walk and he came with her. "My stepfather did nothing wrong."

"While mine was guilty of a great variety of sins." Wat's words were clipped and bitter.

Nan's heart went out to him. Lord Hungerford had been found guilty of procuring the services of a witch to determine how long the king would live and of performing unnatural acts with gentlemen of his household. The latter crime was spoken of only in whispers.

"His own wife testified against him," Wat said. "My stepmother had cause. Father kept her locked up in Farleigh Castle for years."

"His sins are not yours, Wat." They stopped by an arbor, temporarily shielded from prying eyes.

"But I am made to suffer for them, all the same." He gave her a startlingly mature look. "You'd marry me if I still owned Farleigh Castle. I wish I could show it to you. There are high hills all around, and a broad, deep-running stream hard by the castle wall. My father kept seventy head of deer in the park and—"

"There is no sense in pining for what is lost," Nan interrupted. How well she had learned that lesson!

He was silent for a moment. Then, his expression bleak, he said, "I did try to warn you—before your stepfather's arrest."

Nan felt herself blanch. "Warn me of what?" She remembered that he had once tried to speak with her, and that she'd sent him away.

"My master's scheme to replace Lord Lisle with a man of his own choosing."

Shaken, Nan sat on the soft turf covering the nearest garden bench. After a slight hesitation, Wat settled in beside her.

"You will remember that I was in service to Lord Cromwell."

Nan nodded. Later Cromwell had briefly been Earl of Essex, but most people still referred to him by his more familiar title.

"As you must know from your own experience, those who wait on their betters sometimes become so much a part of the background that they go entirely unnoticed, like a piece of furniture. Often they overhear and observe much more than their masters realize. When the plot to overthrow Calais in herring time came to light, I saw how Lord Cromwell reacted. It came as no surprise to him. And when he heard of your stepfather's arrest, he was jubilant."

"As you say, he wanted to replace Lord Lisle with his own man."

"It was more than that." Wat's voice was low and intense. Nan leaned closer, so as not to miss a word. "Long before Sir Gregory Botolph went to Calais, he met in secret with Lord Cromwell. I heard Cromwell coerce the priest into doing his bidding. I heard him say Lord Lisle's name. Then, later, just before his own arrest, Lord Cromwell took steps to thwart the search for Sir Gregory." Wat gripped both of Nan's hands tightly. His eyes bored into hers. "Thomas Cromwell arranged for Botolph to enter your stepfather's employ. He planned it all. I do not believe there was ever any real plot to overthrow Calais, only one to make Lord Lisle look guilty of betraying England."

Nan could hardly breathe. "If this is true, we must go to the king and tell him everything. He'll free—"

"There is no proof." Wat held her in place on the bench when she tried to rise. "If there had been, I'd have reported it at the beginning. I only tried to tell you so that you could warn Lord Lisle to be careful. I thought perhaps he could convince the king of his innocence before Cromwell made his final move against him. But all that I know is comprised of bits and pieces, things seen and things overheard. Cromwell is dead. The conspirators are dead, all but Botolph himself, and no one knows where he is."

"Then why tell me this now?" Nan clutched the front of his doublet. "What good is it to know and not be able to do anything for my family?"

"I . . . I thought you would want to know for certain that Lord Lisle is innocent."

"We must tell the king, even if there is no proof. We will convince him that my stepfather should never have been sent to the Tower in the first place."

"You want me to tell the king that he made a mistake?" Wat asked, putting his hands over hers.

Nan sagged against him. He was right. It would do no good. The king could not pardon her stepfather without admitting he'd been wrong, not only about Lord Lisle, but also about Lord Cromwell. King Henry did not like to be wrong. On the rare occasions when he was, he went to great lengths to avoid admitting it.

"I shouldn't have told you." Wat's voice was full of remorse. "I did not mean to raise false hopes."

"You meant well." Slowly, reluctant to let go, Nan extricated herself from what was very nearly an embrace. "I must go back now."

She fled without another word or a backward glance and once more flung herself headlong into the frivolity of royal life on progress. If Wat Hungerford lingered at Ampthill, she did not see him again.

THE KING AND queen spent Yuletide at Hampton Court, joined there by the king's older daughter, the Lady Mary, and her household. After spending several years sharing a household with her sister, the Lady Elizabeth, the Lady Mary was once more mistress of her own establishment at Hunsdon.

The king was generous with his New Year's gifts, especially to his new wife. Catherine Howard passed them on to her maids of honor to admire— a rope of two hundred large pearls, two diamond pendants, another made of diamonds and pearls, and a muffler of black velvet edged with sable fur.

"There were rubies and pearls sewn into the fur," Dorothy Bray marveled, still impressed hours later, after she and Nan had retired to the bed they shared in the maids' dormitory.

"You received a magnificent pearl yourself," Nan said. The new acquisition was in the form of a brooch. It had been prominently displayed on Dorothy's bosom throughout the day.

"Lord Parr is most generous. And anyone can see how devoted he is to me."

"Dorothy, he already has a wife."

"If the king can have a marriage annulled, so can one of his subjects. Will has not lived with the woman for years and they have no children. He will marry me as soon as he is free."

Nan abandoned the argument and lay on her back in the closed-in bed. It was easy to believe the flattery of courtiers. Too easy.

She thought of Sir Edmund Knyvett. He had nothing honorable to offer her. He not only had a wife, but four sons besides. And Tom Culpepper? He flirted with her, but Nan knew that was all for show. She'd seen the way he looked at the queen when he thought no one was watching. Tom was infatuated with the new queen. He'd fallen in love with the one woman at court he could not have.

Then there was Wat Hungerford, with his hangdog expression and his big, mournful eyes, the picture of unrequited love if his words were to be believed. She sighed. She *liked* Wat, and he was well grown for his age. But it was foolish to wish for the impossible. Besides, Wat was only sixteen and boys his age were notoriously fickle. Then again, so were grown men. So were kings! If not for Catherine Howard, Nan might have been queen.

But an image of the king as he had been at the end of the progress popped into her mind—ill with a fever, his leg swollen to grotesque proportions. His doctors had drained suppurating pus and fluid from the ulcer to bring down the fever.

Nan shuddered. She did not envy Catherine Howard her duties in the royal bedchamber! Or in public, for that matter. The king's temper was more volatile than ever. Nan had been hoping for an opportunity to ask King Henry to pardon her mother and sisters. So far, she'd not dared risk her own position. To make such a request at the wrong time would enrage His Grace and turn him against her.

Resolutely, Nan rolled over and punched her pillow into a more comfortable shape. Then she closed her eyes and willed herself to sleep. She needed to be well rested and alert if she was to thrive at court.

She rose at the usual hour and went to wait on the queen, but on this particular morning, most unusually, Catherine Howard singled her out. "You will take my offering to the Lady Mary," the queen instructed, indicating a small tray on which a box filled with candied fruit had been placed. "I am hopeful it will sweeten her temper."

"Am I to tell her that?"

Nan's tart tone brought a sour expression to the queen's face. Catherine pouted for a moment, then decided to be amused. She beckoned Nan closer. "It is no secret that the king's daughter does not care for me. She does not show me proper respect. But since His Grace seems fond of her, I would have harmony between us. Do all you can to soothe her ruffled feathers."

"As you wish, Your Grace."

"Nan!" The queen called her back.

"Your Grace?"

Queen Catherine waited until she was close enough to hear a whisper. "If she responds well to my offering, you may hint that she will be allowed to reside permanently at court if she . . . behaves herself. You understand me?"

"Yes, Your Grace." This time Catherine let her leave the privy chamber.

The Lady Mary's household was much smaller than the queen's, only about forty attendants, but the king's daughter had been taught by her mother that she would inherit the throne and she knew her own worth, even now that Prince Edward was the king's heir and Mary herself had been relegated to the status of royal bastard. Although she was only a little older than her new stepmother, a regal dignity was as much a part of the Lady Mary as the red in her hair and the low, throaty timbre of her voice.

"So," she said, examining the queen's gift, "she sent you to me with this trifle. Am I to express my undying gratitude now?"

Nan felt the corners of her mouth twitch. "Perhaps a mild expression of rapture?" she suggested.

The Lady Mary looked startled for a moment. Then she narrowed her eyes to take a closer look at Nan. "Mistress Bassett, is it not?"

"Yes, Your Majesty."

A little silence fell. To call Mary Tudor "Your Majesty," a form of address used only by the king, was a risk on Nan's part. For no more than referring to the Lady Mary as "Princess Mary," back when Anne Boleyn was queen, one of Mary's friends had been imprisoned in the Tower of London for several months. But with that single word, Nan had told Mary that she was among those who, in spite of the current law making Mary illegitimate, recognized King Henry's daughter as his legitimate heir, next in line after Edward.

"What does my lady stepmother want?" Mary asked.

"To welcome you to court, my lady. Perhaps to invite you to make your permanent home here, close to your father the king?"

Mary considered this for a moment before she detached a delicate brooch from her own breast and placed it in Nan's hands. "Convey this to the queen with my compliments."

Nan made her obeisance and backed out of the room, clutching the bauble to her bosom. Once free of the Lady Mary's chambers, she smiled. In a small way, she had just won the princess's favor as well as the queen's. Surely that was cause for optimism. The support of one or both of them might make the difference between her family's freedom and their continued imprisonment.

"YOUR MISTRESS HAS acquired more stylish clothes," Nan remarked as she and Cat watched Anna of Cleves—attired in silver lamé striped in cloth of gold—dance with the queen. Catherine wore a gown of cloth-of-gold lined with ermine.

Anna of Cleves had sent her New Year's gift to Hampton Court ahead of her own arrival. Two fine horses with purple velvet trappings had paved the way for a warm greeting from the king, who had welcomed his former wife and current "sister" back to court with a kiss. Then Anna had knelt before her former maid of honor, accepting the reversal of their roles with apparent equanimity.

"My lady delights in buying things and has the wherewithal to indulge herself," Cat said proudly.

"You look very fine yourself. I envy you that crimson velvet. Queen Catherine gifted her attendants with livery to match that of the officers of the king's privy chamber, but black is not my favorite shade."

"You have no cause for complaint. You are just where you wanted to be—at court. Have you done anything to help our mother and sisters?"

"There are good reasons why I have not yet approached the king. His moods are uncertain. I do not wish to incur his wrath. We must be patient."

Cat did not look convinced.

"Are you happy in the service of Anna of Cleves?" Nan asked.

"I am," Cat said. "She is a good mistress. But do not try to change the subject. What are you waiting for? If I were here, in your position, I would have found a way to ask the king for a pardon long before this."

Nan sighed. In the face of Cat's criticism, she had to admit that she had not tried very hard to find the right moment. She'd let fear rule her. But what if there never was a perfect time to ask a boon of the king?

"Soon, Cat," she promised. "I will talk to His Grace soon."

The next day, after dinner, the king presented Queen Catherine with more gifts—two lapdogs and a ring. She thanked him prettily and then, with a look that asked permission first, gave them to Anna of Cleves. Since Nan knew that Catherine Howard was not overly fond of spaniels and that the ring was not nearly as magnificent as the other jewels the king had given her, she supposed that His Grace had approved the gesture beforehand.

The king's honorary sister and Nan's real one stayed at Hampton Court for one more night and left the next afternoon. Cat's disapproval weighed heavily on Nan. Two days later, seeing that the king was in an especially jovial frame of mind, Nan gathered her courage and approached him during one of his visits to the queen's presence chamber. "A word with you, Your Grace?"

"Why, Nan! What a vision you are."

"You are too kind, Your Grace." She slanted a glance at the queen, but Catherine was winning at cards and paid them no mind. "I crave a moment's conversation, if it please you, Your Majesty."

Nan hated to grovel, but it was necessary. When King Henry led her a little aside, into a window alcove, and gestured for his attendants to keep their distance, she essayed a few flattering remarks before she broached the subject of her sisters' confinement in Calais. She was not yet ready to risk asking favors for her mother.

"To whom do you refer, my dear?" The king did not seem to know what she was talking about. Had he truly forgotten that he'd imprisoned most of her family?

"To my oldest sister, Philippa Bassett, and to the youngest, Mary

Bassett. They have been the . . . guests of two citizens of Calais for some time now. If Your Grace would permit them to return to England, they might live at Tehidy in Cornwall, one of the properties my brother John Bassett inherited from our late father." She took care not to mention Lord Lisle's name, or to remind the king that Mary was the one who had illegally betrothed herself to a minor French nobleman.

Peering through her lashes, Nan could not read the king's expression. Was that a frown of displeasure? Or merely the result of intense concentration? Her stomach twisted into knots as she waited for him to speak. She did not dare say more for fear of irritating him.

"Hmmm," King Henry said at last. "I suppose there is no harm in it, so long as they both rusticate in the country upon their return."

"You are most generous, Your Grace." She deepened her obeisance, nearly touching her head to the floor.

He lifted her up, beaming at her, and signaled for Anthony Denny to approach. "Denny, remind me on the morrow to order the release of Mistress Philippa Bassett and Mistress Mary Bassett. They are to be conveyed from Calais to Cornwall at my expense."

"As you wish, Your Grace," Denny said, bowing low.

Well pleased with his own generosity, King Henry returned to his queen's side. She'd noticed his absence and did not look happy to see him in such close proximity to Nan.

When Denny started to follow the king, Nan caught his arm. "Will His Grace keep his word?"

Denny winked at her. "If I have everything ready for his signature and seal, he will not even read what he's signing. He's that anxious to dispense with routine business and return to enjoying the company of his bride."

The Deputy of Calais, my Lord Lisle, hath not been led to judgment; and it is said that he shall be kept prisoner in the Tower for his life, where he is somewhat more at large than formerly he was. And in truth, Sire, certain noblemen of this Court have said to me that on several occasions they have heard the King their master say that the said Lord Deputy hath erred more through simplicity and ignorance than by malice.

—Charles de Marillac, French ambassador to England, to the king of France,
18 July 1541

15

Ned Corbett started his search for Sir Gregory Botolph in Louvain, then moved on through the Low Countries until at last he located his quarry in a nondescript tavern in an obscure Flemish town.

"So, Botolph," Ned said to him, "we meet again."

With extreme caution, Botolph reached up, took the point of Ned's knife between his fingertips, and eased it away from his own neck. Ned sheathed the weapon and slid onto the bench opposite Botolph's stool. All around them he heard the fragments of conversation and the bursts of laughter typical of a dark, noisy tavern. This one was much like the places Ned had frequented in London and Calais, but here the language being spoken was not English.

"My man, Browne, is right behind you, Botolph, should you decide to flee."

"Where would I go, Ned? Indeed, I am glad to see a friendly face in this godforsaken place."

"I've no desire to be your friend and every inclination to spill your blood for what you did to me and to Philpott and to the others."

"What I did?" With exaggerated calm, he took a swallow of beer, watching Ned over the rim of the tankard. "I did not coerce anyone. I used no force or violence. Clement Philpott brought disaster down upon his own head by betraying all he believed in." He sipped again and grinned, unrepentant. "Indeed, if all had gone according to plan, my *friend*, you'd have been the one to cry foul treason to Lord Lisle."

After following Botolph's trail for six months, Ned was not inclined to rush the other man's explanation. He signaled to the tavern keeper for a beer of his own and one for Browne and motioned for his servant to take a seat on the other side of Botolph.

"I want the true story," he said when he'd downed enough of the dark, frothy brew to take the edge off his thirst. "All of it. Your mad scheme cost good men their lives and forced others into exile."

Botolph shrugged. "I am not the villain here, but the man responsible is beyond your reach."

"Who?"

"Thomas Cromwell."

"Cromwell's dead."

"Precisely."

Ned's initial reaction was disbelief. He already knew Botolph was a practiced liar. But something about the fellow's demeanor made him think that, unlikely as it seemed, he might be telling the truth. "Start at the beginning."

"I stole some plate when I was a canon. In hindsight, a grave miscalculation, but I needed money. Lord Cromwell found out about it and summoned me to his house in London. We met in secret in the dead of night and he made me a proposition I was unable to refuse. My freedom and my reputation for helping him bring about Lord Lisle's fall from grace."

"He wanted to fill Lisle's position in Calais with his own man." That much had been obvious for years.

"Not only remove the lord deputy, but make it seem as if he had betrayed the king, betrayed England. Cromwell wanted him imprisoned, at least for a time." Botolph grinned. "Cromwell intended to tell the king the whole story, admitting he'd entrapped Lisle to prove how unfit the fellow was for his post. Then he'd have interceded for Lisle with the king, persuading His Grace that Lisle was merely incompetent for allowing treason to prosper, not a traitor. Lisle would have been freed and restored to his title and honors, but he'd never again have been given any responsibility. And I'd have been pardoned."

"And Philpott? He's dead, Botolph. Hanged, drawn, and quartered. As I would be had I not been helped to escape."

Botolph shrugged. "I warrant Philpott would still have been executed one day, for heresy if not for treason."

Ned's fingers itched to throttle Botolph. His former friend showed neither guilt nor remorse. "You could have come forward. Saved him. Saved us all."

"From what? Your own stupidity? Those who were arrested *did* conspire to commit treason, no matter if it was a real plot or not. Besides, once Cromwell was arrested, who would have believed me? His execution ruined everything." He drank deeply.

"You knew your friends would suffer for believing in the scheme. Left to his own devices, Philpott would never have plotted treason."

"It was *all* Cromwell's plan," Botolph repeated.

"Even your meeting with Cardinal Pole and the pope?"

Botolph laughed. "I never went to Rome, Ned. Why should I?"

"For the gold?" Ned drained his tankard and signaled for another.

Was this possible? Was *everything* Botolph had told them an invention?

"That, too, was supplied by Lord Cromwell. I did as I was told and I received my reward. Two hundred gold crowns. Enough to help me elude pursuit. There was to have been more but, as matters turned out, that will not be forthcoming."

"Two hundred crowns is the rough equivalent of fifty pounds." John Browne spoke for the first time, his voice a harsh monotone. "A man can live comfortably on a tenth of that per annum. Monks pensioned off when their monasteries closed are managing on far less."

Botolph drank again and stared at the dregs. "I was never a monk. I never wanted to be a priest, either, but I was the fourth son. What else was there for me? And then I fell into Cromwell's clutches."

"You could go back," Ned suggested, unmoved by Botolph's whining. "Perhaps the king will reward you for your honesty. Lord Lisle surely will, since it will mean his freedom."

Botolph started to laugh. "What kind of fool do you take me for? I may not be able to live in luxury, but I still have my head."

For a moment, a red haze distorted Ned's vision. His hands curled around the ceramic tankard and squeezed as the urge to kill Botolph grew stronger, all but overcoming his common sense. He wanted to shift his grip to the other man's throat and snap his lying neck.

The tankard cracked with a sharp, splintering sound. Ned stared at his beer-soaked fingers, at the growing puddle on the table. Slowly, he shoved himself away from the table.

When he had control of himself again, the mess had been cleared away, and he had a fresh tankard of beer—pewter this time—he looked Botolph in the eye. "If you will not voluntarily go back to England to face the king's justice, then Browne and I will take you there, bound and gagged, if necessary."

"You'd forfeit your own freedom for revenge? I do not think so. You cannot return home any more than I can."

"Gregory Sweet-lips" still possessed the silver tongue that had led so many men astray. Within a quarter of an hour, he'd convinced Ned that, with Cromwell dead, there was no one left who would believe the true story.

"Then give me one good reason not to kill you here and now," Ned said.

"Only one? I can give you a hundred. And I can make it worth your while to go away. Cromwell paid me two hundred crowns. Half of that is yours to forget you ever found me."

"While you stay here, living under a new name, enjoying your new life?" He would disappear again, to lead other men into trouble, or perhaps to rob another church of its plate. Ned considered the situation while he finished his beer. The decision to take all a man's money, along with his life, was not one that could be made lightly.

In early February, the king went to London, leaving his bride behind at Hampton Court. It was the first time they had been separated for any length of time since their marriage, but King Henry had been growing ever more unpredictable. Nan did not think he'd tired of his young bride, but perhaps he needed a respite from her company.

Queen Catherine scarcely seemed to miss him. She occupied herself as she always did, with dice and cards and dancing and a steady stream of entertainers to provide distraction.

The gentlemen the king left behind flocked to Her Grace's presence chamber like moths to flame. Will Parr was there to be with Dorothy Bray. Sir Edmund Knyvett came sniffing around Nan. Tom Culpepper was among Nan's admirers, as well, but his heart wasn't in it.

A frown knit Nan's brows as she watched Culpepper watch Catherine Howard. His open admiration filled Nan with concern for his safety, but that was nothing to what she felt when she saw the amorous look in Her Grace's eyes. How fortunate that a queen was never truly alone! With so many witnesses surrounding her, she could not do more than lust in her heart for a virile young man.

As Nan continued to watch, Queen Catherine turned her back on Tom Culpepper. Nan told herself she'd imagined Her Grace's prurient interest. Since it was never safe to speculate about such things, she put the incident out of her mind, but her uneasiness returned a few days later when the queen suddenly dispensed with the services of her maids of honor, sending them away for the rest of the afternoon.

"Go and enjoy yourselves," she ordered. "Lady Rochford is all the company I need while I rest."

"How she can stand that prune-faced Lady Rochford, I do not know," Dorothy Bray said as she and Nan and Lucy Somerset made their way to the tennis court. Will Parr was to play in one of the matches that afternoon.

"She likes the way Lady Rochford abases herself," Lucy replied. "She's so willing to please that she'll do anything the queen asks of her."

"We all serve the queen," Dorothy said primly. "If she wants us on our knees to hand her an apple, we go down on our knees."

"But Lady Rochford would gladly crawl," Nan said. There was something not quite right about the older woman. Her face customarily wore a look of quiet desperation and her eyes were always darting this way and that, as if she expected someone to jump out at her from behind an arras.

When they entered the enclosed tennis court, Nan anticipated hearing the crack of tennis balls against racket and floor and wall. The sound of a scuffle reached her ears instead. A man grunted. Another swore. The three maids of honor came out into the gallery in time to see several courtiers pull Sir Edmund Knyvett away from another gentleman. The second combatant swabbed his freely bleeding nose.

A sudden terrible silence fell over the entire company. Nan lifted her hand to her mouth to hold back a sound of distress. To strike another person, especially to draw blood, was an offense against the king when it occurred at court. This was far more serious than a simple brawl.

Will Parr came up to them, a stricken look in his hazel eyes. He was a tall, well-built gentleman with a long face and wore both hair and beard close cropped. Like his sisters, Anne Herbert and Kathryn Latimer, his normal disposition was cheerful, but at the moment he showed no sign of lightheartedness. "You'd best leave, my love," he told Dorothy. "They'll come to arrest him now. There will be no more tennis this afternoon."

"What will happen to him?" Nan whispered. She had refused Sir Edmund's offer to make her his mistress, but she bore him no ill will for suggesting that role for her. In fact, she was grateful to him for opening her eyes to her altered status at court.

"Knyvett must forfeit the hand he used to strike the blow."

Parr's blunt words made Nan's stomach roil. "Is there no remedy?"

He shrugged. "The king can pardon him, but I do not think he will. His Grace's leg has been causing him a great deal of pain these last few days. He is not in charity with anyone but the queen."

Queen Catherine, Nan remembered, was Sir Edmund's kinswoman. She could intervene. More times than she could count, Nan had seen Catherine tease and cajole her husband out of the foulest of tempers. His Grace was as besotted with her as he had been before they were wed. All the queen had to do was smile in order to twist him around her little finger. Picking up her skirts, Nan hurried back to the queen's apartments, but Lady Rochford barred her way.

"Her Grace is resting!" she said in a voice loud enough to wake anyone on the other side of the bedchamber door.

"She will want to hear my news. It concerns the impending arrest of her cousin."

Lady Rochford blanched. "Cousin? Which cousin?"

"Sir Edmund Knyvett."

The other woman's obvious relief made Nan wonder who she had supposed Nan meant. The queen had a large family. There were Howards on her father's side, and her mother—her mother had been born a Culpepper.

Nan was relieved to find Her Grace alone in her bedchamber when Lady Rochford at last permitted her to enter. In a few terse sentences, she told Queen Catherine what had transpired at the tennis court.

Catherine listened and expressed concern, but she refused to intervene on Sir Edmund's behalf.

"The king has been in a volatile mood of late," she said by way of an excuse. Catherine toyed with the gem-encrusted brooch pinned to her bosom. "Perhaps you should ask the king yourself when he returns to Hampton Court."

Catherine would like that, Nan thought. She'd be delighted if the king lost his temper with a woman who had once been his mistress. Although she had no cause, Catherine was apparently still jealous of Nan.

"I have not Your Grace's . . . influence with King Henry," Nan said carefully. "Surely Your Grace will be able to find an opportunity to plead for your cousin, perhaps when the king is in a mellow mood."

"Perhaps my cousin should consider asking me himself. Go and fetch my cloak, Nan. I have a sudden craving to walk in the gallery for exercise." As far as the queen was concerned, the subject was closed.

JUST AS WILL Parr had predicted, Sir Edmund Knyvett was brought before the Court of the Verge in the Great Hall of the palace and sentenced to have his right hand amputated and to forfeit his lands and possessions for having drawn blood at the royal court. On the morning the sentence was to be carried out, courtiers crowded around the windows overlooking the appointed courtyard. Nan stood next to Anne Herbert, fighting the urge to bolt.

Two forms had been set up. One held instruments and supplies, the other wine, ale, and beer.

"For the witnesses," Anne explained.

"Oh, yes, let us drink to the horror!"

"Hush, Nan. There's still hope of a pardon. And if not, well, there is a sergeant surgeon in attendance."

"This is no surgical amputation." And even with a skilled surgeon, the removal of a limb often led to death from loss of blood or from fever. She watched, wide eyed, as the sergeant of the woodyard brought forth a mallet and a block.

"A sergeant of the larder will set the blade right on the joint," Anne said. "A master cook will wield the knife. When the cutting is done, a sergeant farrier will use searing irons to sear the veins."

Nan looked at the pan of fire used to heat them. A chafer of water stood nearby—to cool the ends, she supposed. And a yeoman of the chandlery was in attendance, ready to supply sear cloths to dress the stump. The only person whose presence Nan could not comprehend with chilling clarity was the sergeant of the poultry. "Why has he brought a cock?"

"The bird will be beheaded on the same block and with the same knife. To test the equipment, I presume." Anne did not seem unduly upset by what they were about to witness.

Nan's stomach churned. She tasted bile. When the knight marshall brought Sir Edmund out, she pressed her fists to her mouth.

Sir Edmund was in shirt and breeches, wearing neither doublet nor gown in spite of the February chill in the courtyard. His face was as white as the patches of snow on the cobblestones.

Sir Edmund went down on his knees to confess his crime. In a last, desperate effort to save his hand, he begged the knight marshall to go and plead with the king for mercy on his behalf. "Ask His Grace if I might lose my left hand rather than the right," Sir Edmund called after him as he entered the palace, "for if my right hand be spared, I may hereafter do much good service to His Grace."

Proceedings halted. Nan prayed for Sir Edmund's deliverance but, in her heart, she knew that it was not God's mercy that he needed. It was the king's.

After what seemed an eternity, the knight marshall returned from speaking to King Henry, who had come back from London the previous day. "His Majesty is impressed with your loyalty, Sir Edmund. He will grant your request." He turned to the master cook. "Take off his left hand."

Nan could not help herself. She pressed closer to the window, watching in sick fascination as Sir Edmund's hand was positioned on the block.

The blade was aligned. The cook took hold of the knife's handle. A thin line of red appeared on Sir Edmund's wrist.

At the last possible moment, a man ran into the courtyard—a messenger from King Henry. "On the king's command," he shouted, "you are to stay the execution of the punishment until after dinner!"

Nan rested her forehead against the window glass. Not a pardon. A delay. She had underestimated the king's capacity for cruelty.

Three hours passed while the king dined. Then His Grace made his way in person to the courtyard where Sir Edmund and all the officers still waited. They must be nearly frozen by now, Nan thought, resuming her post by the window. She heard someone come up beside her but did not turn around to see who it was. She assumed Anne Herbert had returned.

King Henry moved with slow, ponderous steps, using a staff to help him walk. He had rarely been without the accessory since the winter began. "Have you anything to say to me, rogue?"

Sir Edmund spoke in a low, trembling voice, beaten down by fear and the cold. "I desire Your Grace pardon my right hand and take the left, so that I might hereafter do such good service to Your Grace as shall please you to appoint."

A smug smile appeared on the king's face. At her side, Nan heard a little sigh of relief. She glanced at her companion. Only then did she see that it was not Anne Herbert who stood next to her. It was the queen. Nan started to drop into a curtsy, but Catherine caught her arm to keep her upright. "His Majesty is about to speak. Listen."

"In consideration of your gentle heart, Edmund, and your long service to the Crown, I grant you pardon. You shall lose neither hand, land, nor goods, but shall go free at liberty."

Catherine clapped her hands in delight. "See how His Grace grants my slightest wish!"

"His Majesty loves you, Your Grace," Nan whispered. As relieved as she was that Sir Edmund had been spared, the queen's display of jubilation filled her with dismay. Without stopping to think how her warning would be received, Nan blurted out, "His Grace once loved your cousin with equal passion."

Instantly infuriated, Queen Catherine slapped Nan's face. "Insolent wench! All the world knows that Anne Boleyn bewitched him."

"And that she was unfaithful," Nan added in a whisper. Her cheek stung, but she could not seem to stop speaking. "Queen Anne was beheaded for indiscretion. There was no pardon for her."

Catherine's face twisted into an ugly sneer. "Taking lovers was not her greatest mistake. It was that she railed at His Grace and made his life a misery. I never contradict him, only sweetly persuade him to do my bidding. I know how to please a man."

"Your Grace, have a care! There are ears everywhere."

But Queen Catherine seemed to lack both common sense and any instinct for self-preservation. "I am queen," she boasted. "I do as I please."

It was Catherine's good fortune that, this time, only Lady Rochford, lurking a short distance away, was close enough to overhear.

As part of the usual revelry that preceded Lent, there were masques at court on two consecutive nights. The king failed to attend either.

"Have you heard?" Dorothy whispered on the second night, after she and Nan were closed into the relative privacy of their bed.

"Heard what?" Nan was exhausted from the dancing that had followed the masque. Sir Edmund, having survived a close brush with disaster, was more importune than ever about making her his mistress. There were times when, out of equal parts pity and loneliness, she was tempted to give in.

"The king's ulcer suddenly became clogged. It has closed up and is causing him great pain. He has a high fever, too."

Nan prayed for the king's deliverance. His heir was a child. If King Henry died, England would be plunged into chaos. Worse, there would be no queen at court. If there was no queen, there would be no place for a maid of honor.

The next day, Queen Catherine was banned from her husband's bedchamber.

"The king refuses to see anyone, Your Grace," Tom Culpepper told her. "And I doubt Your Grace would want to see the king. At one point, His Grace's face turned black. The doctors feared for his life until one of the surgeons drained fluid from the ulcer. Then the swelling went down and His Grace's health improved considerably, but not, I fear, his temper."

"Word of Henry's violent outbursts has already reached us," the queen said.

"He even railed at me," Culpepper admitted with a rueful grin. "His Grace called me a lying timeserver and a flatterer who looked only to my own profit. But then he also said he knew what his councilors were plotting and that he would take care that their projects should not succeed."

"It is the pain talking," Anne Herbert murmured in Nan's ear. "What a good thing it is that men do not have to endure childbirth. They would be quite unfit to live with if they did." Anne had left court briefly the previous year to give birth to her first child and considered herself an expert on the subject.

"His Grace's misery is so great," Culpepper continued, "that he will not even allow music to be played in his bedchamber."

That news alarmed Nan more than anything else she had heard. King Henry loved music. He'd even written several songs himself. That he found his musicians annoying and preferred silence to the distraction of their playing was deeply disturbing.

Culpepper lowered his voice, but that only made the maids of honor stretch their ears. "His Grace bemoaned the loss of Lord Cromwell. He said that his councilors, upon light pretext and by false accusations, conspired to turn His Grace against the most faithful servant he ever had."

How strange, Nan thought. Did the king truly feel regret? Could it be that His Grace was capable of admitting he could make mistakes?

Nan pondered that possibility during the next ten days. All the while, the king kept to his rooms and refused entry to all but a few trusted gentlemen. Nan was unable to go to him, unable to ask him to pardon Lord Lisle.

His pretty young wife was also kept out of the king's apartments. More alarmingly, courtiers were sent home in droves. Those who remained sank into a gloom that was the equal of the king's.

But then, with as much suddenness as His Grace's health had failed him, he was himself again. He summoned Queen Catherine. He was ready to plan her long-delayed official entry into London.

NED CORBETT SECRETLY returned to England a few weeks after he ran Sir Gregory Botolph to ground. He chose yet another new name for himself and stayed well away from court, but he was not content without employment. When he heard of a wine merchant's widow who needed a secretary, he decided that such a position had possibilities.

Ned expected to be interviewed by an aged crone who had depended upon her late husband for everything—someone Ned could flatter and impress. The woman seated behind a table piled high with ledgers and correspondence did not fit that image.

She was young, no older than Ned. Even in the unrelieved black of mourning dress, she was attractive. Her skin was milky white, her figure was rounded in all the right places, and her eyes were the exact color of violets.

Once he got over his surprise, he also recognized shrewd intelligence in those eyes. The widow was examining him every bit as thoroughly as he'd categorized her attributes. Sending a taut smile his way, she gestured for him to sit.

Intrigued, he complied. She had questions. He answered them, most of them honestly, faltering only when she demanded to know if he was a displaced priest.

"No monastery would have taken me," he told her, and dared a wink.

She blinked, then slowly smiled. "You are wondering why I asked. As it happens, most of the applicants for this position have been monks turned out to fend for themselves when their monasteries were dissolved.

They were pensioned off, but the paltry sums they were allotted are not enough to keep body and soul together. I feel sorry for such men, but I do not want to employ one."

"Why is that, madam?" Ned asked.

"As a rule, they do not approve of women, especially women who wish to manage their own businesses."

"I have no such failing. I am ready and willing to assist you." He'd quite enjoy working for her.

"Not all men are so open-minded. Indeed, most of those I have encountered believe that women are incapable of anything more complicated than brewing, baking, and needlework."

"That is shortsighted of them. I have been privileged to observe many accomplished women in my . . . travels. I am certain that you can succeed at anything you choose."

"You show a remarkable degree of confidence in someone you have only just met."

Ned grinned. "I am in need of a job, madam. But though I say it myself, I am also an excellent judge of character." The smile faded when he remembered Sir Gregory Botolph. "I did make a mistake once, but it is not one I am ever likely to repeat."

Her stare bored into him, as if she were attempting to look at his soul. He had to fight to keep from squirming, but he met her intense scrutiny with surface calm until she dropped her gaze to the papers in front of her on the desk.

"Do I meet with your approval, madam?"

"Have you wife or children?"

"No."

"A mistress?"

"Not at present." Ned narrowed his eyes at her. "What has that to do with employment as a secretary?"

"I require one thing more," she said bluntly. "In order to ensure that the business my husband left me continues to prosper, I require a husband."

* * *

IN MID-APRIL, SHORTLY after the court moved to Greenwich Palace, a sickness ravaged the land. For some it was no more than a mild stomach complaint—Queen Catherine mistakenly believed herself to be with child when she came down with it—while others became deathly ill. Tom Culpepper was among them. So was Nan's oldest brother, John Bassett.

Nan considered this news, wondering if she could use it to her advantage. She was not close to her brother. She had seen him only once after she'd been sent into France to be trained. Before that, the Bassett sons and daughters had largely been raised apart. But John's sickness, she decided, was a valid excuse to approach the king, especially if she exaggerated how ill her brother was.

She did not attempt to see King Henry alone, but chose a time when His Grace was visiting Queen Catherine's apartments to approach them both. The king was in a cheerful mood, in spite of his grossly swollen and throbbing leg, which rested on a jewel-studded stool. The bandages on his leg were more noticeable than they had been, as if it required additional layers to contain seepage.

King Henry smiled benignly down at Nan when she knelt before him to ask a boon. "What would you have, my pretty Nan?"

"Your Grace, I have received word that my brother is sick and like to die." His smile vanished. Belatedly, Nan remembered his aversion to illness. He did not even like to hear about those who were ailing. She rushed on, hoping to make her case before he turned against her completely. "Sire, I beg you. He is at Lincoln's Inn. If you could permit my mother to go to him in his hour of need, it would be a great kindness."

The king's face turned an ugly shade of red. Suddenly afraid, Nan fell silent. She did not dare say more. She had no need to in any case, for the king knew full well who her mother was and why she was unable to go to her son's deathbed without royal permission.

"You ask me to set a traitor free?" His voice was harsh. He glared at her through small, hard eyes devoid of compassion. Piggy little eyes, Nan thought, and then was horrified lest he somehow guess what was in her mind.

Nan bowed her head and waited for the next blow to fall. She clasped her hands tightly together in a futile attempt to keep them from trembling. He was going to refuse. She had no doubt of that. But what if there were more serious repercussions? What if His Grace decided he did not want a traitor's daughter at his court?

"I have already done you the favor of freeing your sisters," King Henry reminded her.

"Yes, Your Grace. Your Grace has been most benevolent." She sent him a beseeching look.

"That is all I am prepared to do. I will hear no more of this matter." The finality in his voice left Nan close to tears. She'd waited so long to choose her moment and now she'd chosen wrongly. She stumbled as she backed away from him.

The king watched her. She felt his eyes upon her on and off for the remainder of his visit to Queen Catherine. The queen prattled on, as she always did, talking of inconsequential things. Once or twice she made His Grace laugh, but his good mood was much diminished.

A week later, Nan's brother died.

Tom Culpepper recovered.

AS SPRING ADVANCED, the queen was full of plans for the next progress. They were to set out from London at the end of June and head north, visiting Lincolnshire and Yorkshire, counties where there had been uprisings a few years earlier over the king's decision to dissolve the monasteries. Another outbreak of dissension caused a furor at court. The small band of rural rebels was quickly quashed by well-trained royal troops, but King Henry's response did not end there. He ordered the execution of the old Countess of Salisbury. Cardinal Pole's mother, who had been held in the Tower of London since shortly after her older son was executed, was beheaded.

When Nan heard of it, she went straight to Anthony Denny, hoping for reassurance. "Are there to be other executions?" she asked. "Is my stepfather in danger of losing his head?"

"Not to my knowledge." But the pity in Denny's eyes told her that the situation could change at any moment.

When days turned into weeks and nothing more happened, Nan began to feel more confident. Once on progress, she thought, the king would forget all about Lord Lisle and his wife.

They set out as planned, but then the skies opened and rain fell in torrents, turning the roads into quagmires. As the caravan traveled from Dunstable to Ampthill and on to Grafton Regis, the king's councilors advised him to abandon the journey.

King Henry would not listen. His annual progress was the means by which he showed himself to the people and gave them the opportunity to present him with petitions. Besides, he and the queen slept warm and dry every night. They were not much concerned that hundreds of others, those of lowest rank like Nan's Constance, spent the hours of darkness in tents pitched in the sodden fields and the days shivering in wet shoes and damp cloaks. Nan's maidservant was a sorry sight, but there was little she could do to relieve the girl's discomfort.

The progress stopped in Northampton, then left there in the third week of July to spend a few days at the king's house at Collyweston. In early August, the entourage reached the outskirts of the city of Lincoln. Tents were set up seven miles south of the gates, at Temple Bruer, where the king enjoyed his dinner under a canopy before continuing on into Lincoln itself.

He changed into garments of Lincoln green for the ride to Lincoln Castle, where he and the queen and their closest attendants would be housed. The queen was carried in a litter. She kept the curtains closed for warmth and privacy. Her maids of honor rode behind. On horseback there was little protection from the elements, especially since Queen Catherine had commanded that they put aside their cloaks to better show off their elegant black livery.

Nan was drooping with fatigue by the time the procession neared the castle. She was weary of travel, tired of the rain and unseasonable cold, worn out by nagging fears about the future that never quite went away.

She barely glanced at the large crowd gathered to see the king pass through the city. King Henry's subjects had collected in large numbers all along the route of the progress. Their faces had become a blur. And yet, just as Nan was about to ride through the castle gate, her gaze fell on one particular man in the crowd. For an instant, his face was clearly visible. Nan's breath caught and her heart stuttered.

Imagination, she told herself. Ned Corbett could not be in England. Besides, the fellow she'd seen was clean shaven. Ned had always had a very fine beard.

But the incident left her shaken. More than once in the course of the evening, she caught herself wondering what her life would have been like if she'd gone with Ned into exile.

VERY EARLY THE next day, Constance slipped into the chamber assigned to the maids of honor and touched Nan's shoulder to wake her. Constance held her finger to her lips, reminding Nan that the slightest sound might wake her bedfellow. Quietly, she rose, closing the hangings behind her, and dressed with Constance's help. Whatever her tiring maid had on her mind, it was clearly important or she would not have left Temple Bruer before dawn and walked seven miles in the dark.

Carrying her shoes, Nan tiptoed out of the chamber and followed Constance along corridors and through antechambers until they stepped out into a courtyard. There were already scores of people stirring, preparing for a day of festivities, but no one took any notice of Nan and Constance as they scurried through the gate and out of the castle.

"This way," Constance whispered, and hurried downhill, into the town.

"What is this about?" Nan demanded as she followed. "Where are we going?"

But Constance only walked faster, forcing Nan to do likewise, and led her to a large and prosperous-looking house of the sort owned by wealthy merchants or lawyers or physicians.

A violet-eyed woman wearing an expensively decorated French hood let them in, examining Nan with blatant curiosity as she escorted her into a large and finely proportioned hall. She did not stay with them, but rather disappeared back behind the screen that shielded the room from drafts. Two men stood at the far side of the room, beneath an oriel window and near an unlit hearth. The diffuse light of early morning shone down on them, showing them in silhouette.

Nan gasped. For a moment the room around her dimmed. She pulled herself back by sheer willpower. A spurt of anger drove away any remaining chance that she would faint. "What are you doing in England?" she demanded. "Have you lost your senses?"

Ned Corbett turned as she stormed toward him. She *had* seen him the previous day. Except for the lack of a beard, which revealed a strong, square jaw, he was just the same—brown haired and blue eyed, with laugh lines around his eyes; a head taller than she was and well proportioned, if a bit leaner than she remembered.

"I could not abide foreign parts," Ned said when she stopped only inches from him.

"But the risk—"

"Very small. I have been here in Lincoln for the last five months and no one has questioned my identity."

She reached out, placing a hand on his cheek. He felt real, warm and solid. His scent was the same wonderful mix that had drawn her to him so long ago.

It had been nearly four years since she'd come to England to become a maid of honor, and just over one year since she'd helped Ned escape from the Tower of London and set sail on that Dutch merchantman. Just over a year since their son had died.

Nan closed her eyes against the sudden pain of that memory. It was difficult to think of Jamie. Far easier to pretend he'd never existed.

That made her feel guilty, but not so guilty that she stopped trying to forget.

"Nan?"

Her eyes popped open. Hope flickered to life. If Ned was back, safe, then they could—

But no. Nothing had changed. She could not leave court without arousing suspicion.

"Nan?" This time she heard a smile in his voice. A grin overspread his familiar features. "You are thinking too much. Just ask me what you want to know."

"How? Why did—?" She stopped short of asking him why he had not contacted her. Why should he? She had sent him away and refused to go with him.

Belatedly, she noticed Constance. Her maidservant stood a little apart, wrapped in the arms of Ned's companion. John Browne had returned to England, too.

"You should not be here, Ned. There are others who might recognize you. The Countess of Sussex. Lady Rutland. The—"

"I will stay out of sight until the progress moves on, but I wanted to see you once more. I did not intend to talk to you, even after you saw me in the marketplace, but Browne went looking for Constance, and although she has agreed to marry him, she would not stay in Lincoln unless I told you everything."

"Constance?" She turned to her tiring maid in surprise. "Are you certain?"

"Oh, yes, mistress. Never more so."

"Then you have my blessing, but I will miss you terribly." And she envied Constance, Nan admitted to herself.

"Nan, I've something to tell you." Ned was no longer smiling. "Constance says you know already that Lord Cromwell was behind Sir Gregory Botolph's plot."

"You *knew*?"

"Not until I caught up with Botolph on the Continent. It took months to locate him, but finally, in January, I tracked him down. He confessed everything, how the entire plot was a ploy to discredit your stepfather and oust him from Calais."

Just as Wat Hungerford had said. "So many men dead. So many lives ruined. And for what?"

"Greed. Power." Ned shrugged. "All the evils of the court. I am glad to be well away from such things."

"And Botolph? Can you tell the king's men how to find him?"

"He's dead." The stark words and the hard look on Ned's face discouraged questions.

Nan's heart sank as her best chance to help Lord Lisle died, too.

Ned glanced up at the window as a beam of sunlight struck his face. "The morning advances apace. You must go back to the castle before your absence is noticed."

"Will I ever see you again?"

"No, Nan." His voice was gentle and a little sad. "Best you do not. I have yet another new name now. And I have a wife."

"The violet-eyed woman," Nan said slowly. Suddenly details of her appearance, barely noticed a few minutes earlier, came back to Nan with crystal clarity. Ned's wife was young and pretty and she wore her gown unlaced at the front, as women were wont to do when they were with child.

For a moment, Nan couldn't remember how to breathe. She felt as if she'd lost both Ned and Jamie all over again.

"Nan?" Ned sounded worried. "I never meant to hurt you. I owe everything I have now to you. I owe you my life."

She drew in a deep breath. "I am happy for you." She forced herself to look away from Ned and focus on Constance. "For all of you. And you are right. We must not meet again."

In haste, before she could lose her fragile control of her emotions, she bid them farewell and fled. Back into Lincoln Castle. Back to her duties as a maid of honor to the queen.

Order must be also taken with the Maidens that they repair each of them to their friends there to remain, saving Mistress Bassett, whom the King's Majesty, in consideration of the calamity of her friends, will, at his charges, specially provide for.

—Order of the Privy Council, November 1541

When the progress left Lincoln, it moved on to Hatfield Chase, in Yorkshire. Both the king and queen were mad for hunting and Hatfield Chase contained a large, enclosed area rich in game. The company rode through scrub and woodland to take down nearly two hundred stags and deer. Then they ventured into the river, ponds, and marshes and killed enough young swans and other waterfowl to fill two boats.

Nan was numb to the wholesale slaughter. She felt as if she'd left pieces of herself behind in Lincoln, one with Ned and another with Constance. She knew it did no good to dwell on the past. She had made her choices. Only the present mattered. But she had never felt so alone.

Pavilions had been set up to house the court. These tents were lavishly furnished. The one that served as the queen's privy chamber even had walls and windows.

Nan returned there after the hunt and was about to enter when the back of her neck prickled. Certain she was being watched, she turned slowly, her gaze sweeping the other tents as well as nearby alcoves and doorways. It came to rest upon a young man standing in the shadow of a pillar. Wat Hungerford.

Nan sighed. Another reminder of the past.

Wat stepped out into the daylight. His dark, wavy hair fell over his eyes and he impatiently shoved it aside with the back of his hand. "Good day to you, Mistress Bassett."

"Master Hungerford. Have you come to ask the king to restore your estates?"

He scowled. "I came in the hope of spending time with you, Nan."

Her eyebrows lifted when he addressed her with such familiarity, but she did not reproach him. His open admiration was a balm to her wounded pride. Discovering that Ned was married had come as a shock. Even though she'd rejected him, she'd somehow imagined he would be true to her forever, refusing to marry anyone if he could not have her. How foolish! Ned had always been on the hunt for a wealthy bride. She should be happy for him that he'd found one.

She regarded Wat Hungerford's young, eager expression with skeptical eyes. "We will never make a match of it, Master Hungerford. You need a wife with a fortune and I want a husband with money and a title."

Nan felt a pang of regret when she saw that her blunt words had hurt him, but he had the resilience and self-confidence of youth. He would recover.

"I will be Lord Hungerford one day," he said as she turned away. "My estates and title will be restored. You could wait for me."

Nan stopped just inside the silken pavilion, one hand pressed to her heart. Unwanted tears filled her eyes. If only he were a few years older. If only she were not so jaded.

When Nan had herself under control again, she joined Dorothy and Lucy where they sat sewing in a corner of the pavilion. She saw at once that they both looked worried. "What is wrong?" she asked in a whisper.

Dorothy's gaze shot to Queen Catherine, who stood looking out a window. "Her Grace is watching Tom Culpepper cross the open expanse between the king's pavilion and this one."

In itself, this was not disturbing, but Nan had too often seen the expression of naked longing on the young queen's face when she looked at her distant cousin. The other maids of honor had noticed the same thing.

"Someone should warn the queen that it is not wise to make the king jealous," Lucy murmured.

Dorothy snorted. "And who would be so foolish as to try to tell Her Grace anything she does not want to hear? She is too headstrong, too spoiled, and too stupid to listen. Besides, the king has no idea what his wife is doing."

"Hush, Dorothy. Someone will overhear." Nan looked over her shoulder, but no one appeared to be close enough to eavesdrop on their conversation.

"If matters continue as they are," Lucy predicted, "His Grace is bound to notice her infatuation."

"It is more than infatuation," Nan said, "but Dorothy is right. Her Grace does not care for unsolicited advice." Her hand went to her cheek, remembering the sting of the slap Queen Catherine had given her.

"I do not see how it could be more," Lucy said. "Her Grace is never alone. Dalliance requires privacy."

Dorothy snickered.

"She could not have—"

"Could and has, I'll wager. Have you not noticed how Her Grace sends most of her ladies away when she retires to her bedchamber?"

"The king—"

"Does not stay long. In and out!" Dorothy gave a nervous giggle. "And sometimes His Grace does not visit her at all. Then the queen is left to her own devices, free to . . . entertain whatever . . . person she chooses."

Two things Nan had observed suddenly took on an unsettling significance she'd heretofore missed. Wherever they'd gone on this progress, there had always been an inner stair or an outer door that gave private access to the queen's bedchamber. And Lady Rochford was always on duty at night.

"Whatever we suspect," she said aloud, "it is no more than speculation."

The pretense of ignorance seemed the safest course for all of them. Nan turned a blind eye to the queen's flirtation with her husband's gentleman of the privy chamber. She told herself it was not her place to interfere, or to offer advice. Nor could she betray her mistress by telling tales to the king. No one ever thought well of one who brought unwelcome news. Besides, she did not think he would believe her.

THE PROGRESS MADE several more stops before arriving at Pontefract at the end of August. It was there that Queen Catherine acquired a new member of her household. A fellow named Francis Dereham took the post of private secretary. Within a week of his arrival, he was at odds with one of the queen's gentlemen ushers, going so far as to brawl with him and shove him to the ground.

"Lucky for him the king did not hear of it," Anne Herbert said to Nan as they strolled in the gardens to enjoy a rare glimpse of the sun.

Nan shuddered, remembering what had almost happened to Sir Edmund Knyvett. "I have noticed that Master Dereham is careful to efface himself when the king is nearby."

"How odd. Most men thrust themselves forward. They want His Grace's attention."

"He has the queen's." Nan had observed that Dereham had a most familiar manner toward Queen Catherine. "Where did he come from?"

"He was recommended by the old Duchess of Norfolk."

"The same one who raised the queen?"

Anne nodded. "Someone told me that this Dereham was a member of the duchess's household when Queen Catherine was a girl in her keeping."

A remark Catherine Howard had once made, back when she was a maid of honor, niggled at Nan's memory. She did not wish to examine it closely. It was not safe to know too much, she reminded herself again. Nor was it wise to speculate.

THE PROGRESS MOVED on to York, arriving there in mid-September. Two weeks later they were in Hull and traveling slowly south once more. On the twenty-sixth day of October, they reached Windsor Castle, and then it was back to Hampton Court.

Home, Nan thought. As much as any one place could be to an itinerant entity like the royal court. The king was in high spirits. The queen smiled a great deal. Francis Dereham appeared to have taken himself off somewhere, to the great relief of everyone in the queen's household.

And then, on Friday the fourth of November, the king's guards appeared in the queen's apartments. She was informed that neither she nor her ladies were to leave her rooms for any reason.

"How dare you!" Queen Catherine shouted. "I will go to the king. He will tell you that you have no right to confine me."

But they would not let her pass and, in the morning, one of the yeomen of the guard let slip to Nan that the king had left Hampton Court for Whitehall.

The next two days were filled with wild speculation. Nerves frayed and tempers snapped. It was almost a relief when Archbishop Cranmer arrived, together with the Duke of Norfolk and several clerks with quills and paper. They closeted themselves with the queen.

Dorothy Bray was pale as death. "They are interrogating Her Grace," she whispered.

"They will ask us questions, too." Nan exchanged a look of panic with Dorothy. All the queen's secrets seemed likely to come out.

Should she lie and pretend ignorance? Or tell the truth? Either course might result in being charged with treason.

THE NEWS THAT Catherine Howard was being questioned at Hampton Court spread like wildfire. It did not take long to reach the household of her predecessor at Richmond Palace, and it filled Anna of Cleves's ladies with such elation that they had difficulty restraining themselves.

Cat Bassett had been fond of Lady Rutland, but she'd come to love Anna of Cleves. In Cat's eyes, her mistress could do no wrong. She had felt frustrated and angry on the Lady Anna's behalf when, to Anna's detriment, she'd heard people singing Queen Catherine's praises. Word of the king's domestic troubles therefore pleased Cat mightily. It seemed only right that King Henry should suffer in retribution for all the sorrow he had caused others.

"His Grace should never have put Queen Anna aside," Cat's friend Jane Ratsey said. "Pray God he will see sense when he's rid himself of Catherine Howard."

"What! Is God working to make the Lady Anna of Cleves queen again?" Cat rather liked the idea, although she pitied any woman married to King Henry.

Jane was convinced of it. She rattled on while they sat and wrought, praising Queen Anna's virtues and making rude remarks about her successor. "It is impossible that so sweet a queen as the Lady Anna could be utterly put aside," she declared, just as they were joined by Dorothy Wingfield, one of Anna's bedchamber women.

"I would think the king has had wives enough already," Dorothy said, stitching industriously at the hem of a handkerchief.

"That is why he should take the Lady Anna back," Jane insisted. "It would be as if Catherine Howard never existed."

"What a man the king is!" Cat said with a laugh. "How many wives will he have?"

"Four and there's an end to it," Jane said firmly. "Catherine of Aragon, Anne Boleyn, Jane Seymour, and our own Lady Anna."

"That's only two," Dorothy pointed out, "as the law says neither of the first two marriages ever existed."

"Why, the poor man," Cat said. "He has scarcely any acquaintance with matrimony at all!"

THE DUKE OF Norfolk waited in a tiny, dusty, windowless room. Nan was not the first person to be interrogated there. The place smelled of sweat and terror.

On trembling legs, she stood in front of the table where the duke sat. A clerk was hunched over a sheaf of papers at its far end, ready to take down whatever damning evidence Nan might have to give.

Norfolk was frightening enough in normal situations, with that hawk nose and long, deeply lined face. His eyes were devoid of emotion, dark and flat and utterly without mercy. Under his stare, Nan remembered hearing that his own wife had accused him of physically abusing her and putting his mistress in her place. Norfolk had also turned against his own niece, Queen Anne Boleyn, and presided over her trial at the king's bidding, even pronouncing sentence of death upon her. It appeared he was prepared to do the same thing again to a second niece. Nan did not expect him to show any mercy to her.

Confined to their dormitory, the maids of honor had heard no details of the charges against Queen Catherine, nor had they dared speculate to each other. It was too easy to be overheard. They had pretended, to themselves as well as to others, that they had never noticed anything amiss. Nan prayed she had sufficient talent at deception to convince the duke of her innocence. She could not bear to think about the alternative.

"You are Mistress Anne Bassett, maid of honor to the queen?"

Nan had to swallow before she could answer. "I am, Your Grace."

"Your mother is currently a prisoner in Calais and your stepfather is confined to the Tower of London."

At his accusatory tone, Nan felt her spine stiffen. Her lips compressed into a hard, thin line. She answered with a curt nod.

"And Mistress Catherine Bassett, a maid of honor to the Lady Anna of Cleves, is your sister?"

That question caught her off guard. There was a quality in the duke's voice warning her that he was not just verifying Cat's identity. "She is."

"Has Mistress Catherine Bassett ever spoken to you of the King's Grace?"

Nan hesitated. It would be peculiar if she had not. "I do not understand the question, my lord."

A flash of impatience darkened his features. "Has your sister ever said to you that Anna of Cleves should be queen again?"

"No, my lord." That question, at least, she could answer honestly.

When he continued to ask questions about Lady Anna of Cleves, Nan wondered what the king's former wife had done. There had been a rumor, following the king's visit to Richmond a few weeks after his wedding to Catherine Howard, that he had gotten Anna with child, but like so many of the stories told of King Henry, there had been no truth to that one.

Nan gave careful answers, then offered an unsolicited remark. "My sister and I are not on the best of terms. She has been envious of me ever since I was chosen to be a maid of honor to Queen Jane and she was not."

"You have made a profession of courtiership, I perceive."

"As many have before me, Your Grace." Until that moment, Nan had never thought of her position in quite that way, but it was an excellent description.

"You are an observant woman."

"I like to think so, Your Grace." Dangerous waters here!

"What have you noticed about Master Francis Dereham's behavior in the queen's presence?"

Nan had been prepared for questions about Tom Culpepper. She had not expected to hear Francis Dereham's name. At her evident astonishment, the duke frowned.

"Well?" he prompted her.

"Master Dereham is somewhat forward." Once again, Nan chose her words with care.

Norfolk made an impatient gesture with one hand. "Is he intimate with the queen?"

"I know of no improper familiarity between them, my lord. Why, Master Dereham only joined the queen's household during this summer's progress. And he came recommended by the old duchess—I mean, by your stepmother, Your Grace."

Only by a slight tightening of the lips did the duke betray his annoyance. Then the questions continued. He kept at Nan for the better part of another hour, badgering her to supply the kind of details that would damn the queen.

Nan gave him little satisfaction. Anything she had suspected, she kept to herself for her own protection. The longer the interrogation continued, the more she realized that, in truth, she had observed very little of what must have taken place.

At last the duke seemed satisfied that he had wrung every drop of information out of her. He turned his cold, implacable gaze on her one last time. "You will not be returning to the maids' dormitory, Mistress Bassett. The queen's household has been dissolved. Your belongings have been searched and secured. They will be released to you when you leave Hampton Court."

Nan started to protest that she had no place to go, but stopped herself in time. The Duke of Norfolk had no interest in her fate. Nor did she want him to. She'd prefer it if he'd forget he'd ever heard of her.

Drained of energy, as dazed as if she'd taken a blow to the head, Nan turned out of habit toward the queen's apartments. Guards blocked the door to the presence chamber, effectively preventing her from reaching the privy chamber, bedchamber, and the other smaller rooms beyond.

Nan descended to the kitchens instead. She gave no real thought to where she was going until she found herself at the foot of the small spiral staircase that linked the two floors and allowed servants to deliver food to the queen without actually entering the royal lodgings. There she stopped, wondering where she thought she was going.

She had no place with Queen Catherine anymore.

She had no place anywhere.

The queen's household had been disbanded, her attendants questioned and sent away . . . or to prison. Nan tried to take comfort from the fact that she had her freedom, but that did not solve her immediate need for a roof over her head.

Could she throw herself on Cousin Mary's mercy? Or ask charity of Jane Mewtas or Joan Denny? Each of them had been kind to her, befriended her, but at the time there had been some personal advantage to them in coming to her aid. Now there was none. There might even be a stigma attached to offering her a home.

Where else could she go? Not to Ned, that much was certain. Not Calais. That left only Tehidy, the Bassett seat in Cornwall, where her sisters now lived with Frances, their widowed sister-in-law. Spending the rest of her life rusticating in the country was not acceptable. There had to be an alternative.

Nan was still dithering at the foot of the stairs when she heard the patter of rapidly descending footfalls. Anne Herbert appeared on the landing. Her eyes widened when she saw Nan. She glanced behind her to make certain they were not observed, then made little shooing motions to indicate that Nan should step out of her way.

"The pond garden," Anne mouthed as she passed.

A short time later, they met near one of the sunken fishponds that gave the Pond Garden, located between the palace and the Thames, its name. Surrounded by low walls, the ponds housed fresh fish slated for the king's table. From this vantage point, Nan and Anne had a clear view of anyone approaching.

"What has happened?" Nan demanded. "I've been told nothing, only questioned and ordered to leave."

In the bright November sunlight, Anne's face looked ravaged. She had been crying. "Oh, Nan. It is all so dreadful. How could it be that no one knew about the queen's past?" Anne sank down on the stone-topped brick wall. "They say she took lovers when she was a mere girl."

"Francis Dereham?" Nan guessed.

"And another man, too. She was no virgin when she came to the king, but she deceived him into thinking her innocent. No wonder he is in a rage."

Nan's stomach clenched and she leaned for support against one of the stone beasts that decorated the wall at intervals. If the king had seen through Catherine's falsehoods, he might now suspect that Nan had also lied to him. She would truly be ruined if that were the case.

"And there is more," Anne said. "The queen is accused of taking Tom Culpepper as her lover *after* she was queen. That is treason and the king will have her head for it! The old Duchess of Norfolk and her son, Lord William Howard, have been arrested and taken to the Tower. So have Lady Rochford and two of the queen's chamberers. The queen herself is to be imprisoned in the old abbey at Syon." Anne gave a humorless laugh. "I am to be one of her jailers. I am to accompany her there."

"As jailer . . . or prisoner?"

Anne fiddled with her sleeve. "No one who served the queen is free of suspicion. I suppose I will be both until I prove my loyalty."

As the king's spy, then. Nan kicked at a loose clod of earth. "Have you heard any rumors about Anna of Cleves? Or about my sister?" She was worried about Cat. If Anne's husband, Will Herbert, or her brother, Will Parr, knew what was going on at Richmond, Nan was certain they'd have told Anne.

Anne's puzzled frown was answer enough. "What has Cat Bassett to do with Queen Catherine?"

"I wish I knew. The Duke of Norfolk asked me if she'd ever said anything to me about the Lady Anna desiring to be queen again."

Anne caught Nan's arm. Her expression was as somber as Nan had ever seen it. "There are those who think the king should never have divorced the Lady Anna. If I were you, Nan, I would stay away from Cat. In fact, do nothing that could call attention to yourself."

It was good advice, but Nan did not think she could follow it. "Unless I wish to starve or freeze to death for want of a roof over my head, I must be bold," she said. "Is the king still at Whitehall?"

Anne's eyes widened in fear for her friend, but she nodded.

NAN HIRED A boat to take her downriver from Hampton Court to Whitehall. She disembarked at the water stairs and entered the palace through the gallery that ran from the water gate to the queen's privy lodging. No one tried to stop her. She was not important enough to worry about.

The king's presence chamber was crowded, as usual. Nan searched for the familiar faces of the king's favorite gentlemen, but she saw no one she knew well enough to approach.

Confident that someone would eventually appear who could give her entrée to the king, Nan waited. Her nervousness increased as one hour stretched into two. The yeoman of the guard on duty cast suspicious glances her way. After another quarter hour, he approached her.

"What is your business here, mistress?"

"I have come to see the king."

"Impossible. Be off with you." He took her by the arm, set to evict her in spite of her tears and pleas. He froze at a command issued in the familiar voice of Anthony Denny.

"Yeoman, unhand Mistress Bassett, if you please."

"She has no business here, Master Denny."

"I will see to her," Denny promised, and caught Nan by the same arm the yeoman had just released. He steered her rapidly out of the presence chamber and down a flight of stairs. "You should not have come here," he said in a low, urgent whisper as he hustled her through the nearly empty Great Hall and out into the courtyard that lay between it and the chapel.

"I had to come to Whitehall! I had nowhere else to go. Would you have me repair to my sister at Richmond?" Her words came out in short bursts. Their rapid progress had her gasping for breath.

"That would not be wise," Denny muttered.

"Why not?" Digging in her heels, Nan forced him to slow his pace. She could not imagine Cat in trouble, but then she'd never have guessed that Mary would cause so many problems for the family, either.

Denny closed his eyes briefly, as if gathering strength. They had reached a secluded corner of the courtyard. He all but shoved Nan onto a bench and stood in front of her as if he hoped to block the view of anyone passing by. Clearly, he did not want to be seen talking to her.

"What has Cat done? I must know," she added when she saw the reluctance in Denny's expression. "How else am I to keep myself safe?" And how was she to help her sister?

Denny kept his voice low. "She wondered aloud if Anna of Cleves would be queen again and asked how many wives the king would have."

Nan was certain a great many people had been thinking the same thing, but to voice those thoughts could be construed as treason. Was Cat already in the Tower? The last thing Nan wanted was to join her there, but she had to know more. "Is she . . . where is my sister?"

"Still at Richmond, and still in the service of Anna of Cleves, but it was a near thing. She and two other women in attendance on the Lady Anna were examined by members of the Privy Council. They could have sent her to prison . . . or worse. Just now, the king has reason to be furious at everyone connected to either Catherine or the Lady Anna."

"Why the Lady Anna?"

Denny checked again for potential eavesdroppers. "Your sister's comments came to light because privy councilors were already at Richmond.

They were sent to investigate the persistent rumor that Anna of Cleves has borne a child."

"Oh, that old story!"

"No, a new one. In this version, King Henry is not the child's father. Now, if you have no more questions, be off with you. Take my advice and stay out of the king's sight. Do nothing to call attention to yourself."

"That is what everyone keeps telling me." Tears pooled in Nan's eyes and she was not too proud to hide them. "But where is it I am to go? I no longer have a place at court. My mother is a prisoner in Calais. My stepfather is held in the Tower. I would be ill advised to join my sister at Richmond."

"You have kin in the West Country."

"Including some I share with your wife."

He paled at the reminder.

"Do not worry, Master Denny. I have no way to travel to Devon or Cornwall, even if I wished to go there."

When a look of resignation replaced Denny's scowl, Nan thought he might be about to invite her to use one of his houses. Instead, he offered her his arm. "I suppose there is no help for it. You must speak with the king."

At a brisk clip, he led her back into Whitehall, only this time he bypassed the Presence Chamber. She found herself in the small, sumptuously furnished room where she had once before met the king in private. This time there was no beautifully illuminated Book of Hours in sight, nor was the king waiting.

"Stay here," Denny instructed.

Left alone, Nan was suddenly not at all sure it was wise to throw herself on King Henry's mercy. She could think of a dozen reasons why this was a very bad idea indeed, but it was too late to change her mind.

Her nerves were strung tight by the time she heard a small sound at the door. A moment later, King Henry limped into the room, the corset he wore to contain his bulk creaking with every step. Nan sank into a curtsy, bowing her head until it almost touched the floor, and held that pose until the king's grotesquely swollen fingers appeared in front of her nose and tugged her upright.

"Have you reason to be terrified of me, Nan?" His voice was deceptively mild. His small, suspicious eyes were a truer reflection of his mood.

"No, sire. But I am frightened for my future." She dropped her gaze. "I am without resources, Your Grace. Without family or friends, saving only Your Majesty. I have nowhere to go now that I have no place at court."

A long, tense silence followed. Nan could barely contain the trembling in her limbs.

"I do not blame you for anything that has transpired," the king said at last.

She dared peek at him through her lashes. The thoughtful expression on his face contained neither anger nor annoyance.

"Your Grace," Nan said, greatly daring, "I beg your pardon for troubling you with this trifling matter, but I have no home to go to, no one to take me in."

He reached out with one pudgy, beringed hand to caress her cheek. She barely managed not to flinch in revulsion. The sight of those fat, white fingers was bad enough—they looked like sausages, only not so appealing—but his touch was worse. His skin was so cold that it put her in mind of a corpse.

"Did you think I could forget you, Nan?" the king said. "That I would ignore your plight? You must not worry. I will have Denny escort you back to Hampton Court and there you will stay. You will have new lodgings, something fitting for a member of the Lady Mary's household."

Lightheaded with relief, Nan swayed. "Your Grace is most generous."

"I mean to spend some time in North Surrey," the king continued, drawing her closer and planting a smacking kiss on her lips. "Beddington, Esher, Oatlands, Woking, and Horsley. I will be at Greenwich for

Yuletide, as will Prince Edward and my other children. That will be most convenient, will it not? I will be able to see you, my dear, anytime I visit my daughter Mary."

NAN SETTLED INTO Mary Tudor's household with surprising ease. She already knew several of Mary's attendants, including Bess Jerningham, Lady Kingston's daughter.

In late December, the court moved to Greenwich for the holidays. Anna of Cleves remained at Richmond. Some said she still hoped the king would marry her again, but Nan doubted it. Anna had all she could ever want, without the trouble of a husband.

Anna was fortunate, Nan thought. She was no longer queen, but she had wealth and position. And she had the freedom to do as she pleased, so long as she did nothing to annoy the king. Unlike Catherine Howard, who was now imprisoned in the Tower of London, awaiting execution.

Yuletide passed quietly and, although the king gave Nan a pretty brooch as a New Year's gift, he did not send for her to warm his bed. Nor, to her relief, did he appear to notice that she no longer had the ruby ring he'd once given her.

In January, the court moved on to Whitehall, where the king was to host a series of suppers and banquets. On the twenty-ninth, the guests were all young ladies who were also invited to spend the night at the palace. King Henry spent the entire morning inspecting the chambers they would occupy, even examining the furniture and bedding to be certain they were the best he had to offer.

"The king is looking for a new wife," Anne Herbert said. Since she had permanent lodgings at Whitehall—those assigned to her husband—she had invited Nan, Dorothy Bray, and Lucy Somerset to spend the afternoon with her before attending the festivities that evening.

Dorothy visibly shuddered. Lucy sighed. Nan did not react at all. That King Henry would marry for a sixth time seemed inevitable. She hoped it would be soon. She had not yet been summoned to His Grace's bedchamber, but she doubted her luck would hold much longer.

"Why else do you think you are here?" Anne, the only one of them who was safely wed, took a piece of marchpane from a tray and passed it on to Lucy.

"Are we to be paraded before His Grace like prime horseflesh?" Dorothy asked. "King Henry knows already what we look like."

"He has invited several young women who have not previously come to court. There is Lord Cobham's daughter, Bess Brooke, and—"

"That one's no better than she should be," Dorothy broke in. "You should have seen all the gentlemen gaping at her when she arrived. It was as if they had never seen a female before."

In other words, Nan thought, Will Parr—Baron Parr of Kendal— had admired Mistress Brooke, and Dorothy was jealous. Dorothy had been Parr's mistress and he her devoted slave for a long time, but with Queen Catherine's arrest and the disbanding of her household, the two lovebirds had been separated. The spell had been broken. At least it had been for Anne Herbert's brother.

"Bess Brooke is a mere child," Lucy protested.

"Only a year younger than you are," Dorothy shot back.

"Old enough to be wedded and bedded, but her virginity has been strictly guarded." Anne lowered her voice. "My sister tells me that there is a bill before Parliament to require that any woman who agrees to marry the king must declare, on pain of death, that no charge of misbehavior can be brought against her."

"What if a prospective queen reveals her past and confesses all her sins and the king still wants to marry her?" Dorothy asked.

"I do not believe Parliament considered that possibility, but they did have sense enough to realize that a woman in such a situation might lie. Another provision in the law states that anyone else who knows the truth about the king's intended bride must come forward with it if the would-be queen is not forthcoming. The penalty for failing to do so is imprisonment for life."

"If they are found out," Dorothy said.

"It is never wise to deceive the king." Lucy ignored the marchpane but took a handful of nuts from a nearby bowl, slanting a look at Anne as she did so. "Your sister is Lady Latimer, is she not? Did she come to London with her husband when the lords gathered for Parliament?"

Anne nodded. "They have taken a house in Blackfriars. I hope she will soon be able to visit me here at court."

"No children yet?" Lucy asked.

Anne's face fell as she shook her head. "Kathryn has been unable to give her husband an heir. She did not conceive during her first marriage, either."

"Lord Latimer already has an heir." Lucy's sharp tone drew every eye her way. She blushed.

"I had forgotten. Lord Latimer has children by his first wife." Anne's lips twitched as she fought a smile. "As I recall, the eldest son is a toothsome lad."

It would be a good match, Nan thought. Lucy was the younger daughter of an earl, and young John Neville, Latimer's heir, would one day be a baron. In the not-so-distant past, Nan would have been jealous of Lucy's prospects, but during the last few months she had become ambivalent about many things. If the king wanted her for his mistress, she'd have to force herself to comply. What choice would she have? Only by pleasing King Henry in bed could she ever hope to secure her own future.

A sigh escaped her. The ambitions she'd had when she left Calais had died a slow death in the years since. Now there were times when she almost wished that Queen Jane had chosen Cat to serve her.

Shaking off her self-pity, Nan began to attend to the babble of feminine voices around her. Lucy had been teased into admitting a romantic interest in John Neville and the conversation had moved on to news of marriages and births and deaths. Nan had little to contribute. She was glad when it was time to leave for the king's supper.

TWENTY-SIX LADIES SAT at King Henry's table and thirty-five at a second one close by. The seating was arranged by precedence, so that the highest-born ladies were closest to the king. Nan, whose status remained uncertain so long as Lord Lisle was a prisoner in the Tower, was placed next to a young woman she'd never seen before, a pretty girl with blond hair and blue eyes and a vivacious manner.

She reminded Nan of Catherine Howard.

"Have you tried this syllabub?" the young woman asked. "It is most delicious."

Nan spooned up a small portion, tasted, and agreed, all the while studying her companion. The girl wore a copper-colored gown, richly embroidered. "Mistress Brooke?" Nan guessed. "Lord Cobham's daughter?"

The girl's smile was brilliant. "I am. And you are Mistress Bassett, are you not?"

Nan agreed that she was and thawed a bit in the face of Bess Brooke's friendliness. They chatted amiably throughout the meal.

At the banquet, which was much less formal, the king made a point of speaking to each of his guests. He did not linger long with any of them until he came to Lucy Somerset. By the time he moved on, there were already whispers that he had singled her out to be his next queen.

Nan watched uneasily as King Henry made his way in her direction. He stopped to talk to this one and that, but it was clear he was headed straight for her. She sank into a curtsy as he closed the distance between them.

"My dear Nan," he said as she rose. "You are thriving in my daughter's household."

"She is a most kind mistress, Your Grace."

"And you value kindness?"

"I do, Your Grace." She dared meet his eyes, expecting to find a sensual invitation there, or at the least a spark of admiration. Instead she found speculation, as if he were considering a matter of grave importance.

"I can be surpassing . . . kind," the king said after a moment. "But I expect kindness in return."

"That seems only fair," Nan murmured, but she was confused. It was not like the king to speak in riddles.

"I mean to pardon your mother and stepfather," he said.

Nan caught her breath in surprise. "That . . . that would be a most kind act indeed, Your Grace."

He chuckled, patted her hand in an almost avuncular way, and moved on to Bess Brooke. "And who is this beautiful blossom?"

The king's question, issued in a booming voice, caught the attention of everyone in the hall. Nan was able to retreat unnoticed and slip away soon after to her own small chamber in the Lady Mary's apartments. Did His Grace really mean to free Lord and Lady Lisle? And if he did, she wondered, what "kindness" did he plan to demand in return?

The King had never been merry since first hearing of the Queen's misconduct, but he has been so since, especially on the 29th, when he gave a supper and banquet with twenty-six ladies at the table, besides gentlemen, and thirty-five at another table adjoining. The lady for whom he showed the greatest regard was a sister of Lord Cobham. . . . She is a pretty young creature, with wit enough to do as badly as the others if she were to try. The King is also said to fancy a daughter . . . by her first marriage, of the wife of Lord Lisle, late deputy of Calais.

—Eustace Chapuys, imperial ambassador to England, to Holy Roman Emperor
Charles V, 9 February 1542

Although Nan had told the king that his daughter was a kind mistress, she lived on the periphery of the Lady Mary's household. She had no official position and few duties. She was puzzled when Bess Jerningham told her that Mary wanted a word with her and even more bemused when Mary, who was walking for exercise in a long indoor gallery, sent her other attendants away.

"You may wonder why I asked for you." The princess set off at a brisk pace. As she walked two or three miles every day after breakfast, Nan had to scramble to keep up.

"It is not my place to wonder, Your Grace."

Mary laughed. "I doubt that stops any of my ladies from speculating in the privacy of their own minds. No matter. I have observed you for some time now, Nan Bassett, ever since Lady Kingston first presented you to me."

Nan remembered that day. Queen Jane had been struggling to give birth to Prince Edward.

"Why did the king, my father, send you to me?"

The blunt question took Nan aback, but she had her answer ready. It was nothing but the truth. "I had nowhere else to go, Your Grace. My stepfather is still in the Tower and my mother is held prisoner in Calais. Two of my sisters are dependent upon my widowed sister-in-law and the third serves the Lady Anna of Cleves."

"Did His Majesty send you to spy on me?"

"No, Your Grace." Nan was genuinely shocked.

"Then perhaps he wished us to become friends. It is no secret that my father intends to marry again, or that he is encouraged to do so by his advisors, who want him to produce more sons to secure the succession."

Nan remained silent. She knew enough of Mary's history to understand that, until King Henry had divorced Catherine of Aragon and married Anne Boleyn, Mary Tudor had been heiress presumptive. She had been raised by her mother to rule England. Then she had been disinherited and declared illegitimate. The king might someday restore her to the succession, but in the meantime it must gall her to contemplate the prospect of yet another stepmother, yet another rival for the throne.

"A few days ago, you were summoned to a banquet at Whitehall, Nan Bassett."

"I was, Your Grace."

"I am told by the imperial ambassador that the king was particularly attentive to three of his guests. You were one of them."

Mary strode purposefully along and Nan had to walk quickly to keep pace with her. She was beginning to tire.

"He was kind enough to say that he means to release my stepfather from the Tower, Your Grace." He had not yet done so.

Mary paused to stare at Nan with her nearsighted squint as she considered that information. "There is more, I think, to His Grace's interest in you. There are some who believe he considers that you would make him a most excellent queen."

"I do not think such an outcome is likely, Your Grace."

"Why? Because you were once his mistress?"

Nan shrank back before the vehemence of the question. She was not physically afraid of Mary. The other woman was small and spare, almost delicate looking, and very thin, while Nan, for the most part, enjoyed robust good health. But Mary had an air of authority about her. A sense of power as yet unleashed. There was no safe reply Nan could make. She could not deny that she had been intimate with the king, but telling his daughter that they'd coupled only once did not seem like a good idea.

With admirable calm, Mary resumed her daily exercise. At the end of the gallery, she stopped and turned, framed by a wall of glass and a view of the snow-covered garden beyond. "You were at the king's banquet and I was not. You were singled out for His Grace's attention. I have no doubt that you took note of which other ladies he favored."

"He took care to speak with each of his guests, Your Grace."

Mary made an impatient gesture. "The ambassador tells me that His Grace showed the greatest regard for Lady Wyatt. How is that possible?"

Nan blinked at her in confusion. "Lady . . . Wyatt?" She did not recall meeting anyone by that name.

"Sir Thomas Wyatt's wife, a woman he put aside some years ago with the claim that she'd committed adultery."

Nan frowned. "The king would never consider marrying a woman with such a scandal in her past. Besides, her husband is still alive." And, ironic as it seemed, given the reason for the rift, it was nearly impossible to dissolve a marriage in England now that King Henry had broken away from the church of Rome.

"She was described to me as a pretty young thing," the Lady Mary said.

"That cannot be Sir Thomas's wife." Nan remembered a little about the old scandal now. "She has a son older than I am."

"But who else could she have been? The imperial ambassador told me that the woman in question was Lord Cobham's sister, Elizabeth Brooke."

Nan stifled a laugh. "Your Grace, there is a second Elizabeth Brooke, a girl of fifteen or so. She is the current Lord Cobham's daughter. Lady Wyatt is her aunt."

"Ah, I see." Mary's thin lips twitched and there was laughter in her bright brown eyes. "Yes, that makes more sense."

His Grace *should* consider an older woman, Nan mused. Someone who could nurse him as he himself advanced into old age. She did not express that radical thought aloud.

"Who was the third?" Mary's abrupt question brought Nan back to her surroundings.

"The third lady in whom he is interested? I am not certain, Your Grace."

The princess's expression was rueful. "I fear the ambassador is not always reliable when it comes to English names, his native language being Spanish. He identified her as the daughter of Madam Albart, but I know of no such woman. And he said she was Sir Anthony Browne's niece."

Nan struggled to recall if the king had paid special attention to anyone in particular. After a moment, the pieces of the puzzle fell into place. "I believe, Your Grace, that he meant Lady Lucy Somerset, the Earl of Worcester's daughter. Worcester's secondary title is Lord Herbert of Ragland." Herbert and Albart, she reasoned, sounded enough alike to cause a foreigner to err.

"And is she Sir Anthony Browne's niece?"

"Her father's second wife, Lady Lucy's stepmother, is Sir Anthony's sister." Nan was grateful for her mother's coaching in the relationships between courtiers. It was often useful to know who was kin to whom.

"You have been most helpful. I am in your debt, Mistress Bassett."

"I wonder, Your Grace . . ."

"Yes."

"How was I described that you could identify me?"

"That is no mystery. The ambassador called you a daughter by her first marriage of the wife of the former deputy of Calais. Who else could you be?"

Philippa, Cat, or Mary, Nan thought.

The princess dismissed her with further expressions of gratitude, leaving Nan with no duties to take her mind off the implications of what she'd just been told. She'd denied the king's interest in her as a potential wife when the suggestion came from her friend Anne, but if even King Henry's daughter believed it was a possibility . . .

Nan told herself this was another mistake on the part of the imperial ambassador, akin to identifying the wrong Elizabeth Brooke, but she did not believe it. That night she tossed and turned, unable to sleep, unable to stop worrying about the future. *Did* the king want to marry her? Was that why, even though she had been given her own small chamber, he had not sent for her? Was that why he planned to release her mother and stepfather—so that he would not be marrying a traitor's daughter?

She *was* young and pretty. And His Grace had known her longer than he had known Lucy or Bess. Perhaps he felt more comfortable with her. No doubt that made her more attractive to him.

"But I do not want to be queen," she whispered into her pillow.

KING HENRY HELD another banquet a week after Catherine Howard's execution. Once again, he flirted openly with Nan and set tongues wagging. Nan put on a brave face and flirted back, but inside she was quaking. Only the fact that this gathering, on the twenty-first of February, was right before Lent kept her from yielding to panic and fleeing the court.

Nan had come to the conclusion that she must find a way to deflect the king's amorous interest. It was not only that she'd developed an ever-increasing distaste for his person. Her life might well depend upon it.

Parliament had passed the law Anne Herbert had spoken of in time for the king to use it to condemn Catherine Howard to death. Under that law, Nan's situation was the same as the late queen's. If anyone investigated Nan's past—questioned Kate Stradling, talked to Mother

Gristwood—Nan's life could be forfeit for deceiving the king about her virginity.

Another week passed. Nan slept poorly at night. Lord Lisle had not yet been released. In weak moments she selfishly hoped he would not be.

On the first of March, as Nan's newly acquired maidservant laced her into her garments, Nan realized she had lost weight. After she dismissed the girl, she studied her face in her looking glass. A stranger looked back at her—hollow eyed, pale, haunted.

It was her beauty that had attracted His Grace. Lose that and she would lose his interest. Nan only wished she could! But if he stopped wanting to please her, there could be even more wide-reaching consequences. Until her mother and stepfather were free, she must go on as she had been.

She combed her hair and donned a French hood, steeling herself to face the day. But before she could leave her lodgings, Anthony Denny appeared at her door.

For a moment, she thought he'd come to escort her to the king's bed, although early morning seemed an odd time for a tryst. Then she saw the grave expression on his face.

"He's gone, Nan," Denny said. "Lord Lisle died in the Tower early this morning."

A bone-deep chill swept over her, leaching warmth from her limbs and her face and leaving her dizzy. "Executed?" she whispered.

Denny's eyes widened in surprise. "Never think it! Lisle received word of his pardon last night. The shock of learning he was to be released must have been too much for him."

Guilt washed through her. "I should have gone to visit him when the king first promised to set him free. I could have prepared him for this news." She had not wanted to raise false hopes, or so she'd told herself. The real truth was that, just like everyone else at court, she'd shied away from associating with an accused traitor.

"He was an old man," Denny said kindly. "He lived a long, full life."

Tears blurred her vision as she struggled to come to terms with what had happened. "But he *was* pardoned? There is no longer any taint on his name?"

"A full pardon. By now Lady Lisle has been freed. I expect she will leave Calais and return to England within the next few days."

"And the lands and property confiscated by the Crown?"

Denny avoided her eyes. "I . . . uh . . . there was no provision made to return them."

Nan swallowed the lump in her throat. She did not look forward to facing her mother. Lord Lisle dead. Property lost. Nan's failures would far outweigh her success.

TWO WEEKS AFTER Lord Lisle's death, Nan was still far from ready to deal with her mother. Lady Lisle had sent word that she would not come to court. This struck Nan as a bad sign. It meant that Honor Lisle felt no gratitude toward the king for her release. Doubtless, she blamed King Henry for her husband's death. Nan could only hope she would not say or do something that would land her back in prison facing new charges of treason.

It was a woman Nan had never seen before who fetched her from the Lady Mary's presence chamber at Greenwich Palace. She introduced herself as Lady Hungerford. "So," she said, radiating disapproval from every pore, "you are the one my stepson thinks to marry."

Taken aback, Nan was at a loss for words. She remembered that Lady Hungerford had accused Wat's father of imprisoning and mistreating her. Nan did not recall Wat having ever said anything else about his stepmother. It seemed unlikely that Lady Hungerford held Wat's wardship. She'd not have had the wherewithal to buy it from the Crown after her husband's attainder. That meant she had no say in arranging his marriage. A good thing, Nan thought.

"You know the boy I mean," Lady Hungerford continued. "He is too young for you, mistress, even if either of you had a feather to fly with."

Even though her words echoed what Nan had told Wat, she resented the unsolicited opinion and was tempted to tell this odious woman that she fully intended to marry her precious stepson. Nan's better judgment prevailed before she blurted out something she'd regret.

"I am certain that young man has forgotten all about me," she said instead. "I have not seen or heard from him since a chance encounter at Hatfield Chase on the last royal progress."

"I do much doubt it. He is the most stubborn fellow in all creation. I hope you will have the good sense to keep refusing him." Without giving Nan a chance to reply, Lady Hungerford abruptly changed the subject. "I am on my way to Lady Garney's house, in the village of Greenwich. Your mother is staying there and asked that I bring you with me."

A short time later, they were on their way. "Is Lady Garney a friend of your mother's?" Lady Hungerford asked.

Nan nodded. "Before Sir Christopher Garney's death, he and his wife lived in Calais for many years. But you, madam—what is your concern in this? I have never heard my mother mention your name."

"I was Elizabeth Hussey before I wed. My sister, Mary, is your mother's waiting gentlewoman. Tell me, where will your mother go now that she is free?"

"To Tehidy in Cornwall, or so I suppose. That is where my sisters are living."

"And will Lady Lisle have a place there for my sister?"

In that instant, Nan realized that Lady Hungerford's situation was no better than Lady Lisle's. In truth, it might be worse. Lord Hungerford had not just been accused of terrible crimes, he had been executed for them. At least Nan's stepfather had died a natural death. Worse, Lady Hungerford and Mary Hussey were also the daughters of an executed traitor.

"That will be my mother's decision to make," Nan said, "but if they spent months imprisoned together, they have either become fast friends or your sister is ready to chew off her own arm to escape spending another moment in my mother's company."

Mary Hussey was waiting for them at the door to Lady Garney's house. She rushed into her sister's arms. "I have missed you so!" Mary cried. "Please say you have come to take me away with you."

Lady Hungerford went stiff as a poker. "I am about to remarry. I—"

"Then you will want some of your own kin with you." Mary beamed at her. "I will help you set up your new household."

Lady Hungerford's glance shot daggers at a grinning Nan, but then she unbent sufficiently to speak kindly to her sister. "Are you certain Lady Lisle can spare you? You have an obligation to remain in her service if she still has need of you."

"Mistress Hussey," Nan interrupted, "do you wish to be free of my mother?"

"More than you can know!" Mary clapped both hands over her mouth, but it was too late to call back the tactless words.

Nan patted Mary's arm to reassure her. "Go with your sister with my blessing. Indeed, you may leave as soon as you are packed. There is no need to tell my mother. I will let her know that you have gone." If Lady Lisle lost her temper over Mary Hussey's departure, it might dilute some of her anger toward Nan.

Nan found her mother waiting for her in Lady Garney's solar, a sunlit upper room used for needlework and reading. Lady Lisle was clad entirely in black and seemed smaller than Nan remembered. Her face was pinched and her eyes had a bruised look, but the fervor that burned in them had a manic quality.

"Well," she said in a soft, dangerous voice, "here you are at last, my failure of a daughter."

"What would you have had me do, Mother? Offend the king and be banished from court? I'd be no help to anyone then."

"You are high in His Grace's favor these days, or so I hear. Lady Garney may not frequent the royal court, but by living in Greenwich, hard by one of the king's favorite palaces, she is in a position to hear rumors."

"I am one of several ladies whose company the king enjoys."

"Just how much does he enjoy it?" Honor demanded.

Nan felt herself flush.

"So, that is the way of it, is it? Then I wonder even more that you could not persuade King Henry to do right by your kin."

Nan had to bite her lower lip to keep silent. Protestations of any kind would only make matters worse.

Silence hung over the room like a funeral pall, ominous and oppressive. Nan fought not to fidget as the seconds crawled past. She studied her mother's face, seeing there the unmistakable signs of an overwrought mind. Honor's mouth worked. Her eyes blinked rapidly, although she shed no tears. Then she turned a look of sheer maddened hatred on Nan.

Involuntarily, Nan took a step back. Her mother had always had a volatile temper, always been quick to cast blame and slow to forgive. But Nan had never seen her like this. Had Lady Lisle's imprisonment and the death of her much-loved husband caused her to run mad?

Nan's mother blinked. The contortions in her face smoothed out. "Well," she said, "what's done is done. Best make what you can of it. If the king wants you for his mistress, so be it, but marry him if you can. I waited upon Anne Boleyn in the days before she wed His Grace. Once she let him into her bed and got herself with child, he'd have done anything for her."

Nan stared at her mother in alarm and dismay.

Honor leaned forward in her chair and caught one of Nan's hands in a clawlike grip. "Whatever woman the king marries has influence over him. Play your cards right, my girl, and you can convince him to return England to the true faith."

Horrified at the thought of meddling in matters of religion, Nan sputtered out a protest. "His Grace does not tolerate opinions that differ from his own." Moreover, the king grew more irascible, intolerant, and despotic with every passing day.

"If you wish to leave the court," Honor said in a disgruntled voice, "I will take you back to Cornwall with me."

Anything would be better than that! "I will remain where I am, Mother. I will do what I can for the good of the family, but do not expect more of me than I can accomplish."

Honor wagged a gnarled finger at her. "Mark my words. If you are the king's mistress and do not go on to become his wife, you'll be sent packing as soon as he tires of you."

And if she married the king, Nan thought, she'd likely end up with her head on the block!

Nan returned to court in a troubled frame of mind. If even her mother had heard the rumor that the king wanted to marry her, she had to take it seriously. And she had to take action at once to prevent His Grace from proposing to her. There was only one practical solution. To save herself, she had to divert King Henry's attention to some other woman.

THE KING PAID regular visits to his daughter's lodgings at court. Although he spent some of his time with the Lady Mary, he spent more flirting with her ladies. When his game leg permitted the exercise, he danced with a great number of them, but Nan was his most frequent partner. He kept her with him when he played at cards or dice. And it was to Nan he complained when his ulcer caused him pain. It was Nan he took aside, into any convenient alcove, to fondle and kiss.

Nan seized upon every opportunity to praise the charms of Lucy Somerset and of Bess Brooke, but His Grace did not take the hint. Since neither was at court, it was a simple matter for him to forget that he'd once admired them both.

Nothing had been resolved by early June, when the king went off to inspect havens along the coast. The Lady Mary returned to her own house at Hunsdon, taking Nan with her. It was there that Anne Herbert's sister, Lady Latimer, joined the Lady Mary's household.

They were back at Greenwich on the nineteenth, in time to meet the king on his return from Harwich. The court soon swelled with visitors. Among them was Wat Hungerford. He made a point of dancing with Nan.

"You are as lovely as ever, Mistress Bassett."

"And you have been polishing your flattery, Master Hungerford." He had continued to fill out since she'd last seen him. She could not fault his looks. Indeed, if she had not known better, she'd have taken him for a man of her own years.

They danced apart and then together again. "I have been restored in blood by an act of Parliament," he said.

"I am pleased for you."

Apart. Together.

"It is likely that, in time, my title will be restored as well."

Apart. Together.

Nan's heart rate speeded up. She was about to receive a proposal of marriage, and from someone who might yet be a nobleman. How ironic. Even if there were no other arguments against the match, she did not dare accept him now. Not while the king appeared to be courting her. Wat Hungerford would have no future at all if King Henry saw him as a rival.

She spoke before he could. "It is dangerous to us both to consider more than friendship, Master Hungerford."

Apart. Together.

"I will take any crumb you let fall, Mistress Bassett. I accept your offer of friendship."

He set out to be good company and entertained her for the rest of the evening with a seemingly endless supply of amusing stories. He also managed to coax Nan into sharing some of her fondest memories of childhood. She could not help but be flattered by his attention and decided that it was just as well that he could not marry without permission until he turned twenty-one. Otherwise, she might be tempted.

The next day she returned with renewed determination to the task of finding a wife for the king. Mistress Brooke seemed the best prospect. She had a pleasing personality and a love of music and dance and rich clothing. She had been carefully brought up, shielded from temptation, and so was undoubtedly a virgin. Surely the king would see what an excellent bride she would make him.

He might have, had she been at court, but Lord Cobham had heard the rumors, too. He kept his daughter safe at Cooling Castle, in Kent.

Fortunately, the king did not seem in any rush to remarry. Although his advisors urged him to wed again and produce more heirs, one son being considered insufficient to make the realm secure, His Grace said nothing to Nan. She went from day to day by rote, performing her duties for the Lady Mary, flirting with the king, hating the sameness but at the same time dreading that her situation might change.

It was war with Scotland that finally broke the routine. In August, an army was sent north to fight England's traditional enemy. Lord Latimer was one of the commanders and Kathryn prayed daily for his safe return. She was devastated when, just after the Battle of Solway Moss, she received word that he had fallen ill.

"At least he was not wounded," Nan said.

But Kathryn could not be consoled. When Latimer returned to London, she took a leave of absence from the Lady Mary's household to nurse him.

In late November, the Earl of Sussex died at Chelsea. Nan felt sorrow for Cousin Mary's loss. In spite of their age difference, Mary had been fond of her husband. Then it occurred to Nan that the widowed Countess of Sussex might make an excellent wife for the king of England.

The countess did not cooperate. Like Bess Brooke, she stayed away from court. So did Lucy Somerset. Lord Latimer's declining health might mean his son would soon inherit the title. Nan was certain her friend would prefer a young and virile husband to the aging, ailing king, but she did not let that stop her from mentioning Lucy to His Grace at every opportunity, and Mary and Bess, too.

They moved to Hampton Court in December. The Lady Mary's lodgings there had been newly refurbished since her last visit, no doubt because the king meant to spend more time in those apartments than in his own. Nan continued to be the focus of his attention. He hinted that he had a special New Year's gift in mind for her.

Nan grew increasingly nervous as the Yuletide celebrations commenced. Everyone around her seemed cheerful and full of optimism. She avoided most of them, but she found herself drawn to Kathryn Latimer, who had returned to her duties but showed as little enthusiasm for the festive season as Nan.

"What is wrong, Kathryn?" Nan asked. "Is your husband still ailing?"

"Lord Latimer is dying," Kathryn said bluntly. Her fingers clenched so hard on the book of prayers she held that she left little pockmarks in the purple velvet cover.

"You should be with him."

Kathryn burst into tears. "He will not allow it. He insisted I return to court."

Nan comforted her, surprised all over again, as she rocked Kathryn in her arms, at how tiny the other woman was. She had a delicate build and attractive features, something people rarely noticed because she did not thrust herself forward. With a bevy of vivacious ladies surrounding the princess, she went virtually unnoticed.

Kathryn Latimer did have her enthusiasms, Nan remembered—dancing, jewelry, hunting with a crossbow. And she was by nature gentle, generous, and kind.

Nan stepped back to better study her friend. Kathryn had experience in nursing an ailing spouse. She was experienced in the bedchamber, as well, but no one could fault her for that because she'd gained it through two lawful marriages. She was thirty years old, but still young enough to have children.

The red-rimmed eyes were temporary. Once Lord Latimer was dead, Kathryn would mourn, but she'd recover. She'd undoubtedly remarry. Widows did.

Nan smiled to herself as she offered Kathryn Parr a handkerchief. Unless she was very much mistaken, she had just found the perfect candidate to become King Henry's sixth wife.

... since he learned the conduct of his last wife, [the king] has continually shown himself sad ... but now all is changed and order is already taken that the princess shall go to court this feast, accompanied with a great number of ladies; and they work night and day at Hampton Court to finish her lodgings.

—Eustace Chapuys, imperial ambassador to England, to Mary of Hungary, regent of the Netherlands, December 1542

n New Year's Day, Nan avoided the annual gift giving by pleading a megrim and staying in bed. She did not expect to see anyone but her maid. She knew the king would not trouble her, not with his aversion to illness of any kind.

"Nan?" Kathryn Latimer's soft voice pulled Nan from a light doze. "I have brought you a poultice."

Inwardly, Nan groaned. "I only need sleep," she protested, but Kathryn had already shoved the bed hangings aside.

The smell of herbs tickled Nan's nose—vervain, she thought, and betony. A moment later a damp, warm cloth settled over her forehead and eyes. Nan felt the feather bed depress as Kathryn sat.

"When you have warning of the onset of a megrim, you might try eating raisins. My first husband often found that effective."

"Warning?" Nan echoed. Kathryn's nurturing was so unexpected, so overwhelming, that she had difficulty thinking clearly.

"With a megrim there are usually some signs in advance of the onset. Problems with vision. Nausea. Clumsiness. There are those who say the ailment is akin to the falling sickness, in which case it may be cured by drinking spring water at night from the skull of one who has been slain."

Nan pushed the poultice aside to stare at the smaller woman. "You must be jesting."

"Indeed I am not. But there are many other remedies you might try if that one offends you. Lavender flowers in a bag—red silk for noblemen and plainer stuff for others—with bay, betony, red roses, marjoram, clove pinks, and nutmeg blossoms. Put that on your head and it will soothe the pain of most headaches. An infusion of cowslip juice, taken through the nose, can destroy some megrims. Or you might prefer a tisane of mead-owsweet, feverfew, lavender, lemon balm, ground ivy, woodruff, melilot, lady's bedstraw, or pennyroyal."

"Kathryn, I just want to sleep."

Through her lashes, Nan saw Kathryn's eyes narrow. "Or, we could open the middle vein in your forehead."

Nan's eyes widened. She blinked when she saw the expression on her friend's face. It was no use pretending any longer. Kathryn knew she was not ill. Nan removed the poultice from her forehead and sat up. "I have my reasons," she said in a defensive tone.

"I am certain that you do. And I am pleased to know that you are not in any pain."

"You will not . . . tell anyone?"

"Why should I?" When Kathryn started to slide off the bed, Nan caught her arm.

"Wait. Please. You . . . you seem to know a great deal about herbs and cures."

"No more than any other countrywoman in charge of a large

household. I am the one Lord Latimer's dependents come to when they need care. To me, or to the village cunning woman. Physicians are in short supply in rural areas and cost money besides."

"My mother once had similar responsibilities," Nan said, "but I have never spent much time in the stillroom. Tell me, what would you recommend for the king's ulcer?"

Kathryn's face paled. "I would never presume to make suggestions. His Grace has an army of doctors at his beck and call. Those gentlemen frown on consulting healers, especially uneducated females."

"You may not have studied medicine at a university, Kathryn, but you are scarcely unlettered."

"I would never presume—"

"Yes, yes, I understand. But you must have seen grievous wounds, been called upon to nurse a man gored by a bull or a lad injured at sword-play."

"There was a fellow once who'd been attacked by a wild boar. He did not live." Kathryn scrambled off the bed and hurried toward the door. "I must return to my duties, as you have no need of my care."

Nan lay back against the pillows and stared up at the tester overhead for a long time. Could she trust Kathryn not to betray her? She would have to. But she would have to be very cautious in implementing her plan to bring the soon-to-be-widowed Lady Latimer to the king's attention.

WHATEVER KING HENRY had intended to give Nan as a New Year's gift, he had apparently reconsidered by the time she recovered from her megrim and returned to the Lady Mary's presence chamber. His Grace greeted her warmly and demanded that she join him to play the card game Pope July, but he made no reference to her absence, nor did he present her with any bauble.

The return to court of Sir Thomas Seymour, the late queen's younger brother, provided the next diversion. Sir Thomas looked just as Nan remembered him—tall, dark, and handsome. Feminine heads turned as he strode across a room. He even attracted the attention of those who were usually immune to the charms of flashy courtiers, Nan herself and Kathryn Latimer.

Sir Thomas noticed Kathryn, too.

"Lady Latimer is married," Nan warned him when she next had occasion to dance with Sir Thomas.

"I hear her husband is on his deathbed," he countered. "She'll soon be ripe for the plucking."

Not by you, Nan vowed as she watched him head straight to Kathryn to ask for the next dance.

Nan kept close to Kathryn after that, although she could not be with the other woman every moment. And when the king asked Nan to sup with him, she took Kathryn along.

King Henry frowned at the sight of two women when he'd invited only one, but he accepted Kathryn's presence with good grace. "Two beautiful ladies," he boomed. "I am truly blessed."

Another place was hastily set and, with the king's permission, they sat and supped. Kathryn, as was her wont, said little during the meal. Nan encouraged King Henry to do most of the talking. He was in exceedingly good spirits until he rose from table and put weight on his bad leg. He gasped in pain.

"Your Grace," Nan whispered, appalled. "I believe your bandage needs to be changed." A horrible yellow stain, streaked here and there with red, had seeped through the king's hose. The stench that rose from it made Nan's supper try to climb back up her throat. She stepped quickly away, barely managing not to gag.

The king's gentlemen surrounded him. Someone brought fresh bandages. A moment later, they fell back as the king roared, "Incompetent bumblers! Can no one change a dressing without causing me more agony?"

A low, soothing voice answered. "I can, Your Grace." Moved to pity by his suffering, Kathryn Latimer slipped gracefully through the crowd of courtiers and knelt at the king's side.

* * *

By THE END of the third week in February, King Henry was visiting his daughter's apartments two or three times every day. It was no longer Nan he came to see. To Nan's great relief, His Grace now wanted Kathryn beside him when he played cards or threw dice. Soon he began to send her gifts, small tokens of his esteem.

Lord Latimer obligingly died at the end of February and was buried on the second of March. His widow mourned, but she did not put on widow's weeds. "The king insists that I continue to wear bright colors," she confided to Nan.

"Then you must do as he wishes."

"It is no hardship." Kathryn managed a shy smile. "I am particularly fond of red."

"And the king," Nan murmured, "seems particularly fond of your company."

"I did not set out to draw him away from you, Nan. You must believe that."

"I never thought any such thing," Nan assured her. "And I ask no more than to see King Henry be happy."

"He is . . . very kind to me."

"May I be blunt, Kathryn? The king is lonely. He would like to take another wife, but he wants neither a foreign princess nor a slip of a girl. He wants a companion. Someone to comfort him in his declining years."

"There were many who said he wanted you."

Nan shook her head. "I am familiar to him. Like an old shoe." She forced a laugh. "And I am not brave enough to deal with him when his leg pains him or his temper is short. I fear for my family at those times. What I do here at court has repercussions as far away as Cornwall."

"I have family, too."

"But your brother and your sister are both at court and already in favor with the king. He even remembers your mother fondly, from her days in service to Catherine of Aragon. When he thinks of my mother, he remembers Botolph's conspiracy against the Crown."

Nan took note of the pity in Kathryn's eyes. She told herself that was good, nearly as useful as sympathy. Kathryn must believe her when Nan said she did not want the king for herself.

"I do not think I am suited to be queen," Kathryn said quietly.

"You are as well born as Anne Boleyn or Jane Seymour or Catherine Howard."

"That is not what I mean." Color stained her cheeks and she did not meet Nan's eyes. "There was . . . someone else who showed an interest in me during my husband's illness. Someone I would . . . prefer to the king."

"Sir Thomas Seymour, I presume. Kathryn, Tom Seymour is a notorious womanizer."

Nan could have gone on categorizing Seymour's flaws, but if Kathryn had fallen under that clever rogue's spell, she was not likely to listen to warnings. Criticism would only make her more determined to have him.

"If you truly care for Sir Thomas," Nan said instead, "you must have no more to do with him. The king has a jealous nature. He would rather destroy you both than let another man have what he desires."

"Surely not!"

"I have seen the way the king looks at you, Kathryn. He'll not let another man have you."

"But . . . but I am not suited to be his wife. I cannot give him children. I have been married twice and never conceived. The fault is clearly mine."

"The king has heirs enough." Nan lowered her voice. "It is possible he lacks the ability to sire more children. He has not . . . we have not—"

She broke off when she saw the shocked expression on Kathryn's face. Checking carefully to make sure no one was near enough to overhear, Nan leaned closer to her friend.

"Could you bring yourself to marry the king if you did not have to couple with him?"

"I . . . I do not know. But surely, if he is incapable—"

"I cannot be certain, but I think that is why he has not sent for me. Not once since before his marriage to Queen Anna."

"But with Catherine Howard—"

"If he satisfied her, why did she risk everything to be with Tom Culpepper?"

Kathryn's brow furrowed in thought. "There was a story that Lord Latimer told me. About the trial of George Boleyn, Lord Rochford, before the House of Lords. He was handed a slip of paper and asked if his sister, the queen, had ever made such a claim. Rochford knew already that his life was forfeit. The king was that desperate to rid himself of Anne Boleyn and marry Jane Seymour. So he pretended to misunderstand. He read aloud what was written on the paper—that the king was well nigh impotent."

The two women stared at each other in silence for a long moment.

"It is possible his ailments took away his capability, or at least his desire," Kathryn mused. "Or mayhap the treatments were responsible."

"In any case, what he wants in a wife is a nurse and a companion, not a lover. You have already proven yourself capable of fulfilling his needs, Kathryn. And he told me himself that you have the gentlest touch of anyone, man or woman, when it comes to tending his leg."

As MARCH TURNED into April, Kathryn heeded Nan's advice and avoided Tom Seymour's company, but she also took care not to push herself forward with King Henry. It did no good. His Grace was determined to have her, and since she was a kind-hearted woman who hated to see anyone in pain, she went to him when he was ill, nursed him and comforted him. She was, Nan readily admitted, a much better person than Nan was.

On the twelfth of July, twenty witnesses gathered in the private oratory of the Queen's Closet at Hampton Court to watch Kathryn Parr, Lady Latimer, marry King Henry. Nan was not one of them. She took herself off to the gardens to think about her own prospects.

She left the palace by the southern entrance, with its view of the river landing, but she ignored the path that passed between the pond and privy gardens and ended on the bank of the Thames. Instead she turned east, skirting the privy garden to reach the knot garden. She hesitated there. The knot garden was situated between the gallery wing and the chapel, with the gallery overlooking the garden from the north. The area was too public to suit her present mood.

She continued on, circling the palace but staying inside the moat. A desire for solitude drove her away from the occasional cluster of courtiers. By the time she reached the orchard, the only person in sight ahead of her was one of the mole catchers employed to keep pests out of the gardens.

In common with every other space on Hampton Court's grounds, the orchard was decorated with numerous heraldic devices. Twenty-five carved beasts—antelopes, harts and hinds, dragons and hounds, gilded and painted—stood on green and white bases. At least here, among the apple and pear trees, they were not so overwhelming. In the privy garden there were 159 heraldic beasts, all aligned with rails painted green and white—the Tudor colors—to surround twenty garden beds. There were twenty sundials, too, but the centerpiece of the whole was a huge stone tablet with sculpted figures of the king's beasts holding up the royal shield.

Nan wandered past the first rows of trees. The orchard was one of the newer additions to the palace grounds, much of it planted less than a dozen years before. Apple, cherry, pear, and damson were interspersed with oak and elm, medlar and holly, and the open places were planted in grain. It grew high just now, but it would be mowed at harvesttime.

Nan had wandered nearly to the far side of the orchard before she looked back toward the palace. She was taken aback to discover she was not alone among the trees. A man stood the length of a tennis court away from her, leaning casually against an oak tree.

Sunlight winked on the jewel in his velvet bonnet and dappled his dark hair, shaded face, and court gown. Nan squinted, certain she knew him but unable to see his features well enough to identify him. Whoever he was, he was blessed with a sturdy physique and excellent taste in clothes.

Then he moved, and she recognized Wat Hungerford. As she watched him stride confidently toward her, she could no longer doubt that the boy had grown into a man. He was, she realized, just the same age King Henry had been when he'd succeeded to the throne and married Catherine of Aragon, a woman six years his senior. And that marriage, no matter that it had ended badly, had lasted nearly twenty-five years, most of them in harmony.

"Mistress Bassett." Wat grinned and seized both her hands. "Nan."

"Wat. I did not expect to see you here." She laughed softly. "I did not expect to see anyone here."

"I had just arrived at the landing when I saw you leave the palace. I followed you. I hope you don't mind."

She should, Nan thought, but in truth she was glad to see him. It had been just over a year since they'd last met. At odd moments during those long months, she had wondered about him—what he was doing, if he had become fascinated with some other woman.

They began to walk among the apple trees. Above their heads the fruit was ripening. "I have heard rumors," Wat said.

"Have you?"

"They say the king is about to marry again, and not to you."

"They say true, for once." She glanced back toward the palace. "By now, the deed is done and Kathryn Parr is queen of England."

"Then His Grace can have no further objection to someone courting you."

She had not thought Wat understood why she'd insisted upon limiting him to friendship. She had underestimated him. It appeared that his advanced maturity was not only physical.

"There are still good reasons why you and I should not—"

"I will not be put off this time." Wat seized her by the shoulders and turned her to face him. His eyes locked on hers. "I wish to marry you, Nan Bassett. Do you want to marry me?"

She had to swallow hard before she could speak. Wat Hungerford had grown into a man she'd quite like to marry. Her heart thrummed as he drew her close. Her breath caught, but she managed a strangled answer. "No."

He relaxed his grip but did not release her. "Liar."

Nan swayed closer to him, inhaling his fresh scent. For just an instant she wished she could throw it all away, run off with him, escape the lies and deceit and danger of life at court. But she could not. Whether King Henry was married or not, she was the only one of her family who had his ear, the only one who might yet persuade him to restore lost properties to her two surviving brothers, her three as yet unmarried sisters, and her mother.

"You are still too young to wed without your guardian's permission, and I have insufficient dowry to win anyone's approval."

His slow smile melted her heart. "Then say you will wait for me until I am of legal age to make my own decisions. Some three years more, Nan. Not so very long, not when I have waited for you nearly twice that long already."

When she stepped back, he let her go. "I have no plans to marry anyone else," she said, and began to walk again, in through the pear trees, heading toward the cherries. He followed a few steps behind.

In three years' time, she thought, King Henry might be persuaded to restore Wat Hungerford to his father's title. She could have everything she'd wanted, and Wat as well.

"I vow I will keep asking you to marry me until you accept."

She glanced over her shoulder. "Then, one day, I may surprise you by accepting."

Delight flared in his eyes, quickly followed by desire. This time when he reached for her, she had to push with both hands against his chest to stop him from kissing her. "One day," she repeated. "But not yet. I can make everything right again, Wat, but only if I am here at court, close to the king, close to those the king loves. When the time is right, I can ask for the return of lands and properties forfeited to the Crown. Lisle lands. Hungerford lands. The Hungerford title."

"And if he refuses?" Wat's hands caressed the small of her back, sending shivers of delight all through Nan's body.

In a dizzying moment of self-awareness, she realized that she could envision spending her life with him, title or no, fortune or no. She could imagine giving him a child.

"Nan?"

"Keep your vow, Wat. Keep asking me."

"Marry me now."

But she shook her head. For a moment, she thought he might pick her up, toss her over his shoulder, and make off with her, but he thought better of it. With an exasperated groan, he took her hand and they started walking again, but this time they headed back toward the palace.

He treasured her, Nan thought, clinging to him. That was a great gift. She had once thrown away her chance of happiness with a man who cared for her. She would not repeat that mistake, especially since she was coming to treasure Wat in return. And she realized, suddenly, that although Ned Corbett had been her first love, Wat Hungerford would be her last.

Nan returned to her duties with the new queen with a sense of purpose. She would be patient. She would plan carefully. She might no longer be the youngest of the maids, now that she was twenty-two. Nor was she still the prettiest girl at court. Bess Brooke now had that distinction. But Nan had earned the gratitude and friendship of both the king and the queen. She was right where she belonged and where she needed to be. Until the day when she and Wat Hungerford could marry, she was content to be a maid of honor to the queen of England.

There is no doubt but she shall come to some great marriage.

—Lady Wallop to Lady Lisle (referring to Anne Bassett), 8 August 1538

EPILOGUE—
1554

On the eleventh day of June, near the end of the first year of the reign of Mary Tudor, a thirty-three-year-old Nan Bassett, waiting gentlewoman to the queen, accompanied her royal mistress to the queen's chapel for the last time. Queen Mary's face was wreathed in smiles, as Nan knew her own must be.

"This is an auspicious day," the queen said.

"Yes, Your Majesty," Nan agreed.

"Will you miss being at court, do you think?"

"I will miss my friends, Your Grace, and it will seem strange not to be in Your Grace's company every day."

"But you will have a loving husband, as I soon shall. And children to complete your life."

The queen was to marry King Philip of Spain as soon as he arrived in England. He was expected toward the end of July, only a bit more than a month hence. Queen Mary's happiness at her betrothal had, at last, persuaded her to part with Nan. And to grant her, as a wedding gift, a goodly number of the properties that had been confiscated by the Crown at the time of Lord Hungerford's attainder.

As they approached the chapel at Richmond Palace, where Nan's wedding ceremony was to be performed, she could not help but think back over the years since she'd first waited upon Mary Tudor. She'd left Mary's household to serve Kathryn Parr, content to wait until Wat Hungerford reached his majority before she married. But King Henry had become more and more difficult as his health failed him. He was so unpredictable that even Queen Kathryn had once been in danger of arrest for carelessly expressing a wrong opinion. Although Nan had never given up hope that she would one day achieve her goals, neither had she ever dared ask the king for the restoration of the Hungerford lands and title.

Seeking favors from Jane Seymour's son, Edward, a boy not yet ten years old when he succeeded to the throne, had been even more impossible. His reign had been difficult to endure. Since Edward VI had been too young to rule on his own, England had been governed by his advisors. They'd been radical in their religious beliefs, so harsh in their suppression of papists that even though Mary Tudor was the king's half sister, she had feared for her life.

Nan's choices had been limited at the start of Edward's reign. He'd had no queen for Nan to serve. There had, however, been a powerful woman at court. Queen Jane's brother, Edward Seymour, Earl of Hertford, had been named lord protector and elevated in the peerage to Duke of Somerset. In all but name, he was king and his wife a queen. But just as Cat Bassett had shied away from entering the then Countess of Hertford's household when the two sisters first came to England, so Nan had been reluctant to place herself at the mercy of a woman reputed to be a vicious, vindictive virago. Nan had always thought it a great pity that her mother had wasted the gift of her own pet linnet on such a notoriously bad-tempered noblewoman.

Instead, Nan had returned to the Lady Mary, this time as a lady-in-waiting. Mary Tudor had been out of favor, but until King Edward married and had children of his own, she remained next in line to inherit the throne of England. Nan had joined her fate to that of King Henry's oldest daughter and had never looked back. She and Wat had been patient, and when Mary Tudor finally succeeded her brother, Nan once again became a gentlewoman in the service of a queen.

This time the queen was a queen regnant, a woman with power. And Queen Mary believed in rewarding those who had been loyal to her.

Nan drew in a deep breath as they reached the chapel. Wat Hungerford of Farleigh waited just inside, together with the Catholic priest who would perform their wedding ceremony. Wat was no boy now, but a man in his prime. And yet the look in his eyes as he watched her approach was the same as it had always been. He had never wavered in his devotion, never stopped proposing marriage, never grown tired of waiting until the day—today—when, at last, they could be united in holy matrimony.

Friends and family filled the chapel, gathered to celebrate Nan's nuptials. She felt a moment's sadness for those who could not be with her. As she well knew, death could take away the young and healthy as well as the old and infirm. Her good friend Anne Herbert had died two years earlier. Anne's sister, the widowed queen, Kathryn Parr, had been lost to childbed fever less than a year after her marriage to Sir Thomas Seymour. Jane Mewtas was gone, too, and both Joan and Anthony Denny.

But I am alive, Nan thought. *And I have a bright future ahead of me.*

Close to the spot just within the chapel door where she and Wat were to take their vows stood the members of Nan's immediate family. She scarcely knew her brothers, George and James, but they had come to attend the ceremony. Nan's mother was present, too. For once, she looked pleased with her daughter's accomplishment. And why not? The queen had promised that Wat would be knighted. Less certain was that he would be restored to the title of Baron Hungerford, but that no longer mattered to either Nan or Wat. Such honors were not as necessary as Nan had once believed. It had taken her years to realize it, but loving and being loved by a good man was far more important.

Nan's sister, Cat, stood beside their mother. Cat's husband and six-year-old son were with her. They lived in Kent, near enough to the queen's favorite palaces for Nan to have visited them often. Whatever rivalry had once existed had been set aside long ago.

Nan's oldest sister, Philippa, was also on hand. She, too, was accompanied by a husband and a son. The youngest Bassett girl, Mary, as yet unmarried, sniffled into a handkerchief, but she managed a watery smile for her sister.

Elsewhere in the chapel, Nan caught sight of Lucy Somerset, now Lady Latimer, and Cousin Mary, who had remarried and was now Countess of Arundel. Most of the maids of honor Nan had served with in Mary Tudor's household, both before and after Mary became queen, were also present to celebrate with her.

Nan took her place beside Wat, standing at his left hand. The queen herself blessed their union and gave Nan into the keeping of her future husband.

Throughout the solemn, scripted ritual that followed, Nan could only think how glad she was that this moment had finally come. She did not regret her time at court, but she was ready to leave the service of royalty behind. She wanted nothing more than to spend the rest of her life at Farleigh Castle as Lady Hungerford.

Wat took her right hand in his right hand, his grip firm and confident. He'd never once doubted that they belonged together.

"I, Walter, take thee Anne to my wedded wife, to have and to hold from this day forth, for better or worse, for richer for poorer, in sickness and in health, till death us depart, if holy church will it ordain, and thereto I plight thee my troth."

As the ceremony demanded, Wat withdrew his hand and Nan took it back again to make her own vows: "I, Anne, take thee Walter to my wedded husband, to have and to hold from this day forth, for richer or poorer, in sickness and in health, to be bonair and buxom in bed and at board, till death us depart, if holy church will it ordain, and thereto I plight thee my troth."

Bonair and buxom, she thought, smiling slightly, words that meant courteous and kind. She would have no difficulty with either. Not with Wat as her husband.

The priest blessed the ring, which had been placed on a book along with a monetary offering. When he'd sprinkled it with holy water, Wat took the ring in his right hand, using three fingers, and held Nan's right hand in his left. Then he repeated the priest's solemn words: "With this ring I thee wed and this gold and silver I thee give; and with my body I thee worship, and with all my worldly cattle I thee honor."

He placed the ring on Nan's thumb, "in the name of the Father," moved it to the second finger—"and of the Son"—and on to the third finger: "and of the Holy Ghost." When he placed it on her fourth finger, he concluded with, "Amen."

Nan looked down at her hand, wondering if it were true that in the fourth finger there was a vein that ran straight to the heart. Overwhelmed by the emotion she felt at this moment, she was certain there must be a connection.

Together, Nan and Wat moved to the step before the altar for the nuptial Mass and blessing that would precede a wedding breakfast in the royal apartments—another mark of favor from the queen. Nan scarcely heard a word for the haze of happiness that surrounded her.

When all the prayers were done, Wat received the pax from the priest. The final act of the ritual was to convey it to Nan by kissing her. "At last," he whispered just before their lips met.

At last, Nan thought, relishing his touch, basking in her sense of belonging and the sheer joy of mutual love and respect.

The kiss Nan gave Wat in return told him everything that was in her heart.

A NOTE FROM THE AUTHOR

I chose to end Anne Bassett's story on a happy note. Sadly, she did not live long after her wedding. In common with many sixteenth-century wives, she bore her husband two sons who died young and was dead herself sometime before June 7, 1557, the date of Walter Hungerford's remarriage.

For those who want "the real story," it is to be found in M. St. Clare Byrne's excellent six-volume edition of *The Lisle Letters*. I have drawn my own conclusions about certain events in Nan's life and about Lord Cromwell's involvement in the Botolph conspiracy, but overall I have worked within the historical record. I did choose to omit a number of details of the Botolph conspiracy simply because they made the scheme too preposterous for a modern reader to believe.

Maids of honor may have waited on the queen in shifts, with two on duty for each eight-hour period, but since no one knows for certain, I often have all six in attendance on the queen at the same time. The identities of these "damsels" are also open to question. Many more women are said to have held the position than is possible, even with a great number of them marrying and leaving the ranks. Some young ladies, like Elizabeth Brooke, as the daughters or sisters of courtiers, lived at court without having any official position.

For more information on the real people who populate this novel, see the Who's Who section that follows this note. You will find more mini-biographies of Tudor women at my website, KateEmersonHistoricals.com. The only characters in *Between Two Queens* who are entirely products of my imagination are Nan's maid, Constance; the midwife, Mother Gristwood; Jamie and his adoptive parents; and Ned Corbett's violet-eyed wife.

A WHO'S WHO
OF THE TUDOR COURT
1537–1543

Anna of Cleves (1515–1557)
Henry VIII married his fourth queen on January 6, 1540. She was persuaded to accept an annulment on July 9 of that same year. She retired to Richmond and Bletchingley, properties granted to her in a generous settlement, and was thereafter treated as "the king's sister." A false rumor, circulated in 1541, claimed she'd given birth to a child. She was present at ceremonial occasions throughout the reign of Mary I. She was buried in Westminster Abbey. Her portrait by Hans Holbein the Younger still makes her appear, to modern eyes, the most attractive of King Henry's wives.

Arundell, Jane (d. 1577)
Jane Arundell, older half sister of Mary (below), was one of Queen Jane's maids of honor when Anne Bassett first came to court. She was at least thirty years old at the time, since her mother had died before 1507. After Queen Jane's death, Jane Arundell joined her half sister's household. Nothing further is known of her.

Arundell, Mary (Countess of Sussex) (1517?–1557)
Mary Arundell was Anne Bassett's cousin. Their mothers were sisters.

She was at court as a maid of honor to Queen Jane Seymour until she became the third wife of Robert Radcliffe, Earl of Sussex, on January 14, 1537. Mary remained at court as one of Queen Jane's ladies until Jane's death and returned to court as one of the great ladies of the household under Anna of Cleves and Catherine Howard. She had at least one son by Sussex, born in March 1538, but he seems to have died young. After the earl's death, Mary became the second wife of Henry FitzAlan, Earl of Arundel, marrying him on December 19, 1545. She was once thought to have translated Greek and Latin epigrams, but it is now believed that scholars confused her with her stepdaughter, Mary FitzAlan.

Astley, Jane (Mistress Mewtas) (1517?–1551?)

Jane Astley was a maid of honor to Queen Jane Seymour until she married Peter Mewtas. The wedding took place after Easter but before October 9, 1537. Jane is the subject of the sketch by Hans Holbein the Younger labeled *Lady Meutas*. Jane and Peter had several children—Cecily, Frances, Henry, Thomas, and Hercules. Anne Bassett lived with them in their house in London after she left the Countess of Sussex's household.

Bassett, Anne (1521?–1557?)

Anne was the third daughter of Sir John Bassett and his second wife, Honor Grenville. When her stepfather, Arthur Plantagenet, Lord Lisle, became deputy of Calais in 1533, Anne was sent to Pont de Remy to live with the family of Tybault Rouand, Sieur de Riou, and complete her education. In 1537, she became one of Queen Jane's maids of honor but her stay at court was short. She was sworn in only one day before the queen went into seclusion to await the birth of Prince Edward. Following the queen's death from complications of childbirth, Anne went to live in the household of her cousin Mary Arundell, Countess of Sussex. Later she resided with Peter Mewtas and his wife and then, at the king's suggestion, with Anthony and Joan Denny. The king took a particular interest in Anne and at one point gave her a horse and saddle as a gift. Upon Henry VIII's marriage to Anna of Cleves, Anne resumed her post as a maid of honor. She entered the household of Queen Catherine Howard after the marriage to Anna was annulled. When Queen Catherine's household was dissolved, the king made special provision for Anne Bassett, although exactly what provision is unclear. At the time, her mother and stepfather were both being held on charges of treason in connection with a plot to turn Calais over to England's enemies. Their continued imprisonment did not seem to affect the king's fondness for Anne. At a banquet where he entertained some sixty ladies, she was one of three singled out for particular attention, leading to speculation that the king might marry her. When Kathryn Parr became Henry's sixth queen, Anne resumed her accustomed post as maid of honor. She left court during the reign of Edward VI, but returned as a lady of the privy chamber to Queen Mary in 1553. In June 1554, Anne married Walter Hungerford of Farleigh, a gentleman some years younger than herself, in the queen's chapel at Richmond. The queen granted the couple a number of properties that had been lost when Hungerford's father was attainted and executed in 1540. Anne bore her husband two sons who died young and had died herself before June 1557, when Hungerford remarried.

Bassett, Catherine (1517?–1558+)

The second daughter of Sir John Bassett and Honor Grenville, Catherine was in competition with her sister Anne for one position as a maid of honor to Queen Jane in 1537. When Anne was chosen, Catherine was taken into the household of Eleanor Paston, Countess of Rutland. There was talk of placing her with Catherine Willoughby, Duchess of Suffolk or with Anne Stanhope, Countess of Hertford, but Catherine apparently preferred to remain where she was. A marriage was proposed for her with Sir Edward Baynton's son, but the Bayntons thought Catherine's dowry was too small. In 1540, she joined the household of Anna of Cleves, but by then Anna was no longer queen. In 1541, Catherine was heard to wonder aloud how many wives the king would have. This comment led to her examination by the Privy Council but she does not seem to have been charged with any crime. On December 8, 1547, she married Henry Ashley of Hever, Kent. They had a son, also named Henry. The date of Catherine's death is unknown, but took place sometime between 1558 and 1588.

Bassett, Mary (1522?–1598)

The youngest daughter of Sir John Bassett and Honor Grenville, Mary was, according to Peter Mewtas, the prettiest of the four sisters. She joined the household of Nicholas de Montmorency, Seigneur de Bours, in Abbeville in August 1534. Her stepfather, Arthur Plantagenet, Lord Lisle, attempted to find her a place in the household of the young Elizabeth Tudor, but nothing came of it. Mary suffered from ill health and returned to Calais in March 1538 to be nursed by her mother. Gabriel de Montmorency, who had become Seigneur de Bours on his father's death in 1537, paid a number of visits to her there and eventually proposed marriage. They kept their betrothal secret, with disastrous consequences. When her mother and stepfather were arrested and all their papers seized, Mary attempted to destroy Gabriel's love letters by throwing them down the jakes. She was caught and her unsanctioned engagement to a Frenchman was taken to be one more proof of treason in the household. It was a crime to conspire to marry a foreigner without the king's permission. It is not clear where Mary was confined in Calais or when she was released. The next record of her is her marriage to John Wollacombe of Overcombe, Devon, on June 8, 1557.

Bassett, Philippa (1516?–1582)

This oldest Bassett daughter remained in Calais with her mother. There was talk of a marriage to Clement Philpott, but nothing came of it. She was arrested with her mother and sister but it is not clear where she was held or when she was released. She had married a man named James Pitts by 1548.

Botolph, Sir Gregory (d. 1540+)

Botolph is the mystery man of the story. He was a younger son from a respectable Suffolk family and became a priest. He was a canon at St. Gregory's in Canterbury in the mid–1530s and later confessed that he stole a plate from the church during that time. He went to Calais in April of 1538 to become one of the three domestic chaplains employed by Lord Lisle. There he shared quarters with Clement Philpott, who joined the household at the same time. He has been described as both a fanatic papist and an unscrupulous rogue. He was known in Calais as "Gregory Sweet-lips" for his ability to talk people into doing what he wanted. He claimed to have made a very fast, very secret trip to Rome to meet with the pope and Cardinal Pole in early 1540, but there is no evidence to back up his story. He was, however, clearly the instigator of a plot to deliver Calais to England's enemies in "herring time" and he did recruit Clement Philpott and Edward Corbett, among others, to help him. The plan probably would not have succeeded even if Philpott had not betrayed the conspirators. Botolph escaped being arrested when his coconspirators were taken by English authorities because he was already in "the emperor's dominions." He may have been taken into custody there, briefly, but he was never returned to England to stand trial for treason. He disappears from history after August of 1540. Further details about the Botolph conspiracy can be found in volume six of M. St. Clare Byrne's *The Lisle Letters*.

Bray, Dorothy (1524?–1605)

Dorothy Bray was either the youngest daughter or the fifth of six daughters of Edmund, Baron Bray, and was at court as a maid of honor to

Anna of Cleves in 1540. She served Catherine Howard and Kathryn Parr in the same capacity. She was involved in a brief, passionate affair with William Parr, brother of the future queen, in 1541, but during Kathryn Parr's tenure as queen, Parr's interest shifted to Dorothy's niece, Elizabeth Brooke. Dorothy later married Edmund Brydges, Baron Chandos, by whom she had five children. After his death she wed Sir William Knollys, a much younger man. Late in life she was known as "old Lady Chandos."

Brooke, Elizabeth (1525–1565)

Elizabeth Brooke is sometimes confused with her aunt, Lady Wyatt, with whom she shared her name. This younger Elizabeth, however, is most likely to have been the "sister of Lord Cobham" to whom Henry VIII paid attention at a supper and banquet at court in January 1542, leading to speculation that he might marry her. Elizabeth was accounted one of the most beautiful women of her time. Late in the reign of Henry VIII, she captured the heart of Queen Kathryn's brother, William Parr. For more on this fascinating woman, see the extended biography at my website, KateEmersonHistoricals.com.

Browne, John (d. 1540+?)

Edward Corbett's servant, Browne was accused of treason right along with his master. There is a record of his attainder and his exemption from the general pardon, but not of his execution.

Carey, Catherine (1523?–1569)

As the daughter of Mary Boleyn, long Henry VIII's mistress, Catherine may in fact have been the king's child, but he never acknowledged her as such. Catherine came to court as a maid of honor to Anna of Cleves in January of 1540, but she married Sir Francis Knollys on April 26 of that same year and gave up the post. They had fourteen children. Catherine returned to court when Queen Elizabeth took the throne.

Champernowne, Joan (Mistress Denny) (d. 1553)

Joan Champernowne came to court as a maid of honor to Catherine of Aragon and remained at court during the tenures of Henry VIII's next five wives. Married to Anthony Denny, by whom she had at least ten children, she was called upon by King Henry VIII to take Anne Bassett as a guest in her house in Westminster so that Anne could enjoy the country air and take long walks. Joan was one of the ladies sent to greet Anna of Cleves upon her arrival. While serving Kathryn Parr, she was accused of sending aid to Anne Askew, who was later executed for heresy. Joan was an ardent Protestant, but nothing treasonable or heretical was ever proved against her. In May 1548, Princess Elizabeth and her household were sent to stay at Cheshunt with the Dennys. They remained there until autumn. Some accounts say Elizabeth's governess, Katherine Champernowne Astley, was Joan's younger sister. Others believe they were only distantly related. Joan was considered a great beauty.

Corbett, Edward (d. 1540+?)

Very little is known about the real Edward Corbett except that he was a gentleman servitor to Lord Lisle at Calais and frequently carried messages to Honor Lisle's daughters in England and ran other errands for his master. He became close friends with Clement Philpott after the latter's arrival in Calais in 1538 and was recruited by Sir Gregory Botolph to participate in a plot to overthrow Calais. His failure to report what Botolph suggested made him guilty of treason even though he did not actively aid the conspirators. He was arrested, questioned in Calais, then taken to England and imprisoned in the Tower. He was attainted and exempted from the general pardon but there is no record of his execution. He simply disappears from history. He may have been one of the "others" executed at the same time as Clement Philpott. His relationship with Anne Bassett is my own invention, but it *could* have happened.

Cromwell, Thomas (1485?–1540)

Henry VIII's chief advisor after the death of Cardinal Wolsey, Cromwell was the driving force behind the king's marriage to Anna of Cleves. Henry's displeasure with his new bride was undoubtedly what cost Cromwell his life. Cromwell created difficulties over money and property for Lord and Lady Lisle and was probably responsible for Lisle being implicated in the Botolph conspiracy, even though Lisle knew nothing about it before Philpott confided in him. Cromwell was arrested on June 10, 1540, and executed on the same day Henry VIII married Catherine Howard.

Culpepper, Thomas (d. 1541)

Described as "a beautiful youth," Thomas Culpepper was at court as a page in 1535 and by the time Henry VIII married Catherine Howard, Thomas's sixth cousin once removed, he was a groom of the privy chamber and had the unpleasant duty of dressing the ulcer on the king's leg. Culpepper was high in favor at court as early as 1537, when Honor Lisle sent him the gift of a hawk in the hope he might use his influence with the king on her behalf. Whatever his relationship with the queen during the progress of 1541, it was foolish in the extreme to have met with her in private. He was executed on the charge of treason.

Denny, Anthony (1501–1549)

By 1536, Denny was a groom of the privy chamber to Henry VIII, yeoman of the wardrobe of robes, keeper of the royal palace at Westminster (Whitehall), and keeper of the privy purse. Later he was a gentleman of the privy chamber. He was one of the king's most trusted servants and the recipient of frequent grants. He had houses in Aldgate in London, where he was a neighbor of Hans Holbein the Younger, and in Westminster. It was to the latter that Anne Bassett came as Denny's guest in October 1539. Denny was present at Kathryn Parr's wedding to the king in 1543 and was knighted on September 30, 1544.

Prince Edward (1537–1553)
The baby prince's mother, Jane Seymour, died of complications of childbirth when Edward was twelve days old. He was for the most part raised away from court. He succeeded his father in 1547.

Princess Elizabeth (1533–1603)
Elizabeth makes only a brief appearance here, at the christening of her baby brother. For most of the period of this novel, she was regarded as the king's illegitimate daughter and therefore not in line to inherit the throne. She shared a household with her older half sister, Mary, for part of that time and succeeded Mary to the throne in 1558.

Grenville, Honor (Lady Lisle) (1494?–1566)
In 1515, Honor Grenville married Sir John Bassett and by him had three sons and four daughters. Her second husband was Arthur Plantagenet, Viscount Lisle and lord deputy of Calais. She was one of the "six beautiful ladies" who accompanied Anne Boleyn to France in 1532 and at least two of her daughters, Anne and Mary, were renowned for their looks. In 1540, when accusations of treason were made against Honor and her husband, in part because she continued to cling to the old ways in religion, she was placed under house arrest in Calais and held there until her husband's death in the Tower of London in March 1542. Following her release, she retired to Tehidy in Cornwall. Rumor had her going mad while in captivity, but this is not supported by any reliable source.

Harris, Isabel or Elizabeth (Mistress Staynings) (d. 1543+)

Isabel had four children under the age of six by 1534, when her husband was sent to prison for debt. One of her children was named Honor, after Isabel's aunt, Lady Lisle. Left in poverty and pregnant with her sixth child when her husband died in 1537, Isabel entered the service of Mary Arundell, Countess of Sussex, as a waiting gentlewoman. She was invited to join Lady Lisle's household in Calais but declined. She may later have remarried, to a man named Thomas Gawdie.

Henry VIII (1491–1547)

King Henry was forty-six in 1537 and still in relatively good health, although he was already portly. He was over six feet tall and had introduced the square-cut beard into fashion a few years earlier. By 1543, he had lost his looks. His waist measured fifty inches and his chest forty-five. His beard was sparse and flecked with gray and his hair was thinning. He weighed over 250 pounds and sometimes wore a corset. He used a staff to walk and wore a felt slipper on the foot of his game leg. Rumors that he was impotent began as early as his marriage to Anne Boleyn. He may have suffered from syphilis, but his symptoms are also consistent with land scurvy, which is caused by poor diet. Henry died less than four years after marrying Kathryn Parr.

Herbert, William (1506?–1570)

A Welshman, Herbert was at court as a gentleman pensioner by 1526 but in 1527 he killed a man in a brawl and was not heard of again until he reappeared in court records as an esquire of the body to Henry VIII in 1535. He married Anne Parr in early 1538, shortly after Queen Jane Seymour's death. After Kathryn Parr became queen, Herbert rose in favor and was created Earl of Pembroke in 1551.

Howard, Catherine (1521?–1542)

Raised by her father's stepmother, the dowager Duchess of Norfolk, Catherine was allowed to run wild as a teenager. When she came to court as a maid of honor to Anna of Cleves, her vivaciousness had as much to do with attracting the king's attention as her petite form and pretty face. Henry VIII fell in love, had his marriage to Anna annulled, and married Catherine on July 28, 1540. Eventually, however, Catherine's past came to light. An investigation into former lovers also turned up Thomas Culpepper, who had been meeting with Catherine in private during the royal progress of 1541. Catherine was arrested and sent first to the former Syon Abbey and then to the Tower. On February 11, 1542, Parliament passed a law making it a crime for an unchaste woman to marry the king. Catherine was executed the next day.

Hungerford, Walter (1525?–1596)

Hungerford, whose father was given the title Lord Hungerford of Heytesbury in 1536, was a member of Lord Cromwell's household by 1538. In 1540, however, both Cromwell and Lord Hungerford were attainted and executed. The charges against the latter included unnatural sexual acts. It is not clear where young Walter went at this point, although he would probably have become a royal ward. He could not marry or inherit until he was of age at twenty-one. He married Anne Bassett on June 11, 1554, at Richmond Palace. He was younger than she, but estimates differ on how many years separated them. After Anne's death he remarried, but his second marriage was unhappy and ended in a scandalous separation.

Husee, John (1506?–1548)

Lord Lisle's man of business for seven years, operating primarily in London, Husee was also a "gentleman of the King's retinue at Calais." His father was a vintner. He turned down the offer to become Lisle's steward. He is well represented in *The Lisle Letters* but disappears from the correspondence without explanation in March of 1540, just before the Botolph conspiracy came to light.

Hussey, Mary (d. 1545+)

Because of the treason of her father, Baron Hussey of Sleaford, Mary lost any hope of a good marriage. At the end of May 1539, she went to Calais to become a waiting gentlewoman to Honor Grenville, Lady Lisle. As a result, she was part of that household a year later when Lord and Lady Lisle were arrested and all their correspondence seized. Mary Hussey helped Mary Bassett destroy her love letters and appears to have remained with Lady Lisle during her imprisonment in Calais and been released with her after Lord Lisle's death in March 1542. She later married and had children. Her sister, Elizabeth, was Lady Hungerford, unhappy second wife and later widow of Walter Hungerford's father.

Jerningham, Elizabeth (before 1515–1558+)

A waiting gentlewoman to Anne Stanhope, Lady Beauchamp, until January 1537, Elizabeth became a maid of honor to Anne's sister-in-law, Queen Jane Seymour, at that time. Later she was a maid of honor to Queen Mary. In this, she was following family tradition. Her mother, Mary Scrope, first as Lady Jerningham and later as Lady Kingston, was a member of Catherine of Aragon's household from the beginning of the reign.

Kingston, William (before 1476–1540)

Constable of the Tower of London from 1524 until his death, Kingston was responsible for many high-ranking prisoners, including Queen Anne Boleyn and Lord Lisle. There is no record that he ever helped anyone escape from the Tower.

Knyvett, Edmund (1508–1551)

The king's sergeant porter, a cousin of the Earl of Surrey, Knyvett married by 1527 and had four sons. In 1541 he almost lost his hand for striking another man within the precincts of the royal court. The king waited until the last moment to pardon him. Accounts of exactly when and where this happened differ. Later in life, Knyvett was involved in a scandal with a married countess.

Manners, Thomas (Earl of Rutland) (1492?–1543)

Lord chamberlain to Anna of Cleves, the Earl of Rutland was the one who convinced Anna to agree to annul her marriage to the king. Rutland's second wife, Eleanor Paston, was a friend and correspondent of Honor Lisle's and took Honor's daughter Catherine Bassett into her household. Rutland's primary residences were the former Benedictine nunnery of Holywell in Shoreditch, just outside London, and Belvoir Castle.

Princess Mary (1516–1558)

The only child of Henry VIII and Catherine of Aragon to survive infancy, Mary became queen on the death of her brother, Edward VI, in 1553. She restored Catholicism to England with disastrous results. Her marriage to Philip II of Spain produced no children, and upon her death she was succeeded by her younger half sister, Elizabeth. Queen Mary was so fond of Anne Bassett, one of her ladies, that Anne was married in the queen's chapel at Richmond Palace and the wedding breakfast was held in the royal apartments. As a wedding gift, Mary granted the couple a goodly number of properties that had been confiscated by the Crown when Lord Hungerford was attainted.

Mewtas, Peter (d. 1562)

Peter Mewtas was a gentleman of the privy chamber to Henry VIII and held other posts as well. In the spring of 1537 he was in France, nominally in attendance on Stephen Gardiner and Sir Francis Bryan, but he was really there to carry out King Henry's orders to kidnap and murder Cardinal Pole. This plot failed. Later that year, Mewtas married Jane Astley, one of the queen's maids of honor. They had a house beside Our Lady of Barking in Tower Street, where Anne Bassett was their guest in 1539. Mewtas was knighted in 1544.

Norris, Mary (d. 1570)

The daughter of Henry Norris, who was accused of being one of Queen Anne Boleyn's lovers and was executed on that charge, Mary was a maid of honor during the tenure of Anna of Cleves and probably during that of Jane Seymour. She may also have been a maid of honor to Catherine Howard. She married Sir George Carew, admiral of the Fleet, and was with King Henry at Southsea Castle on the day in 1545 when the *Mary Rose* sank. She watched in horror as her husband and hundreds of others drowned. Mary's second husband was Sir Arthur Champernowne of Dartington.

Parker, Jane (Lady Rochford) (d. 1542)

Infamous for her part in bringing about the downfall of two of Henry VIII's six wives, Jane may simply have been the victim of bad press. That is the contention of a recent biography, *Jane Boleyn*, by Julia Fox. The daughter of Baron Morley, Jane was unhappily married to George Boleyn, Queen Anne's brother, and evidence Jane gave was used against him. Contemporaries, however, cannot have thought too badly of her. She was back at court as a waiting gentlewoman to Jane Seymour, Anna of Cleves, and Catherine Howard. That her connivance allowed Catherine to meet with Thomas Culpepper in secret is well established, as is the fact that she paid for this lapse in judgment with her life. She was executed in 1542.

Parr, Anne (Mistress Herbert) (1515?–1552)

Anne Parr's mother was a lady-in-waiting to Catherine of Aragon and Anne became a maid of honor to Queen Jane Seymour. In early 1538, she married William Herbert and as Lady Herbert she was keeper of the queen's jewels for Catherine Howard. She should not be confused with Lady Herbert of Troy, who was in Elizabeth Tudor's household, or with Mrs. FitzHerbert, who was chief chamberer to Jane Seymour. Although Anne left court briefly to give birth to her first child in 1540, she was back in time to attend Queen Catherine during the latter's imprisonment at Syon House and in the Tower of London. When Anne's sister, Kathryn, became queen in 1543, Anne was part of Kathryn's household. Anne's husband was created Earl of Pembroke in 1551. At the time of Anne's death, she was one of Princess Mary's ladies.

Parr, Kathryn (Lady Latimer) (1512?–1548)

There are a lot of silly stories about Kathryn Parr's first two husbands. Neither was a sick old man. The first, Edward Borough or Burgh, was twenty-two years her senior and the second, John Neville, Lord Latimer, was about nineteen years older than she was—in other words, still in the prime of their lives. Lord Latimer was in good health until the Scottish campaign of 1542, after which he was known to be dying. It was at this point that King Henry began to send Kathryn gifts. She was also courted by Thomas Seymour, Queen Jane's brother, but not until he returned to England in January of 1543. Latimer was buried on March 2, 1543. Kathryn married the king on July 12, 1543. After Henry VIII's death, Kathryn wed Thomas Seymour. She died after giving birth to a daughter, Mary. Susan James's *Catherine Parr* is an excellent account of her life.

Parr, William (1513–1571)

Brother to Anne and Kathryn Parr, William Parr was at court even before his sister became queen. He was married as a boy of thirteen

to Ann Bourchier, age ten, the only child of the Earl of Essex. Parr
expected to be granted the Essex title when Ann's father died. Instead
it was given to Thomas Cromwell and lapsed upon Cromwell's execution. Parr was engaged in a passionate love affair with one of Catherine
Howard's maids of honor, Dorothy Bray, in 1541, but later he fell in
love with Elizabeth Brooke. Since his wife was still living, he could not
marry either woman, but eventually he was able to divorce Ann and
wed Elizabeth. This marriage was declared invalid during Mary Tudor's
reign and reinstated under Queen Elizabeth. Parr was created Earl of
Essex in 1543 and Marquis of Northampton in 1547. After the deaths
of both Ann and Elizabeth, he took a third, much younger wife, but
survived that marriage by only a few months. He had no children by
any of these unions.

Paston, Eleanor (Countess of Rutland) (before 1496–1559)

As the second wife of Thomas Manners, Earl of Rutland, Eleanor gave
birth to eleven children. In between, she served as a lady of the privy
chamber to Jane Seymour, Anna of Cleves, and Catherine Howard. In
1536 the Rutland house in Shoreditch was the scene of a triple wedding—three child marriages uniting Henry Manners, age ten, with Lady
Margaret Neville; Anne Manners with Lord Neville; and Dorothy Neville
with Lord Bulbeck, the Earl of Oxford's heir. Catherine Bassett lived in
the Rutland household from 1537 until 1540.

Philpott, Clement (d. 1540)

The younger son of a Hampshire knight, Philpott joined the household of Lord Lisle at Calais as a gentleman servitor in April 1538 and
became good friends with Lisle's chaplain, Sir Gregory Botolph, who
arrived in Calais at the same time, and with Edward Corbett, who was
already there. Philpott was devoted to Botolph and privy to his plans to
overthrow Calais, but at the last minute he lost his courage and revealed

the plot to Lord Lisle. He was arrested; questioned in Calais; sent to the Tower of London; tried for treason; and hanged, drawn, and quartered at Tyburn on August 4, 1540. He has been variously characterized as a dupe and as a dangerous fanatic.

Plantagenet, Arthur (Viscount Lisle) (1462?–1542)

The illegitimate son of King Edward IV, he was thus Henry VIII's uncle. He had three daughters by his first wife. By his second wife, Honor Grenville, Lady Bassett, Lisle acquired four stepdaughters and three stepsons. The oldest of the boys, John Bassett, married Lisle's oldest daughter, Frances Plantagenet. The extensive correspondence of Lisle and his family while he was lord deputy of Calais has been preserved by virtue of being seized when Lisle was arrested and charged with treason in 1540. He died in the Tower of London shortly after being told he had been pardoned.

Radcliffe, Robert (Earl of Sussex) (1483–1542)

When his first family was grown, Sussex married a young maid of honor, Mary Arundell, as his third wife. Anne Bassett lived in their household for a time following the death of Queen Jane Seymour. It was the Earl of Sussex who was sent to Calais to arrest Lady Lisle and seize Lord Lisle's papers.

Scrope, Mary (Lady Jerningham; Lady Kingston) (d. 1548)

One of nine sisters, two of whom married earls, Mary made a career of courtiership. She was at court from 1509–1527 as Lady Jerningham, one of Catherine of Aragon's ladies. At the beginning of 1532, she took as her second husband Sir William Kingston, constable of the Tower. During the imprisonment of Anne Boleyn, Lady Kingston was called upon to hear the queen's apology to Mary Tudor and deliver it to the king's daughter after Anne's execution. Lady Kingston carried Mary's train at the christening of Prince Edward. According to some accounts, she served the first four of Henry VIII's queens and also spent time in the household of Princess Mary. She may have been in charge of the joint household of Mary and Elizabeth from March 1538 until April 1539. Several of her children, including her daughter, Elizabeth Jerningham, entered royal service.

Seymour, Jane (1509?–1537)

Jane came to court as a maid of honor under Catherine of Aragon and also served Anne Boleyn. Henry VIII married her shortly after Anne's execution. She collected poppets (dolls). She died as a result of giving birth to Prince Edward.

Skipwith, Margaret (1520+–1583)

Rumored to be Henry VIII's mistress in 1538, Margaret married George, Lord Talboys, in April 1539. He was the son of Henry's former mistress Elizabeth Blount. After Talboys's death, Margaret married Sir Peter Carew, and following Carew's death took Sir John Clifton as her third husband. She had no children by any of them.

Somerset, Lucy (1524–1582)

Although she was identified as one of three young women to whom Henry VIII paid particular attention at a supper and banquet in 1542, Lucy was never seriously in the running to become wife number six. She was the daughter of the Earl of Worcester and was a maid of honor to Catherine Howard. In 1545, she married Queen Kathryn Parr's stepson, John Neville, Fourth Baron Latimer, and was part of Kathryn's household as Lady Latimer. She and Latimer had four daughters.

Stradling, Katherine (1513–1585)

Orphaned by the death of her father in 1535, Katherine entered the service of Mary Arundell, Countess of Sussex. She was there at the same time as Anne Bassett and became the subject of a heated correspondence between Anne and her mother, Lady Lisle, because Anne had shared a gift of pearls with Katherine. Katherine was one of the English maids of honor assigned to Anne of Cleves at the beginning of 1540, but soon after that married Sir Thomas Palmer of Parham, Sussex. Their first child was christened on August 23 of that same year.

Zouche, Mary (1512?–1542+)

In 1527, Mary Zouche wrote to her cousin the Earl of Arundel to complain about her mistreatment by her stepmother. She asked to be taken into royal service in order to escape Lady Zouche's cruelty. As a result, she came to court as a maid of honor, probably to Catherine of Aragon. She was definitely at court as a maid of honor to Anne Boleyn and Jane Seymour. Some accounts say she never wed, but others give her a husband named Richard Burbagge. She is probably the "M. Souch" in the sketch by Hans Holbein the Younger.

READERS CLUB GUIDE

Introduction

Anne Bassett (Nan) is about to become one of Queen Jane Seymour's maids of honor and has been taught for all of her sixteen years that this is the opportunity of a lifetime. She has no great dowry, but she is very beautiful. At the royal court she'll have a chance to catch a wealthy and titled husband. Even the king has found wives among the maids of honor, first Anne Boleyn and then Jane Seymour, and Nan is encouraged when the king notices her. But the day after Nan wins her post at court, the queen and all her ladies go into seclusion. Jane is about to give birth to King Henry's heir. When Queen Jane dies after birthing the future Edward VI, Nan's hopes are dashed. She will not be able to catch anyone's eye if she isn't at court, and as long as there is no queen, there is no need for maids of honor. Uncertain of her future, she goes to live with her cousin Mary.

Nan is young and headstrong, but she knows the king will most likely make a foreign marriage and it may take years before there is a new queen. Even then, there is no guarantee Nan will still be wanted as a maid of honor. Visits from her stepfather's servitor, Ned Corbett, bringing news from her family's home in Calais, soon become the highlights of her days.

What begins as a simple rebellion—slipping out through the gate to see the sights of London with Ned—quickly grows more complicated. Combined with a conspiracy plotted against her family, Nan's future at court becomes more and more unlikely.

For Discussion

1. How did the letters that opened each chapter impact your reading experience?

2. Consider Nan's reflection: "How odd, she thought, that her mother believed bribes of wine or quails or jewelry were acceptable, but that offering one's self in return for favors was a sin" (page 124). Do you agree with Nan's suggestion of her mother's hypocrisy, or do you think the form of bribery that Lady Lisle engages in is comparatively innocent? Why or why not?

3. What is your impression of Nan's mother, Lady Lisle? Do you believe that she uses her daughters for her own advancement, or are her actions necessary for survival? Is she more powerful than her husband, Nan's stepfather?

4. What does the conversation a young Wat Hungerford eavesdrops on between Lord Cromwell and Sir Gregory Botolph foreshadow?

5. Ned plots to court Cat so that he may continue seeing Nan (pages 54–55). What, if anything, do you think this says about his character? How does Ned evolve in this story? What effect does his innocent involvement in Cromwell and Botolph's plot, including his subsequent imprisonment in the Tower, have on his character?

6. Compare Nan and Ned. Although their destinies diverge, do they share similar ambitions? Would they have made a successful marriage, had Nan accepted Ned's proposal?

7. Nan's priorities and desires change throughout the course of the novel. What events account for the change in her sense of purpose? Can you identify any particular turning point for her character?

8. Why does King Henry befriend Nan and grant her favors, even after he marries Catherine Howard? How do Nan's interactions with Henry maintain his respect and favor toward her?

9. When Catherine Howard's flirtations with other men in the court begin to get noticed, Nan vows to stay uninvolved. "A remark Catherine Howard had once made, back when she was a maid of honor, niggled at Nan's memory. She did not wish to examine it closely. It was not safe to know too much, she reminded herself again. Nor was it wise to speculate" (page 287). To what remark is Nan referring? What dangers does Nan avoid by refusing to make further conjecture?

10. Why does Nan surreptitiously orchestrate Henry's marriage to Kathryn Parr?

11. What does Nan's marriage to Wat Hungerford indicate about her development as a character?

Enhance Your Book Club

Author Kate Emerson drew inspiration for this novel from M. St. Clare Byrne's *The Lisle Letters*. Read it as a companion text.

To see a Who's Who of Tudor Women and additional information about the time period and the author, visit KateEmersonHistoricals.com.

To learn more about many of the royal and historical sites featured in the novel, including Hampton Court and the Tower of London, visit www.hrp.org.uk/.

Read the first book in Kate Emerson's Secrets of the Tudor Court series, *The Pleasure Palace*.

A Conversation with Kate Emerson

1. When Nan first came to your attention as a historical figure in *The Lisle Letters*, as mentioned in your Author Note, did you immediately begin to imagine the arc of her story line for this novel? What was your process for developing the fictional version of this woman from the historical references?

    The plot of *Between Two Queens* was inspired by a combination of things. I've written a number of historical mysteries and novels of historical romantic suspense, so I'm always on the lookout for a good, real-life conspiracy/spy story. I've also written biographies, so the stories of interesting women tend to appeal to me. That said, I didn't immediately fix on Nan as the protagonist. Her mother is the central character in *The Lisle Letters* and Nan's youngest sister Mary is the one with the most romantic story. But Nan, in addition to being at court and having caught the king's attention in real life, also had more interesting gaps in what is known about her. In developing a fictional character from a real woman, I try to answer all the questions that aren't answered in the historical record. Was Nan the king's mistress? Did he really consider marrying her? If so, why didn't he marry her? What happened in Nan's life between the events recorded in *The Lisle Letters*? What secrets might she have that would make her fear marriage to Henry VIII?

2. Are the letters that open each chapter in *Between Two Queens* real letters that were exchanged between these historical figures? When you set out to write this novel, did you plan from the beginning to include a character Who's Who?

    The letters are all real. I've modernized some of the spelling, but otherwise they are just as they were written. As for the Who's Who, I did plan that from the beginning, since almost all the characters in the novel are real people. There will be a Who's Who in each of the books in the Secrets of the Tudor Court series.

3. **Nan and her sister are in competition with each other in the beginning of the novel. With whom did you find yourself sympathizing more as the novel progressed? Was competition within families for status and reputation a common occurrence in the Tudor Court?**

I can't really say I sympathize with either Nan or Cat, but since Nan is the protagonist, I was always more in tune with her feelings and reactions. Competition within families was indeed common and there were often pairs of sisters at court, vying for the same suitors, if not the same posts.

4. **It seems that so many maids of honor became mistresses to Henry VIII. Do you believe that the women who entered court often expected that the position would result in a wealthy marriage or romance with the king, or did they more often go to court with only the intention of serving the queen?**

Almost all courtiers, male and female, were at court to advance themselves and/or their families. The maids of honor were unmarried, so they were particularly interested in finding husbands; but there were many more women, most but not all of them married, who made a career of courtiership. They earned wages and were not averse to taking bribes to whisper a word in a royal ear.

5. **Nan's stepfather, Viscount Lisle, was the illegitimate son of King**

Edward IV. What determined the royal court's response to bastard children?

Royal bastards were either acknowledged or not. Those acknowledged by their fathers (Lord Lisle; Henry Fitzroy) enjoyed a privileged upbringing. Those who were not, were raised as the children of their mothers' husbands. Either way, there does not seem to have been any stigma attached.

6. How likely do you think it is that Nan would have been able to rescue Ned from the Tower? Are there historical records that indicate that prisoners were able to escape?

In writing the Tower scenes I studied details of two real escapes, that of Alice Tankerfelde in 1534 and that of William Seymour in 1611. Both were successful, but Alice was later captured because she aroused suspicion by being dressed in men's clothing.

7. In the description of Anna of Cleves in the Who's Who at the end of the novel, you state that Hans Holbein the Younger's portrait of her "makes her appear, to modern eyes, the most attractive of King Henry's wives" (page 335). Is there evidence to suggest that King Henry truly annulled his marriage to Anna of Cleves because of her lack of beauty? Why would Holbein have misrepresented her in the painting? Based on Holbein's portraits and what is recorded in history about the appearance of Henry's other wives, have perceptions of beauty changed since the Tudor era?

All the evidence suggests that Henry had a strong negative physical reaction to Anna of Cleves. He was even willing to state in public that he was impotent with her. Perhaps the chemistry was just wrong between them. And perhaps Holbein was not affected by the same elements. It is true, however, that what constitutes beauty changes from era to era. It is also true that three of Henry's wives, the three Catherines, were all petite and had fair coloring with red or light brown hair.

8. How did King Henry's ability to charge his subjects with treason, including those who used to be his closest and most commanding advisors, like Cromwell, affect his rule and life at Court? Was Henry's power also self-destructive?

    Henry VIII became increasingly paranoid and self-destructive as he aged. He was always supremely self-centered and capable of great self-deception. Truthfully, I feel sorry for him.

9. It is suggested in the novel that Anne Boleyn bewitched Henry. Was this a commonly held speculation at the time? How prevalent was the general belief in witchcraft during the Tudor era? Was witchcraft an ability (or curse) attributed only to women?

    Almost everyone in the sixteenth century believed in the supernatural, including the miracles of saints as well as the power of witches. Witchcraft, however, was not a civil crime in England until the Elizabethan era. Men could be witches, but women were more likely to be accused.

10. In literature, film, and television, so much attention has been paid to the Tudor Court. Why is this time period in British history so popular among modern audiences? Were there royal kingdoms that existed elsewhere in the world during the Tudor reign that would provide equally entertaining material?

I'm not sure I understand the Tudor craze myself, although I've been fascinated by the era since I was a teenager. The court of Francis I of France was every bit as full of scandal and intrigue, but England seems to hold a special place in readers' hearts.

11. **What will the next book in your Secrets of the Tudor Court series be about?**

Next up is *By Royal Decree*, the story of Bess Brooke, another of the three young ladies (along with Nan Bassett and Lucy Somerset) in whom King Henry took an interest at that banquet that followed Catherine Howard's fall from grace.